The Distance Between Stars

The Distance
Between Stars

A NOVEL

JEFF ELZINGA

Water's Edge Press LLC

This is a work of fiction. Names, characters, businesses, places, events and incidents are either the products of the author's imagination or used in a fictitious manner. Any resemblance to actual persons, living or dead, or actual events, is purely coincidental.

Printed in the United States of America

Water's Edge Press LLC
Sheboygan, WI
watersedgepress.com

ISBN: 978-0-9992194-7-8
Library of Congress Control Number: 9780999219478

Credits:

William Stafford, "Ask Me" from *Ask Me: 100 Essential Poems*. Copyright © 1977, 2014 by William Stafford and the Estate of William Stafford. Reprinted with the permission of The Permissions Company, LLC on behalf of Graywolf Press, Minneapolis, Minnesota, www.graywolfpress.org.

Stanley Moss, excerpt from "Ransom" from *New & Selected Poems 2006*. Copyright © 2006 by Stanley Moss. Reprinted with the permission of The Permissions Company, LLC on behalf of Seven Stories Press, www.sevenstories.com.

Cover art and cartography by Monique Brickham

Chapter image licensed through Getty Images, iStockphoto.com.
A WATER'S EDGE PRESS FIRST EDITION

For Valérie, Eliot, Céline, and Paul

Some time when the river is ice ask me
mistakes I have made. Ask me whether
what I have done is my life.

From "Ask Me" by William Stafford

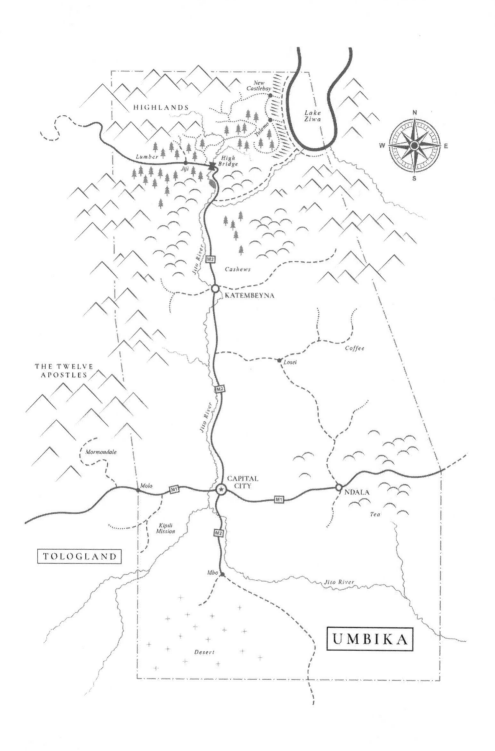

Chapter 1
Looking Back

Years ago, and in someone else's country, I lived an uncomplicated life. I was not motivated by the typical temptations of ambition and wealth, nor by the intimate comforts that family or love might offer. All that mattered to me was doing my job well. Back then, I was an American diplomat, a career Foreign Service Officer, living alone and serving as the U.S. Consul in Umbika, a vast unstable country in East Africa, a place most Americans had never heard of. Or if they had heard of Umbika, the place meant nothing to them. But for me, Umbika was the only world that mattered.

My job was caring for American lives, our citizens who travelled to Umbika or resided in-country. If a baby was born on my watch to American parents, I certified his U.S. birthright. If an American died in Umbika, I made sure her remains were shipped to family back home. And for that unknown length of time we live between birth and death, I was responsible for everyone's safety. No days were ever predictable. Every morning arriving at my office, I dug into an in-box of unforseen problems waiting to be solved. A host of new challenges. So, on that cloudless afternoon in late October when the "Hightower cable" arrived from Washington, I shouldn't have been surprised. I should have been ready for anything. But I wasn't. I was stunned.

In fact, all the officers at the Embassy were staggered by the news. The words in the Department's message had hit us like a flurry of punches, pummeling the senses, taking our breath away.

After our African employees knocked off for the day and left for home, we Americans gathered nervously around the water cooler on the third floor of the Chancery. It was half past five.

"Why, of all the places, would Mo Hightower come here?" I asked. "It must be a mistake."

"The Department doesn't make mistakes," said Alice Jones, our petite Admin officer. "But you're right, Joe. Something's wrong." Normally, Alice's wide smile and breezy Georgia accent made even the worst news sufferable, but not this day. Alice had lost her smile. Instead of lifting us up, she looked down at the floor and shook her head over and over again, while the dull amber wall behind Alice, its paint's humorless color the very emblem of American bureaucracy, towered over her uneasy pose. Complaints from other officers ramped up quickly. It was tough separating one hot voice from another.

"Hightower's visit will ruin us," they said. "The man's unpredictable. He's crazy is what I'd call him. No, the Department is crazy for sending him. We're the crazies if we put up with this nonsense. But what can we do? Yeah, what can we do? Well, we tell them to send him somewhere else!"

None of it made any sense. Blake finally took charge.

"Settle, people, settle!" he commanded. "What's done is done." Blake was someone you paid attention to. He directed our Political Section, one of the most important offices in the Embassy. Blake studied his watch. "Hightower is already on his way to the airport. Forty-one hours from now, he'll be landing here. That's Sunday morning our time." Blake's precise math was meant to calm us, but the inevitability of Sunday morning, and what would happen once our visitor was on the ground, only reinforced the anxiety we were all feeling.

"Men like that," said Connie Saunders, our new press attaché, "you can't trust them." Connie was a first-tour junior officer, a sweet young woman fresh out of grad school, in-country only three months. "I won't work with him." At first it seemed understandable, Connie being as tense as she was.

Umbika was her first Foreign Service posting abroad. The Hightower visit would be her first VIP affair, and working with someone as high profile as Mo Hightower would be stressful for any officer. But as her words sank in, Connie's outspokenness surprised me. I had not seen her so agitated before, or so afraid.

Since I had many questions of my own, and no ready answers from the group, I returned to my office two floors below, where I dialed the stateside number for Benny Cohen, our desk officer in the Department. Benny and I went back several years, one tour overlapping in Addis, another in Niamey, and four months of training together at the Foreign Service Institute. I was hoping he might see a way out of this mess for us.

My call to the U.S. connected on only the third try. A crisp "Hello" greeted me from the other end of the line, a lady's voice, middle-aged, black. "Hello, this is the Africa... is the... Bureau... the Africa Bureau... how may I direct... may I... your... direct... call... your call?" The connection could not have been worse. Every word the poor woman said was repeated two seconds later, creating a cascade of gibberish. It was a phenomenon we all knew as the East Africa echo.

"This is Joe Kellerman at the Embassy in Umbika," I said slowly, enunciating each word, but already preparing to hang up, which was all anyone ever wanted when hearing the echo. "I need to speak with Benny Cohen. But I'm hearing the echo. Tell him I'll call on the STU-3 in five minutes. Five minutes from now. The STU." I did not wait for the woman's jumbled reply. I hung up and hurried upstairs to our Communications Unit.

Back then, awful telephone connections were common throughout Africa. Depending on the country, you could hear anything from a droning hum to the whine of a police siren. Some places you might get quacking ducks or songbirds chirping over the line. In Umbika, we lived with the echo, though it only happened with international calls, and not all of them. Unfortunately, you never knew when the echo was coming, though when it did, the experience was frustrating as hell. Ex-pats blamed the problem on Umbika's Special Security Service and how they eavesdropped on all calls made to Europe and the U.S. Triple S's spying on foreigners was well known and ubiquitous throughout the country, and it seemed a plausible explanation for the problem. A year earlier, however, just before I arrived in country, a specialist from the Department had come to Umbika with a suitcase full of secret electronic gear. He checked every line going in and out of the Embassy, and even though Umbikan agents were indeed listening in on our phone calls, he discovered that the echo had nothing to do with their snooping. A mismatch of technology was causing the problem, a telecommunications gap between the sophisticated electronic equipment used in the Western world and the old devices from the colonial-era still in place in Umbika and its African neighbors. The echo was simply a by-product of old meeting new.

"Is this some kind of joke?" I asked Bennie on the Secure Telephone Unit line.

"I'm sorry, Joe. It's no joke. The visit took us by surprise too." He went on to say the White House had been working the deal for days, but as usual didn't tell the Department until the last minute. We both knew the White House and Congress treated U.S. Embassies and their career officers like hired help, polite when they needed something, but never with the respect they deserved.

"This is beyond surprise, Benny. People here are flipping out. Level with me. Why are we bending over backwards for Mo Hightower? He's a nightmare."

Benny's voice hushed. Someone must have been standing near the cubicle where he was talking. I had to listen carefully to hear him.

"It's polling numbers," he whispered. "They're closer than anyone expected." He explained that the President might not be re-elected.

"Come on, that's not possible."

"Believe me, Joe, it's possible. A second term is no sure thing."

I had not been following the presidential race. As far away as I was from the U.S., it didn't matter to me who won or lost. But I was surprised to hear the President was no longer a shoe-in for a second term. I asked what had happened.

"The other side is gaining in the South and Midwest. If they flip enough of the black vote, they'll win some states they were expected to lose."

"I thought blacks liked the President."

Benny assured me they did. Everyone thought the President would get eighty percent of the black vote. But Hightower had been hammering the President in his newspaper column, and now the White House would be lucky to get thirty percent, unless things turned around fast.

"Hightower's only one guy, Benny."

"Yeah, one guy with a newspaper column read by three million people. They say he's the most popular black journalist ever."

I asked what Hightower's gripe was with the President.

"His gripe is with you, Joe. Everyone out there at the Embassy. He's telling his readers the Embassy is in bed with the rebels, running a secret war against J.J. He says you're planning a coup."

I forced a laugh, though nothing seemed funny right now. We agreed it all sounded like typical Hightower paranoia.

"Why haven't we heard anything, until now?"

"We weren't paying attention to Hightower, not until the White House pulled us in. Normally, they would ignore someone like that. Too far out in left field to take seriously. But we found the smoking gun." Benny's voice came back to full volume. Whoever was standing near his STU cubicle had left. He said the real pressure was coming from the Congressional Black Caucus. They wanted to silence Hightower as much as the President did. Hightower had been telling his readers the Caucus was as guilty of undermining J.J. as the President was.

"For god sakes, Benny, J.J. Mulenga is a dictator – one of the worst."

"That's not how Hightower sees him. They go way back." Benny described how Hightower was portraying President Mulenga as Africa's last great champion of good over evil, David against Goliath. He was telling his readers to throw out every incumbent in Congress who had said anything bad about Mulenga – both white and black. It was possible that if Hightower got a good portion of his readers to vote his way, or stay home and not vote at all, it might be enough to swing a few states.

"You're telling me the White House is afraid Mo Hightower can turn an election?"

"No, not really turn it. But who knows? He's one of twenty fires the White House is trying to put out. With less than three weeks before Election Day, they're taking every fire seriously." Benny cleared his throat. "That's why he's on his way to you. The White House thinks the best way to muzzle Hightower is to let him go to Umbika and see for himself what's happening on the ground. You can prove to him we're playing nice over there."

I asked Benny what the White House thought Hightower was going to see here. The local protests were grassroots and serious. Mulenga had been a tyrant since independence. "He hates Tologs, and they hate him," I said. "J.J. doesn't need the American Embassy to undermine his government. He does fine on his own."

"You're preaching to the choir, Joe. Just give Hightower the king's tour. Once he sees our hands are clean, maybe he'll write about something else, and then the White House can move on to another fire."

"You know Hightower, Benny. He'll write whatever sells newspapers, and he doesn't care who he steps on."

"Just so you know, he'll be J.J.'s guest in Umbika too. Remember, he and the Life President go way back."

"This won't end well. No one can work with that guy."

"That's why the Department chose you as the control officer, Joe."

Being control officer meant I would tag along with Hightower wherever he went. Part tour guide, part handler. "That wasn't in your cable."

"Come on, who else would the Department pick? The Assistant Secretary said if anyone can make chicken salad out of chicken shit, it's Joe Kellerman."

"I'm touched, Benny."

"You always come through, Joe. A week from now, Hightower's visit will be ancient history."

It was half-past six when I hung up with Benny Cohen. I went back to my office. The other Americans had all left the Embassy. I sat and read the Department's cable again. My eyes lingered over the last line on the yellow page: "Mr. Hightower is the personal guest of POTUS. All officers should provide full courtesy and hospitality without question/delay/exception."

These were the lines that had caused my coworkers to panic. We knew the kind of person Maurice Hightower was and so did the Department. Any mistake or embarrassment during a trip organized by the White House could affect the trajectory of an officer's career, even an Ambassador's. This visit would be a precarious test for all of us.

The year Hightower visited Umbika marked my fifteenth anniversary since joining the Foreign Service. I had spent all of those years in Africa. They floated me across the continent, one country after another, dispatched to any U.S. Embassy where an important consular problem needed fixing. Very early in my career, the Office of Personnel Management had decided that problem solving was my strong suit and put a purple star on the jacket of my employment file. Colors meant everything to a person's career path in the Department. When junior officers completed initial training, a senior review panel gave each a colored star. Color assignments were secret; not even the officer himself was supposed to know for sure what he was. But we knew. Yellow stars meant exceptionally strong skills at compromising. Blue stars went to those best suited for a Western country. Red stars, of course, were those sent behind the Iron Curtain. Green, superb language ability. And the few who were found to be hot-headed or disagreeable, they got black stars, not long before they were selected out of the Service.

The very few who rated in the top five-percent of a training class, those for whom the Department thought only the sky was the limit of their potential, got a purple star and were referred to as kites. "Kites had rights because they soared above the lights," the saying went. Kites were assumed to be special, to possess organizational talents beyond the good judgment and diplomatic temperament all officers were recruited for. With the purple star, the Department had identified me as one of their most able problem solvers, a critical thinker they could depend on to fix things when they broke. But that was all myth.

Maybe the notion of special talents was true for other kites, but I had known from the beginning that I wasn't smarter than other officers, and certainly not better. Two things the senior raters might have mistaken for special talents were my tendency to work longer hours than my classmates and my drive to see a problem through to its end. Hard work and perseverance were behaviors I owed to my father. He had always emphasized the importance of perspective, and he said work was never about who did the job, only about the excellence that went into it. He believed beauty was revealed not in notions of taste, but in matters of precision. Not in how good the finished product looked, but in how well the work to get there was performed.

For all his adult life, my father was employed in the aviation industry, calibrating altimeters for jet airliners. Until the day he died, at the early age of forty-six, he never missed an hour on the job and never accepted second-best in the quality of his work. When the pilot of a passenger plane landing in a thunderstorm needed to know exactly the number of feet he was from the ground, the altimeter my father calibrated had to work perfectly. There was no room for second-best with a plane full of people. The pilot in that storm probably thought he was betting his life and the lives of his passengers on a complicated mechanical instrument. My father knew the truth: their lives depended on my father and the quality of work he had done.

My father was even-tempered and never made me feel guilty for mistakes I made as a child. All he ever said, after I finished a chore, was, "How could you have done that better, Joe?" By the end of high school, he had taught me that, regardless of what others might say, a job done well was its own reward.

So, when Maurice Hightower's visit to Umbika went sour, when everything fell apart at the end, and I was ordered back to Washington to answer for what had happened, I never protested or complained. A review board met and ordered me to "walk the halls for six," as they say. That meant six months without an office or anything to do, a consultant without clients – Department purgatory. Six months that went on forever. But I accepted the consequences for what had happened. And looking back, there was nothing I would have done differently to arrive where I did.

Still, I can't say for sure why things turned out the way they did, even though I was the one closest to what happened with Hightower. All the Department and I could agree on is that the choices we make, we own. And we all know, of course, that choices can have consequences. Or as they say in Umbika – When you pick up one end of a stick, you pick up the other end too.

Chapter 2
Guess Who's Coming to Umbika

Before Hightower arrived, my coworkers at the Embassy were concerned about more than just making a good impression on a controversial VIP sent by the White House. They were worried about Maurice Hightower's unpredictable and confrontational personality, behaviors that always make diplomats uneasy. Even at sixty-six years, an age when many journalists have put their pens aside and welcomed retirement, Hightower was still on the battlefield, harping about the United States and what he called the government's "genocidal fascination with black folk." Hightower's pen had skewered U.S. Presidents for forty years, his rage always hitting the same sharp notes – government and big business conspire to tilt privilege and opportunity towards those with the lightest skin color, at the expense of those with the darkest. There was no American Dream for a black man, Hightower claimed. There were only nightmares for them, and the blacker the skin, the more disturbed the sleep.

Hightower's polemics about race first appeared as essays during the war, in far-left magazines such as *First of May* and *Workers Standard*. Over time, his crusade reached a wider and wider audience. His newspaper column was eventually syndicated in 150 newspapers across the country, including the *Post* and the *Times*. In the late Sixties, Hightower reached true celebrity status, when his article "Recipe for Subduing a Black Man" appeared in the *Atlantic*. "Recipe" became part of the lexicon of anyone in the U.S. talking seriously about race, even among those who never read the article. In short, Hightower's "recipe" went like this: Take one part welfare for sustenance, two parts affirmative action for justice, mix in three parts black fantasy for hope – that is, the Hollywood fairy tale that any kid of color can escape his lot in life by either becoming a professional athlete, recording artist, or movie star. Stir slowly for generations. You now have what Hightower called the Black Dream Elixir. "Except, my brothers and sisters, it ain't no dream potion you want to drink," he wrote. "It's a nightmare created by your government. It's a deadly concoction, an intoxicating and irresistible lie. And shamefully, our children are swallowing it every day."

Hightower's central thesis never changed after "Recipe" was published: Black people in the U.S. are kept alive by handouts, tricked into thinking life can be fair, and deluded by false hopes. Nothing had changed in America in a hundred years, Hightower argued, and under a white regime, nothing ever would. He implored his audience to "get real." Even though Hightower's "get real" mantra was disturbing to many Americans, awards committees recognized his talent as a writer. He won several prizes, though at the U.S. Embassy in Umbika we were not thinking about his writing honors. We were worried about what his newspaper column might say about us, after he left. Career government employees never want to see their names highlighted on the front page of the *Times*, especially not in a spotlight held by someone as angry as Maurice Hightower.

Hightower's star had been rising for decades. Before he was thirty, he won a Pulitzer for an exposé on the treatment of black Marine Corps recruits at Montford Point, North Carolina. Like all his work, the Marine Corps piece was explosive, leading to a class-action lawsuit, the early retirement of a dozen Marine officers, and significant revisions in the USMC Code of Conduct. My colleagues brought up the Montford Point lawsuit and much of Hightower's personal history that afternoon when we gathered around the Embassy's water cooler to talk about Benny Cohen's telegram. Everyone seemed to know at least one odd fact about Hightower's career. One story, however, was prominent in all of our memories. You could say it was the genesis story of Maurice Hightower.

When Hightower was sixteen, he was convicted of tossing a Molotov Dr. Pepper bottle at a police cruiser during a labor disturbance in Mississippi. Still a minor, Hightower was sentenced to six months in county jail. A month before his release, Klansmen drowned the 32-year-old white woman his twin brother had been sleeping with. It took a week for the vigilantes to find Hightower's brother, but when they did, they hanged him from a hundred-year-old oak in front of the county courthouse.

After his release from jail, Hightower was heartbroken about his brother, and he began investigating the two murders. The local sheriff had been unable to find any leads in the case, but after four months of digging, Hightower uncovered a ton of evidence. In a magazine article surprisingly well written for a high school dropout, Hightower laid out a convincing case for KKK and law enforcement involvement in both murders. Barely seventeen now, and already a convicted criminal, Hightower was hailed among New York elites as an important new voice in the field of investigative journalism. Hightower's writing career was born. Fifty years later, Hightower was on his way to Umbika in search of another exposé, and his influence, particularly among black readers, had never been higher. Educated white people rarely objected to the issues Hightower wrote about; his work was always well-researched and accurate. What made so many whites uneasy was his apparent hatred of all things white. In interviews with white politicians and business executives, Hightower turned even the most innocuous conversation into an argument about race. Using guilt, shame, and intimidation, he constantly forced his opponents into retreat. Along the way, Hightower never compromised, never backed down, never apologized – which was why he scared the hell out of a lot of people.

After hanging up with Benny Cohen, I sat at my desk for a while, thinking about what was in front of me. The secret to being a successful control officer for a VIP visit was to act professionally at all times. Provide excellent service.

Never get drawn into an argument. Always take the high road. And at wheels-up, make sure the guest leaves feeling like he's been treated as royalty. Unfortunately, I had no idea how I could possibly make any of that work with someone like Maurice Hightower.

Chapter 3
Der Glückliche Löwe

Every night, twilight covers the roads in Africa with long shadows in melancholy colors, a reminder for ex-pats and diplomats alike of being cosmically adrift and far from home. The evening of the Hightower cable was a Friday. I was dead tired after a busy week of work yet feeling anxious over what was to come. I swung by the Happy Lion on my way home, expecting some friends to be there to relax with. The Happy Lion was the tavern of choice for Westerners living in the capital city. Not only did it have the best food in town, but it also was the only public space where agents of President Mulenga's Special Security Service steered clear.

The owner of the Happy Lion, Jürgen Schneider from Munich, had retired in Umbika after working as a mechanical engineer on the High Bridge project in the Northern Province. Jürgen had a passion for preparing fine food and was proud of his reputation for never serving a weak drink. He personally prepared every plate he served: schnitzels, sausages, and Bavarian chicken. Jürgen's bartenders were also Germans who had worked on the High Bridge. They all believed that Africa was one of the last places on earth where a little money could still buy a lot and where the average man could still feel important.

When I entered the Happy Lion, the noisy crowd stood shoulder to shoulder around the bar, their chatter the sound the workweek makes when it finally relaxes. The scent of disinfectant met me just inside the door. After years in Africa, I had come to rely on the smell of disinfectant to gauge the cleanliness of whatever a business was offering. Like security lights around buildings, the scent of pine cleanser drew me in, embraced me, and made me feel safe. Jürgen never skimped on the disinfectant.

A cluster of pink-faced men were laughing at the far corner of the room. They saw me come in and waved. They were members of a local running club, offspring of colonial plant managers and entrepreneurs. Their families were among the few who had stuck around after the exodus following Umbika's independence. Though I didn't run anymore myself, I knew the men from visas I had issued for their travel to the U.S. Now, they had formed a circle around one of their own, a bearded man standing on a chair. He was trying to finish in one go a glass boot of maroon-colored ale, while those around him sang a drinking song and cheered him on. Beer overflowed the man's mouth and ran down his chest, soaking his tee-shirt printed with the words "Drinker with a Running Problem." When the glass boot was empty, he inverted it atop his head and held it there while his mates applauded. I gave the man a thumbs-up.

To the left of the bar and down a few steps was the dining room. The dining room was also filled with breathless talk. Jürgen's German wife was the head waitress, and she led me by the arm through the room to where Connie, Blake, and the Hardys were sitting around a table. Blake spotted me and got up. "I was just telling Connie one of my favorite Foreign Service stories," he said, "but let me get you a drink, Joe. You're already a couple rounds behind."

I placed my order, and Blake left. Jürgen's wife brought me a chair, and I sat at the table between Blake's empty seat and Dave Hardy, the Embassy's economic officer. Like Blake and me, Dave Hardy was in the middle of his career. Next to him sat Jill, his wife, a kind woman with a girl-next-door smile. Jill wore her wheat colored hair in a ponytail, just as a farm girl from Iowa might, which is where the Hardys were raised. In front of me on the table was a thick round candle surrounded by plastic sprigs of Edelweiss, the candle's hearty flame spreading yellow light over a green-checked tablecloth. Connie sat directly across from me, her high cheekbones lit by the candle's soft glow. Tall and pretty and holding a journalism degree from Northwestern, Connie was the youngest public affairs officer I had ever known and the youngest officer at the Embassy.

Blake returned with my drink and a tray for the others. "Let's get this party started," he said and handed us our glasses, keeping a bottle of German dark for himself.

"A toast!" Dave Hardy announced and raised his glass. "To L-B-H. Life-Before-Hightower." Glass was clinked. Everyone drank.

"Finish your story," Connie said to Blake.

Blake set down his beer and leaned over the table. In many ways, he was the most valuable member of the Ambassador's staff. As political officer, he was always on top of what was happening in and out of government and had contacts everywhere in Umbika. Blake was the grandson of Sicilian immigrants, so with his dark hair and light olive skin he could move unnoticed through any crowd, even those in Africa. Depending on how Blake chose to dress, he could pass for an English professor or a day laborer. Such versatility made it easy for him to interact with people of any background.

"So, we're back in Bangladesh," Blake said. "The Embassy driver in Dhaka had just picked up the junior officer, his wife, and their two kids from the airport. He drives them to their new house in the city. They stand outside the house, admiring the size of the place. It's amazing, a mansion, and they'll be living in it for the next two years. Unfortunately, it's lunchtime when they get to the house. No one's there, so they have to wait for the front door key to arrive." Connie's brown eyes grew larger, hanging on every word of Blake's story. "While waiting outside, the junior officer looks up at this huge tree they're under. He sees rats sitting on the branches, dozens of rats looking down at him from the tree."

"Rats?" Connie asked. "You mean, they had rats in their tree?"

"That's right. Big, fat Bangladeshi rats. And the rats are staring down at the junior officer and his family. The young officer looks higher in the tree. He sees even more rats." Connie and Jill Hardy squirmed in their seats, which only encouraged Blake's desire for drama. "In fact, he realizes there are rats on every branch of the tree – all the way to the top – hundreds of them.

"'My God!' the junior officer says to the old driver who had brought them from the airport. 'There're rats in the tree!'"

Connie put down her drink and sat on her hands.

"The old man stared up into the tree. Then, he looked over at the junior officer and his family." Blake paused to drink from his beer, holding the bottle so loosely by the neck you would have thought any second it would drop to the floor. Jill Hardy moved to the edge of her seat and fidgeted with the end of her ponytail. Blake shifted his voice into a perfect South Asian sing-song accent. "'Of course, there are rats in the tree,' says the old driver, though he doesn't sound like a common chauffer anymore. He's a sage now, wisely addressing one of his most curious students. The sage smiles at the young officer. Then he says, matter-of-factly, 'In Dhaka, our rats live in the trees – because of the snakes on the ground.'"

Dave Hardy burst out laughing.

"That's disgusting, Blake," Jill said and rubbed goose bumps off her arms. "And it's not funny, David. You know how I hate snakes."

"Joe hates them, too," Dave Hardy said.

Everyone looked at me. I nodded, smiled.

Blake added, "I've been telling Joe it's time to get the hell out of Africa – before a snake finally gets him. But he won't listen."

"I'm content here," I said.

Blake shook his head, unconvinced. He pulled from his beer again.

"It doesn't matter," said Dave Hardy. "They'll never let Joe leave AF. He's too valuable."

An older woman's voice echoed through the dining room, a privileged sound, infused with an upper-crust British accent. "Constance! Oh, Constance!" We rotated our attention towards the voice. Vigilance Weatherly, the wife of the British High Commissioner, was plowing through the dining room on her way to our table. Two women I didn't recognize followed close behind. A fourth was still at their table, settling the bill with Jürgen's wife. Blake pushed back his chair. I was following his lead, starting to get up, when

Mrs. Weatherly called, "Don't jump to it now, boys. I'm coming around."

Mrs. Weatherly was a head taller and pounds heavier than her companions. Despite her favored position as the spouse of an ambassador, she presented herself in a common manner, forgoing makeup, pinning her silver hair with cheap barrettes, and never going out of her way to be stylish. Yet despite these provincial tastes, Mrs. Weatherly was a force to be reckoned with. Her hands touched the purse strings of every charitable organization in Umbika, including the biggest charity of all, the Blue Sky Society. The Society's official costume – blue dresses, white gloves, and red hats – was what the four ladies were wearing. I figured they were either coming from or on their way to a charity event.

"It's nice to see you, Mrs. Weatherly," Connie said and extended her hand.

"Dear, you must call me Vidge. Dougie's mother is Mrs. Weatherly." The woman ignored Connie's hand and embraced her in a smothering hug, like a grandmother on a holiday visit. "I hope you can join us at our fundraiser next week. As the new girl in town, Constance, you'll meet a lot of important people."

"I'm definitely considering," Connie said and brushed back her hair, tucking the shoulder-length strands behind her ears. "I almost have my feet on the ground."

"Just remember, dear. All postings are not alike. After a successful tour on the Dark Continent, you're sure to get something cheerier for your next post. After our first time in Africa, Dougie and I were off to Hong Kong. Three years in heaven. Those were the days." Mrs. Weatherly folded her arms over her chest. She surveyed the table, as if it were an inspection. "Good evening, Joseph. Blake. Mr. and Mrs. Hardy."

"Hello, Vidge," I replied. Dave Hardy raised a glass.

She then stepped to our side of the table and bent between Blake and me, steadying her balance with a hand on my shoulder. Her lips nearly touched my ear. "Gentlemen, my sources are chirping a storm." She exhaled deeply, and I caught the sweet scent of Riesling on her breath. "They say the Americans are about to get prickly with His Excellency. They say Washington is upset how the Life President is handling the agitators in the North."

"If we're getting prickly, ma'am," I whispered back, "I can assure you, the American Consul is always the last to know."

She peered at me slyly and then at Blake. "Don't look at me," Blake said and raised his hands in surrender.

Mrs. Weatherly set her oversized handbag on our table, shuttering the light reaching us from the candle. Mrs. Weatherly's companions could not hear anything she was saying, and even Connie and the Hardys could make out only a few words. "Tell Warner this," she whispered, referring to our Ambassador, L. Warner Durhlmann, "Umbika is a fine place, one of the finest places on this bloody continent." Her eyes never blinked. The tiny black pupils moved back and forth between Blake and me. "Jimmy Mulenga runs a tight ship. But this is Africa. He's the model others need to follow. These poor people have to walk before they can run. Washington has to remember that. We need Jimmy Mulenga."

American and British diplomats agreed on most international issues, but not on policy regarding the dictatorship of Jim Jimmy Mulenga. His atrocious record of human rights abuse was more than the U.S. government could stomach. And because Mulenga's record had been getting even worse, business contacts between the U.S. and Umbika had spoiled in recent months.

"We must pitch in and help Jimmy," she said, "not those bloody UFreeMo buggers in the North. The last thing we need is the Life President looking to the Reds. We've seen where that road ends." The volume of Mrs. Weatherly's voice had been slowly rising. Now was the time to steer the conversation in a different direction.

"My biggest concern is the safety of our citizens," I said.

"Pooh-pah. Dougie and I spent two years in Salisbury, you know. Has everyone forgotten what happened to Smitty?" I politely shook my head. We all remembered what had happened in Rhodesia, now named Zimbabwe. Civil war between whites and blacks had left thousands dead. Ian Smith had been Rhodesia's white leader. "Dougie was our press man during the worst, you know. The Foreign Office had him trying to please both the coloreds and the whites. But their plan was daft, a tub full of idiots in Whitehall." The fourth sister with a red bonnet had arrived at our crowded table. "Throw 'em to the curb!" Mrs. Weatherly added. She moved her hand across her face in a gesture I had never seen before, but it complemented her disgust. Mrs. Weatherly let go my shoulder. As intoxicated as she was, I half-expected her to topple onto the table. But she stood perfectly fine, only a modest lean. "There's a lesson to be learned, boys. White or black, don't let the Communists get their noses on." Mrs. Weatherly raised her hands chest high and tugged on her white gloves, as if she were heading into surgery. She leaned towards Blake and me again. "Jimmy Mulenga won't let criminals destroy this country," she whispered. "And neither will Britain."

Mrs. Weatherly, then, steel-straightened her back and pivoted one-eighty on her heels. With a turn of the head, she smiled at Connie again and said, "Did I mention you look heavenly, my dear?" before leading her companions out of the dining room, in single file. We watched silently until the heavy door opening onto the parking lot had closed behind them.

"I'll write that up," Blake said, shaking his head. Jürgen's wife brought us another tray of drinks.

"I talked to Benny before I left work," I said. "They've designated me control officer for the visit."

Dave Hardy smiled. "You thought they'd pick someone else?"

"Does that mean you'll be with him all the time he's here?" asked Jill.

"More or less," I said.

"Does the Ambassador know he's coming?" Connie asked. Her voice carried a new sliver of dread. "Maybe he can stop it."

"The Ambassador was out all afternoon," Blake said. "Tonight he's at a reception. I'll drop by the Residence on my way home."

"I feel for you, Joe," said Dave Hardy.

"I'll be fine."

"Don't be so sure. This guy's a big prick with a short fuse."

"David!" Jill sounded more annoyed than ever.

"Okay, okay. I never said that, whatever it means. But you know what I'm getting at. Mo Hightower supports a damn dictator over his own country – a country that's still a democracy, by the way."

"People think Hightower is nothing but a bully," said Blake. "I saw him speak in college, at the Boston Garden. He's an unbelievable showman – and very clever."

"What did he do?" asked Connie.

"We weren't disappointed!" said Blake. "I can tell you that."

For ten minutes, Blake explained how he and some friends waited shoulder to shoulder for two hours to get front row seats to see Hightower speak. When Hightower strolled in, half an hour late, a thick white towel covered his head, like a prizefighter. He bobbed and weaved through the aisles, jabbing at phantoms on his way to the stage. Once on stage he took off his shirt. His sweaty skin sparkled in the spotlights. He showed off his muscles. Black guys in the crowd went wild, screaming and pumping their fists.

"Hightower grabbed the microphone and yelled, 'Black!' and the crowd shouted, 'Power!' They all knew the routine. He yelled louder, they answered louder. This went on for two or three minutes. The sound was shaking the walls."

"I bet you were scared," said Jill.

"Yes and no. We were caught up in the moment. It was a circus, and Hightower was ringleader and main attraction. Everything was about him. He commanded the center of attention. At one point, he faced a group of white kids, sitting not far from us. 'You boys and girls from those fancy colleges,' he said, 'you listen carefully to Uncle Mo. I'm here to build bridges, not burn them down. Under the skin, you and me, we're all God's children.' Then, Hightower ran across the stage and pointed to a far corner of the Garden. He called out, 'Can you hear me back there, brothers and sisters? I just told these white children down here, I'm about building bridges. You know what I'm saying?'"

Connie was listening to every detail. Blake pulled his chair closer to the table.

"Someone in the back corner of the Garden – like on cue – started chanting, 'Burn, baby, burn!' The chant spread like wildfire around the whole Garden. 'Burn, baby, burn!'"

"I would have left then and there," Connie blurted out.

"We were okay," Blake assured her. "We were cocky college kids from

Cambridge, Mass. We thought we'd live forever. Besides, Hightower wouldn't let anyone hurt us. We were props in his play."

"He hates people like us. He's said so on TV," Connie protested. "White people are the cause of everything bad. It's all he talks about."

"He's an angry man. But anger is how he makes a living," Blake said. "It's part of his show."

"It's not our fault," Connie interrupted, as if she hadn't heard a word Blake just said.

"Of course not," Blake agreed. He took a long drink from his beer. "Of course not." Blake set his bottle back on the table. "The most interesting part was when he analyzed why black men desire white women."

"He did what?" said Jill.

"It was just a few comments. The program ended before Hightower explained himself. Someone threw a smoke bomb onto the stage. Then, a lot of black guys stormed out of the building, knocking over chairs and pushing people out of the way. Hightower was hustled off stage. By the time my friends and I got outside, the streets were insane. Windows on a liquor store had been smashed, and a car was on fire. Sirens were coming, so we ran to the T and got a train back to campus."

Connie gaped at Blake. "Somebody tell me why we're letting this person come to our Embassy," she said. "He's crazy." Connie's comment sounded extreme, but she had had a lot to drink.

"VIP visits are about power," said Dave Hardy. "We have none. The Department has none. The White House has the rest."

Connie was not the only one who had reached her alcohol limit. I counted five empty glasses in front of Jill. "In Washington last summer," Jill said, "I saw Mr. Hightower on the news. He's a handsome man, you know."

"What!" Connie gasped. "You're joking."

"No, really, he reminds me of – what's his name, David?"

"I don't have a clue."

"Come on, he's famous. You know the one I mean. But his skin is not as dark." We tossed around several names, but no one could identify the person Jill was thinking of.

"I'm telling you," Dave Hardy said, chewing the last of the ice in his glass. "The Department can call it fact-finding or familiarization or whatever the hell they want, but we're going down like the Titanic."

For a while no one said a word. Our evening had run its course. We were the only customers left in the dining room. Connie picked her fork around the piece of pineapple cake she had ordered but not eaten. Jill played with the wedding band on her ring finger. Blake looked over at me and raised his eyebrows, as if to say, no use fighting City Hall. Maybe it was because I hadn't drunk as much as the others, but I had grown less worried about Hightower's visit since arriving at the Happy Lion, not more. Our best strategy still was to stick to the high ground and act like the diplomats we were. It was the only way to keep the visit on track and keep Hightower from seeing us as the enemy. Whatever happened in the November elections was not our concern.

Blake was the first to get up from the table. The rest of us followed. "He's going to do something crazy when he's here," Connie warned, as we were leaving the dining room. "And we'll all suffer for it." I noticed a young black girl sitting alone at a small side table near the doorway to the kitchen. She had a large stack of pressed cloth napkins in front of her, and she was calmly folding each one into the shape of some exotic white bird.

Chapter 4
Grief

Normally, on a Saturday, I slept until seven or eight, but my phone rang at six-fifteen this morning. Our duty officer at the Embassy informed me that Ambassador Durhlmann had called a Country Team meeting for 9:00 to discuss the Hightower visit. I got to the Embassy by seven. No other cars were in the lot. Early morning sunlight was coaxing open the purple blossoms of a massive bougainvillea vine climbing the back wall of the Chancery. Anything with leaves grew well in Umbika. Flowers best of all. Once in my office, I jotted notes to my weekly to-do list and scoured overnight cable traffic. There was nothing new regarding Maurice Hightower. By eight, other department heads were drifting in.

At 8:45, I was about to head upstairs for the meeting when my phone rang. Immediately, I recognized the caller's voice. He was a Mormon priest living not in Umbika, where Mormon proselytizing was banned, but just over the border in Tologland, the neighboring country to the west. I had met him and his wife twice since I had been in Umbika. First was at the Ambassador's 4th of July picnic, and then a few weeks later when I visited their compound in Tologland. They were part of a dozen American families that had built a Mormon mission deep in the bush. Because they lived 400 miles from the

U.S. Embassy in Tologland, and we were only 140 miles away, my office served their official needs.

"Mr. Kellerman, I wasn't sure what to do," the man said, hopelessly. "That's why I called you."

"Tell me what's wrong," I said. The phone line went silent for a moment.

Finally, the man said, "My nephew died here this morning." My stomach sank under the news. "Our phone at the mission wasn't working. I'm calling from the Customs Office at the border." I knew the gloomy shack he was in. It dated to the colonial era. In an instant, I could visualize the cracked cement floor, chipped paint, and patina of brown grime waist-high around the room. The cracks and chips and stains all served as testament to decades of comings and goings and no budget for house-keepers or repairs. I pictured two Tolog bureaucrats in ancient threadbare uniforms, sleepwalkers sitting in the Customs Office, inspecting bills of lading for every piece of freight entering and leaving Tologland, stamping forms in triplicate.

"We always tell the kids not to walk around the hippo pond," the priest said. "But my nephew only arrived last night. I hadn't warned him yet." The man went on to explain how his nephew was visiting from Texas and had gone for a walk at sunrise, before anyone else was up. Apparently, the teenager had gotten himself between a mother hippo and her newborn. Sensing a threat, the mother attacked the boy, crushing him with her powerful jaws. The boy had died almost instantly. One powerful scream had alerted the other Americans. The priest began to cry and said the boy's death was his fault.

"No, it was a terrible accident," I told him. "You can't blame yourself. Things happen here we can't predict."

The immediate problem now was getting the boy's body on a plane to Texas as soon as possible. The man knew he needed special paperwork from the Embassy to get the body back into the U.S. He had already called his sister in Texas and broken the terrible news. The boy's parents would make arrangements on that end and be waiting for the body to arrive. "I'll leave right away," I said. "I'll be at your place by early this afternoon." I hung up but before I could do anything else, I put my head in my hands. Death cases were the worst. My brain was pounding. My stomach felt sick. A few minutes later,

I contacted my counterpart in Tologland and brought him up to speed on what was happening.

In the hallway outside the conference room, I met the Ambassador just as Country Team was about to begin. "You're looking kind of pale, Joe," he said. I told him about the dead Mormon boy and my need to drive to Tologland right away. "That's a son-of-a-bitch," the Ambassador said. "You sure you're all right?"

"This kind of news, it just takes the wind out of me sometimes," I said.

"Be sure to tell the family how sorry I am."

"I will."

"You'll be back in time tomorrow to go with me to the airport?" he asked.

"I'll be back tonight, sir."

For an official trip out of town, I normally used an Embassy vehicle with an Umbikan driver. But leaving at the last minute on a Saturday morning, I had no time to find a driver. I took my own vehicle and drove alone. Traffic was light on the M-1 that morning. The weather was good, no clouds anywhere, and temperature better-than-average for the dry season. It would have been a beautiful Saturday morning if not for the reason I was heading to Tologland. Handling death cases was the toughest part of my job. Taking official custody of the body of a deceased American was the ultimate responsibility for an American Consul in a foreign land. Repatriation was a tricky business. There was no room for error. Family back home depended on the U.S. Consul to stand in for them. They counted on him to make sure the body was treated with dignity and respect, that a cause of death was determined, that the body and personal belongings were returned to the family. They expected him to have perfect judgment, to do all the right things for them. In a rugged and underdeveloped corner of the world, like the land along the border of Tologland and Umbika, that important work was all the more challenging.

Once outside the capital city, stress from the priest's phone call had left me. My stomach felt fine again, my head had stopped pounding, and my thoughts focused only on the tasks awaiting me at the Mormon mission. Two hours later, I had made it to Molo, the frontier town on the Umbikan side of the border. Red tape typically delays travelers an hour or two when crossing an African border, but my white diplomatic license plates got me out of Umbika and into Tologland in five minutes. I then left the surfaced road and headed northwest on a wide rolling trail of reddish dirt, the particles so fine I could have been travelling over paths of ground cinnamon. I passed through picture book scenes of Africa. Tall women carrying silver water pails on their head. Flat-top Acacia trees soaking up sunlight. A man dressed only in shorts, mixing mud for bricks. I passed skyward pointed noses of termite mounds, the tips reaching taller than the roof of my car. For a while these colorful images let me forget why I was traveling the path I was on. I continued mile upon mile of empty bush land. In one small village, young men sat in the shade of a baobab tree, their backs against the wall of a market shop. The men looked bored and discontent. The white pine boxes stacked out front of the coffin-maker's business next door brought my thoughts back to why I was on that road – the family of a teenaged boy from Texas.

When the Mormon property came into view, all I saw at first were white specks in the distance, at the foot of the Twelve Apostles, a hundred-mile mountain range meandering along the border between Tologland and Umbika. One particularly high sunny peak rose above the compound. I drove onto the property of a dozen or more whitewashed brick and mortar buildings. The priest and his wife were waiting for me, standing side-by-side in the shade of a brick archway at the front door of their home. Their shoulders leaned one against the other, two pillars shaken by grief and regret. The support they provided each other was all that kept them from collapsing to the ground. I parked at the back of the house. African villagers had already queued up, waiting in the traditional way to pay respect to the family. A hundred yards behind the house was the calm green water of the hippo pond where the boy had died. Nothing in my view gave a hint of the tragedy that had taken place there only hours earlier.

The couple took me inside their home. On a twin bed in a back room, the dead boy was lying under a white, knit bedspread. A doctor was already there. A mortician arrived after me, and while I helped the pastor complete form

DS 2060, Report of Death of an American Citizen Abroad, the mortician and the doctor prepared the body for transport. Although the priest had been led to believe at the Customs Office that the body would be embalmed before travelling, the mortician said that was not true. Embalming was not possible this far out in the bush.

"Custom Office knows this," the mortician said. "No pressurized casket. If the family wants that, they order from Luceyville. It takes one week." Waiting a week was not an option. Someone would need to let the funeral home in Houston know to be ready for the change in color. Depressurization would turn the boy's white skin purple and black during the high-altitude flight home. The shock someone got opening the casket in the U.S. could be overwhelming if they were not warned ahead of time.

The boy's body was generously wrapped in cotton sheets. We lifted him into the standard casket the mortician had brought with him. I roped the four sides in a prescribed manner, with a special white cord I had brought from the Embassy. I pulled the strands taut and threaded the cord through the official document pack. I knotted and joined the ends in melted red wax, which I pressed with my official seal. Mormon families were crying in the living room when we passed through with the casket. They followed us outside to a police van waiting in the yard. We slid the casket inside. Two policemen drove the van, followed by the priest and his wife, in a Jeep Cherokee. Another family followed in their small red sedan. They were on their way to Tologland's international airport, nine hours away. The paperwork needed to get the body to leave from Umbika would have taken a few days to process. I had called ahead so that the American Consul in Tologland would meet the family at the airport, and the casket would be put on the midnight flight through Amsterdam.

I stayed a while longer to talk with the rest of the Americans at the mission. Some were concerned about rumors they were hearing, of unrest in the Northern Province of Umbika, vandalism and arson mostly, but also of missing persons. When I finally left, the sun was only a small gold orb atop indigo-shaded hills to the west. Shadows covered most of my return to the border. At one point, a dust devil to the south funneled dry earth up into the sky, a fantastic red tornado framed by a cloudless sky. By dusk, the frontier had come into view again. Its gray chain-link fence stretched north and south as far as the eye could see. Like all borders in Africa, the line separating Tologland and Umbika meant little to the locals who lived on either side of it. A hundred years earlier, Africa's borders were invented in Berlin by European lords and generals using nothing but the outline map of a continent, a pen, a straight edge, and their shared sense of entitlement. Actual fences and checkpoints came later. Not until my third posting in Africa did I realize what Africans had always known – foreigners understood little how the Continent really worked. Fences and frontiers were fine for Europeans to manage their interests, but boundaries created by outsiders would never change how one African tribe felt about another. Only the locals themselves knew where the real borders lay.

I steered my white Land Cruiser through a final curve in the highway and then up a short incline towards the border on the crest of a treeless hill. Downshifting, I slowed my speed by half. I passed the Customs Office, where the Mormon priest had phoned me hours earlier. Lying in easy reach on the seat beside me were my black diplomatic passport and blue Umbikan residency card. A scrum of Tolog kids with leathery bare feet was standing along the border fence, kicking up particles of red dust. Tologs were the majority tribe in Tologland and the people in East Africa with the darkest skin. The kids' long ebony fingers clung to safe spots on barbed-wire strands strung along the chain fence, their eyes gazing east across the frontier.

The sound of my approach grabbed the children's attention, and they turned. Their eyes widened when they saw me, a *mzungu*, smiling through my open window. I rolled to a stop at the border gate. The kids darted to me, forming a ring around my car. Their rough hands reached in through the open window. "*Pipi! Pipi!*" they shouted. Candy.

The gate guard, wearing the familiar green shirt and khaki pants of Tologland's border police, blew a whistle dangling from a lanyard attached to his shirt pocket. "Get out of that!" he barked at the kids. The guard carried no firearm, but his fist clenched the handle of a baton he cracked against a gatepost. "Don't play with the fire!" he shouted. The kids ignored him and remained close to my car. When the guard feigned a step towards them, they jumped back from my fenders. A moment later, their fingers were again at my window. I dropped a few hard candies from my glove compartment into their outstretched hands.

"Get away!" the guard shouted. He cracked his baton again and advanced on the kids. They shuffled back to the fence, stuffing treats into their mouths and purposefully kicking up clouds of red powder in protest. The guard unwound a rusty chain and swung open the heavy gate, letting it fly with considerable force against the chain links, exactly where the children had been standing a second earlier. Clack! the gate sounded, but it touched not one of the quick-footed kids.

I inched forward into the narrow opening. The Tolog guard recognized me from earlier in the day and waved me through without asking for papers. I rolled off the sharp end of the paved road and dropped onto a wide crust of dry earth separating the two countries. When I passed the fence line, the man closed the gate and re-wrapped the chain. During the coming rainy season, this middle ground would turn into a marsh, and thistles with colorful flowers would grow in the depressions. But not now. Now the ground was dry and hard. I pressed forward another thirty yards, my heavy tires rising and falling over ruts carved into the moonscape.

I pulled up in front of a second gate and sounded my horn. Unlike the transparent wire fence on the Tolog side of the border, Umbika's fence looked like an impenetrable wall, the chain-links interwoven with vertical slats of bamboo. A round brown face appeared through a slit in the gate, his cautious eyes signaling a routine I knew well. These eyes were judging my status, analyzing my license plate for color and number code. Once the color and code had confirmed my status as an American diplomat, the Umbikan guard swung open the gate. A police corporal, he waved me forward. I drove slowly, until my wheels caught asphalt again. Once through the opening, I braked to a stop and shut off my engine.

The corporal scurried to my window and peered inside the vehicle. While looking into the front and rear seats, he nervously caressed the stock of the automatic rifle slung over his shoulder. He called to a green tent pitched nearby. Seconds later, an officer with the same caramel skin emerged from the tent. His gray uniform was neatly pressed. A shiny black holster rested high on his waist. I held my papers out the window. The officer brushed past my hand and strutted to the front of the car. At the front bumper, he paused mid-step and shouted something to the corporal, who had returned to the gate. The corporal hurried to the officer and fell to his knees in front of him. He covered his ears with his hands and cowered on the ground like a frightened animal. The problem was one I had witnessed before. The corporal had failed to inform his boss that my car had diplomatic license plates. If the corporal had told him, the pompous officer would not have ignored my outstretched hand and insulted me like he did. My official position and the color of my skin were a dual humiliation – an officer embarrassed in front of his underling not only by a *mzungu*, but by one with special status.

The officer slapped the corporal on the side of the head and pushed him with his boot so hard the man tumbled backwards to the ground. The officer returned to the side of my vehicle and saluted crisply. He used the familiar military style gesture made popular by British colonialists, lifting one leg in a slight hop, bringing the leg back smartly to the ground with another hop, and raising a flat hand in salute. The officer then said to me, while holding his pose, "His Excellency, the Life President, sends greeting." Flecks of fine red dust caught up in the salute settled slowly over the officer's black boots.

"It's almost dark," I said. "Looks like I made it, just in time."

"You are most welcome," replied the officer.

Chapter 5
Preacher

African countries routinely close borders at sunset, and the gate between Umbika and Tologland was no exception. My Land Cruiser was the last vehicle to enter Umbika this evening. If I had arrived ten minutes later, the frontier would have been sealed, and even my diplomatic passport would not have provided leverage enough to get me back into Umbika until daybreak. Knowing how close I had cut it, having stayed longer with the Mormons than anticipated, I considered myself lucky. It was essential I returned to the capital now. The Ambassador was counting on me to meet Maurice Hightower with him the next morning when his plane touched down in the capital city.

Up the road a stone's throw from the border was a petrol station. I pulled in and got out of my car. The station was typical for a frontier town: two pumps – one gas, one diesel – a stack of used tires, a small office of concrete blocks and a tin roof. Long ago, the walls on the station had been painted in vertical stripes of green and white, but the stripes were barely visible now. There was a new coat of paint under the roof line, however, a yellow horizontal stripe printed with red lettering: "Bata Petrol Ltd. Welcome to Molo, Umbika. Land of Fine Roads." An Umbikan flag, frayed and faded, hung like an ancient greeting from an arm of old pipe above the front door. The town of Molo was splayed out behind the station, rows of thatched roofs and mud walls, a few whitewashed shops and tin roofs. Blue smoke from cooking fires drifted over the town. I enjoyed the smell of wood smoke in the evening. The sweet scent still seemed mysterious and alluring to me, even after fifteen years.

An elderly Umbik man was standing beside the door to the petrol office, chewing on a fist of sugar cane, when a Tolog boy of nine or ten years sprinted through the doorway. He ran to my Land Cruiser. I had seen the dark-skinned boy on previous trips through Molo.

"His Excellency, the Life President, sends greeting, Boss," the boy said in Umbik, with a lisping Tolog accent. I spoke neither Umbik nor Tolog, but had memorized Umbika's national greeting and customary response.

"I am honored," I replied in Umbik.

The boy smiled and wiped his hands on a rag pulled from the waist of his shorts. He admired my vehicle. He tapped his knuckles on the front fender and gave me a thumbs-up approval. "Toyota," he said. "Fill-hup?"

I nodded, and the boy went to work. The old man in front of the station, I noticed, was spitting sugar cane pulp to the ground with more urgency and determination now. His gaze was focused on the border fence. A commotion of some sort appeared to be brewing beyond the fence line. In the barren strip of dirt between the two countries, I saw through broken and missing slats in the fence, a couple of dark Tolog men were arguing with the brown-faced Umbikan officer who had saluted me. The border gate was open a foot or so, and the officer had positioned himself in the opening to keep the two from entering his country. The Umbikan corporal was standing behind his boss, pointing his rifle towards the two men. By the look of their clothing, these Tolog men were drifters, vagrants. One was holding a suitcase bound by yellow rope, the other a pink plastic sack slung over his shoulder. The loudness of the men's shouting carried into Molo. Townspeople had come to see what the commotion was about. I stood next to the old man at the station. I asked him what the problem was at the gate.

"Ha!" he laughed and spit out a mash of cane pulp. "The officer said to them, 'Look up, you foolish Tologs. Can you see the sun? It is night. Go away. Umbika is closed.'" The old man's grin was brimming with Umbik pride.

The drifter with the pink sack pushed against the gate with his shoulder. The officer pushed back, but the small Umbik was unable to match the Tolog man's size and strength. The gate opened another foot. The officer grabbed his corporal's Billy club and beat it Clack! Clack! Clack! against the gate pole, just in front of the intruder's nose. The warning was enough to stop the dark man's advance.

Then, both drifters began pushing at the gate, forcing the officer back another step. Sensing defeat, the officer pulled out his pistol and touched the barrel to one drifter's temple, the tip only an inch off the man's ear. Throughout Africa, I had witnessed confrontations similar to this. When police got involved in a disturbance, the possibility of someone getting hurt was high. What saved countless lives in Africa each year was not diplomacy or donor assistance, but the fact that most countries were too poor to give every policeman his own firearm.

"You think he'll shoot?" I asked the old man next to me. He grinned, not realizing I was being facetious. The intruders backed away from the gate. I watched the two men set down their luggage on the hard ground between the two countries. One began to dance in a circle around the bags on the ground. He flapped his long shadowy arms as if they were giant wings, his pivot foot tracing a circle in the dirt. His companion clapped in time and shrieked whenever the birdman changed direction. Bush theater at its best. A protest play everyone understood but me.

"What kind of bird is he supposed to be?" I asked the old man.

"Turkey vulture," he said. His voice no longer sounded amused. "They dishonor our police with their dance." His body language grew angrier. "They have no right!"

Tologs on the other side of no man's land had arrived at their fence and were watching the dance too. An old man in the Tolog crowd started clapping in rhythm with the birdman's companion. Soon, dozens of Tologs had joined in. On my side, Umbikans watched in silence, waiting for their officer to regain his honor. Before the officer could distinguish himself, the birdman howled and fell to the ground. He lay motionless on the hard earth. Tologs burst into cheer, some whistled, a wave of unruly noise rolled across the border and into Molo. Their humiliation complete, Molo townspeople turned and walked briskly away. The drifter got up off the ground, dusted himself off. The two wanderers walked to the gate to Tologland with their belongings, where the sentry let them enter.

The young boy filling my gas tank had been watching the commotion too and failed to notice that fuel was overflowing my gas tank's spout. The clear liquid gushed down my side panel and was soaking the ground around my rear tire.

"It's full already!" I shouted to the boy.

He quickly shut off the flow and removed the nozzle. "It'th full, Bawth," he called back, nervously. He locked the pump handle back into its housing and put his rag to work soaking up streaks of fuel on my fender. He continued to rub the stain, even after it was dry, and looked in my direction, waiting to see what punishment I would hand down for his costly error.

Three Umbik men I hadn't noticed earlier emerged from the purple shadows near the fence line and approached the gas pumps. Because the daylight was so far gone, it was difficult for me to make out their faces. I paid the old man for my gas and was walking back to my car. I could feel the eyes of the three men measuring me. Even though I had walked with a limp for years, I never saw it as a handicap. Still, I knew there was enough unevenness in my stride to attract the curiosity of those seeing me move for the first time.

The air around my car smelled of evaporating fuel. "It's dry," I said to the youngster still passing a nervous rag across my fender. "You can stop. It's okay." I pulled five bills from my wallet and handed them to the pump boy. His face brightened and his shoulders shook at the sight of so much money. With his thumb and index finger, the only full fingers he had on the hand, he accepted my gift and formed a half fist around the bills.

"Bawth," he said and darted away.

"Save some for a rainy day," I called, but he had already disappeared into the station.

In Africa, you get so accustomed to unknown people hanging around, doing nothing, waiting for something to happen, you tend not to see them anymore. I had not been closely watching the three Umbik men approaching the gas pumps, but somehow they had come right behind my Land Cruiser. I opened my door and started to get into the car, when one of them spoke in a commanding voice. "That is too much to gift a pumper," he said.

The men were positioned like a triangle in the narrow space between the gas pump and my rear bumper, hardly more than two arm-lengths away. The speaker stood in front of his pals, close enough for me to see the details of his rough face. His brown eyes were darker than his skin, and an ugly scar cut across his forehead. He carried in his small hand a well-worn black book, thick like a Bible. It was Saturday, and church services on Saturday afternoon were common in this region of the country. I figured he was a preacher. His clothes seemed to bear out that conclusion – peach colored dress shirt with sleeves – dress pants, dark gray and cuffed – white tube socks filling the space between the cuffs and a pair of brown shoes – a blue blazer, missing all but one brass button.

"It is wrong," the preacher advised, "to let them see themselves as more than God intended. That one is a pumper. He will always be a pumper. He will never be more."

"Excuse me?" I said. The moment the words left my mouth, I regretted saying anything. I knew better than to get into a confrontation with a stranger. Keep your mouth shut. It was one of the first rules of Africa, especially at night. The preacher moved closer. His scar shone as a hideous reminder of some previous encounter, curving violently around one eye and ending at his ear. Bible in hand, the man rested his forearm against my side window. He said, "When you pay so much to a Tolog, you make him think he is something better than he is. Did you not see his failing?" The man's deeply bloodshot eyes pointed at the dark petrol blot on the ground.

"I saw the gas, if that's what you mean. The overflow was an accident. It means nothing."

"It was his error," said the preacher. "That is what it means. But now the boy does not know what it means. You have confused him. He acts with recklessness, and you give him a reward."

"I've been through here before," I said. "I know that boy, and I'll give him whatever I want. He loves his job."

"He does not love a job," said the preacher. "He does not know how to love like that. What he knows is you and other *mzungu* will pay a Tolog pumper more than he is worth. He knows you are ignorant. The boy has learned that." I was tired and hungry, and the most important VIP visit of my career was kicking off in the morning. All I wanted was to get home and crawl into bed. I had no zeal to debate a stranger over my generosity or his tribal politics.

"I'm ignorant?" I said. "Whatever you say, chief." I got into my car. The powerful Land Cruiser engine started with a roar, and I pulled away from the pump. As I left, three brutal sounds arose from the back of my car. Bam! Bam! Bam! I quickly braked and checked my side mirror. In the purple haze of evening, the three strange men were nothing more than shades in the distance, but they were walking towards me with great purpose. This time, however, I would avoid an argument. I accelerated forcefully and kept an eye on my mirror. The men chased my car but were swallowed up in a cloud of dust. In seconds, I was on solid pavement again, and soon the town of Molo had disappeared behind me.

I drove east towards the capital city, a hundred and ten miles to go. I wondered what transgressions I had committed to cause three strangers to act so aggressively. All I did was give the equivalent of two U.S. dollars to a dark-skinned, barefoot boy, a kid who owned nothing of his own, who survived day to day on the generosity of strangers, a child who pumped gas without all of his fingers and lived among people not of his own tribe, all in a back corner of the world few people cared about.

T-I-A, I thought to myself. This is Africa.

Chapter 6
Pulley

East of Molo, a wide swatch of darkly-bruised clouds swirled in front of me in the eggplant sky. They were the first clouds I had seen in months. I switched on my head lamps, the powerful beams spreading a carpet of white across the dim roadway. Umbika had only two paved highways of commercial grade in the country, the east-west M-1 that I was on, and its sister the M-2, which ran north-south. Both were jewels, among the best roads in Africa. The M-1 stretched from Molo, at the western frontier, 350 miles to the eastern edge of the country. The M-2 started in the mountains in the North and meandered across the central plain, dropping 3,000 feet in altitude from north to south.

Before the British arrived in the late 1800s, these two thoroughfares had been foot paths, hard-scrabble trade routes pressed into the bush. The spot where they intersected developed into the commercial hub of the territory. In the 1920s, British engineers began leveling the paths and paving them with asphalt. After the British awarded the native Umbikans political independence in the 1960s, the Danish government offered to build the new nation a pair of modern highways to pull together all four corners of the developing country. The Danes were not major players in global affairs then and had not ventured into Africa in any significant way before. Yet they were fully committed to the idea of African self-determination, and they wanted to do their part to assist that vision.

The Danes chose *Umbike Vej Planlaegge*, or Umbikan Roads Project, for their first humanitarian initiative on the continent. It took the builders four years to complete the two highways. They insisted on using only the most exacting European expertise and materials for the work. Unlike most roads in Africa, the tarmac surface of the M-1 and M-2 was mirror smooth, the pea-gravel shoulders wide and deep. The craftsmanship overall was so perfect that Umbika became known in East Africa as "the land of fine roads." Even though the country's other thoroughfares were nothing but dirt.

I arrived in Umbika nine months before Maurice Hightower's visit. The Danish Government had just announced it would no longer repair Umbika's two stellar highways, something Denmark had been doing for 20 years, ever since the roads were constructed. Vivid written accounts and photos in the Danish press of recent human rights abuses committed under the dictatorship of Life President Jim Jimmy Mulenga were so unpleasant to the average Dane that the Danish Parliament was forced to suspend all financial and material assistance to Umbika. The Life President was furious, so he did the only two things he could: he cut off water to the Danish ambassador's residence and he canceled the teaching contract of a visiting math professor from Copenhagen University. During my nine months in Umbika, I had not noticed any deterioration in the surfaces of the two highways, but as I had seen happen in other African countries, it was only a matter of time.

The surface of the M-1 was a joy to drive on. That night after I left Molo the highway's white centerline became a beacon guiding me home. Without that line down the middle of the road, and my powerful headlights, I would have been lost in darkness. Few villages along the M-1 were connected to Umbika's electrical grid, so it was impossible for me to know in the surrounding darkness if I was passing a farm, a settlement, or just empty bush. The U.S. Embassy had a rule prohibiting us from driving long distances at night; they called it, "driving dark." In fact, the Department's policy for all of East Africa stated that American diplomats must never venture out of a major city after sunset. For officers posted here for the first time, the order seemed harsh, but highways in East Africa became death traps after dark. Fatality rates were ten times those in Europe. Why? Because Africans rarely pushed disabled vehicles off the road and most drivers at night were either drunk or unlicensed. I did not want to drive dark this night, but my need to get back to the capital city left me no choice.

I glanced at my dashboard. The bright clock assured me I was making progress. But I was feeling tired. I kept my right wheels close to the centerline, concentrating on what lay ahead on the road, even as my thoughts drifted to Hightower. I had read an article about him in *People* magazine a few years earlier, published after he appeared on a late-night talk show. Hightower had written a book that included a chapter on the KKK. Wherever Hightower went on his book tour, Klansmen picketed him, including at an Atlanta TV station. The program from Atlanta was broadcast live. When Hightower was introduced, he ran barefooted onto the stage, wearing only a white Klan hood and a pair of ruby red basketball shorts. Printed in magic marker under one eyehole on the hood was the word "Truth," and printed under the other hole was the word "Lies." According to *People*, Hightower pranced across the stage like a big black stallion, taunting his critics outside. Inside the studio, the audience clapped and whistled. Lucky for us, I thought, as I drove deeper into the darkness, Umbika had no TV stations.

The first rain to arrive was only mist on my windshield. Minutes later, the drops came with more determination. Isolated cloudbursts were common at the end of the dry season, splashing the blacktop for a minute or two before disappearing. This night, the rain started that way too, but it didn't stop there. Soon, the drops were falling with greater velocity, hitting the windshield with considerable force. I turned on my wipers and leaned forward, over my steering wheel, to get a better look ahead. Water whipped across the pavement, and the rain pounded against the Land Cruiser like a thousand tiny hammers. I dimmed my headlights to reduce reflection and kept the centerline as my anchor to the highway. Then, the steering wheel began to drag to the right, pulled by an unknown force, so I reduced speed. The wheel continued to tug me over the centerline. I eased back on the gas, cutting my speed another third. In a heavy sheet of rainwater, I lost track of my position on the road, unable to see anything ahead. I was driving blind. Then, just as quickly as I had lost the road, the white line reappeared.

Whump – whump – whump – whump. A new noise bellowed from the back of the 4x4. I knew something wasn't right. Whump – whump – whump. The pull on the wheel was more than I could handle. I lifted my foot from the accelerator and engaged the clutch, letting the car coast along the pavement. The odd noise continued, though with less urgency. I applied more brake and steered to the shoulder, coming to a stop with two wheels on gravel and two on tarmac. I punched the emergency flasher, charging the black air around me with one-second bursts of amber light. I had no rain gear in the car, only a U.S. Embassy umbrella. I took it and a flashlight from my glove box and stepped outside.

Rain drenched the front seat before I could shut the door. The umbrella kept only my head and shoulders dry. Within seconds, I was soaking wet from the waist down. The rear tire on the driver's side, I saw, was shredded, its metal rim smoking hot and hissing in the rain. The air was smoldering with the odor of burning rubber. The Land Cruiser's spare that I needed was concealed behind the rear bumper and locked in place by a crank and pulley system. It was only accessed by inserting a long rod with a key-shaped end into a similarly-shaped hole above the bumper. The rod worked as a crank to lower the spare from its harness. According to the car manual in the glove box, the rod was stored with the jack beneath the rear seat. I found the jack, but the rod was missing. Its anchoring clips were there, but the clips were empty. I shined my flashlight across the back floor, under the seats, and in the cargo bay. Nothing. Without the rod, I could not engage the pulley and lower the spare. Without the spare, I was stuck with only three good tires.

I bent down to get a better look at what I was facing. Water gushed around the spots where my knees touched pavement. I shined my flashlight on six steel bolts anchoring the pulley to the chassis, each bolt looking as big as my thumb. But I had no tools to remove them. No way to get at the spare tire. My situation was hopeless. Rainwater washed across the highway and over the gravel shoulder, carving rifts through the pebbles like miniature canyons. The quick streams disappeared in savannah grass lining a nearby ditch. I pointed my flashlight beyond the waist-high grass, searching for a village or even one hut, but my light was not strong enough to penetrate the storm. Up and down the M-1, the highway was deserted. No lights. No cooking smoke in the wind. No human sound, only the drum of falling rain and the tap-tap-tap of an idling engine. I had spent my entire career in Africa. Fifteen years. I had endured malaria twice, dysentery once – seen floods and famine – survived civil war and personal loss. But I had never before been stranded in the dark, in the middle of nowhere, alone.

Something on the rear wheel caught my eye. The inflation valve, that long plastic stem protruding from the rim, was cracked along one side and bent at a ninety-degree angle. Only a powerful force could cause such damage. The valve was too far from the ground for the blow to have been caused by the highway. A hard kick, however, directed against the plastic stem, could cause it to split apart, just like what I was seeing. Compressed air would bleed out of the crack until the tire was deflated, ten or twenty minutes later. Then, the spinning rim would cut through the rubber tire like a circular saw, and a driver not reacting quickly enough, especially at high speed, could easily roll the vehicle. Even in the U.S., an accident like that would be fatal.

I recalled the three strange men at the filling station, the men who had confronted me over the spilled gas, and the banging sounds when I pulled away. The preacher had worn heavy dress shoes, with thick heels. Shoes that could cause considerable damage. Had he been angry enough to want me dead, or to just delay my travel? An answer did not matter. I would never see the man again or know for sure what he was thinking.

Chapter 7
Mr. Mkandawire

Having decided to sleep in my vehicle, I retreated from the rain. In the morning, I would hitch a ride to the capital city. I shut down the engine, turned off my headlights, but let the emergency flasher continue to spread bursts of hope into the darkness. Reclining the angle of my seat, I noticed a tiny halo of light moving at the corner of my side mirror. At first, the orb was faint, an insignificant distraction in the vast dark sea behind me. I could not tell if the image was an actual light or a phantom reflection. I continued to follow the sphere, as it grew in size, until I was seeing the lone headlamp of a small pickup truck approaching. I went back into the pouring rain. The truck's cab listed precariously to one side, perhaps carrying an uneven weight or broken spring. With rainwater flowing across the pavement, the small vehicle looked more like a boat than a truck. Its captain was doing all he could to steer a course through the waves.

I was not sure if anyone inside the pickup had seen me, so I vigorously waved my flashlight until the truck rolled to a stop directly behind my car. At the steering wheel was a brown-skinned man about my age, wearing a straw hat and white shirt. Next to him sat a younger woman, her hair threaded with colorful beads. A *chitenji* was wrapped over her shoulder, the fabric supporting a bundle that I realized was a baby. The driver got out and walked towards me. Even with his straw hat, he was a head shorter than I, but heavier. "His Excellency, The Life President, sends greeting," the man said, his voice barely able to penetrate the storm. He extended a hand in the formal Umbikan way. "I am Mkandawire. You are experiencing something of difficulty."

"I've got a bad tire, but I can't reach the spare. It's under there," I said, pointing to the back of my car. "I don't have the special tool to crank it down." Without my inviting him, Mkandawire rested his hands and knees on the wet pavement. I handed him my flashlight. Moments later, he stood again.

"That one has us." He gave me back the light.

"I figured as much," I said. "I was supposed to be back in the capital already."

"You will get there, sir. I can be of assistance."

"You mean you can fix it?" Mkandawire nodded. "How will you get at the spare?"

He smiled. "It is not the size of our work, sir. It is the size of our desire." Mr. Mkandawire returned to his truck. He spoke to his female passenger and handed her his straw hat. Reaching behind his seat, he took a while to find whatever he was looking for. Finally, he returned to where I was waiting. "This will grab it," he said and held up an adjustable wrench no bigger than his hand.

"Okay," I nodded, not believing the little tool could unlock much of anything, let alone my spare tire. He took my flashlight and lay on the pavement, his back flat to the wet surface. He wiggled under the rear of the 4x4, until only his pants legs and shoes were showing. Seconds later, he eased his head out and gave me back the light.

"Point the torch there, sir," he said, motioning towards the savannah grass bending in the wind. "We must keep vigilant for snakes," the last word a familiar reminder. On the continent there could always be something dangerous moving in the dark. My heart raced at the thought of a snake nearby. I flooded the pea gravel with light, knowing that snakes did not care about rainy weather or time of day. In Africa, if a cobra or mamba wanted to find you, it could.

A week earlier, the Ambassador's secretary had gone into her bathroom and discovered a yellow-bellied sand snake wrapped around the showerhead. Her gardener killed it with a machete. A month before that, a pit viper entered the ground floor apartment of the Embassy's housing officer, slipping in through a crack in the drainpipe and making itself at home in the toilet bowl. Fortunately, just before sitting down, the officer had noticed movement in the bowl. In the U.S. it was common to worry about mice and cockroaches coming in where they shouldn't. In Africa, it was snakes. I walked a continuous loop around my Land Cruiser, shining the bright beam out across the shiny pavement, my eyes alert to even the slightest movement. In one of my circles, the young woman in the pickup was watching my bad leg, her gaze captivated by the rhythm of my limp. When she realized I had spotted her, she quickly looked away.

Mkandawire's right hand reached out from under the car and dropped a steel bolt on the pavement. Plunk! Then, a second and a third. To save me, this man, who I had already concluded would fail, was taking apart the back of my car. He was working piece by piece, in the dark, by touch alone, his hand surrounded by edges sharp enough to slice through his skin like a razorblade. His fingers turning the wrench a fraction of a rotation, resetting, and turning again, over and over. "Is everything okay?" I asked.

"We are experiencing progress," replied the African, his words barely audible, as rain continued to pound the pavement around us.

"Don't worry about snakes," I said. "I haven't seen anything move out here."

"You must remain attentive, sir. Darkness brings out the worst of their kind."

The first African snake I had come across was fourteen years earlier, on the third fairway at the Ikoyi Golf Club in Lagos. On its way to a nearby creek, a gray python had crossed in front of my foursome and held up play for ten minutes. Two years later, in Brazzaville, I watched from my kitchen window as a flock of finches fought off an emerald green boomslang that was circling up a mango tree towards a nest of chicks. That same year, I found a red cobra asleep under the hood of my car, its fat body coiled around the carburetor.

Africa was filled with stories of snakes, and like everyone else, I had my share.

I collected five bolts off the pavement and placed them inside the Land Cruiser. After Mkandawire removed the sixth, he pushed the spare tire out from under the car and wiggled after it. Together, we mounted the new wheel, then faced each other between our vehicles. It was ten o'clock now. I would be sleeping in my own bed tonight, not in the front seat of my car.

"No snakes," I smiled.

"That is a good sign," Mkandawire replied. "When snakes find us in an early storm, it means too much rain for our crops."

"Let me put something on those," I said, pointing at his bleeding knuckles. "I have a first aid kit in the car." While Mkandawire held the umbrella over us, I covered each wound with a band-aid, and then wrapped his entire hand with white gauze and tape. I had taken the Department's first aid course.

For the first time since I had pulled to the side of the road, the rain was beginning to let up. "Thank you for helping me," I said. "I'm not sure what would've happened if you hadn't come along." I handed him two American twenty-dollar bills, the equivalent of a month's salary in Umbika. Mkandawire did not accept the money immediately, but bowed with his hands together, as if to pray, a traditional sign of humility.

"Those are too much for one puncture," he said.

"Please," I countered, extending the gift. "Take it for your family. I know you'll find good use for it." He reached one arm towards me, supporting the wrist with his other hand, a sign of gratitude.

"You are most welcome, sir," he said and tucked the bills into his shirt pocket, the green money showing through the thin, wet fabric.

"Tell your wife I'm grateful too," I said. "It's a terrible night to be out."

"That one is my daughter," said Mkandawire, proudly. "The girl, she is much like her mother, but my wife passed some time now."

As I drove on, the pavement on the M-1 remained slick, even after the rain had stopped. In low spots along the road, whiffs of steam rose in the cooler air. I held the Land Cruiser to a reasonable speed, given the darkness and uncertain road conditions. Every few minutes, I checked my rearview mirror to make sure the small pickup was behind me. It was reassuring on a deserted road in a foreign country to know that a man who was skilled enough to take apart a car with only his fingers and a small tool was close by.

At one point during the drive, my thoughts drifted. Maurice Hightower was arriving in the morning. I made another to-do list in my head. I needed to be ready. The next time I checked my mirror, the lone headlight that had been following me was gone. I slowed to a crawl and checked the mirror again. There was no sign of Mkandawire's pick-up. I stopped in the middle of the empty road, my wheels straddling the centerline. I got out and looked back up the M-1 as far as I could see, all the way to where the centerline dissolved into nothingness. Fearing I had somehow lost track of my speed and gotten too far ahead of the pickup, I stood in the road for ten minutes, then waited another five, but the small truck never re-appeared. Mkandawire and his daughter and infant grandchild had turned off somewhere, perhaps a side road only locals knew.

Chapter 8
Arrival

Another day in paradise is how Blake would describe a Sunday morning like this one: azure sky like blue honey – shirtsleeve temperatures – air as quiet as a church. The intoxicating scent of jasmine wafted in through my bedroom window and circled my head. A day in paradise, indeed, if not for the fact Maurice Hightower's plane was touching down in a couple of hours. I lived in the American Residential Compound, the ARC, as did all American diplomats, a cluster of low-rise apartments adjacent to the Ambassador's Residence. The entire property was well-guarded and surrounded by a ten-foot brick wall topped with razor wire. After breakfast, I walked the neatly groomed brick path to Ambassador Durhlmann's stately home. Near the house, I spotted Connie already there, deep in thought and pacing between the Ambassador's tennis court and his black Sedan de Ville. The limo was decked out in a recent waxing and small American flags had been fastened to the front fenders. When I was beside the Cadillac, I called to Connie. "Beautiful morning!"

She looked up, but it took a moment for her to gather her bearings. "I guess it's okay," she said, pushing errant strands of hair behind her ears. Connie was an attractive woman, especially true in the soft morning light. If I had been ten years younger, I would have taken a stronger interest in her, but the difference in our ages made any future together impractical.

"You seem stressed," I said to Connie as she walked towards me.

"This is Maurice Hightower," she said under her breath. "Of course, I'm stressed. Aren't you?"

"Not really. He'll be gone before we know it."

"Ha."

The hood of the Ambassador's car gleamed in the spatters of sunlight falling between the leaves and branches of an old jackalberry tree next to the Residence. The Ambassador's driver, Timbu, was behind the wheel of the limo. He nodded at me. "I still get a kick riding with the flags," I told Connie.

"This is my first time," she replied sadly and motioned for me to follow her.

"What's wrong?" I asked at the back of the limo.

"I've had problems before, with men like him."

"What kind of men?"

"Black men." She avoided eye contact.

"Hightower's a troublemaker, but he's nothing to be scared of."

"You don't know, Joe."

"Believe me, Connie, this visit isn't the end of the world."

"I'm not a complainer, Joe."

The engine of the Cadillac roared to life. The Ambassador was closing the front door to his house. He saw us and waved. "Just stick to what we do best," I said.

"If Dave Hardy's right, you'll end up in Port Moresby or worse. Is that the next post you want?" Connie said.

"It'd get me out of Africa."

Connie looked away, not appreciating my attempt at humor. "And what about me?" she said as we got in the backseat.

The snap of the flags flying on the fenders turned the heads of pedestrians we passed on the road to the airport. Connie sat next to the Ambassador, with me facing them on the jump seat. The Foreign Minister had called the Ambassador that morning to say Hightower would arrive through the VIP lounge and not the main terminal. No reason for the change was given. We breezed past the police checkpoint at the airport gate, the white-gloved officers saluting as we passed. The VIP Lounge was a one-floor building beyond the main terminal, Umbika's exclusive doorway for dignitaries arriving by air. We parked under a wooden pergola, its mahogany beams smothered in spiraling vines dotted with enormous white flowers. A valet in shiny black pants, white shirt, and red waistcoat opened the door for us. Beside him stood a functionary from the Office of Protocol, an older man in a gray three-piece suit. The valet bowed. "His Excellency, the Life President, sends greeting," he said.

The man from Protocol moved forward. "It is most regrettable, Mr. Ambassador," he said. "The flight from Paris is delayed thirty minutes."

The Ambassador nodded and called to his driver, "Bring me my crossword puzzles, Timbu!" And so started the visit.

The VIP lounge was an amazing example of too much of everything. We walked up steps clothed in sapphire blue carpeting, entered a long rectangular greeting room with teak walls varnished to a mirror finish and ceiling panels sculpted in plaster. Bamboo fans fitted with ostrich feathers twirled overhead. There were door hinges gilded in gold and clay pots overflowing with hibiscus and birds of paradise. Even the wastebaskets were striking, each carved in the shape of a lion from its own block of ebony. We were seated on over-stuffed leather couches. Ladies brought us spiced tea in white porcelain cups edged in gold. In light of the dismal conditions in which most Umbikans lived, such extravagance seemed shameful.

I recounted my flat tire experience for Connie and the Ambassador. When I finished, the Ambassador leaned close to me. I expected a light comment, maybe a joke about the rain, but his whisper was serious. "You notice anything unusual on the M-1?" he asked. "Anything out of the ordinary?" I told him I saw nothing like that. "What about army vehicles or Explorers?"

"I saw nothing but the pickup that stopped to help. Is something going on?"

"We're hearing chatter," the Ambassador said. "Something's in the wind.

Don't know what. Something up north, it seems. I'm just wondering what the government knows."

A picture window looked out onto the gray strip of asphalt that was the airport's only runway. Beyond the runway was a chain-link fence, and beyond the fence nothing but red earth and acacia trees pressed up against the horizon. A Kenya Airlines jet landed and parked near the terminal. Passengers descended an open staircase and climbed into shuttle busses on the tarmac. On the side of one bus was a billboard photo of President Mulenga, smiling with open arms. "You Are Most Welcome!" the caption read. On another bus was a picture of a stern-faced police officer with folded arms. "Pull no stops! Fight corruption!" the poster said. The loaded busses drove to the main terminal.

Ambassador Durhlmann continued to fill in squares on his crossword puzzle, comfortable in that pose on the leather couch, as if relaxing at home in his den. He appeared confident, not showing even a hint of anxiety over what could be one of the most precarious visits of his career. Connie was absorbed in the task she had set for herself, meticulously pinching off split ends on her long strands of hair, pausing every ten minutes to visit the restroom. A bare-footed Umbik woman was organizing rows of crystal stemware on a table in the middle of the lounge. She clapped, and two Tolog ladies entered through a side door. They lugged a steel tub filled with ice and bottles of Coke and Orange Fanta into the room. They set it on a mat beside the glassware table. That was when it struck me. There were way too many glasses and soda bottles for the arrival of one American VIP.

"Mr. Ambassador, the flight from Paris will touch in five minutes," said the man from Protocol. The Ambassador closed his puzzle book and tucked it inside his jacket. The three of us stood at the picture window, watching the wheels of an Air France 747 kiss the runway. Four Umbikans wearing brown suits and yellow ties, the uniform of the Special Security Service, entered the lounge. They took positions at the doorway leading out to the tarmac. Three immigration officers I knew from previous visits to the airport came in after them, each carrying a stack of white cards and a rubber stamp. A dozen drivers entered the lounge and stood in a corner.

"Something's up," I said to the Ambassador. "This isn't for our guest."

The room remained eerily quiet, like the silence before a horse race. Then, the double doors leading from the tarmac burst open. Five soldiers of the National Explorers Group, President Mulenga's paramilitary guard, strode into the room. They wore black jumpsuits and dark sunglasses, machine guns clipped to heavy white straps slung over their shoulders. At best, NEGs were regarded as clichés by Western diplomats in Umbika, at worst as clowns. On the other hand, the average man on the street in Umbika feared them completely. NEGs had the Life President's consent to use "any means necessary" to stop dissent and keep Umbika's citizens in line. And they did.

From the tarmac, VIP passengers began entering the lounge, African men, women, and children. Their voices were buoyant, glad to be back on familiar ground. They handed duty-free shopping bags to the drivers. Children spotted the pop and scurried over to it, snatching bottles and sweet biscuits off a silver tray. "What the hell's going on, Joe?" the Ambassador asked.

"Someone very important must be on that plane," I said.

Connie was first to spot Hightower. A head and a half taller than the Umbiks around him, he was hard to miss. Plus, his skin was darker than theirs and he was wearing an immaculate yellow suit with white shirt, two buttons undone at the neck. A thick gold chain dangled in the open space. Hightower's hair was silver-blue, like moonlight falling on fresh snow at night. He was a fit man, with muscular shoulders, and he looked nothing like someone in his late sixties, despite the color of his hair. As Jill Hardy had reported, he was an unusually handsome man. But it was how Hightower carried himself across the room that made the strongest impression on me. He glided over the expensive oriental carpet when he walked, his long strides graceful and effortless, his head held high, his back erect. It was remarkable poise for someone who had just traveled halfway around the world.

A photographer popped flashes, not at Hightower, but at the attractive Umbikan lady walking beside him. In her early forties and very finely groomed, she wore a richly-tailored African dress and matching head scarf. Thick gold bangles encircled her wrists and smaller versions hung from her ears. "That's Catherine Phiri," I said to the Ambassador.

"Who?" he asked.

"The Life President's youngest sister. She's married to an Asian businessman."

The Ambassador pushed forward, into Hightower's path. "Welcome to Umbika," he said to the journalist. "I'm Warner Durhlmann, the American Ambassador." He turned towards the pretty figure, whose hand was intertwined with Hightower's. "Mrs. Phiri, I don't believe I've had the pleasure until now."

"We are thrilled Maurice has come home to Africa," she said. She raised Hightower's hand to her lavender-painted lips and kissed it, a gesture I had never seen an Umbikan do in public, man or woman. The security men behind Mrs. Phiri flinched. "We will talk again soon," she said and departed.

"How was your flight?" the Ambassador asked Hightower, who was watching the Life President's sister walk away.

"Things got better on the flight from Paris," he said and winked. "Met her on the plane. Imagine that."

Ambassador Durhlmann nodded, but I could tell Hightower's answer confused him. "I want to assure you, my staff and I will do everything we can to make your visit exactly what you hope it to be," he said.

"Thank you. The White House promised I'd be able to get around the country, see things for myself. That's all I ask."

Durhlmann introduced Hightower to Connie and me. Connie stayed half a step behind my shoulder, so Hightower went to her and shook her hand. Then, he shook mine. "They told me in Washington you're the best damn guide in Africa," Hightower said. He had soft hands but a strong grip.

"I'm here to help, any way I can."

"We'll sit down and talk," he said.

"The program we planned—"

Hightower interrupted me. "I have a meeting this morning at the Presidential Palace."

"A meeting today? Sunday? With President Mulenga?" the Ambassador asked. The news took us all by surprise.

"I arranged it in New York before leaving. They didn't tell you?"

"This is the first we've heard of it," the Ambassador said.

"If it's too much trouble, I can catch a ride with Catherine."

"It's not a problem," the Ambassador assured our guest. "My car is outside." Of course, we would never let such a high-profile guest as Maurice Hightower out of our sight. The White House had made it perfectly clear what they expected of us. Connie had drifted away, to the edge of the room where children were clinking bottles and munching sweets. I waved to her that we were leaving. Durhlmann and Hightower were already at the door, but I waited for Connie to catch up. She looked out of sorts. "What's wrong?" I asked.

"When he looked at me, I could tell what he was thinking." Connie was clearly upset, her hand covering her chest.

"I think you're reading too much into this visit," I told her. "The poor guy just got here."

Hightower and the Ambassador were already in the limo when we got to the car park. I took the jump seat, facing them, and Connie got in front, next to the driver. We made small talk during the fifteen-minute ride from the airport to State House, but Connie said nothing, never turned around, just twirled the same strands of hair round and round her finger.

Chapter 9
State House

President Mulenga had four palaces, though State House, in the capital city, was the most elaborate and where he spent most of his time. Its front gate was spectacular, mounted with large brass finials in the shape of lion heads. Ceremonial guards dressed as bush warriors, wearing leopard skin loin cloths and headdresses of ostrich feathers and long grass, cuddled chrome-plated AK-47s at the gate. As we passed, they saluted our American flags rippling in the wind. A hundred Umbik ladies in colorful wraps and scarves were gathered at the foot of stone steps. Seeing our car, they erupted in high-pitched tongue calls. A traditional drummer, hidden somewhere behind the staircase, began an African beat, and the ladies started chanting and undulating their hips to the sound. Security men hovered on a patio at the top of the steps.

Fenton Mabviko, Umbika's Foreign Minister and first cousin to the Life President, was waiting for us at the bottom of the steps. Mabviko's skin was darker than the average Umbik, his build narrower, shoulders drooping. Thick glasses on his skinny nose made him appear timid, inconsequential, though he was anything but. Mabviko was a true believer, part of Mulenga's inner circle. People learned, sometimes the hard way, to take him seriously. After customary introductions, he took Hightower's hand and held it, as close friends do in East Africa, all the way up the staircase and into the palace. The Ambassador and I trailed them. Connie waited outside, next to the car.

"Mr. Ambassador," Mabviko said, stopping abruptly in the foyer, "His Excellency the Life President, wishes to confer privately with our guest. Afterwards, time permitting, His Excellency, the Life President, will enjoy tea with you." Before the Ambassador could respond, two aides appeared and escorted Hightower to the far end of the room. We watched him disappear behind tall doors guarded by stone-faced NEGs. Mabviko scurried away in the opposite direction.

"This is bullshit," the Ambassador said. "We've been outmaneuvered. Now we can't refute anything Mulenga says." I pointed to a comfortable chair, but the Ambassador declined, preferring to pace the room. An hour passed before the door to the President's suite opened again. Hightower emerged with Mabviko at his side. They walked briskly towards us.

"Mr. Ambassador," Mabviko said, "the Life President wishes you a good day, but regrets he is too busy to have tea." Hightower walked right past us, talking over his shoulder. With his long strides, he was already far enough away that I could not understand what he was saying.

"That's it?" the Ambassador said to Mabviko. "We waited here an hour." The Ambassador was extremely agitated and wanted to take his anger out on the Foreign Minister, but Hightower was already quite a ways across the foyer, on his way back to the car. The Ambassador abandoned Mabviko and hurried after our guest. I trailed by several steps, due to my leg. Hightower must have noticed and stopped.

"You okay with that foot?" he asked.

"I'm fine," I said.

"They told me you're the one who handles visas."

"My staff processes the applications, and I approve them."

"Good," Hightower said and pulled an Umbikan passport from his jacket pocket. "I have a favor to ask." He handed me the passport. A standard American visa application had been folded in half and slipped inside the front cover. "I just met a man whose son needs a visa to the U.S. I told him I didn't think it'd be a problem." I unfolded the form and saw the surname printed in black ink across the top of the page. ANDELEBE. It was not a common name in Umbika, yet one I knew. Below was printed the applicant's first name – WILLIAM. We arrived at the steps leading down to the Ambassador's limousine.

"Lovemore Andelebe gave you this application?" I said.

"You know the Colonel?"

"Not personally, but I've chatted with him at diplomatic functions."

"Lovemore Andelebe is commander of the National Police and head of Special Branch," Ambassador Durhlmann said, jumping into the conversation. Hightower started down the staircase.

"The Colonel has an important perspective on what's happening here, especially when it comes to the rebels," Hightower said, then paused at the bottom of the steps and looked up at me. "We don't discriminate against police officers when it comes to visas, do we?"

"Of course not," the Ambassador said.

As I came to the bottom of the stairs, I held out the application. "The form says William wants a tourist visa."

"He's planning a grand tour, you know. Disney World, Times Square, the Rocky Mountains."

"It says he wants to stay six months."

"The Colonel said it's his son's first trip abroad. If he likes the U.S., he might come back. He asked for something called 'a multiple-entry visa.'"

We reached the Cadillac. Connie was back in the front seat, still fidgeting with her hair. Later, I wished I had told Hightower the rest of the story right then, that twice the police chief's son had applied for a visa and been denied. Maybe Hightower already knew that, and State House was testing us to see how far his influence might carry. What they surely would not have told Hightower, what the Embassy already knew, was that Triple S had been grooming the Andelebe boy to spy on Umbikan dissidents in the U.S. His real mission was to befriend Umbikans living there and report to his father anyone who spoke unkindly about the Life President. Through beatings, lost jobs, and imprisonment, family members back home would learn the consequences of having relatives who criticized J.J. Mulenga, regardless of where they were in the world.

Back on the road again, the Ambassador's limousine passed through the market district. "Who's this fellow up north causing problems for the Life President?" Hightower asked.

"You mean Wisdom Chitsaya," the Ambassador said. "He's a cashew farmer."

"Is he on trial?"

"The trial starts this week," said the Ambassador. "It's not here in the capital, but up in Katembeyna, in the North."

"I heard he might hang for what he did. What's the official American position on that?"

"They haven't convicted him yet," I said. Hightower smiled knowingly, as if he were privy to more than he was letting on.

"Didn't he plot to overthrow the President?"

"Hopefully, the truth will come out in court," I said.

"Our government supports the rule of law," said the Ambassador matter-of-factly. "Chitsaya deserves a fair trial."

"You already told the press he's innocent," Hightower said. "You've undermined a fair trial before it even begins." The Cadillac was moving quickly towards the center of town. We passed warehouses and empty lots, overtook bicycles piled high with firewood, wove around crowded minivans unloading passengers.

"We've seen no evidence Chitsaya is guilty of anything," said the Ambassador.

"All he said was he wanted more than one choice when he voted. That doesn't sound outrageous," I added.

"I'd like to go up there and see for myself," Hightower said, looking out his window, watching the heart of the city pass by. "Maybe I'll write an article about the trial."

"Katembeyna is five hours by car," said the Ambassador. "Joe knows the lay of the land up there and can help you get around. Tonight, we've planned a dinner for you with the diplomatic community." Hightower nodded. We were almost to his hotel. He looked out his window again. I interpreted his agreeability as a good sign. Maybe the visit was starting out better than expected. Hightower leaned over the front seat and put his hand on Connie's shoulder.

"Miss Saunders," he said, "since you're the press attaché, maybe you can go north with us. I'd be interested hearing another journalist's perspective about this country." Our driver was just arriving at the Intercontinental Hotel. I waited for Connie to say something. When the silence became awkward, I turned in my seat to look at her.

"Here we are," said the Ambassador. "It's the nicest hotel in town."

Hightower took his hand off Connie's shoulder and eased back into his seat.

Chapter 10
Reception

The word "Umbika" roughly translates to English as "gift from Heaven." The country was one of the last British colonies in Africa in the 1960s to gain independence. By the time it was cut loose, Britain had grown tired of struggling to hold onto its old outposts. Jim Jimmy Mulenga, then a young lawyer educated in Ghana, led the delegation to Windsor Castle that received the official declaration of sovereignty from Queen Elizabeth. With a few strokes of her pen, the young royal ended nearly a century of subjugation for two million Africans. Their optimism for a free and fair life was short lived. The sorry truth was that liberty and justice rarely replaced colonial repression. In the New Africa, homegrown dictators were as ruthless as their European predecessors, sometimes worse. When I joined the Foreign Service, near the end of the independence movement in Africa, I was perplexed over how it was that so many well-educated people in the West could not understand why the new African leaders were so cruel and intolerant. As if peace and justice were the natural order of things.

During the first months of Umbika's independence, rival political factions took six months to agree on a parliament. When it was time to select the nation's first president, the vote was deadlocked between two old men. A compromise candidate was eventually floated, J.J. Mulenga, the young lawyer who had led the independence delegation to England. Mulenga was abrasive and arrogant, but the common Umbiks loved him. They remembered him from the impassioned BBC radio address he gave before accepting the Queen's decree of independence. In that speech, he spoke about Umbiks having been slaves to the colonialists for too long and now was the moment for seeking their destiny in a new world order. It was all about hope and the future. Parliament elected J.J. Mulenga as Umbika's first president on their next ballot.

Within the next year, Umbika's economy was crumbling. Three-quarters of the white population had fled the country. Thriving businesses were abandoned or turned over to black supervisors who were never taught how to organize a payroll or balance a ledger. All senior managers at the electric company, the water works, and the central hospital were gone. By the time Parliament amended the Constitution to allow Mulenga to use harsher methods to slow the exodus of skills and capital, only fifty-nine holders of a university degree were still living in Umbika. Shady black-market entrepreneurs conspired with corrupt officials in government to divert donor assistance to their own foreign accounts. President Mulenga threw some of the bandits in prison. He promised his countrymen that if Parliament gave him enough power, he could root out the other crooks and protect the people from more corruption and thievery. Desperate to stop economic free fall in the new nation, Parliament made J.J. Mulenga President for Life and gave him complete control over the treasury, police, and courts. Only thirty-six years old at the time, Mulenga was one of the most powerful men in Africa.

For Hightower's first night in Umbika, we had planned a reception for him at the Ambassador's Residence, with forty couples from several embassies and international organizations. All of those invited accepted the invitation, except for the South African Ambassador and his wife. This was not unexpected. Hightower had recently written a cutting op-ed piece condemning apartheid.

That night, I walked to the Residence from my apartment in the ARC and arrived an hour before the guests. A five-piece orchestra was already setting up on the large patio, across from a temporary bar. Several dining tables lined the perimeter of the patio, with a generous space left open in the center for dancing. A buffet table was covered in white linen and set with silver serving dishes. The Ambassador's wife found me on the patio, listening to the musicians tuning their instruments. She said Connie was ill and would not be attending. After what had happened in the car from State House, I was not surprised, but I felt disappointed in Connie. If she was going to make it in the Foreign Service, she needed to be able to put aside her opinions about someone like Maurice Hightower and focus on her work. Our responsibility at an event like this was to circulate among the guests and make small talk, make the guests feel welcome and build relationships. Her absence made everyone else's job a little tougher.

Seven bureaucrats and wives from the State Media Office were the first to arrive, even before our guest of honor. Attending an event at the U.S. Ambassador's home was the thrill of a lifetime for a mid-level functionary. The fancy plates edged in gold and the unlimited food and drink made a strong impression on these men and women. Connie was the one who had invited the Media Office bureaucrats, hoping they would eventually turn into sources of information for her during her stay in Umbika. In her absence, Blake and I took turns talking with them.

Hightower was brought from his hotel by the Ambassador's driver and took his place in the receiving line. He looked refreshed in a charcoal suit, pink shirt, and maroon tie. He said he had been able to nap a few hours after his long flight. After passing through the receiving line, which consisted of Hightower, the Ambassador, and Mrs. Durhlmann, the African guests headed to the bar and then gathered with their drinks in the living room. The Europeans clustered on the patio, talking or listening to the band. Blake and I stood off to one side.

Between arriving guests, Hightower walked over to me and stated, "Warner says we're visiting a tea plantation."

"Yes, on Tuesday," I said. "The Ministry recommended it, to give you a look at Umbika's agricultural sector and the struggles its workers are facing."

"Don't forget, I want to see that trial up north."

"I haven't forgotten. It begins Thursday."

Ambassador Durhlmann lifted two flutes of champagne from a waiter's tray and offered one to Hightower. Hightower raised his hands, palms out, as if bracing himself against a fall. "I haven't had a drink in eleven years," he said. "Alcohol is a hazard of my profession, that and being tarred and feathered." The Ambassador laughed and motioned for Blake to come closer.

"I'd like you to meet the head of our political section," the Ambassador said. Blake extended his hand.

"It's a pleasure, Mr. Hightower."

"The political section," Hightower remarked, but ignored the offer of a handshake.

"Yes, sir. I hope you enjoy your visit to the Land of Fine Roads."

"I think I'll find it hard to enjoy anything in Umbika, including the fine roads, as long as the United States continues to undermine a democratically-elected president." The change in Hightower's demeanor caught us off guard. The Ambassador and I exchanged looks of surprise.

"You're aware that Umbika's president has been appointed for life," Blake said, not missing a beat. "He's not elected anymore."

"From what I hear, the people love him."

"Some do. But there's only one political party, so it's hard to tell. You can't really call Umbika a democracy." The Ambassador said nothing, while balancing a full glass of champagne in each hand, but he was watching Blake closely.

Hightower called to the black couples sitting in the living room, "Brothers and sisters, come closer!" Some of the Umbikans sitting there got up and stood in the foyer with us. "I fear for Umbika's future," Hightower began, addressing his new congregation. "The Americans insist on supporting the insurgents in the North, who are nothing but common criminals. Why do the Americans do this? you ask. Why do they choose provocateurs and thugs who want to destroy your beautiful country and your peaceful way of life?" The Africans looked at each other, both amazed and wary. They had never heard a foreigner so brazenly criticize his own government.

"We are not assisting UFreeMo," Blake said.

"Is that an official denial?" Hightower asked, looking not at Blake, but the Ambassador.

"It's a true statement," answered Blake. "We give them nothing."

"That depends on which end of the horse you're looking at."

"I'm not sure I follow you," Blake said.

"After the drought last year, people here were starving, but the United States stopped sending food to Umbika. Is turning your back on the needy supposed to punish the Life President? Are you trying to pressure the hungry people in the villages to accept UFreeMo?" Blake stared silently at Hightower.

The Ambassador cut in. "We stopped sending maize because everything we sent disappeared. We had entire caravans go missing, even the trucks."

"The thefts were too well-organized for common thieves to pull off," Blake added.

"So, who are you accusing?" Hightower said.

"Your guess is as good as mine," said Blake. "What we know is that workers we hired to unload the grain were threatened, some were beaten. The home of one American was burned to the ground. The government here refused to investigate."

"You're claiming President Mulenga is letting his people starve." I saw the trap coming, and Blake did too, but he took the bait anyway.

"Only his people in the North," Blake said.

"That's outrageous!" Hightower scoffed. "The Life President – letting people starve?"

"You can add two and two as easily as me," said Blake. All Africans from the living room had joined us now. They watched our guest intently.

The Ambassador interrupted, "Let's be clear. Blake's not accusing President Mulenga of stealing donor grain or harassing workers. We have no idea who's doing it." The Ambassador was lying, but with reason. Over the previous two months, the Embassy had collected solid information pointing to Umbikan officials using NEGs to hijack aid trucks and intimidate workers. We had not found the missing maize, but we knew how it had been taken.

"Nothing gets a poor man's attention like an empty stomach," Hightower said to Blake. "The rebels steal the food you send, but Umbikans are told it's the Life President who's doing it. Washington gets high-and-mighty about human rights and says it's time for the Life President to step down. Tricksters in Washington have done this before. They've done it all over the world."

"The United States isn't starving anyone," Blake said. "Many governments are calling for free and fair elections in Umbika, not just us."

"Are you aware of food sacks being stamped, 'A Gift from the U.S.A. – Long Live Multiparty Democracy'?" Hightower asked.

The Ambassador stepped forward. "Maurice, there are people on the patio who'd like to speak with you."

"In a minute," Hightower said, dismissively. "My friend is making a point."

"What I've heard," said Blake, "is anyone who's caught with maize coming from the U.S. goes missing."

The Africans from the living room pressed closer around us, a crowd of twenty or so. Hightower was a head taller than Blake. He leaned in close to Blake, their bodies almost touching. The Ambassador and I were close enough to hear what Hightower was saying, but those behind us could not.

"I know about people like you," Hightower said. "I know who you are, what you do. You people believe you can get away with whatever you want, simply because you want it."

"Everyone's stealing maize," said the Ambassador, loud enough for the Africans to hear. "American grain is turning up on the black market. We know some sacks are making it to the opposition in the North. You can probably find stolen U.S. maize right here in the capital, at the city market."

Hightower stepped back. He suddenly seemed tired of the argument. "I'm sure it's a complicated problem, Mr. Ambassador," he said in a conciliatory tone. He then leaned in close to Blake again, right at his ear. "There's one thing I want your people back at headquarters to remember," I heard Hightower whisper. "You're slandering an African patriot. The people on this continent won't forgive you, and neither will I."

"I think you have me confused with someone else," said Blake.

Chapter 11
Samahani

Blake refused to turn away from Hightower's cold stare, but he said nothing more. Hightower put his hand on the shoulder of a man with light brown skin, standing an arm's length away. He drew the man to his side. "Tell me, sir. What do you think of the Life President?"

It took the Umbikan bureaucrat a moment to get his sea legs, having never expected to be asked in public such a hazardous question. Then, reciting from memory, the man said the only safe thing he knew to say, "His Excellency, the Life President, is the father of our country. He is our blessed leader and provider." The man held a large cocktail glass in his hand, a turquoise concoction with an extra-long straw and a skewer of pineapple chunks and maraschino cherries the size of quarters. The exotic drink was invented for a cruise ship, not something normally ordered at a diplomatic reception. The men and women around him were holding similar colorful creations. He added, "His Excellency, the Life President, is the first son of Mother Africa. He is part and parcel of all goodness that shines on our people."

"Thank you, my brother!" Hightower proclaimed and turned towards the others. "Today, I had the honor to speak privately with President Mulenga." A chorus of oohs and aahs rippled through the African crowd.

"He explained what had happened when the colonialists abandoned Umbika. How the Europeans fled like white bandits in the night. Taking with them the wealth Umbiks had accumulated over a hundred years. The British were the worst. They removed every chair and desk from your offices, every trailer and plow, every shovel and hoe from your fields. They took your seeds and fertilizer. Emptied every garage and shed." The intonations in Hightower's voice became rhythmic, like waves meeting shore – a Bible-belt preacher warming up his congregation before the offering – high pitches, followed by low growls, then repeat.

"You know the rest of the story, my friends. Jimmy Mulenga – a young, hard-fighting lawyer – a nationalist – statesman – and visionary. you must never forget how he grew up, what he had to overcome. Jimmy Mulenga was a child of Colonial Africa. Dirt poor, no electricity at home or clean water – no modern sanitation – no privilege. School was an hour away."

"Up hill, both ways," Blake said to me under his breath. The Ambassador shot us an admonishing look.

"I first met Jimmy Mulenga twenty years ago in London. He told me his life story – the white bosses keeping him locked in place – stealing from him – cheating him. But Jimmy Mulenga never lost hope. As my friend here said, the Life President is the son of Mother Africa. The only leader who can give you a better life. Jimmy Mulenga is a hero to all Africans!"

The room burst into cheer. Out on the patio, the orchestra had started a swing tune, their playful notes barely audible over the noise in the foyer. "Listen, listen," Hightower continued, "I apologize for the greed and the mistakes of the United States. I am an African by blood, but I was born a captive in America. The United States embarrasses me, my friends. It makes me angry."

"Why do you criticize your country, sir?" asked a diplomat from Kenya, who was standing at the back of the crowd, a man almost the same age as Hightower. He did not seem to be enjoying the revelry of the younger Africans around him.

"I tell it like it is," Hightower replied. "It is written in the Book of John, 'Ye shall know the truth, and the truth shall set you free.' I'm a journalist, sir.

I'm only looking for the truth."

Blake later confided that he wished he had remained silent. "In your newspaper column," Blake started, "you've argued for massive reconstruction aid for Africa, like the Marshall Plan. You say the United States and Europe should pay for it. Can you explain that?"

"You've read my column," Hightower said, his laugh sounding cynical. "I want a Marshall Plan for Africa, but I want it bigger. It has to be bigger. The only way Africans will ever recover from hundreds of years of exploitation and sacrifice is through a massive infusion of dollars. I'm talking billions and billions of dollars, nothing less." Hightower looked to the Africans standing near him, ignoring Blake now. He took a couple by the hand. "This is a great problem, my friends. It requires a great solution!"

Most of the Africans nodded and clapped. "Yes! Yes!"

"You and I have suffered unimaginable horrors," Hightower went on. "It's no secret white people caused that suffering. We agree on that, don't we?" Hightower waited for objections, but there were none. "I'm not claiming the white people here in this house caused that suffering. I'd be a fool to say that. But in Africa, as in America, white hands have been stained with the blood of black women and black men for more than three hundred years. Time is up. The guilty must repay the victims. They must give back what they've taken."

Before anyone could respond, a commotion erupted at the back of the dining room. "*Samahani! Samahani!*" It was Miriam, the Ambassador's wife, calling in Swahili. She led eight helpers out from the kitchen, each man barefooted but dressed in white pants, white shirt, and a black bow tie. "Excuse us! Excuse us!" she repeated in English. The men carried silver platters over their heads, wide trays of steaming roast beef and grilled chicken, heaping mounds of rice, towers of bread and a hill of green salad. Miriam guided the servers towards the buffet table. The sweet smell of a feast passed in front of Hightower and the Africans. In an instant, the listeners gave up Hightower and headed towards the long buffet table, forming an irregular queue.

The sudden departure of his audience seemed to tip Hightower off balance. "Warner, I want to apologize," he said to the Ambassador, recovering. "Sometimes my passion gets the best of me. I hope I didn't offend you."

The tone in Hightower's voice sounded sincere, not the confrontational or arrogant adversary he had been with Blake. But who knew what to believe?

"Umbika is a complicated place," the Ambassador said.

"I barely have my feet on the ground and already I'm making judgments," Hightower said. He offered his hand to Blake. "I hope we have more time to talk about the politics of developing nations." Blake politely shook the journalist's hand.

"Let's find our table," the Ambassador said and pointed Hightower to the patio. He handed me an empty and a full glass of champagne. "Thank Miriam for me," he whispered in my ear.

After everyone finished dinner, I was standing outside alone, leaning on an iron railing overlooking the Ambassador's swimming pool, a short walk from the house. Underwater spotlights had been turned on, coloring the shimmering water aqua blue and complementing the darker starry-night sky above.

"I was wondering where you went," Blake said, coming up behind me. He took a spot beside me at the railing. "The boys are done clearing tables," he said. "Guests are starting to dance."

"We won't be out of here before midnight," I said. Light from two Tiki torches behind the diving board covered the redwood deck in a soft blush of yellow.

"Did the Ambassador say anything to you?" Blake asked.

"You mean about Connie calling in sick?"

"No, about me."

"He said nothing about you. Why?"

"He kept tossing me dirty looks at dinner. I should've kept my mouth shut with our guest."

"I don't think you were out of line. Whatever Hightower got, he asked for."

Blake reached inside his suit coat and pulled out a white business envelope. The flap was not sealed, and there were no markings on the outside. "These cost an arm and leg. But they're interesting as hell," he said and passed the envelope to me. "Too bad it's all I could get on short notice."

I pushed back the flap and removed four black and white snapshots from the envelope. Seeing the first photo, I felt a surge of excitement, like warm oil, course through my chest and dance down my arms. It was the most alert I had felt in days. The photo was taken in a private room at State House. Hightower and Mulenga were sitting on a sofa and drinking coffee from demitasse cups. Mulenga family photographs adorned the wall behind the men. "Damn," I said, impressed by Blake's access to such private information.

In the second picture, Hightower and Mulenga were on the sofa, but Catherine Phiri was sitting between them now, everyone laughing, like friends sharing a joke. Her hand was on Hightower's knee. A third photo showed Mulenga standing with his right arm raised high in the air, fist clenched. Hightower was on the sofa, writing in his notebook. The final shot showed the two men in front of a half-opened door, shaking hands and smiling. At the edge of the photo, half of the body of a woman had been cut off the frame, but clearly it was Catherine Phiri, her elegant hand holding onto Hightower's free arm. I looked over at Blake.

"You don't want to know," he said, before I could ask. He slid the photos into the envelope and returned it to his coat pocket. "Let's get a drink."

Chapter 12
Slow Dance

We entered the screened-in patio from the back yard. Couples were on the dance floor, swaying to a Dean Martin standard. We crossed the room to the far side where the bar was set up. "The boss looks in a better mood," I said to Blake. Ambassador Durhlmann was sitting at the head table, whispering in the ear of his German counterpart, who was stroking his trim gray beard. Both men laughed.

"Maybe I'm off the hook," said Blake.

I scanned the crowded room. Votive candles on the tables gave off just enough light for guests to discern faces across from them, but inky darkness separated one table from the next. Maurice Hightower was on the dance floor, paired with the wife of the French Ambassador. Madame Lavoisier, a former model, was the prettiest spouse in the diplomatic corps in Umbika.

"Hightower knows how to pick them," I said to Blake. We watched the couple move together, not one dip or twirl out of place. Both were excellent dancers. When the song finished, Hightower led Madame Lavoisier back to her table. He then took the hand of the wife of the Spanish Chargé d'Affaires and brought her to the dance floor. After her, it was Mrs. Weatherly of the UK, surprisingly spry, not the two left feet I expected. Everyone seemed to be having a good time.

"He has stamina," Blake said and set his empty beer bottle on the bar. "But I've got to circulate, Joe. Catch you later." Blake went over and sat with a table of Ugandan diplomats. I watched Hightower take on three more partners, instructing one less-experienced lady how to move her hands and feet a certain way. The woman responded well to Hightower's instructions. After a brisk Cha-Cha, they left the dance floor. Hightower came alone to the bar and ordered a ginger ale. Perspiration glistened on his forehead and beaded in the hair around his ears. He withdrew a maroon handkerchief from his chest pocket and dabbed at the moisture.

As the bartender set a glass on a napkin in front of him, he said to me, "the breeze feels good. Are the nights always cool here?"

"Only now, in the dry season," I said. "When the rain comes, the nights will heat up, but we never get too hot, because of the altitude." Hightower finished half his ginger ale in one long drink. "You look like you're having fun."

"Music was the center of my mother's life," he said. "When I was a boy, she made me sing in the church choir and take dance lessons. I'm glad she insisted because I sleep better now after dancing. You should go out there yourself. Is your wife here?"

"I'm not married," I said.

"I've been married three times, divorced three times," Hightower said. His question had stirred memories in me, but they lasted only an instant. "I see plenty of ladies in this room who'd love to dance. That limp doesn't hold you back, does it?"

"Not really."

He leaned closer to me, like a confidential source speaking off the record. "Look at those men out there," he said. "As far as I can tell, they have no passion, Joe. They move like robots." He twisted his arms stiffly back and forth. "Tonight is probably the first time their wives have danced with someone like me. You know, someone who lives the music – someone with soul."

"You're probably right." It was all I could think to say at the time.

"Let me put it another way," Hightower said. "How you dance is how you live." He set his empty ginger ale glass on the bar. "If you dance without passion, you live without it, too. And if you live without passion, then tell me, what's the point?" Hightower did not wait for my reply. He walked away. I watched him glide from table to table, his superior height making it easier for me to track him across a room without much light.

At the table of the Foreign Minister, Hightower seemed intent on getting Fenton Mabviko's wife onto the dance floor. She refused him several times. He finally took her small hand in his and coaxed her out of her seat. The tiny lady looked dreadful, standing awkwardly beside the giant. She sat back down and put her hands in her lap. Hightower did not know that an Umbikan lady never dances with a man in public, not even her husband. She can join other women in traditional dances, but you will never see an Umbikan couple dancing in front of friends or strangers. Hightower moved to another table and then another. Bored, I turned away and organized another to-do list in my head. I had a busy week ahead.

A while later, Hans Heinzen approached me at the bar. Hans was the vice-consul at the German Embassy. Unlike most German diplomats I had known, Hans was vulnerable and deferential, like a puppy recently weaned. His short hair and round spectacles made him appear even younger than his twenty-seven years. He had been in Umbika about six months.

"What do you think of this dirty business?" Hans asked me.

"I'm sorry," I said, trying to reorient my thoughts. "I didn't see you there, Hans."

"This business, Joe."

"What business are we talking about?"

"This scandal show," insisted the young German officer, tilting his head towards the dance floor.

"Help me out, Hans. What am I looking for?"

"My ambassador."

In the candle glow at the head table, I found the German ambassador sitting beside Durhlmann. His suitcoat off, he wore an elegant blue shirt with white collar and gold cuff links. "I see him," I said. "Herr Bergen looks elegant tonight."

"He is not happy, Joe. Do you see Frau Bergen?"

It took me a while to find the man's wife; she was not at their table. I finally spotted her across the room, on the dance floor with Hightower. They were almost in total darkness. "I see her," I said. "She's dancing."

"She is with your newspaperman. My ambassador is angry."

"What's he angry about?"

"Can you not see, Joe?"

It took a moment for my eyes to adjust to the shifting shadows. Frau Bergen was an attractive lady with thick blond hair. Her given name was Brigetta, and she was many years younger than her husband. Brigetta's big natural curls bounced in slow motion when she moved. She was wearing a thin creamed-colored dress reaching mid-calf, though the hem opened to her knees. Her head was resting on Hightower's shoulder, and she moved so slowly I thought she had fallen asleep in his arms. I looked back to the German ambassador. He was scanning the patio. We had a much better view of the couple from our place at the bar than he did. The German ambassador did seem agitated, as Hans had claimed, but it seemed it was because he could not find his wife in the crowd, not because she was dancing with Hightower.

"Your ambassador has every right to be upset," said Blake, who was now beside us. "I've been watching them for ten minutes. I already learned a couple new moves I'm dying to try."

Hans gave Blake an admonishing look. "She drinks too much wine," said Hans. "You must do something, Joe." Hightower and Frau Bergen continued to sway as one body with the sleepy beat of the orchestra.

"What do you want me to do?" I asked. "She's on her feet. Half the women here can't get out of their chair anymore."

"The other women are not dancing in such a way, with a black."

The German ambassador had a reputation for a volcanic temper, but I was not about to interrupt the dancers. The embarrassment I might cause Hightower could be worse than the German ambassador's fit. "Nothing is going to happen," I assured Hans. "Our guest has been dancing all night. Ladies like dancing with him. He's a good dancer."

"Your newspaperman does this with purpose," Hans insisted. "He knows the effect he makes on the females."

"Huh?"

"Here she goes again," said Blake. Brigetta's arms had strayed from Hightower's shoulders and were edging down his back. She slid her hands inside his suit coat and appeared to grip his waist, above the hips. The dance floor was crowded, so only someone watching from the bar could see it when her hips came alive. She seemed to press her waist against Hightower, moving to the orchestra's slow, strong beat. It was difficult in the shadows to know the extent of contact between them, but I thought she had crossed the line. "This is unbelievable," Blake said, sounding more amused than worried. "At least he's not encouraging her."

I looked to the German ambassador again. He had spotted his wife, but had a bad angle on her, so he did not see when she took Hightower's hand and moved it to her lower back.

"That's not good," said Blake.

Hightower refused his partner's invitation, lifting his hand back to her shoulder. Frau Bergen tilted back her head and laughed.

"This is your problem, Joe," the German vice-consul pleaded. "You must control that animal spirit."

"What am I supposed to do, Hans?"

"Ha!" Blake said. "You're the control officer, Joe. Control them."

I didn't find Blake funny at the time. I made my way around the dinner tables and out onto the dance floor. Halfway into the crowd, I stopped when the slow song ended. The dancers clapped, politely. I clapped too, a feeble disguise. I continued across the floor. Hightower was on the move too. One arm held Frau Bergen at the waist and the other had her elbow. He guided the intoxicated woman over to her table. She fussed for a moment, but her protests were weak and uncoordinated. Hightower steered her into the empty chair beside her husband. When she was safely back where she belonged, Hightower bowed his head to the German ambassador and then returned to the bar. Hightower said nothing to Blake, who was there alone. By the time I returned to the bar, Hightower had his drink and was walking away.

Blake and I stuck around after the last of the guests had left for the night.

Once Hightower was on his way back to his hotel, we informed Ambassador Durhlmann what had happened with the Germans, how close we were to an incident. He told us to forget it and stay focused on keeping to Hightower's good side. Then, he dismissed us, and Blake walked with me to our apartments in the ARC. The walkway directing our course was outlined by little umbrellas of pink light, like a long narrow runway. Thick clouds had moved in and obscured the stars. The sky was solid black. Off the path and beyond the reach of the pink light lived shadows of indeterminate consequence, dark holes stretching deep into the government-owned property. I opened the heavy metal gate to the compound.

"This was one helluva reception," I said, re-latching the gate once Blake was through. "The business with Frau Bergen..."

"Yeah," Blake laughed. "You can't make up something like that."

Chapter 13
Speaker

At the center of the capital city was the largest roundabout in Umbika. It sorted major traffic moving through the city, vehicles coming from the north, south, east, and west. The perimeter of the roundabout was lined with flower beds, wide and neatly maintained, a rainbow of colors and a cornucopia of shapes and sizes. The inner circle of the roundabout contained a hill of earth covered in buffalo grass, a knob of a place named Statue Park. At the summit of the hill stood a bronze sculpture of President Mulenga – four times life-size. Mulenga's right arm pointed towards the desert to the south, the direction to his home village, the heart of the Umbik tribe. His left arm rested across his chest with an enormous hand clutching a book. Umbikans debated whether the book was the Bible or the nation's constitution. Cynical ex-pats joked it was the ledger for the Life President's bank accounts in Zurich. For Umbikans of all walks of life, the roundabout at Statue Park, with its colossal statue in bronze, was both the geographic and symbolic epicenters of the country.

On weekday mornings Statue Park roundabout was the busiest intersection in the country. The access road coming off it to the north was Kenyatta Avenue, the city's main thoroughfare. Kenyatta Avenue ran ten miles to the international airport. All major embassies and businesses were located on it or adjacent to it. Beyond the airport, it became the M-2 highway and went another 480 miles north to the frontier. West from Statue Park roundabout was a residential neighborhood for government officials, fed by Presidential Way, which ended at State House. After that, the road became the M-1 highway all the way to Molo, where my tire had been damaged by the preacher. To the east, Jubilation Drive ran through the market and hotel districts and then another 200 miles to the hill country and tea estates around Ndala. Finally, leading into the desert to the south was a beautiful highway almost no one other than President Mulenga and his entourage ever used.

Every morning, under the pointing arm of J.J. Mulenga's statue, young boys who should have been in primary school peddled newspapers and sticks of chewing gum to motorists passing through the roundabout. To the side of the road, vendors sold almost anything a person might want, from matches and ostrich meat to pineapples and living room furniture. The U.S. Embassy sat on a large parcel of land on the northwest corner of the roundabout, property astutely purchased before Umbika's independence. Across the road from the U.S. Embassy was the British High Commission. The morning after Hightower's reception at the Ambassador's Residence, I bought a newspaper at the roundabout and then continued around the circle, turning onto a narrow street at the far side of the U.S. Embassy's property. At the end of that side street was the rear entrance to the Embassy, an opening most people were unaware of.

The Chancery was the Embassy's main building. From a distance, it looked like an enormous white shoe box, rectangular, sharp corners, unremarkable – a thoroughly boring structure. Up close, however, its architectural subtleties and security features were more interesting. Windows were creatively protected by whitewashed concrete buttresses and steel grids. Doorways were narrow and recessed for protection. Security lights ringed the building. The entire compound was surrounded by a 14-foot iron fence. Higher up, thin strands of copper wire, strung at various heights from aluminum poles, crisscrossed the Chancery's flat roof, like dozens of clotheslines glistening in the early sunlight. The lines were not there to air the Embassy's laundry; they were sophisticated radio antennas connecting this distant outpost to the Communications Center in Washington, 24 hours a day. I parked in my assigned spot not far from the Chancery, on a shaded island of asphalt from which a curved yellow brick sidewalk lined with palm trees led to the building.

Grass grew thick and rich under the shade palms. Colorful flowers thrived in well-tended raised beds along the way, including wine-red proteas with their star-burst spines, purple hibiscus as large as dinner plates, and traditional white American daisies. A cement archway draped in a cherry red bougainvillea vine framed the front entrance of the Chancery, the thorny strands climbing all the way to the roof. As I did on most days, I walked to the front door so I could enjoy the colors in the gardens, even though a rear door was closer to the parking lot. Corporal Vince, a U.S. Marine security guard, was inside the lobby at Post 1 when I entered. It was Monday morning. He was setting up a line of gold stanchions for the visitors' chute that would direct walk-ins to a reception desk.

"Good morning, Vince," I said. "How's your little girl feeling?"

"She doesn't miss those tonsils one bit, sir."

I greeted another Marine, this one standing at the end of a long countertop where visitors were logged in. "I like the haircut, Johnny."

"Roger that, sir."

At the end of the lobby, a Marine sergeant sat behind a window of thick glass, next to the electronic door he controlled. He pressed a hidden button and the steel bolt clicked open for me. My office was a suite of small rooms on the first floor. Inside, I set my lunch bag on my desk and draped my suit coat over my desk chair. In an adjoining room, I opened curtains covering a picture window that looked out onto the lobby. On one wall of the lobby was an American flag, on another a framed photograph of the U.S. President, and next to my picture window hung a red, white, and blue sign printed with the words:

CONSULAR AND VISA SERVICES

9AM – 12PM

MONDAY – THURSDAY

At eight o'clock I was comfortably behind my desk, reading the morning cable traffic, when my office assistants, Grace and Violet, arrived for work. I was already on my second cup of coffee. Grace was the heavier of the two ladies and had the more outgoing personality. She talked almost non-stop and preferred bright African headscarves and traditional floor-length wraps, over Western clothes. Violet, on the other hand, was reserved and dressed in European style clothes, typically navy blue blazers and gray pleated skirts below the knees. She had always seemed to me the more thoughtful and sympathetic of the two. Both ladies were of the Umbik tribe. They had worked as administrative assistants at the Embassy since Umbika's independence, prized jobs in Africa, especially for women, since they were rarely hired for anything other than housekeeping or childcare. The American Embassy was known for its generous wages, the best health care, and a standard of fairness not seen at other embassies or businesses in the capital.

There was one disadvantage to working for us, however. Locals were relentlessly harassed by Triple S. If an Umbikan refused the Security Service's request to spy on us, her family members were beaten or imprisoned. Consequently, we assumed all of our local employees were spies, telling their handlers any information they could about the work we did or our personal lives. We had to lock our safes and desk drawers when we left a room. We always watched what we said. And locals were never permitted higher than the first floor in the Chancery, not even to clean a carpet or change a light bulb. No one ever spoke about this reality, the wide chasm separating the Americans from the Umbikans; no one ever needed to. It was simply a fact of diplomatic life. This morning, the two ladies curtsied when they came in, as was Umbik custom, and then continued into the next room.

Umbika was a fine assignment for me and was lasting longer than others I had had. It felt good to stay in one place for a while. Ambassador Durhlmann had been aware of my work in Cameroon and had requested me when his previous Consul suffered "a nervous breakdown" and was ordered home. The man's collapse came after Triple S found him naked and passed out in a hotel room with three bottles of duty-free Scotch and four homeless African boys. Durhlmann personally escorted the officer onto a flight home and made sure the wheels were up before leaving the airport. I arrived the day after the disgraced officer had flown out. I found the Consular Section in shambles. The Consul's out-box was stuffed with work orders never delivered. The in-box held tasking cables a month old. A comprehensive inventory revealed several classified documents unaccounted for. Visa equipment was missing or damaged. Neither Grace nor Violet could remember the last time office supplies were ordered. It took me five minutes to find a working pen. That first day, I shredded the nudist magazines I discovered at the back of the safe and flushed seven vials of prescription drugs down the toilet. When a team from the Inspector General's Office flew in from Washington three months later, I had scrubbed the Consular Section clean. They nominated us for the Turn-around-Post of the Year Award.

Grace brought me a third cup of coffee and told me about her children, her husband, her nieces and nephews, and her mother-in-law. I reviewed an inventory of forms and booklets, completed a printing order, and made a note to call Benny Cohen once the sun was up in Washington.

"You busy?"

I looked up to see Blake standing in my doorway. He came in and shut the hallway door behind him and then the door to the room where Grace and Violet were working. "You never could've known it," he said and pulled a chair close to my desk. "But Saturday, when you got that flat tire on the M-1, UFreeMo was a quarter mile from your car."

"UFreeMo was on the M-1?"

"They were – probably in the weeds, watching you change the tire."

"Come on. They've never been this far south."

Blake went to the large relief map on the wall behind my desk. He put his finger on a spot marked The Highlands. It was a mountainous area, a mosaic of brown contours in the Northern Province, at the top of the map. He motioned me closer. "A few days ago, ten UFreeMo soldiers left the Highlands in a minibus. They crossed the M-2 outside of JiJi and drifted south down this valley, on back roads." Blake's finger meandered along a trough shaded in green, bordered by rows of elevated beiges and browns. The valley on the map descended a quarter of the way down my wall. "They left their vehicle here and traveled by foot through the Twelve Apostles."

I followed the invisible path he made along the border between Umbika and Tologland, until Blake's finger stopped on an empty green area just east of the border town of Molo. A bold black line, the M-1 highway, ran horizontally under his finger.

"They camped here, late Saturday afternoon," he said.

"That's where I stopped." Blake nodded. "I didn't see anything."

"There's good cover there. It's the best place to cross the highway without being noticed."

"Why didn't they rob me?"

"They're not thieves. They probably saw your CD plates. They consider us the good guys."

I looked at the map, the long distance these ten soldiers had travelled. "What's UFreeMo doing so far south?" I asked.

Blake smiled. "That's what I'm trying to figure out."

By ten that Monday morning we had already processed fifty visa applications. Violet was the first to notice Maurice Hightower enter the lobby, one of the Marines pointing him to our interview window.

"I want to see Kellerman!" Hightower shouted at Violet through five inches of special security glass. The Umbikans waiting in line in the lobby moved to the side to give space to the angry man. The Marines took an interest in the commotion, but they were unsure how to respond. Like the rest of us, they had been briefed that Hightower was a guest of the President of the United States. When he saw me, he cursed, "You are the lowest creature!" his long index finger pointing my way, like an archer's arrow. "You were smiling at me yesterday – you patronizing-son-of-a-bitch – all the while knowing you weren't giving that boy a visa!" Somehow, Hightower had found out that earlier that morning I had denied William Andelebe's visa application. I had sent a driver with the boy's passport back to his father's office at the Ministry of the Interior. "You're a coward. Do you know that? Did you think

I wouldn't find out?"

"Will you come in my office and talk about this?" I asked, my heart beating rapidly.

Hightower pushed his pointing finger against the window glass. "I've got nothing more to say to you. I'll take my complaint to someone who can do something for me." He turned to leave, but he stopped and looked at me again. "One more thing – I don't appreciate you people sneaking into my hotel room and going through my things."

It did not take long for the Ambassador to summon me to his office. Hightower was seated at one end of a coffee table, the Ambassador sitting across from him. A tea pot and cups rested on a silver tray on the table. "Have a seat, Joe," the Ambassador said. I took the chair between them. "Someone entered Mr. Hightower's room last night, during the reception. They went through his things. Whoever it was didn't try to hide the fact. His suitcase was left open." The news surprised me. I looked at Hightower, who was glaring at me. "I assured Mr. Hightower no one from here would ever enter another American's hotel room. The National Police Chief and the Foreign Minister have also assured him that no one from the Umbikan government would do that either. Police investigators are at the hotel right now, gathering evidence." For a moment, I imagined the poorly-trained, unequipped, and ham-fisted police investigators stumbling around Hightower's hotel room. A sophisticated police investigation in Umbika was an absurdity. "Do you have any idea who might be behind this?" the Ambassador asked.

"I haven't been in his room, if that's what anyone's thinking."

"Of course, not – no one's suggesting that."

"If someone was in there, it's either Explorers or Triple S. I suspect Explorers. They do stupid things all the time. People from the Security Service would have had enough sense to close the suitcase."

"What do you mean, Explorers?" Hightower asked.

"The National Exploring Group," I said. "Sometimes, they're called NEGs." I spelled it out for him, N-E-G. "They're President Mulenga's personal army. He calls them his 'Boy Scouts.' They're just punks with little education and a mean streak in them. He recruits orphans and street kids, gives them food, fancy uniforms, and power. All he asks in return is they do whatever he tells them. The Explorers answer to no one but Mulenga."

"The Life President has no reason to search my room," Hightower said.

"It could be a burglary," offered the Ambassador.

"I disagree, sir. Burglars don't work the InterContinental Hotel. It's too high profile. President Mulenga would hang them himself." I turned towards Hightower. "What was missing from your room?"

"Nothing. They just moved things around. This isn't the first time someone's entered my room. The FBI used to do it all the time." Silence expanded through the tense air.

I looked at the Ambassador and shrugged. "Is there anything else, sir?"

"There is," Durhlmann said and poured himself and Hightower another cup of tea. "Can you explain why you refused William Andelebe a visa?" This was what I was waiting for, the real reason I had been summoned. An Ambassador questioning a Consul's judgment about a visa was almost never done in the Foreign Service. Yet here it was, and in front of someone from outside the Embassy. The pressure Durhlmann was feeling from Washington must have been immense.

"I'm not sure what you want me to say."

"Mr. Hightower has convinced me this young man is not a risk to the U.S. He has a round-trip air ticket and plenty of money. Mr. Hightower will vouch for him, if that'll help." The Ambassador and I knew that the Department had a standing order not to give U.S. visas to foreign police informants. We also knew William Andelebe had been recruited by Triple S to spy on Umbikans living in America. "What's really at issue here, Joe?" Durhlmann pressed me. I took a deep breath.

"Sir, I looked at his application and checked our records. The young man had applied twice before, both times denied. I saw no new information about his situation. He isn't married and has no children. He's not a student. He has no job. So, by INS definition he has no strong ties to Umbika. In my judgment, he's an overstay risk, two-fourteen B."

"That's ridiculous!" Hightower said, raising his voice. "I know two-fourteen B. That kid's not a vagrant. You think he'll go on welfare, ask for food stamps? He's the son of this country's chief of police, for god sake. If his father tells the boy to come home, he'll come home. What does it hurt to give him a damn visa for six months?"

I looked to the Ambassador, but he was offering me no help. "In good conscience, I can't do it," I said.

"Who else here can?" Hightower demanded.

"I'm the only one. William Andelebe can go to the American Embassy in Nairobi or Lilongwe or Dar and apply there. He can have someone there re-evaluate his application."

"Even I know that's not possible," crowed Hightower. "They won't give a visa to an African outside his own country. You're telling me only one person in this embassy approves visas?"

"If I'm unavailable," I said, "the responsibility shifts to our Deputy Ambassador. He's on leave in the U.S. and won't be back for a month."

"Mr. Ambassador?" It was Gwen Sharpe, the Ambassador's secretary. She was standing in the open doorway.

"What is it?" said the Ambassador. I could not tell if Durhlmann was annoyed at the interruption or grateful for its timing.

"Blake just went out," she said. "He wanted you to know that UFreeMo attacked a village this morning, not far from here."

"Attacked?" the Ambassador said. He did not seem surprised by the news, more curious about Gwen's word choice.

"That's the word he used, sir."

"Did he write it up?"

"He said he had to check some things first."

"Okay, thank you."

"It's Enro Muswaya's village."

"Son of a bitch!" the Ambassador said. Enro Muswaya was the Speaker of Parliament and next in line for succession if something happened to President Mulenga.

"Blake thought there might be fatalities," Gwen added.

"Send Blake in here the minute he gets back." Gwen closed the door behind her. Muswaya's village was an hour west of the capital, halfway to

Molo. "You used the M-1 a few days ago, didn't you?" the Ambassador said to me.

"I did, sir. Muswaya's village is about ten miles south of where I had my flat tire." With Hightower in the room, I was not about to share what Blake had said about UFreeMo's having slipped down through the Valley of the Twelve Apostles. Either way, I was certain the Ambassador already knew that. "Please, excuse me, sir. I better make some calls," I said. "We have Americans living near Muswaya's village." Although Foreign Service protocol requires an officer to wait for an Ambassador's permission to leave a room, I got up and moved to the door, while they absorbed the news of the attack. The Ambassador waved me away, and I hurried out of the room.

Chapter 14
Father John

Word of the attack had spread through the Embassy by the time I returned to my office. Grace was sitting on a folding chair in the workroom, shaking from head to toe. Violet was leaning over her, fanning her face with a pink handkerchief. Violet said Grace had gotten a call about the attack from her sister, who had heard about it from a cousin who knew someone who lived a mile from the village. According to Grace's sister, nineteen people were dead, including some from her family, though no one could reach any relatives near the village to confirm that. I knelt beside Grace and took her trembling hand. The skin felt soft and cool. "It'll be all right," I said. "No one knows what's happened yet. I'll try to find out."

Rumors travelled fast in Umbika, but with poor accuracy. I did not have much faith in what Grace's sister was reporting. I went to my desk and phoned Garrett Livingston, our Peace Corps director. He had volunteers in the field near Muswaya's village, but he had not heard the news yet. "I'll call you right back," he said.

Five minutes later, Garrett was on the line again, sounding anxious now. "I talked to my drivers. They say twelve villagers are dead. Twenty rebels were killed. I'm going to drive out there, Joe. I have a couple of girls not far from where this happened."

"Hold off for an hour, Garrett," I said. "Let me see what I can find out. I might go with you."

Seven hundred Americans lived in-country and a hundred more just across the border in Tologland – missionaries, Peace Corps volunteers, business owners, retirees, Embassy families. When I first arrived in Umbika, the Embassy had no efficient system to contact Americans in case of an emergency. So, I designed a scheme using telephones, HAM radios, motor scooters, 4-wheel drives, and bicycles to connect Americans with the Embassy. It worked like branches on a tree. I called it our Early Warning System. All I had to do was make a call to one of my wardens, and an entire branch of the country would come alive, like a chain reaction. One American family got in touch with another, and so on, until every American had received the message sent by the Embassy. In trial runs, I had been able to get a message to 80% of the Americans in-country within two hours.

I pulled a red binder out of my safe and turned to the page for Father Dr. John Wilson, my principal warden for Branch 3, the west-center of the country. A Catholic priest and veterinarian from Indiana, Father John had lived in Umbika for thirty years. He claimed the day he was called to Africa was the happiest day of his life. I dialed his bush clinic, only five miles from Enro Muswaya's village. A female voice answered on the second ring. "Catholic animal hospital," she said, with a light Scandinavian accent. I identified myself and asked to speak to the priest. "I am so sorry, Father has gone out." I started to explain the unfolding situation, but the woman was way ahead of me. "He is there now, Mr. Kellerman," she said. "Father told me you would call. He says he will ring you when he returns."

I thanked her and hung up. Deeper in the red binder I found the number for Herb and Lori Pettigrew, Lutheran missionaries from Wyoming. They ran a couple of churches and lived two miles west of Muswaya's village.

"Kipili Mission, this is Pettigrew." It was Herb's voice answering, but it sounded troubled, the words threadbare and pitched, and coming faster than usual.

"Herb, this is Joe Kellerman from the American Embassy," I said. "We met a few months ago. Have you heard anything about a shooting in Kipili Village?"

"Joe, I saw the bodies – six of them," Herb said. "All were dead – all six."

"You were in the village?" I said.

"We got there right after it happened."

"Okay, Herb. Tell me what you know. Did you see any Americans?"

A woman in the background was talking to Herb now. He told her, "It's Joe Keller from the American Embassy."

"Herb, it's really important that I know if any of the dead are American citizens," I said.

"No, no, all of them were black," he said and then caught himself. "I'm sorry, Joe. You know what I mean. The ones we saw are all from here. Lori and I went to buy tomatoes this morning. It's market day. We got there a few minutes after UFreeMo left. You could still smell the gunpowder." The adrenaline rush that comes with the elation of relaying critical information was now feeding Herb Pettigrew. According to his parishioners who lived in Muswaya's village, he reported, about a dozen Tolog rebels arrived on foot at eight o'clock, mostly teenagers, but four adults leading them. All were armed. "They knew it was Muswaya's village," Herb said. "They made disparaging remarks about the Speaker and tried to set fire to a hut. When that didn't work, they shot a goat."

Apparently, the Speaker had heard the commotion with the goat. He came running from his house on the edge of the village. The rebels acted surprised when they saw him. Parliament was in session, and the Speaker would normally be in the capital city, not in his village. "Muswaya had come back to celebrate his grandson's birthday. I wrote all of this down, Joe. I can get you a copy."

"Tell me what else you heard," I said.

"Well, they said the Speaker was in his pajamas. He confronted the leader of the rebels, got right up in his face. 'You Tolog hyena!' he shouted, and spit on the man. The rebels huddled together, deciding what to do, I guess. The Speaker demanded they leave. 'Get out,' he said. 'Unless you want to clean my latrine or transport garbage to the rubbish pile!'

"The man he spit on raised his rifle, but the Speaker didn't back down. He stepped closer and sniffed the air. 'No matter how you wash a hyena,' the Speaker said, 'it still smells like hyena.' The rebel shot the Speaker between the eyes."

I cannot adequately describe the emptiness and dread I felt at that moment. The magnitude of what Herb had said was beyond imagination for Umbika. The country was a total police state. No one dared step out of line. An attack like this, on the second most powerful man in the country, was unthinkable. I did my best to stay focused. "They shot Muswaya," I said.

"Blew a hole right through his head, Joe. I saw the body myself."

"You actually saw him, Herb, I mean, really saw him?"

"I saw what was left of his head. It's not something I want to see again."

I asked him about the other victims. He said that the rebels went looking for the Speaker's family. They shot his wife and daughter in their front yard. Then, they found his grandson in the house and shot him. They also killed two villagers who got in the way. It did not sound like the rebels had gone to the village to kill anyone, just that things turned ugly, got out of hand, Herb said. The rebels also tried to set fire to the Speaker's house, but the walls and the roof would not burn. They carried out a bed and sofa and lit them on fire.

"We saw the smoke when we were driving there," Herb said.

"Were any Americans in the village?"

"There was the Catholic priest who runs the animal clinic. He got there right when we were leaving. But I never talked to him."

"A couple of Peace Corps volunteers live nearby, Allison and Ruth," I said.

"I know those girls."

"Did you see them?"

"No, not this morning."

"One last question, Herb. Are you completely sure Muswaya is dead?"

A long pause lingered on the other end of the phone line. "My friends said it was the Speaker," Herb said. "I only saw a body." His voice was barely a whisper now, the adrenaline all run out. "It didn't have a face. But it was wearing really nice pajamas – too expensive for normal villagers."

An hour later, Father John called and confirmed everything Herb

Pettigrew had told me. "Our girls are safe," the priest added. "I have them here at the clinic. After we fix them something to eat, I'll bring them to the capital." We talked a few minutes more. "You know, Joseph," the priest said sadly before hanging up, "this attack will change everything."

Chapter 15
Lemons

Enro Muswaya's murder did change everything. President Mulenga had never referred to UFreeMo by name in public before then. He had only alluded to the rebels in speeches, calling them "the disease from the North" or "breakfast for crocodiles." Anyone who supported UFreeMo, or was the least bit sympathetic, he labeled a "confusionist." That all changed. When Mulenga went on radio that afternoon to announce the Speaker's death, he spoke with great conviction.

"The mosquitoes who call themselves United Freedom Movement have fed on innocent blood," he said. "They have murdered six of our brothers and sisters. We can be lazy no more. We must crush them before they destroy us all. We must light the light. Outside agitators have offered our blood to this confusionist-UFreeMo-plague. They also must be held to the account. I will not rest until our martyrs receive justice."

In the Embassy's conference room, the principal officers listened to Mulenga's radio address. After he finished, there was only silence in the room, none of the usual jokes we made about the ornate uniforms he wore, the oversized sunglasses, the funny hats. Umbika was changing. Our lives would change too. We could sense it. President Mulenga did not say it directly, but

Umbika was in a civil war now. He had named his enemy. Maurice Hightower had gone to lunch with some Umbikan reporters, so I did not know if he had heard the Life President's radio speech, but if not, he would hear about it soon enough. Later that afternoon, the Ambassador ordered thirty-seven Peace Corps volunteers living in the north and west to return to the capital as soon as possible. Grace was relieved when she learned that none of her relatives had been harmed, but she was still shaky and speechless. Violet promised to help her get home. It was impossible for any of the locals at the Embassy to get work done once news of the deaths had spread because, it seemed, everyone knew someone who knew someone who lived in Muswaya's village.

Connie came to my office at four o'clock and asked me to read a classified telegram she was about to send to Washington. It contained amazing details of a high-level Umbikan government meeting held earlier in the day. The story had literally fallen in her lap. She said the publisher of Umbika's only daily newspaper had flagged down her car outside the ARC. The man was nearly incoherent, rambling on about how Umbika was heading down a path without forgiveness. He said he was ashamed of his government and told Connie that President Mulenga had called his cabinet into emergency session at noon. The publisher's brother was Deputy Minister for Trade and had attended the session in place of the Trade Minister, who was in Lusaka for a conference. At the emergency meeting, cabinet members begged Mulenga to hang sixty Tologs currently in prison, ten for each person killed by the rebels. They said this should be done from trees on the lawn of Parliament and would send a clear message to UFreeMo that the government was willing to use any means necessary to squash them. The Life President, however, vetoed the idea, worried how the world press would react, though he left the option open. The publisher told Connie he was horrified by the hanging idea, and his brother was too. They would have no part in mass murder.

I handed Connie's telegram back to her. "Good work," I said. "They'll be talking about this on the seventh floor." I considered asking her what she was feeling about Hightower now, but I let it go. She left my office, and I went upstairs to call Benny Cohen on a secure line.

After we talked about the recall of Peace Corps volunteers, Benny said,

"A friend at the *Post* called me last night. Looks like Hightower's out on a limb over a book deal. The book is ready to go to the printer – some back-to-Africa thing – but they're afraid it won't sell enough to make back the advance – two hundred and fifty grand. So, his publisher is getting cold feet."

"They gave Hightower a quarter million dollars to write a book?"

"We're in the wrong business, right? This all got me thinking, Joe. What if Hightower is using Umbika as a publicity stunt, to gin up book sales? You know, do some crazy stuff over there, get a lot of attention. He already promised his readers he'll expose our secret plot to overthrow J.J."

"It sounds like a stretch to me," I said.

"Normally, I'd agree. But I checked with someone I know in New York. Hightower's already booked on talk shows the week he gets back. That's a lot of free publicity, right before the election." I reconsidered Benny's theory. It had a little more weight to it than I first thought.

"You think he really came here to peddle a book?"

"I don't know, but it's possible."

"Have you shared your theory with anyone in the Department?"

"Of course, but everyone is on edge. Poll numbers are so close right now, they say the election's a tossup. No one wants to do anything to rock the big white boat on Pennsylvania Avenue – or to upset your guest."

At six at night, I left the Embassy and drove home. A few weeks earlier, I had made plans for hosting a small dinner party at my apartment this night. When the Hightower visit came up, I thought about cancelling the dinner, but never did. I was glad it was still on. With all we had been through at the Embassy during the day, having a few friends over would be a good way to unwind. Hightower was having dinner with the Ambassador and his wife.

Godfrey, my cook, was waiting in the entry when I walked in. Godfrey was wearing his usual hosting attire, white pants and shirt, thin black belt cinched tight around his narrow waist, red-and-white-checked apron. "You are most welcome, sir," he said, cheerfully.

"Here you go." I handed Godfrey a grocery sack of five rib eye steaks and five acorn squash from the commissary. Godfrey had never cooked acorn squash, so I took a few minutes to explain how to clean, cut, butter, and bake them. I mixed a sugar glaze for Godfrey to brush on at the end.

My guests arrived at seven. The evening was too cool to sit on the patio, so we gathered in the living room. Godfrey brought us a tray of groundnuts and cut vegetables. Trevor Poole, my counterpart from the British High Commission, and his wife, Annabelle, were there, as was Rolf Gunderson, the press attaché at the Norwegian Embassy. Rolf's wife had returned to Oslo for vacation, so Rolf came stag. Finally, there was Heather May, a first-tour officer from the Canadian High Commission, a new friend of Connie's. Connie was invited too, but she was still not feeling up to a night out. I immediately liked Heather May's energy and optimism upon meeting her. She was ready to save the world. Only a year out of graduate school, Heather was analytical and well read. Her dissertation at McGill had focused on the administration of small grant projects in developing nations. "If both sides would hear one another," Heather was saying, when I carried in the drinks, "they could avoid people getting hurt. UFreeMo just wants to be heard."

Rolf Gunderson was holding a handful of nuts. A longtime Africa hand, he loved to share gossip. "Dar Vander Bree at the South African Embassy says British paratroopers are standing by in Nairobi. Is that right, Trevor? Are you getting ready to evacuate your folks, or are the boys coming here to steady J.J.'s nerves?"

Trevor was sitting at such an angle to the group that when he reached for his own handful of peanuts, only I could see his face. He rolled his eyes for me. "There are no S-A-S in Kenya, Rolf," Trevor said. "We are always ready to help, but the Life President has the situation in hand."

"Dar said they're at the military airport outside Nairobi, three planes of them."

Trevor shrugged.

"Because of the Speaker and all, we called in some Peace Corps volunteers today," I said. "We're bringing back about forty – from the Highlands and the lake, down to Kat – plus a few from here to Molo."

"We're sending home three of our volunteers from the lake," said Heather.

"Has there been trouble up north?" asked Annabelle.

"Not that I know of," said Heather, though I could tell she wasn't completely sure, so she looked over at me.

"There's nothing specific we've heard," I said. "We just don't want our volunteers in the middle of it, if things fall apart."

"Tologs and Umbiks biting at each other," said Trevor. "It's a shame. They once lived in peace, side-by-side, you know. That's independence for you."

"Umbika's economy is fragile," Heather pointed out. "This country is a classic example of post-colonial degradation. Research shows its financial system never got off the ground once the British pulled out. In addition, the Umbik tribe had a rough time of it for almost a hundred years. We've seen this before in Africa. It's a familiar story." Trevor accepted the point with a polite nod. He had no zeal for getting into an old argument.

"I ran into Vidge Weatherly at the Happy Lion," I said. "She claims the Americans are single-handedly destroying Umbika."

"Was she potted?" Trevor asked.

"Trevor Poole!"

Trevor smiled innocently at his wife, but he said nothing.

"We have a crop advisor in Katembeyna," Rolf said, proudly. "He telephoned this morning, said he saw six lorries of NEGs drive through town." Rolf's news grabbed my attention, and Trevor Poole's. Heather was too new to the business to recognize the potential value of what Rolf was saying.

"Six trucks?" I said.

"He counted six. They've camped at the teacher training college."

"Explorers?" Trevor asked.

"The trucks were full of them," Rolf said with confidence. "He counted a hundred and twenty when they piled out."

"Hard to believe so many," Trevor said. His skepticism of Rolf's news was common among Western diplomats. Officers from the larger missions steered clear of the Scandinavians as sources of useful information. The Scandinavian footprint in a country was almost undetectable, and the Swedes in particular were mocked for their extreme idealism. I felt different. I saw their low profile as strength, not weakness. They went places where others could not, because no one noticed them. They were almost invisible.

"Our man is observant, very capable," said Rolf. "He said they had new AK-47s – all of them."

"New AKs?" said Trevor. "Anything else?"

"He said he met an American family from the Highlands that was returning to the capital. They think the North isn't safe anymore."

No Americans in the Highlands had notified me they were pulling out. "Which Americans are leaving?" I said.

"He didn't tell me their name. It was a family."

Godfrey had gone outside to collect an evening tea tray from one of the gardeners, an older man. I watched them both through the living room window. They appeared to be arguing. The gardener waved his hand in front of Godfrey's face, as if to dismiss him, and then walked away. Godfrey was a Tolog, the gardener, Umbik. Tribes again. Someone had once told me that nowhere on Earth does dawn arrive with more potential for greatness than in Africa, and nowhere on Earth but in Africa does the sun set with so much potential unfulfilled. Tribalism was destroying Umbika, just as it had destroyed other parts of the planet. I excused myself from my guests and went to the kitchen.

I asked Godfrey, "Was there a problem with the gardener?" I waited as Godfrey washed the gardener's cup and teapot and dried his hands on a dishtowel. He said nothing. "Is Mr. Jumbo still taking sugar from us?" I asked. Godfrey stood at the sink, his eyes fixed on the idle dishtowel in his hands, his body motionless. I went outside and found the gardener standing on a patch of grass along our building. He was washing his honey-colored feet in a trickle of water from a garden hose, pants legs rolled up to his knees. The straps of his bib overalls fell loosely over his knobby shoulders. The man's faced was leathery and wrinkled. I suspected he had been an Embassy gardener for many years.

When he saw me, he dropped the hose and stood at attention, like a barefooted soldier. We faced one another under an avocado tree, the leafy branches shading us from the powerful beam of a security light at the corner of the building. Avocados dangled like green footballs from branches only inches above our heads. Close to Mr. Jumbo, I noticed he smelled strongly of lemons. There was a lemon tree at the back of our building.

"Every morning and night, Godfrey brings you a full bowl of sugar and a cup of tea," I said to him. "And after your tea, the sugar bowl is always empty. That bowl is three times the size of your teacup. How is it possible for one person to use so much sugar every day?"

The man's arms remained stiff at his side. His hands were lined with cracks from work and age. I was a head taller, so the angle between us made it difficult for me to see into his eyes. I had not the slightest idea what Mr. Jumbo was seeing himself, let alone what he was thinking. "Every week, I buy us ten pounds of sugar," I continued. The lemon scent floating around the gardener was becoming intoxicating. "Who on earth uses ten pounds of sugar every week?" My voice was rising in volume, but I was trying not to lose control. "Does your family need sugar? Is that the problem? I'll give you enough sugar for your whole damn village. Just stop stealing it from me!"

Mr. Jumbo never looked up. My gaze drifted out beyond the old man, out across the compound's well-manicured lawn, and farther out past the limit of the security lights, to where there was nothing visible. Somewhere in that dark emptiness was my vegetable garden, the plot assigned to me by the Embassy Housing Board. Mr. Jumbo tended my plot, my rows of tomatoes, peppers, and zucchini – all food for my dinner. I wondered if he had any idea of the point I was making.

"Are we clear? No more stealing."

"Yes, Master," he said.

"All you have to do is ask for sugar, and I'll give you whatever you need."

"Yes, Master."

"And stop calling me master," I said. "I'm Joe or Mr. Kellerman. I'm not your master." I turned back towards my apartment, but still hanging heavily in the air was the fragrance of fresh citrus. After a few breaths, I stopped walking. Mr. Jumbo was still standing in place, motionless as a field post, his eyes locked on the ground. "And the same goes for stealing my lemons," I said.

"Yes, Master," he replied.

Chapter 16
Smoke

My dinner guests were halfway through a second round of drinks when I returned from my detour outside with the gardener. As I sat down, Trevor asked, "What is the story on your newsman, the black from New York? We heard he gets on with J.J."

"Not much else to say," I replied.

"What's his program?"

"Tomorrow, we tour a tea estate. He also wants to see the Chitsaya trial."

"I would love to see the Chitsaya trial," Heather said. "I think it'd be fascinating. But our High Commissioner thought it was too dangerous for me to go."

"He's right, dear. The North is dangerous," said Annabelle. "Lord knows what could happen with UFreeMo running wild."

"Stand clear of Katembeyna," advised Rolf. "It's unpredictable up there – even before what happened here today."

Annabelle sniffed the air. "Does anyone smell smoke?"

I shot out of the room, Trevor and Heather following. A rolling white cloud was escaping from under the kitchen door. I pushed open the door, and a tempest of smoke engulfed us. I rushed into the room, Heather just behind me. The sink was against the wall to the right, opposite the stove. Shoestring potatoes were deep-frying in a pan of oil on a burner, but the source of the smoke was not the stove top. It was the oven door; something inside was on fire. Orange flames were seeping from the edges of the door, stabbing the air above. Then, a larger spear of flame burst out the top. The intensity of the heat forced me back a step. The wooden spice rack anchored on the wall above the stove lit up, and a new flame grew there, licking the ceiling tiles and scarring them with black char. New flames quickly danced across the ceiling, towards the pantry.

I spotted Godfrey through the smoke. He was standing still, his back to the sink, eyes closed. In one hand was a blue-striped dishtowel that he was waving in a circular motion above his head. The absurdity of the sight paralyzed me for a moment. Then, I wrapped my shirt like a mask around my mouth and nose and pulled the pan of fries and oil from the burner. I set the pan hissing in the sink. I then grabbed a fire extinguisher off the back wall. Distant to us, the smoke detector at my front door began to screech.

Heather opened a window above the sink. The fresh air surging in fed more oxygen to the flames already engulfing the stove. They shot out even farther. I blasted the spice rack with the fire extinguisher, while Trevor pried open the oven door with a broom handle. More flames escaped. A long blast from the extinguisher forced them to retreat. I saw that our steaks were on fire, fed by grease burning at the bottom of the oven. I blasted inside the oven again and at stringers of flame skittering up the adjacent wall. Pieces of melted ceiling tile were falling throughout the kitchen like tiny fire parachutes. Three Marines ran in and quickly gained control of the situation with their own extinguishers, covering the oven, walls, and ceiling with white foam. The fire was under control less than a minute later.

Rolf and the Pooles had staged outside on the grass with Godfrey, who was lying on his side. Each time Godfrey coughed, a billow of white smoke escaped his mouth. Heather was bent over on the sidewalk, coughing out smoke as well. A Marine came out of the apartment and over to us. "Everything is out, sir," he said to me. "We opened some windows, but you've got one hell of a mess to clean up."

"Thank you, sergeant."

"It could have been worse, sir. We found a jerry can in the pantry."

"There was gasoline in there?"

"Five gallons, sir. But it's squared away, locked out back in the shed now. Have a good night, sir."

Neighbors who had been watching the drama returned to their apartments. Godfrey was soon breathing better and on his feet. I went over to him. "What happened in there?" I asked. Godfrey stared at the ground, fidgeting with his hands.

"The gravy for the new vegetable cooks too fast," he said.

I discovered that instead of cooking the squash as I instructed, he had baked them for an hour, with a quart of sugar glaze in the pan. The glaze had boiled over and caught fire on the bottom of the oven. Those flames had started the steaks burning. As for the gasoline in the pantry, Godfrey said it was Mr. Jumbo who had put it there. I struggled to find logic in what had happened, why the fire had gotten so bad so quickly, so I went inside and got the smoke detector from the kitchen. It had never sounded during the fire.

"Why didn't you tell us the kitchen was on fire?" I asked my cook. He didn't reply. I flipped open the lid on the smoke detector. I showed Godfrey the emptiness inside. "This is from the kitchen ceiling," I said. "There's no battery. If a battery had been in here, we would've heard the alarm. We could've prevented some of the damage. Do you know who removed the battery?"

Godfrey thought for a moment. "It was the cleaning lady," he said. "She is not to be trusted."

Trevor Poole burst out laughing.

My guests had gone without dinner and were tired, even so they agreed to another drink before leaving. Trevor was still chuckling when we came back inside. "Good show, old chap," he said, patting me on the back. "T-I-A."

Despite the chill in the air, we moved to the patio, away from the smell of smoke.

"We have a wager on the board," said Trevor. "Three are betting you'll sack the lad, but Miss May thinks you'll spare the poor bugger. Is it because of the fine chips he makes?"

Not to anyone in particular, I asked, "What was Godfrey thinking? Flames are at the ceiling. And he's standing there, waving at the smoke with a dishtowel!"

"Sometimes, it simply astounds me," said Annabelle. "They can be so thick headed."

"Oblivious," said Rolf.

"So, what's the verdict, Joe? Are you letting him go or keeping him on?" The thought of firing Godfrey had never entered my mind, until Trevor asked.

"Maybe I should sack him, protect him from himself."

"He might have gone up in flames if you hadn't come in," said Rolf.

"There's the answer!" Trevor said, clapping his hands. "You need a new cook."

"But Godfrey has a family," I said. "Who can say a new cook would react any different?"

Trevor raised his glass to Heather. "All right, Miss May. I see where this is headed."

"Why don't they tell us when they make a mistake?" said Annabelle. "We're here to help."

"That's been a mystery to me for years," said Rolf.

"T-I-A," said Trevor, pausing between each letter.

"T-I-A?" Heather said. "I've heard people say that."

"It means, 'This-is-Africa,'" said Rolf.

"Ex-pats use it when there is no logical explanation for something here," said Trevor.

"Actually, dear," Annabelle interrupted her husband, "education is what Trevor is talking about. People aren't born with common sense. It takes education. Do you think Godfrey's been to school?"

"Not likely," said Rolf. Trevor shrugged, unsure.

"I disagree, Mrs. Poole," said Heather, with that timbre of innocence I was liking so much about her. "The reason Godfrey didn't tell us about the fire isn't a lack of schooling. It's because he thought we're too important to be bothered with a simple problem in the kitchen."

"Keeping a row of flats off the burn pile is no bother to me," said Trevor.

"Heather's hitting on something," I said. "House helpers always act like we're more important than them. Like we're special."

"But we aren't," said Heather. "That's my point. We aren't special or more important."

"Are you certain?" asked Annabelle, in all sincerity. "We never say it in so many words, of course. That wouldn't sound right. But be honest. We do matter more." Heather's eyes widened. "Not in an individual sense, dear," Annabelle continued, "you know, all God's creatures being equal and such. But if you consider the bigger picture, the assistance our countries give these people is much more than what their countries do on their own."

"It's certainly more than they do for us," said Rolf.

"Exactly. Without us, where would they be?" said Annabelle.

"Of course, our work makes a difference," Rolf said. "Otherwise, why are we here?"

Trevor leaned forward and took a long swallow from his glass, finishing it all, a coda on the evening. "There's a simple reason they don't tell us when they botch up," he said, setting the empty glass on the table in front of him. "It's not education. It's not some inferiority complex they have. It's not something random. The reason they don't tell us is because they're afraid. They're afraid what we'll do to them for making a mistake. They'd rather take a chance with their life in a fire, than tell us they buggered the steak and chips."

"You're saying they fear us?" said Heather.

"Terribly, Miss May. Terribly." Trevor rested his hands in his lap. "Sometimes, T-I-A means only that, Miss May – fear."

Chapter 17
Ndala

The trajectory of a diplomat's career in the Foreign Service is determined by his or her performance during two periods of administrative review. The first occurs in Virginia at the Foreign Service Institute, during a rigorous nine-week training course known as A-100. I was fortunate to receive good marks in A-100, completing the course at the top of my class, earning the status of "kite." My classmates voted me "Most Likely to Become an Ambassador," though I am certain they would have selected someone else if they had been able to look into the future and see what would happen in Umbika. The second review of a junior officer happens at the end of his or her first tour overseas. For me, that was after two years in Nigeria. I had rated high again in Lagos and was given a Meritorious Honor Award, vaguely similar in importance to the military's Bronze Star, for finding a missing person. From tour to tour, my standing continued to rise in the Africa Bureau. Embassies started requesting me by name when they needed a consular problem solved. They turned me into a floater, perpetually on temporary duty, my assignments lasting a few weeks to several months. This nomadic life fit me well.

Tuesday morning of the Hightower visit, I was in my office, preparing to leave for the tea estates, when Ambassador Durhlmann appeared in my doorway. "Joe," he said and sat on the sofa in my office. "Benny called me last night. He said he'd just met with Mitchell Watts." Watts was the Assistant Secretary for Africa, a high-level political appointee in charge of all of the American diplomats in Africa. He was the former CEO of a large corporation and the President's roommate in college. "Maurice Hightower phoned the White House yesterday. He complained about the Andelebe boy's visa."

Grace and Violet were in the next room, so I closed the door between us.

"Watts was furious," the Ambassador said. "He told Bennie he'd issue the visa himself if he had to. Of course, he can't do that. But either way, Benny went up to the Seventh Floor. He briefed Watts and the Secretary about Triple S and the kid. It was enough to get everyone to take a step back for a while. But then, before close of business, the White House presented Bennie an offer." Already, I was feeling that Hightower's visit was turning towards the disaster Dave Hardy had predicted. "What the White House is promising is that the FBI will keep an eye on the boy while he's in the States, if you'll issue the visa."

It was all I could do to hold my tongue. I was hoping we had moved past the Andelebe visa, but now the White House was in the middle of it. They were very upset and knew some consular officer in Umbika was causing the problem. Me. "You know what the Life President will do, sir, when he gets the names of dissenters in the U.S."

The Ambassador stood. "What I know is the election is two weeks from today. The President's team is under a lot of pressure. Watts knows they can't afford having Maurice Hightower stir up more trouble for the President. The FBI offer is a plea for help. They're hoping you'll reconsider." The Ambassador smoothed his tie, pulled on his shirt cuffs. He could tell I was uncomfortable, but he had made his point. "Give some thought to what they've promised," he said. "We'll have to get back to the Department in a day or two." The Ambassador extended his hand. "Have a good trip to Ndala," he said. We shook, and then he left my office.

Fred and I listened to President Mulenga speak on the radio during our drive to the Intercontinental Hotel to pick up Hightower. President Mulenga called on Umbiks to assist the police in their search for the murderers of Speaker Muswaya. At the end of the speech he said, "Do not lose hope, my brothers and sisters. No one but God Almighty tells the cock when to crow or the crocodile where to find his breakfast. We must stay strong. God will lead us on the path to justice. We are in His hands. We are His servants. Bring me the confusionists responsible for these murders. With God instructing us, this nation will crow again, and we will feed the crocodile his breakfast."

President Mulenga's hatred for Tologs had roots reaching back a hundred years. Back then, Umbika was nothing more than an empty space on missionary maps, labeled vaguely as Central East Africa. That was when the first Christian missionaries arrived here. Malaria was ubiquitous in the central region and soon drove the British settlers from the lowlands where the Umbik tribe lived, to higher altitudes in the north, where mosquitoes were less common. The north was home to the Tolog tribe. Tologs were an accommodating and superstitious people by nature and got on well with the white pastors and priests. They eagerly learned English so they could read the Bible and become more faithful and more protected. Soon, British authorities needed civil servants for the growing colony, and they chose English-speaking Tologs over illiterate Umbiks. The same was true for British businesses. Tologs received all of the best opportunities. Consequently, uneducated Umbiks became mired in a cycle of poverty and subservience, even though they vastly outnumbered the Tologs.

Jim Jimmy Mulenga carried his own personal dark spot in his heart for Tologs. When he was a boy, he watched Umbiks with his skin color wait on the street in long lines for a few menial labor jobs that paid next to nothing, while dark-skinned Tologs with coats and ties sat in colonial offices, laughing and drinking tea. The inequality taunted his imagination for years. When he became president, he promised Umbiks he would set things right. His campaign began by blaming Tologs for the problem whenever something went wrong. If the electrical grid went down, it was Tolog incompetence. If coffee prices fell, it was Tolog mismanagement. When the rainy season arrived late, it was Tolog bad luck.

After he was declared President for Life, Mulenga announced his National Birthright Policy. No longer could Tologs hold government jobs outside the province where they were born. The army and police were prohibited from accepting Tolog recruits. Tologs were forbidden from working in hospitals. When Mulenga's new National Exploring Group was formed, it was comprised of only Umbik youth. Tolog leaders feared prison or death if they complained too loudly, so most remained silent, but the bravest among them created a secret organization, the United Freedom Movement – UFreeMo. Twenty years after Mulenga's rise to power, Tologs were beginning to fight back.

After the Life President's radio speech ended, I asked Fred what he thought would happen to Tologs now. "I am short on words, sir," he said, sadly. "But we must remember the patience of Job."

Fred Chombo had been my driver since I arrived in Umbika, and he was a good one. I knew little else about him. Almost as thin as the red, white, and blue tie he wore to work every day, Fred never offered information about his family or his life away from the Embassy. I suspected from his skin color he was Tolog. But I did not know where his home village was. It was rumored that his wife was Umbik, but he never revealed that to me. What I did know was that Fred was an excellent choice for a driver. He knew every road in the country, knew when local markets were open, and knew what their specialties were. Fred could find a cold bottle of water on the warmest day and was expert at getting through a police stop without delay. He also spoke several local dialects. In my opinion, Fred was the best driver at the Embassy, perhaps the best I had ever had in Africa. I was lucky to have him.

Hightower was waiting for us at the bottom of the steps to the Intercontinental Hotel when we arrived. It was ten o'clock. He slid in opposite me on the back seat. Fred stowed his overnight bag in the trunk and then steered us onto the M-1 highway, headed east.

"The Speaker of Parliament is murdered, and we're going to see how tea is made," Hightower said.

"We can cancel if you prefer to stay here today."

"No, no," he said, dismissively. "Tea is important. And the Life President thought I should go."

"I want to apologize for what happened with the visa," I said. "I hope we can put it behind us." Hightower said nothing, just stared out his window, his face expressionless. The barrier my briefcase and his leather satchel formed on the backseat between us seemed no less formidable than a wall between two countries. I refused to drive three hours without speaking. So, I started describing what I knew about Umbika's tea region, whether Hightower cared to listen or not.

"The man we're seeing has ties to Umbika going back to the nineteen-twenties," I said. "His name is Pietr Ritt-Boorman."

Hightower said nothing, as rust-red landscape passed outside our windows. We braked for a boy herding a cow with a stick. Off to the side of the road, a man chased his hat in the wind.

"Ndala is the capital of the Eastern Province," I said. "It's an area known for premium-quality tea. The name, Ndala, means 'leather sandal,' but why the town is called that is a mystery." We were on the eastern edge of the capital city. Fred steered our 4x4 around three women walking with buckets balanced on their heads. A minibus in front of us stopped to collect men waiting at the side of the highway. Hightower stared out his window, and my monologue continued. Ndala was a town of fifty thousand, I said, the place where the first cement sidewalk in East Africa had been built. The hills east of Ndala grew the finest tea in Africa, exported around the world. At the height of the Colonial Era, three hundred independent tea plantations had operated there. Other small-scale industries in Ndala manufactured soap, batteries, and cardboard boxes. We then stopped for the first police checkpoint of the trip.

In front of us, waiting to be screened, was a long line of cars and semi-trailers. Fred steered our vehicle over the gravel shoulder and around the queue, towards the front of the line, passing more than a dozen vehicles. Our thick tires stirred up a cloud of red dust. Normally, traffic cops manned these checkpoints, with one or two bored patrolmen waving people through. Now, behind a barrier in front of us stood a screen of NEG soldiers, eight or ten in black uniforms, black berets, dark sunglasses, and shiny AK-47s. "What's going on?" I asked Fred.

"The government is afraid," Fred said, pushing us closer to the front of the line. "They worry the opposition is trying to enter the city."

One NEG soldier noticed us bypassing the queue. He raised his weapon, but a traffic policeman stepped forward and pointed to our diplomatic license plate. He waved us around the barrier, two empty oil drums connected by a long steel pipe. On the passenger's side, a NEG officer bent over to look inside our vehicle as we passed, contempt written on his face. Hightower was looking out that same window; he acted as if nothing happened. He jotted something in his notebook. Once beyond the roadblock, I continued my travelogue of Ndala trivia.

"Tea accounts for ninety-percent of the economy of the Eastern Province," I said. "The estate we're seeing is ten thousand acres, twenty-five million tea bushes." Hightower turned from his window. I thought he was ready to talk, but he didn't look at me, just wrote another line in his notebook. "Working on a new column?" I asked. He closed the notebook.

"You're not going to show me every one of those twenty-five million bushes, are you?"

I ignored the sarcasm, just glad he was talking. "Of course not."

"Good."

"But I wanted you to know how important tea is to Umbika's economy. Every village around Ndala is involved in the tea business. Mostly, people work as pluckers or sorters."

"People 'pluck' tea?" Hightower asked.

"That's right. It takes a worker fourteen hours to pluck fifty pounds of tea. For that, he makes two dollars."

"Sounds unfair – like a cotton field, back in the day."

"I don't know about cotton, but two dollars is twice what the average Umbikan earns." I waited for Hightower to respond, but nothing came. "The biggest danger to a plucker is snakebite." This detail seemed to get his attention. He adjusted his position on his seat. Fred was listening. He turned and smiled at Hightower.

"In Africa, sir," he said, "a dead snake is the only good snake."

"That fellow on trial in the North," Hightower asked, "what tribe is he from?"

"He's a Tolog. Same as Fred, I think. Isn't that right, Fred?"

"Chitsaya is Tolog."

"His first name is odd," Hightower said. "What is it?"

"Wisdom. His name is Wisdom Chitsaya," Fred said.

Hightower picked up his notebook and started writing again. "It takes a hard head to carry a name like Wisdom around with you. Why did he tell people to overthrow the government?"

"He never told anyone that," I said. "He only said Umbika is not a democratic country. He said it would never reach its full potential unless the Life President permitted multiparty democracy. For that idea, the government wants Chitsaya to hang."

Hightower looked over at me, studied me for a moment, and then wrote another line in his notebook. "Chitsaya's mistake was passing out a flyer about multiparty on the street in Katembeyna," I said. "The flyer argued that Umbika was a dying country."

"Sounds to me he was agitating people to overthrow the president. That's being guilty of sedition, not handing out a flyer."

It was so easy to slip into an argument with Hightower. My heart was pounding strongly in my chest, blood pulsating through my neck, whooshing in my ears. "Chitsaya didn't tell anyone to do anything," I said. "He doesn't deserve to die because of his opinion." I expected Hightower to tease the argument to the next level, but he went silent again, paging through his notebook. Finally, he clicked his pen and stowed it in his shirt pocket.

"I don't think a country like the United States, a country that was built on slave labor," he said, "has the moral authority to judge anyone else. Umbika is learning to walk. It doesn't need multiparty democracy. All multiparty will bring is more hatred, conflict, and fighting." Outside, the flatness of the Central Province had started to contort into gently rolling hills.

"Umbika is a dictatorship. President Mulenga rules with an iron fist. Thirty-five political prisoners, not criminals, were hanged in Umbika last year."

"That's an Amnesty International number. I read their report before I came here."

"Our annual Human Rights Report agrees with them."

"When I met with the Life President, I asked him about those numbers. He swore that no one in Umbika was ever hanged because of politics. I take the man at his word, unless you can show me some real evidence."

I could have shown him a file folder full of evidence at the Embassy, a dozen classified reports collected over the years, interviews from credible sources, details about torture and murder, names and locations. We even had a few photos of mutilated bodies, but none of that would ever be seen by Maurice Hightower or anyone else outside the Chancery.

Chapter 18
Traditional Medicine

We entered Ndala at half noon. The drive of 150 miles was long enough to bring out some stiffness in my bad leg, though I had felt worse in those joints. Fred rolled down his window. Cool air from the hills to the north and east washed over us, bringing with it the scent of tea, which Ndala wore like an exotic perfume. A mile from the center of town, Fred slowed to a crawl. Foot traffic on the road was nearly impenetrable. "It's market day, sir," Fred said. Hightower spotted the sprawling trading center at the bottom of a hill, a mosaic of color and frenzy. Crowds moved through open-air stalls from every direction.

"Can you stop?" Hightower asked. "I'd like to take some pictures." Fred found a place to park above the market, in front of a textile shop. A young Asian man stood in the doorway, his arms folded over his chest in a manager's pose.

"I'll stay with the car, keep an eye on our things," I said, though truth be told, my leg was throbbing and would only get worse if I had to push through the market crowd. Fred and Hightower descended the hill and were lost in a sea of buyers and sellers. I sat on a rock the size of a couch, next to our car. It was the perfect perch for following Hightower's silver hair floating above the masses. I eventually lost him at the far side of the market.

Ten or fifteen minutes passed before I saw Fred again. He had returned to the market's entrance, but there was no sign of Hightower. Fred waved to me up the hill, beckoning me to come down to where he was standing. When I reached Fred, he seemed agitated.

"You must collect him, sir," Fred said. "It is not good."

"What are you talking about? Where's Mr. Hightower?" Fred led me past stalls of vegetable sellers and tin craftsmen. Hightower was behind the shoe kiosks, standing among other shoppers in front of four folding tables. Wood bins the size of desk drawers sat atop each table, five or six of them. The drawers were further subdivided into compartments, each holding various roots and dried leaves in organic shades of greens, browns, and grays. Take-away paper bags bound with twine formed a row beside the bins. Three of the tables had elderly men standing behind them. Hightower was standing at the fourth table, taking photos of an old man set back from the table, sitting motionless in the shade of a nearby tree. I could not tell if the man's eyes were open or closed. He was so still he could have been asleep, or even dead. "What's in the bags?" Hightower called to him. The old man didn't answer, didn't move. "I said, these paper bags here, you selling spices or what?" The old man gave no sign he had heard Hightower's question or cared what was going on. Fred began to pace. He was watching the curious shoppers who had taken a keen interest in Hightower.

"We must leave, sir," Fred said to me.

The old man called to Hightower. "Where you coming to?" His voice had more power in it than I expected.

"Sir," Fred pleaded with me.

"Where am I coming from?" Hightower replied. "I'm coming from the capital city."

"B'wanza?" the old man said, shaking his head. "You not in B'wanza. Where you coming to?" Hightower twitched his shoulders and cocked his head. He was growing impatient.

"I want to know what you're selling," Hightower said. "This stuff is for sale, isn't it?"

"We should head to our hotel," I said to Hightower. He poked a finger in each open bin on the table, twirling the roots and leaves, bending down to smell them. He picked up a paper bag and lightly shook it. The crowd backed away.

"Oh, no!" Fred said, his voice showing unusual concern. "You must not touch the pouches." The area around the table had opened up. I saw the wooden sign hanging in front: L. Kudzedze – Traditional Doctor. I explained to Hightower that the old man was an African healer, a medicine man, but he ignored me. I whispered that the man was a witchdoctor, but even that wasn't enough to pull Hightower from the table.

"I'm from New York," Hightower said to the old man. "North America."

"America," he replied, shaking his head. He pushed out of his chair and shuffled to the table, where he picked up a mirror the size of a paperback novel and held it flat in front of Hightower. "Put your hand."

Hightower laughed. The old man placed his own palm against the mirror's glass to show him. "You want my hand on that?" Hightower said. The old man nodded and took a black cloth from the table. He wiped the glass, making it clean again. Hightower seemed amused. He laid his palm against the glass and held it. The old man gently lifted Hightower's hand and studied the imprint left behind, a faint outline of body oil and perspiration. The old man blew across the surface three times. Then, he pulled a dry leaf from one of the bins and crushed it between his fingers. He let the fine powder fall over the mirror. Captivated by the strange ritual, Hightower stepped closer. The old man blew away the dust, revealing the distinct image of Hightower's hand.

"What's the diagnosis, brother?" Hightower asked.

The old man opened an empty paper bag. With a wooden spoon, he apportioned various leaves and twigs into the bag, crushing each with his fingers. Then, he folded the flap shut and handed the package to Hightower. "Tea," the old man said. "Drink three nights, at sleep."

Hightower held the bag up to the sunlight. "What's this for?" He shook the bag at eye level. "I'm in perfect health."

The old man pointed to Hightower's chest, his hand directed at the heart.

He touched his own heart and shook his head. "In here, no good," he said

"What do you mean, no good? What'd you see in that mirror?"

The old man shuffled back to his chair in the shade.

Fred said, "These people think they are doctors. They are not educated, sir."

Hightower dropped a five-dollar bill on the table, but he left the paper bag. Minutes later, we were driving through the gates of the Victoria and Albert Hotel, a semi-circular driveway outlined in small whitewashed rocks. Fred followed the drive clockwise to the foot of a staircase that led to a veranda that circled the front of the building. A black man, dressed like an English butler, came down the steps and opened our doors.

I checked us in, two rooms. Hightower declined my offer of lunch, saying he had some work to do. Fred left to find a petrol station. On my way to the hotel restaurant, the receptionist said, "There is a message, sir." He handed me a piece of hotel stationary. I returned to my room and called the Embassy.

"This morning, the Department issued a travel advisory for Umbika," said the Ambassador's secretary over the phone. "Americans are advised not to visit here. Those in-country should stay away from areas where crowds could gather."

"Thanks for letting me know, Gwen," I said.

"There are a couple more things, Joe. The Speaker's death got national TV coverage in the U.S. And our visitor called the major networks from his hotel last night."

"Do we know what he said?"

"He said more innocent black people will die unless the U.S. stops assisting UFreeMo."

Chapter 19
The Daily Noose

I was annoyed with Hightower for contacting TV stations in New York, stirring the pot, but I let it go. We still had a visit to a tea estate to get through. At two, we left the hotel, heading farther east. The afternoon sky looked wonderful, a soft blue like a robin's egg, and only a few wispy clouds. To the left and right of the highway were rolling green hills. We stopped at marker 1217, where a whitewashed fence post stuck out from a hedgerow. Nailed to the wooden post was a hand-lettered sign, Estate of Glen Allyn – Estb. 1893. Fred turned into a narrow opening barely recognizable in the thick of it. No one would guess he was entering the premier tea estate in all of Umbika, a property ten thousand acres large, home to one of Umbika's most influential businessmen.

We drove around overgrown bushes, under a canopy of feathery trees. Fred steered one way and then another to follow the winding lane. The changing shadows and relentless motion left me completely disoriented, and a little car sick. Finally, we broke free of the dim light and saw a magnificent colonial house standing on a distant hill, its walls plaster white, its roof made of buffed copper.

Two Rottweilers appeared on either side of our car, and then a pair of black and gold German Shepherds. None of the dogs made a sound as they loped beside the car. Pietr Ritt-Boorman was waiting at the house, on a porch at the top of heavy stone steps. When we parked at the foot of the steps, the dogs ran up to Pietr and sat at his feet, their long snouts pointing down on us. Pietr wore a light shirt, gray bush shorts, and black tube socks under dark leather sandals. His shirt was cut tight to his wide shoulders and narrow waist and would have looked silly on most men his age. But not on Pietr Ritt-Boorman. For a man in his sixties, Pietr was exceedingly fit. His skin taut and tanned. "Welcome to Glen Allyn!" he called down to us.

Pietr and I had met at a diplomatic reception six months earlier. I doubted he remembered much about me, but the Ritt-Boorman family history, and Pietr's place in it, was legend in Umbika. He was third generation African. His grandfather was born in the 1800s in South Africa, at Hout Bay, a fishing village on the road from the Cape of Good Hope to Cape Town. The family had operated a successful outfitters store. It was in Cape Town where grandfather Joost met and married his first and only love, Mary Ann, the daughter of an owner of cargo ships.

Travelers passing through the Cape at the time told of a new British colony to the north, a special place where a man with a dream and the capacity for hard work could make a fortune. With financial backing from his father-in-law, Joost and his brother travelled to the new colony and purchased two hundred acres of virgin land near the trading post of Ndala. They planted 5500 tea and 600 coffee bushes. Mary Ann arrived the following year, a few months before Joost's brother died of malaria. By the fifth year, Joost had doubled the size of their property and doubled the number of tea bushes on the farm, but he decided against expanding the coffee business. He built a magnificent house, large enough to raise a family. Mary Ann gave birth to a son everyone called Junior. With the demand for tea continuing to grow, Joost and Mary Ann decided this place would be their life.

For twenty-five years everything went well, more land purchased, more tea planted, two girls born. Then, Joost suffered a stroke. Junior, barely an adult, took over the business. The First Great War began in Europe and spilled over into parts of Africa. Several businesses in East Africa collapsed. Imports and exports were lost at sea. Land changed hands. Yet Glen Allyn survived it all. One reason was blind luck. Another was Junior's skill at bribery, coercion, and intimidation. Junior was also known to be quick with a whip when his workers failed to meet the expectations he had set for them. Five years after assuming control of Glen Allyn, Junior had tripled the family holdings, and ten years after that, he had doubled them again. By the start of the Second World War, Glen Allyn was the premier tea estate in the colony.

In the early 1950s, Junior, his wife, and their teenage daughter were killed in a foggy road accident outside Ndala, their car colliding head-on with a coach bus. Junior's only son, Pietr, a promising graduate student in economics in London, abandoned his studies and returned to Africa. Pietr possessed a warmer and more generous heart than his father's, characteristics more in line with his grandfather Joost. Pietr put his London education to work immediately, becoming the first entrepreneur in the colony to vertically integrate an industry. He purchased warehouses and a short-haul trucking company. He built his own processing plant and packager. Five years after his parents' death, Pieter had made Glen Allyn the top African exporter of premium black tea to the UK, and one of the most profitable companies in East Africa.

When colonial powers were leaving the Continent in the late 1950s and early '60s, Pietr had no interest in starting a new life in South Africa or England or Australia, as many of his neighbors did. Most whites feared a bloody backlash after independence. Not Pietr. His entire life he had known Umbikans to be peaceful and kind, so when the time came, he cast his lot with the new government, gambling his life and everything he owned against the possibility of a racial bloodbath. There was a risk, to be sure, but his choice was not a reckless wager. Pietr was simply following the most important lesson he had learned in London—great entrepreneurs do not let fear decide their business options for them.

Pietr's gamble proved correct. The transition to black rule in Umbika went smoothly, without much destruction of property or loss of life. Pietr had foreseen the end of colonialism in Umbika for what it really was – the chance of a lifetime. Dozens of abandoned properties sold for a fraction of their true value, and Pietr Ritt-Boorman became the richest white landowner in the country.

When we got up to the porch where Pietr was waiting, he said to Hightower, "It's a joy to meet you, my friend." I did not remember Pietr being as tall as he was, only two or three inches shorter than Hightower. "I understand you are here to see how we make a cup of tea."

"Ha," Hightower replied, "and to learn about Umbika. The Life President said you know a lot about your country."

"I'll give it my best," Pietr said and turned to me. He offered his hand. "Mr. Kellerman, from the American Embassy. We've met before."

"Yes, we have."

I followed Pietr and Hightower to a sunroom at the back of the house. We sat on red leather armchairs, in front of an enormous picture window overlooking an expanse of lawn. On the far side was a windbreak of eucalyptus trees, gray and towering over the bright green grass. A house helper who looked a lot like my cook came in with *Kir Royales* in long fluted glasses.

"You're a writer," Pietr said to Hightower. "One of the best in the States, I'm told."

"By trade, a journalist," Hightower corrected. "People want to understand what's happening in the world. I try to help them."

"Three million readers, am I correct?" Pietr said. Hightower nodded. "Your influence on public opinion is difficult for me to imagine."

"My readers don't trust the mainstream press. They know I look for the truth. You probably know that's why I'm in Umbika, to find the truth." Another man from the kitchen set out an elaborate tray of cut vegetables, dipping sauces, and neatly arranged tangerine wedges.

"Is this your first visit to Africa?"

"No," Hightower said. "I travelled to Ghana, years ago."

"The Gold Coast," Pietr sighed. "The slave trade is our sad past... and America's. But the past is just that, the past. I look to the future. If history interests you, you must visit Lake Ziwa in the North. At the shore, there's an old building where Arab traders collected slaves, before sending them to ports on the Indian Ocean. You can still touch the chains."

"I'm planning to go north for that trial."

"Ah, the cashew farmer." Pietr gave a reflective nod. "A simple man who made very poor choices. I think your readers would rather hear about tea, than treason, yes?"

Hightower laughed. I laughed. The visit appeared to be off to a good start.

"Maybe you can explain something to me, Pietr," Hightower said.

"I'll give it a try."

"Why did a simple cashew farmer let himself get into so much trouble?"

"You should ask Mr. Kellerman," Pietr replied. "His embassy carries some responsibility, you know. That poor fellow never heard of multiparty-anything until the Americans started preaching it." I feigned a polite smile. He turned his attention back to Hightower, which suited me fine. "The trial starts tomorrow," Pietr added.

"I thought it was Thursday," Hightower said, looking at me.

"The start was moved for security reasons. I doubt it'll go long. The evidence seems clear." Pietr finished the last swallow of his drink and set the empty glass on the table. "How about we begin our tour while the sun is still high?"

We left through a door off the kitchen, the dogs staying close. We walked across the spacious lawn, towards the windbreak. Behind the trees was a large barn painted white with orange doors and window trim. "Are we going too fast for you, Mr. Kellerman?" Pietr asked, shortening his stride.

"It's not a problem," I replied. "My leg tightens up a little on car rides." At the orange barn door, Pietr took Hightower's elbow and drew him to his side.

"May I speak candidly for a moment?" he asked, his voice hushed.

"Certainly. What is it?"

"What I say is not for publication, at least not with my name attached."

"Say whatever is on your mind. If you prefer confidentiality, no names will be used." Hightower removed a reporter's notebook from his jacket pocket.

Pietr began, "I'm a white man, obviously – though not European. I'm African, and I'm proud every time I say that. Africa is my continent. I was born in Umbika. My father was too. My grandfather was born in South

Africa. My skin color might be different, but I have as much right as anyone to speak about Africa and defend my way of life. Maurice, I hope you can tell me something. What does America want from us?" Pietr put his hand on Hightower's arm, which seemed to discourage an answer for the moment. "I mean, you're a smart man, a journalist. Is multiparty all America wants from Umbika – or is there more?"

Pietr's directness caught Hightower off guard. "America wants control," he said, finally. "It's what America always wants."

Pietr seemed confused, maybe unconvinced by Hightower's answer. "I have a friend in the North. He says white people are slipping over the border, taking soil samples in the Highlands, taking water samples in the lake. There are rumors of great deposits of copper and magnesium and oil up there."

Hightower turned towards me. "Perhaps, Joe has something to share with us."

"I've heard the same rumors," I said. "If Americans were digging up there, we'd all know. You can't keep a secret like that."

"I agree on one point, Mr. Kellerman," Pietr said and slid open the orange barn door. "Secrets in Africa don't stay secret for long." Pietr led us inside the building. "This is our cleaning shed." No one was working inside. The far wall was a face of frosted glass, hundreds of large panes, their translucence making the light soft and calming. Even so, slivers of the sun snuck in through random cracks between windowpanes, the brilliant light illuminating columns of dust particles suspended midair, like ethereal pillars for some ancient temple.

Pietr explained how tea leaves were cleaned, dried, and graded. Then, halfway to the far side of the large space he stopped. "Jimmy Mulenga is a good man – a man whose heart is as big as this shed. Since he was a boy, he could be counted to do what was right for Umbika. I don't say that just because he's been my friend for many years. I say it because he's a true national hero." One of the German Shepherds had found a stick on the floor and was carrying it in his mouth like a prize, teasing the other dogs. "Mr. Kellerman, I read about Umbika in that human rights report your Embassy sent me. You make it sound like we harm people on purpose. We have policemen, of course, who are passionate and occasionally make mistakes. What police force in the world doesn't? Your writers of that report need to remember where we are, Mr. Kellerman. People must learn to walk before they can run."

"I've heard that," I said.

"Let me put it this way," Pietr continued walking, looking at me. "Your government asks a question to an African. In your mind, it's a simple question. You expect answer A or answer B. These are the only choices your government ever considers, A or B." The other three dogs chased the Shepherd with the stick. "But the African doesn't think like that," said Pietr. "He gives you answer C." The Shepherd dropped the stick and another dog picked it up. "The problem, Mr. Kellerman, is that your government is so powerful it can ignore answer C, even if it's the right answer for the African."

The four dogs were all growling now over ownership of the stick. Pietr commanded them to be quiet, which they did immediately. He picked up the stick and carried it himself. "It's what the powerful always do, Mr. Kellerman. They impose choices on the weak. T-I-A. Isn't that what ex-pats say when something doesn't fit their idea of how things should work here? My friends take offense at that arrogance."

I smiled and nodded, not wanting our visit to turn on its side. We had reached the far side of the barn. Pietr slid open another orange door and motioned for us to step outside. Across the next lawn was another barn, similar to the first, except its walls were painted orange and the doors and windows were white. "My government wants two things," I said, as we headed for the next barn. "Let people form their own political parties. Let people speak freely in public."

"Your Bill of Rights."

"That's part of it," I said. "Mr. Hightower is a journalist. I'm sure he believes in a free press and the good it can do." Hightower had a small camera with him and had been taking pictures of the landscape around us. He put the camera away.

"What does that mean, Joe, 'a free press'?" he asked, sarcastically. "Free to do what?"

It felt foolish defending something as obvious as the First Amendment. "Our government doesn't tell a newspaper what it can print," I said. "It prints whatever it wants." We arrived at the orange barn.

"Maybe that's the problem," Hightower said. "People printing anything they want. It amazes me that a diplomat for such a powerful nation is so naïve about his own country's news publications." Hightower was smiling, but it was a mocking smile. "The press in America is free all right – free to exaggerate, free to deceive, free to lie."

"What lies are you talking about?" I said.

"Look, Pietr. I live in New York," Hightower said. He had turned away from me, taking his argument back to our host. "We've got a newspaper there called the *Daily News*. It's the biggest paper in the city. Hell, it's the biggest paper in the whole country. You want to know what black people call it? The Daily Noose. Because every day its white editors are hanging black people with ropes made of lies. Every story about black people is negative. We are drug dealers, muggers, pimps, prostitutes, and crazy folk. When a black man wins an award, there's no coverage of it. Do something good for the neighborhood? Forget it. That's America's free press Joe is talking about. Hundreds of newspapers like The Daily Noose." Surprised, Pietr looked at me for a response.

"I hadn't heard that," I said and shook my head.

The air inside the orange barn was cool and damp because the floor was cement. There was no wall of windows as in the white barn. Light came from hundreds of fluorescent tubes hanging from the ceiling, and a smattering of natural light from a narrow clerestory running the length of the gable roof. In the middle of the barn, black men sorted piles of dried tea leaves at large tables.

"This is where we oxidize the leaves after they've been wilted and rolled," Pietr explained. "Rolling a leaf breaks its resistance, so its juice can escape and mix with oxygen. That starts the enriching process and gives tea its special taste." Black ladies dumped baskets brimming with leaves in front of the men, who spread the leaves on wooden trays. Hightower pinched a clump of leaves between his fingers, raising them to his nose.

"Smells... fertile," he said.

"That's the smell we want. If we aren't careful, we can punish the leaves too much, and the flavor is lost. Then, our market price takes a tumble."

"What kind of tea is this?" Hightower asked.

"At Glen Allyn, we only process black tea," Pietr said.

"Like Earl Grey?"

"Earl Grey is a blend," Pietr said and picked up a handful of leaves. "This is pure black tea, nothing added, the best there is. Black requires more care to the leaf, but it gives the richest flavor. My neighbor across the road makes a respectable business with green tea. Asians prefer green. One estate makes oolong, a cross between green and black." Pietr led us back to where we entered the barn.

"During the colonial period, pluckers were paid poorly," he said as we walked. "They had to grow their own maize and their own vegetables to survive. On special holidays, maybe, the British owners gave them salt and cooking oil, sometimes sugar and dried fish. The workers called these gifts, *thangata*. Literally it meant, 'Thank God.'

"Back then, a plucker's life was miserable. I've heard stories that would make you cry. Even my family was guilty of some abuse years ago. But life is different in Umbika now. My workers are paid a fair wage. They receive weekly rations of maize and other staples for their families." We stepped out of the cool barn and back into the warm sun. Pietr dropped the stick he had carried beside the door and pointed us along a path towards a low hill. Hightower had pen and notebook in hand.

"Has UFreeMo hurt your business?" he asked.

"They haven't hurt us yet. But who knows what's coming? They changed the rules when they killed the Speaker. Enro Muswaya was a good man."

"Do you expect things to get worse?"

Pietr stopped on the path. His dogs sat immediately around his feet. Pietr glanced at what lay behind us, giant barns, the eucalyptus windbreak, a luscious lawn, the sprawling house. Reflected sunlight lit up the home's roof like a copper fire. "It was bad enough my countrymen were starving this year because of the drought. Now, UFreeMo is killing them too. Things are sure to get worse, my friend. Thousands could die before the rebels are stopped. I hope you will write that in your newspaper. Thousands could die. And the irony is that innocent Tologs will suffer the most, not Umbiks."

Hightower was writing in his notebook faster than I had seen before.

"I'm a businessman, not a politician," Pietr said, his hands resting on his hips. "Umbika will always be my home. You must understand, Mr. Hightower, and I want you to know this as well, Mr. Kellerman. I will not let my country fall into the abyss." He bent down and petted one of the Rottweilers. "My closest friends and I have already made arrangements to assist the Life President when he needs us. Jimmy Mulenga will never flee State House. He will not be forced out. The future of what we've built here depends on him."

Pietr stood and continued walking. I knew that analysts up and down the Potomac would be very interested in his declaration of total support for President Mulenga. I was excited to write that cable.

"This is what I wanted to show you. This is where the tea lives," Pietr said. Over the gentle rise in the path, green bushes stretched out in front of us in neat rows, like spokes on some enormous wheel, all the way to the horizon. "We call our plants trees, not bushes, because we grow them unusually large at Glen Allyn. But if you look carefully, you can see they are really a bush."

"It's impressive," Hightower said.

Down one row, we saw young black boys crawling on the ground from bush to bush. They were pulling weeds from around the trunks and tossing them to even younger boys behind, who gathered the refuse and put it into wooden crates they dragged after them with ropes. Pietr stopped beside a thriving bush, its highest branches reaching to his shoulders. From the top, he plucked a small leaf a shade of green lighter than the rest of the bush. He pinched the young leaf between his fingers and brought it to his nose. He breathed in deeply, closed his eyes, and smiled with satisfaction. "For number one grade, you pluck the bud and two newest leaves on the branch," he said. He picked more and handed a bud to Hightower and one to me. I pinched and sniffed. The smell was intense, a bittersweet fragrance, incredibly fresh.

"The new leaves give the most flavor," Pietr said. "It takes many of them to make a kilo." He led us deeper into the grove, closer to where the boys were collecting weeds. Hightower removed his camera from his pocket and framed a photo of the youngsters.

"What about snakes?" I said. "I heard they pose a danger for pluckers."

"Those buggers are around. When we see one, we take it to him," Pietr said with a hunter's grin. Hightower's posture had straightened on the mention of snakes. Now, as we continued down the narrow path between bushes, his body language changed. He tried to squint his shoulders to stay as far from vegetation as possible. Pietr noticed Hightower's posture too. "Don't worry," he said. "We haven't lost a plucker to snake bite in years."

"I don't look favorably on snakes," Hightower confessed, his eyes scanning left and right. "My mother went to country school. At recess one day, boys came up to her with a paper bag. 'Have a piece of candy, Hildie,' they told her. My mother reached in the bag. But there wasn't any candy in there – just a tangle of snakes. She told us that story often. It's a lesson I never forgot."

My eyes began searching for unwelcome movement too. Pietr stopped beside a bush and scanned the top branches, those lit by the sun. "Mostly, we find boomslangs and mambas," he said. "They like branches in the sun, where it's warm. Unfortunately, that's where our pluckers work." He circled to the next bush, scanning the top. "Don't get me wrong, snakes are beautiful creatures. The boomslang is elegant, like a jade necklace. Mambas grow to twelve feet. They're fast as a horse and strong as iron. I've seen a mamba stand as tall as a man."

"But they're dangerous, right?" Hightower said.

"Yes and no. A mamba stays clear of humans. It's not a social snake. If you surprise one, it'll run away. And if it can't escape, it's usually not successful when it tries to bite your body. That's because a mamba's jaw can't open wide enough to get a hold of you, not like a viper can." Mimicking the mouth of a mamba, Pietr created a space between his index finger and his thumb, a gap only as wide as what it'd take to hold a cigarette. "If a mamba lunges at your back or your leg, all it gets is a sore nose," Pietr demonstrated by bumping his thumb and index finger straight against his chest.

"See? A mamba's mouth can't get a hold of you. And its fangs curve backwards." He raised his other hand. "But let it grab something small, like your finger or ear or hand, then you have trouble." Pietr's finger puppet sprang out and locked onto the index finger of his other hand. "We call them, threesteppers. Three steps and you're dead."

We reached the spot where the boys were removing weeds. Pietr spoke in the local language, asking the boys one question and then a second. "No, Bwana. No, Bwana," the boys said, proud to please the estate owner. Pietr thanked them. "They haven't seen any snakes today," he told us, sounding disappointed at having to tell us that news. Farther down the row, Pietr pulled back a branch. He spread the foliage, keeping his face away from the opening. His head bobbed one way and then another, as he peered deep into the heart of the plant. Hightower crossed his arms over his chest and stepped away from the bush. I wasn't feeling much better myself.

"We have vipers too," Pietr said, spreading more branches, searching. "They're dangerous, like your rattlesnake. They attack. When a viper bites, his jaw unhinges, and the fangs hit you flat, like two spears. They go deep into the flesh." Pietr formed a V-shaped arc with his right index and middle fingers, as if he were a veteran pitcher showing a rookie how to throw a curve ball. "Their fangs can penetrate your back, chest, legs, even your face." He pushed the invisible baseball against his cheek, with the finger fangs appearing to enter his mouth through his skin. "You're already bleeding when the viper injects his venom. It mixes with your blood. In an hour, every red blood cell that the poison has touched has turned to porridge. You're dead after that."

Pietr shook another branch, and Hightower and I jumped. Pietr looked under the bush to see if anything had fallen to the ground. Seeing nothing, he let go of the branch, and it whipped back in place. "I'm sorry," Pietr said sadly and put a friendly hand on Hightower's shoulder. "People come to Africa and expect to see snakes – snakes and lions. That's what they want. But today, there's nothing to show you."

Chapter 20
Victims

We stood on Pietr Ritt-Boorman's porch and watched a blood-orange sun slip behind plum-blue hills to the west. Dusk had arrived in Umbika. I thanked our host for his hospitality. He handed each of us a wrapped parcel of premium black tea, each gift topped with a small, white bow. It had been a good visit, all things considered, but leaving as late as we were meant we would be driving during the most dangerous time on a road in Africa, twilight. "Do not worry, sir," Fred promised, as we reached the end of the Ritt-Boorman driveway. "We will arrive before the day is fully gone." He flipped on headlights and steered the Land Rover onto the smooth surface of the M-1. On our way back to the hotel, we watched for truckers drifting over the centerline. We braked for a father and son crossing at a curve. Two girls on the shoulder appeared in the maze of shadows. They were dressed in plaid school uniforms and pushing bicycles heaped with firewood. Fred steered around them.

Hightower and I said nothing for minutes. The only noise was the whine of tires pressing against tarmac. Halfway back to Ndala, Hightower spoke. "What's it like for you, Joe, a white man, living around so many black people?"

At first, I thought I had misunderstood him. "What was it you said?" I replied. Nightfall was upon us, always a gloomy hour in Africa. The visit to the farm was not perfect, but it had gone well enough. I was not expecting problems between Hightower and me.

"I'm curious. What's it like for you, a white man living all the time in a black country?"

"I'm not sure I follow you," I said. I could tell something was not right. Something was coming.

"Someone said you've been in Africa your whole career." I grew worried that Hightower was setting a trap for me. I thought carefully how to reply. I did not want to say something stupid, something that might end up in his newspaper column. I was still thinking over my options, when he spoke again. "You've been here like fifteen, twenty years – am I right? That's a long time for a white man to live where blacks run the show."

"I've been fifteen years in Africa," I said, "not fifteen in Umbika."

"Yes, Africa is what I meant. Is it true what they say about Africa? It's where they send diplomats if they're going nowhere?"

"I've been in Africa my whole career," I said. "I like it here."

"It sounds to me that Washington doesn't think much of Africa. It's a dumping ground."

Hightower was trolling now, hoping to snag an argument. I could disagree with him, but I was not going to indulge his appetite for conflict, especially after a relatively good day. "Like I said, I like it here."

"Missionaries stay, but you're not a missionary. The Ambassador told me you have a knack for fixing things."

"I go where they send me."

"No, I think there's more to it, Joe. He called you a kite. It sounded like something special. What does that mean, a kite?"

Remarkably, we had passed only three other vehicles since leaving the tea estate. Behind us now, the declining sky and the dark land had merged into one pane of nothingness out our back window. In front, though, far in the distance, a wedge of blue light marked the horizon, all that remained of the day. Illumination inside the car came from the gauges on Fred's dashboard – a soft orange light – though there was not much of it, only enough of a glow to make out Hightower smiling at me.

"Why do you want to talk about me?" I said. I rolled down my window halfway. The cool air felt refreshing on my warm skin.

"I'm interested in you, because over here, you represent Americans."

"We don't say it like that, but you're right, I guess. All of us at the Embassy, we represent Americans."

"Then, I'm wondering, how do you, or the others, represent me?" Obviously, he would try anything to provoke an argument. It was the Hightower behavior we were all worried about. "You're nothing like me, Joe – and you know nothing about me."

"I know you're headed somewhere with these questions," I said. Hightower did not respond immediately. I could see he was looking at me, sizing up his next move. "Really, I don't want to get into a quarrel," I added. "We're both Americans. That's all that matters." Hightower leaned across the back seat, his face edging closer to mine.

"My passport says I'm American. But the United States is not where I belong. I'm not really American. America is only a stopping point for displaced people like me. It's where we wait, until something better comes along."

"I don't see it that way." Hightower was close enough for me to smell the exotic scent of his aftershave.

"Get real, Joe. Africans didn't choose America. The slave holders chose us." Hightower waited, as if I was supposed to say something, jump into the fray, but I kept silent. I refused to fall into his trap. "How do I call home a place that kidnapped my ancestors, enslaved them, and killed them? America's done nothing for me or my people. Once a slave, always a slave."

"You're a successful writer, sir," I said. "You live a good life. You're well known. You're the special guest of the President of the United States. America's done that."

"Come on, man. The White House wanted me out of their hair. That's why I'm here. It's election time." We had arrived at the outskirts of Ndala. Atop the radio tower, on the far side of town, a red beacon was blinking a silent code into the night sky. Fred turned off the M-1 and onto the feeder road that went into town. "Don't pretend to look amazed, Joe."

"We are at the hotel soon," Fred said. I detected great unease in his voice.

"Something tells me you're on the run, Joe." He waited again. I would not be pulled into wherever he was headed. "You stayed in Africa all this time because you're trying to get away from something. No white man with talent, especially someone with a bad leg like yours, stays in Africa fifteen years – unless maybe he was born here. Or – he's a missionary, following some calling. Or – he's hiding from something."

"I'm not hiding," I said.

"I haven't figured it out, Joe, but I can read people."

"Believe me," I smiled, trying to ease the tension between us. "I'm not hiding from anything."

"Is it the handicap?"

"No, it's not the limp."

"Then what is it?"

"Look, I have no ties to the U.S. My parents are gone. I have no other family. I like it here. That's it."

"The Ambassador said he had never known any American diplomat to stay fifteen years in Africa, except you."

"I'm useful here – how about that?"

"You could be useful anywhere!" Hightower shot back. He seemed to be getting annoyed now, almost angry, all because a mystery he had invented had no simple ending. "Back in the day, I knew a white boy who surrounded himself with black friends. He dressed like us, talked like us, even tried to dance like us. You would have almost thought he was one of us. I finally figured out why he did it. Being around us made him feel superior. He knew he'd always have white skin privileges – no matter what he did. Is that why you stay in Africa, Joe? White privilege?"

I felt deeply insulted. A man who thought arguing was a sport was clearly trying to get under my skin. When I didn't answer right away, Hightower clapped his hands. "That's it?" he snickered. He may have been joking, playing with me still. I don't know. "It's nothing to be ashamed of," he said. "We all have demons." To this day, I regret the next words I said. There was no need to say them. I should not have said them. Yet once the words started flowing, they would not stop. I am convinced they led to everything that happened afterwards.

"Why is everything with you about race?" I demanded, my voice louder than normal. "Every white person is against you, out to get you. Why do you need to play the victim all the time?" Hightower's silhouette turned rigid, his shoulders arched and jaw pushed out, his eyes wide. He had not expected my attack or my tone. It was the first time I had seen him speechless. "Who chooses to live like a second-class citizen, when he doesn't have to?" I asked. "What demons are you running from?" Hightower slid closer to me, his satchel pressing against my briefcase, which pressed against my hip.

"You need to slow your mouth," he warned. "It's running faster than your brain. I'm not too old to be provoked by your disrespect." I could see rage pooling in his eyes. If he had been testing my cool, he had succeeded at finding the boiling point. My unexpected reply had tested his cool as well. Fred glanced over his shoulder, worried, he seemed, over what might happen next. Then, out of nowhere we caught a break. A barricade loomed ahead. Flashlights waved in the darkness. "Traffic stop, sir," Fred said, relieved.

The police waved our CD plates through without even a look inside the vehicle. Soon we were up to speed again. I should have waited to see what Hightower would say, but I wasn't thinking straight anymore. "I've read your column," I said, feeling free to say anything on my mind. "I know what you think about white people. I know why you're here."

"Then you know I didn't come here to find white folks to argue with. I came here to find the truth."

"The truth? Ha. Slavery ended a hundred years ago. That's the truth."

"You think so?" he chuckled. He was mocking me. "Tell me, how many Americans at your embassy have black skin?" I said nothing. "That's what I thought."

More headlights passing us on the road now. We were in Ndala again. "See? Everything is about skin color," I said. "Jesus, you really believe if your skin was white, people would treat you better?" He stared at me, simmering. "You think an employer would hire a white person who is angry all the time, like you are, someone who's always picking a fight?"

Hightower put one arm over the backseat and his other over the passenger seat next to Fred, angling his body towards me. "That's what you don't understand, young man. You think racism is over because you want it to be. What do you think happens when I walk into an office of white people? I can see what they see. I can see what they're thinking. 'What business could someone-like-him have in here?'"

The intermittent light escaping the doors and windows of passing shops let me see Hightower more clearly. His teeth were bright, but his lips looked odd, almost like a madness or a wretched determination. "In white grocery stores," he continued, "clerks watch me like I'm a thief – some crazy Negro come to rob them. I'm almost seventy, for chrissake! Don't you get it?

"Black people understand racism because we live with it. We know where we ain't welcome. We know what we can't do. We know where our neighborhood ends – and yours begins. We've known that for hundreds of years. You think everything's okay now? You think suffering is over because you're tired of hearing about it? As long as this color is on my skin, it ain't over. Not for me – not in the United States of America."

"Mr. Hightower, I've been in Africa a long time. Like you said, I'm surrounded by people with black skin. But I never feel they hate me because I'm white. I never go somewhere and feel threatened or out of place. But in downtown Washington, black kids on the street used to look at me like they wanted to kill me. I've had them throw things at me. I did nothing to harm them. My ancestors never owned slaves. They were immigrants who worked their way up from the bottom. Why should those kids on the street want to kill me?"

"Your ancestors didn't know what the real bottom was, Joe. The bottom is being kidnapped and never seeing your home again. Being sold to another man and then treated no better than a farm animal. And rock bottom is being lynched because you fall in love with the wrong color woman."

"Your life's been rough."

"Don't patronize me again, young man!"

I breathed in slowly. My head was spinning. I had no idea where any of this would end. "I can't feel guilty about things that happened more than a hundred years ago, things I never did."

"A hundred years ago? And in my lifetime!"

"Sir, I'm not part of the problem."

"Like the wise man said, Joe, 'If you ain't part of the solution, you part of the problem.'"

I sat back on my seat and turned to face forward. We were passing the market again, closed now, just dark random shapes at the bottom of a hill. The hotel was up ahead. I had never spoken like this to anyone before. It made me feel exhausted and frightened, but as strange as it sounds, it felt invigorating too.

"I'm going to drive north tonight," Hightower said. "Go up to that city for the trial." Our VIP guest's unexpected statement sent a shock wave through me.

"It's nighttime. We can't drive in the dark – Embassy rules."

"I don't work at your embassy. I can drive at any time I want, and I want to get to the trial before it's over."

"The British High Commissioner is hosting a special dinner for you tomorrow night. Everyone will be there – maybe even the Life President."

"I've been looking at a map," Hightower went on. "I'll go through Losei. I can hire my own car and driver."

I was thinking as quickly as I could. "You don't want to hire any driver. You can't trust most of them. And the main roads are dangerous at night. Losei's not even on a main road. You should stay here. Really." I realized, finally, I had said too much earlier, crossed over the line of what was appropriate. "Do you want me to apologize for what I said back there?"

Hightower laughed, an odd sound like he was mocking me again. Then he said, "The European press will be at Wisdom's trial. But who knows what they'll write. President Mulenga assured me, that man will get a fair trial. I plan to witness it and write it." Fred pulled up to the hotel steps.

"You should call Ambassador Durhlmann. Talk to him. He's been in touch with the White House." A valet hurried down the stairs and opened the rear door of the Land Rover.

"I'll leave that to you," Hightower said. "In a few days, when I'm back in the capital, the Ambassador can tar and feather me, or take me to dinner." The irony seemed to amuse him.

"Honestly, sir," I said, "Let's put the disagreement behind us. I apologize, sincerely. I was upset. You hit an old nerve, I guess."

"Forget it, man. If you apologize, then I have to."

"Honestly, it's not a good idea to drive at night. The roads here are death traps."

"I give you credit. You're good at your job, just like the Ambassador said, but it's more dangerous for me to drive in Mississippi at night – fifty miles from Vicksburg to Jackson – than it is to go from one end of Africa to the other." Hightower got out of the vehicle. He had his satchel in one hand and the gift of tea with the white bow in the other. He bent down to look back into the car, a movement requiring extra effort – for it appeared he had pain or stiffness in his back, maybe from the awkward way he had been sitting. "Thanks for the ride, Fred," he said and turned to me. A light on the porch illuminated his face. It was the first time I had noticed the age lines around his eyes and the blemishes on his skin. "Don't worry, Joe. What we talked about stays between you and me. You won't see your name in my column. I'm not like that." He closed the door and started up the steps. I knew I had to convince him to stay until morning, but I didn't know how. I was below and behind him as he mounted the stairway. He held his head high, his shoulders square, taking the steps eagerly now, as a younger man might. He seemed not the least bit afraid for what lay ahead – unlike me.

Chapter 21
Dream

There was no activity in the lobby of the Victoria and Albert Hotel when I walked in, though guests were eating in the dining room to the side. Hightower had already gone to his room. On my way up the wide staircase to my room on the third floor, I moved without ambition, my progress slowed by the heavy weight of regret I was carrying in my chest. Why did I have to say what I did? Sure, the man had drawn me in. He had made it personal. But there was no excuse for letting him get to me. I was trained to handle contentious situations. I knew how to avoid a fight. Yet I had let all my training desert me. When I got to my room, I telephoned Ambassador Durhlmann. I didn't want to, but I had to make the call. I briefed him on the visit to the tea estate, and then told him about Hightower's decision to drive to Katembeyna at night.

"He's doing what?" the Ambassador shouted.

I had tried to talk him out of it, I said, but Hightower insisted on going now. Durhlmann said he would call Hightower himself and abruptly hung up. A few minutes later, my phone rang. It was the Ambassador. Hightower had already checked out of the hotel. There was no way to stop him now. He was on his way north, driving dark. Durhlmann said he and I would talk about this again in the morning, after I got back to the Embassy.

That night, I lay in bed replaying in my head our conversation from the car. I fell asleep thinking about Hightower's claim that I had remained in Africa because I was hiding from something. I am certain it is why a familiar dream came back that night. I had had the same dream almost once a year since leaving Lagos. While the details had grown more elaborate over time, the images becoming more vivid, the storyline had stayed the same.

I'm in a big city. It's mid-afternoon on a crowded sidewalk, skyscrapers towering over me. People jostle against me as I walk. Traffic is loud, bumper to bumper. Chaos all around, though the sun shines warmly, a day for short sleeves. I dart across a busy street, zigzagging through traffic. Train tracks appear in front of me. I jump them. I follow a new sidewalk, less crowded than the first. I turn onto a side street and then another. The tall buildings fall away. Puffy clouds roll in, blocking the sun. I'm walking faster now, on edge. I'm in a foreign part of the city. Grayness covers the sidewalk like a filter. Street vendors shout prices over the sound of unfamiliar music. A woman sits on steps going up to a brownstone. Children scrap at her feet. No one has noticed the only white person on the block – me.

I turn another corner. Trashcans overflow with garbage. I pass an abandoned factory, a rusty fence, the skeleton of a car on concrete blocks. Silence now – I tell myself not to worry, a soldier's false confidence growing within me. Dark clouds dip low over the empty buildings, swirl above my head. I hope it doesn't rain.

I hear Claire in the next room, peeing.

Ahead, seven or eight young men jostle one another and laugh, comrades in arms. The tallest is also the thinnest. He's bouncing a basketball. I can't see faces, only black skin, and I know I've wandered into new territory. The young men see me now, stop talking, no surer what to do next than I am. They uncoil in a line, like a dark whip, and strike out.

I call to Claire – Help me, Claire.

My brain tells me, run. My legs respond, not moving in place or stuck to the ground as in some dreams. Here, I'm unusually swift. But my pursuers are just as fast. They come after me, hurling threats and vulgarities like arrows or spears. They want to teach me a lesson, they say. Don't go where you don't belong, they shout. I sprint up one street, cross an empty lot. I follow the side of a building. The dark whip breaks in two. One part disappears around a mountain of garbage. I counter the ploy, cut back to the center. My legs ache. My lungs strain for air. I'm running so fast, but my pursuers have gained on me. They are only an arm's length behind.

I'll be right there – Claire says. Her voice soft, reassuring.

The tip of the black whip is at my back.

I spot tall buildings shining in a wedge of sunlight. Then, train tracks to my left, a train speeding towards me.

I hear Claire's footsteps on the stairs.

The chasing men see the train and turn before it hits.

I jump the tracks, landing on a wide deck of gray cement. A plaza, warm in the sunlight. People smile at me as they pass by. I wake at this moment every time, always frustrated I can't remember even one of their names.

The Victoria and Albert Hotel served a complete English breakfast, starting at 7 a.m. The next morning, Fred was standing in the lobby of the hotel when I finished eating. With Hightower gone, neither of us had slept well. "Mr. Hightower never came back last night, Fred."

"Yes, sir. That one has flown."

We returned to the capital. During our drive, a flock of egrets swooped in low over the M-1, ten or twelve of the angular white birds. They glided above us for several seconds, only yards in front of the Land Rover. "I've never seen so many like this," I said.

"When egrets arrive from the north," Fred explained, as the birds were landing in a nearly-dry marsh beside the road, "it means the rainy season is close. I will alert my village."

An hour later, we were on the outskirts of the capital. Army trucks and soldiers were positioned at major intersections, the soldiers nervously gripping their rifles and frowning at passing vehicles. Back at the Embassy, Violet told me that several Americans had dropped by while I was gone. I spent the remainder of the morning phoning those Americans and reminding them of the travel advisory. At noon, the Ambassador summoned me to his office. He was standing behind his desk, lighting his pipe, when I walked in. "How the Sam-hell did you lose him, Joe?"

I had been thinking since leaving Ndala how I would explain what had happened. "I'm sorry, sir. He's not the easiest person to control."

"Ndala was supposed to be a simple diversion, avoid any controversy and bad press. You couldn't do that?"

"Pietr Boorman told him the Chitsaya trial had been moved up to today. Mr. Hightower insisted on going up by himself. I can drive there this afternoon and find him."

"Blake already left this morning." Durhlmann's voice was starchy, gruff. "He'll keep an eye on him." The Ambassador went over to a credenza against the far wall and poured himself a cup of tea. "I'm disappointed, Joe. Really disappointed. Couldn't you think of something to convince him to come back with you?"

"I tried, sir. I told him how dangerous the roads are. I told him about driving dark, but when he makes up his mind, it's impossible to change." The Ambassador returned to his desk and started searching through a file, lifting out papers, sipping tea. I stood waiting for more questions. After a few minutes of silence, I left the room. I felt bad for putting the Ambassador in a bind and letting down my co-workers. I might have dwelled on these thoughts the rest of the day, if not for a phone call I took, moments after returning to my office.

Chapter 22
Peace Corps

The phone call came in not from the Embassy switchboard, but on my direct line. "Good afternoon, Joseph!" said the familiar voice. It was Dr. Benton Mcheu, a surgeon at Mulenga Central Hospital. Benton and I had chatted several times on the diplomatic circuit. He was always professional and apolitical.

"It's good to hear your voice, Benton," I said. "How are you?"

"I am fine, Joseph. But I need to advise you. We are dispatching an ambulance to a mishap on the granary road. Do you know where the spur crosses the M-2?"

"Sure. There's a Mul-Co grocery on the corner."

"Ayy, that is the one."

I waited for more information. "Benton?"

"I am sorry to bring unfortunance on such a beautiful Wednesday – but I am hearing a white woman, on a scooter, was struck by a maize truck."

"It's serious?"

"You must go there, Joseph, to see on your own."

"I'll leave right now," I said and hung up the phone. During my years on the continent, I had learned that Africans never talk about death head on. They prefer to come at it indirectly, perhaps a way to give the listener time to process the news. From Benton's phone call, I knew two things. A white woman was dead, and she was American. I closed my eyes, momentarily unable to think clearly. I let the weight of my body collapse into my chair, motionless. I could feel nothing in my arms and legs. What might look like meditation to someone watching me, this was what happened to me every time I had to handle a death case, this odd reaction somehow triggered, I guess, by the enormous responsibility I felt about getting everything done right. I breathed deeply and sat there until my mind was able to focus and the episode had passed. Then, I called the Ambassador's secretary and told her where I was going.

Outside the motor pool, Fred was sitting on a bench beside Mr. Goodson, the motor pool supervisor. They were sharing a lunch of rice and fish.

"Mr. Goodson," I said, "I need a vehicle."

"You are most welcome, sir," he replied.

"There's been a road accident, near the granary. I need Fred to take me."

Mr. Goodson's fingers flipped through papers fastened to a clipboard next to him on the bench. "Number eleven!" he called. Fred was already on his way to the vehicle.

The accident had occurred on the M-2 highway, about four miles north of Statue Park roundabout. For the first two miles, Fred and I made good time. Traffic was light. At a crossroad, a dozen soldiers had surrounded a minivan in the southbound lane. Two soldiers were rummaging through suitcases and parcels open on the ground. Other soldiers pointed their rifles at passengers from the van, dark-skinned Tologs from the North who looked terrified as they knelt in a line on the ground beside the van.

"Did the Life President speak on radio again today?" I asked Fred.

"No, sir. But he is turning up the heat."

Just beyond the turn-off going out to the national soccer stadium, traffic heading north had stalled. We were behind a big trailer truck full of used tires. The truck was having a tough time making it up a hill. Fred shifted to 4-wheel drive and steered off the blacktop, crossing an expanse of loose soil, weaving around huts and shops, gardens and borehole wells. It was a hundred vehicles to the front of the queue and twice as many bumps along the way.

We finally pulled into a clearing, absent vehicles except for one large transport truck, its front tires straddling the highway's dotted centerline. Stacked on the truck's trailer were 200-pound sacks of maize, piled high like so many stuffed pillows, the stack as tall as a house. Several sacks had tumbled off the truck and split open on the pavement. White kernels of maize glistened in the sunlight like grains of sand on a tropical beach. Villagers stood elbow to elbow at the side of the road – empty buckets and tubs clutched in their hands – eyeing the white shoreline of corn. Traffic policemen with wooden batons kept the crowd from running onto the road. Other police prevented traffic from moving through the accident scene. Vehicles heading north and south were at a standstill. Everyone was waiting for me to arrive.

Under the massive front tires of the truck lay the twisted frame and handlebar of a moped, a motorized bicycle. A large pool of liquid glimmered rainbow-like on the pavement beneath the truck's engine. The sharp smell of gasoline was everywhere. Three damaged suitcases and their contents had been gathered into a pile in front of the big truck. We slowly drove past this uneven knot of color – what I saw were blue jeans, shirts purple and white, a paperback novel with a yellow and red cover, two balled up pairs of white socks, a pink baseball cap, one black brassiere. Teetering on top of the pile lay a single flip-flop sandal – turquoise green.

On the far side of the rig stood a heavy-set police officer with milk chocolate skin, a gold brimmed cap, and three white stripes angled across the sleeves of his tunic. He towered over the truck driver who had hit the scooter, a skinny Sikh man sitting motionless in the middle of the northbound lane. In one quick stroke, with a stick he had been holding behind his back, the police officer belted the Sikh across the side of the head. The man reacted immediately to the sting, but too late to protect his ear. The officer hit the Sikh again, against his shoulder. Across the highway and tight to a thicket of bamboo was parked an ambulance from Central Hospital, a white station wagon with red crosses hand-painted on each door. A globe of blue light rotated lazily on the vehicle's roof. Two men in white smocks stood at the side of the vehicle, hands on hips, watching us approach.

Fred parked beside the ambulance. I walked over to where the officer stood on the highway. He saw me coming and tossed his stick to the ground, straightened the lines of his uniform, adjusted his cap. He looked not at my face, but at the rhythm of my walk. My limp seemed to mesmerize him. "I'm Kellerman from the American Embassy," I called.

"I know," the officer replied. We shook hands. "Madzedze, Officer-in-Charge." I waited for his report, but an awkward silence ensued. Madzedze made no more eye contact, looking instead towards the moped and the belongings piled on the highway.

"I'm here on behalf of the family," I said finally, recalling Umbikan custom. Madzedze was not permitted to speak about a death to strangers until a family member was first informed. As US Consul and an American citizen, I served as family for the deceased.

"You are most welcome," Madzedze replied, obviously relieved I had said the magic words.

"Where is she?" I asked. Madzedze led me behind the ambulance. A collapsible stretcher had been expanded to waist height, on which a sheet covered the contour of a human shape. The body appeared adult size, though misshapen, its form twisted with unnatural bends in the middle and far end. One of the attendants stepped forward.

"Do you wish to see her?" he said.

"In a minute."

A crimson backpack with white piping along its zipper lay on the ground beneath the stretcher. A stuffed animal, a chimpanzee no bigger than my thumb, dangled like a totem on a key chain anchored to the zipper's metal tab. I picked up the backpack. There was almost no weight to it.

"Did she have identification?" I said. Madzedze unzipped a thin side pocket I had not noticed on the pack and handed me an American passport. The navy-blue cover with gold eagle imprint was familiar worldwide. He handed me a laminated ID card, slightly smaller.

"Peace Corps," Madzedze said, distinctly pronouncing the final p and s.

The ID photo was in color, a smiling young woman in her twenties. Royal blue t-shirt with the word BRANDEIS, in white lettering, stenciled across her ample chest. Black hair in two long pigtails, spilling over the curves. She had been in-country only three months, according to the ID, a teacher in the remote village of Dkata-kota along the lake. I did not remember meeting this volunteer, but I had seen her smile many times – the unvarnished Peace Corps smile. It was what all volunteers had when they first arrived in-country – the look of absolute optimism, rooted in their belief they would make the world a better place. I opened the U.S. passport and studied the black and white photo inside. Here, she looked more professional, not smiling and wearing no pigtails – rather, outfitted in make-up and a salon-style hairdo, long strands wound behind her head in a bun. With a photo like this she could have been employed by IBM or AT&T.

She was Amanda Weinberg. 23. Born in Massachusetts. According to the Peace Corps ID, Mandy for short. I figured she was one of the volunteers we had recalled to the capital after Enro Muswaya was murdered. She had almost arrived, only four miles short of her destination. I motioned the attendant. He pulled back the sheet, revealing Mandy's battered face. Purple and yellow halos settling around the eye sockets made her appear grotesque, as if made up in some macabre costume, asleep at a Halloween party. I compared her face to the ID and passport photos in my hand. "That's her," I said to no one in particular and slipped the documents into my shirt pocket. The attendant pulled back more sheet. A crushed shoulder and arm – the truck had dragged Mandy along the blacktop for a considerable distance. Her green tank top and white bra were shredded. Friction had dissolved tissue from around her right breast down to where her thigh met her torso. She had been wearing an African skirt, a single long rectangle of fabric, beige with black geometrical patterns. Terrible forces had rolled the skirt up her thighs, looking as if she were wearing a mini skirt. White bone poked out from a skin tear at the middle of her thigh. Two bones on her right leg, at the knee, jutted out at a freakish angle. What blood she lost had soaked into her skirt, or was left on the highway. Mandy's other turquoise green flip-flop held to her left foot – the toenails painted cherry red.

I signaled the attendant to cover her again. "Radio the motor pool," I told Fred. "Tell Mr. Goodson we have an AMCIT fatality on the M-2. Gwen should call Peace Crops and have Mr. Livingston meet us at Central Hospital. We'll follow the ambulance."

I walked back onto the highway and began collecting Mandy's belongings, but Madzedze stopped me. "My boys will do that," he said. I waited off to the side as they stowed the items in our cargo bay, along with Mandy's backpack. Madzedze said the maize truck was coming to the city from the north, the same direction as Mandy. The driver had noticed the scooter up ahead, the white woman's long hair streaming behind her. Three suitcases were strapped to the back of the scooter with yellow cord, one atop the other. She was riding close to the shoulder, safely away from traffic, just as she should have. When the driver's turn came to pass her, he had moved towards the centerline. As he overtook the scooter, it veered sharply into his path, like Mandy had suddenly decided to go somewhere else, but without looking first. The driver braked, but he could not stop before the truck had dragged the scooter seventy yards. "Sir, it is a most unfortunate accident," Madzedze concluded.

I thanked him and returned to our vehicle. We followed the ambulance and its lazy blue light leaving the accident scene. Behind us, the officer-in-charge raised his arm, a signal to the villagers waiting anxiously beside the road. Dozens rushed to the dunes of white corn on the highway – scooping handfuls, filling pockets and pails as fast as possible.

Chapter 23
Inventory

At Central Hospital, the ambulance parked first. Fred took an empty spot between it and a gray Land Cruiser already waiting for us, its red, white, and blue Peace Corps logo prominent on the door. Garrett Livingston, our Peace Corps director, was pacing on the loading dock. From a distance, Garrett resembled a modern-day Viking hero, red beard and thick strawberry blond hair, strong neck and shoulders, a fearless stride. But as I got closer, I saw his eyes were weak and confused. He looked wounded, humbled. "Who is it?" he asked me, his voice as fragile as his eyes.

"It's Mandy Weinberg."

"Damn it." He hopped down from the loading dock. "It's Mandy? Damn it all to hell." Umbika was Garrett's first assignment abroad as a country director. I could tell this was also his first dead volunteer. The attendants lifted the stretcher out from the ambulance and locked the wheels in place. Garrett put his hands on the metal frame. He tried to assist the men pushing the stretcher up a concrete incline, but his hands kept slipping off the side rail. He grabbed again, but his uncooperative fingers could get no grip. He ran ahead to hold the door open, leading into the hospital.

"How bad is she hurt?" Garrett asked me. I was not listening carefully to him. Truth be told, I was selfishly thinking how relieved I had felt at the accident scene – once I saw Mandy's Peace Corps ID. It meant someone else would be responsible for her repatriation, not me. "How bad is it?" Garrett asked again inside the building.

I looked Garrett in the eyes. "Well, Garrett, she's dead," I said. "Here's her passport and ID. You'll need them later for your report." He took the documents and stared at Mandy's photos, as if seeing her for the first time.

"Out there, I wanted to look at her face," he said, "but I couldn't get myself to pull back the sheet." He put the passport and ID in his pants pocket. We followed the stretcher down a long, poorly lit hall. Along one side were windows propped open with sticks and rocks. The windows opened onto an inner courtyard of matted dry grass, the color of cardboard. I could smell a cooking fire. Someone somewhere nearby was making porridge.

"Did you know her?" I asked.

"I try to know them all," he said. Garrett's eyes were darting every which way along the hallway. The pitch of his voice fluctuated between high and low notes. "These kids all have unique stories. It's what I like most about my job." We turned a corner. Up ahead, two women were bent over a small fire burning on the cement floor. Wisps of smoke rose over a cooking pot and out a window to the side. "The fact is," Garrett said, "Mandy was one of the best. She had more heart than the average volunteer, which says a lot. Her village loved her."

"Was she called back after Enro Muswaya was killed?"

"We got word to all of them at the lake, yesterday. Told them we'd come and get them. She must have decided to leave on her own. That was just like Mandy – taking the initiative to get something done." The stretcher arrived at the end of another long hallway. The attendants pushed through a pair of faded orange doors with a sign. MORGUE – AUTHORIZED STAFFING PLEASE. I paused with Garrett outside the doors. "I'll let you take it from here," I said. "Good luck."

Garrett took hold of my elbow. His eyes were glassy and moist. "I don't know what I'm supposed to do, Joe."

"This is your first death case?" Garrett nodded. "Peace Corps has a protocol, doesn't it?"

"They do," he said. "Ten pages of it. I read it on my way here. Writing the cable to Washington isn't a problem. It's what to do in there." He pointed past the orange doors.

Back in my office, a pile of paperwork was waiting for me, and I was still desperately worried about Hightower. I had already been away from the Embassy for two hours. This was not my case anymore. It was a Peace Corps matter. "I want to do it right," Garrett added.

He was biting his lip and running his hand through his beard, waiting for me to respond. I could have given him a pep talk and left him to figure it all out, which he would have. But he reminded me of me in Nigeria – fifteen years earlier – and the first death case I had had to deal with. I ended up doing it all by myself, and it had not been easy. "How about we do this one together?" I said.

"Thanks," Garrett smiled and pushed open the orange door for me.

On the other side, Dr. Mcheu was waiting for us. He greeted me with a warm African handshake. I introduced Garrett and mentioned that this was his first repatriation. Benton nodded sympathetically. Mandy's body was waiting on a stainless-steel table at the center of the room. The sheet from the stretcher lay in a pile on the floor. The room was poorly lit, typical of an African hospital, not the acute brightness of an American morgue, where observing minute details was a priority.

Benton had the passport and was comparing its photo to the face on the table. He took a black permanent marking pen from his coat pocket and removed the sandal from her foot. On her sole he wrote the date. On her other foot, he printed "WEINBERG, A." – referring to Mandy's passport to get the spelling correct. "Everyone is light on the bottom," Benton said to Garrett. "Black people, brown, Asians – always lighter. Makes it easier to write." I moved closer to the table, but Garrett held back.

"We take possession of everything she has, so we can send it to her family," I said to Garrett. "And we need to make an official inventory of it." He seemed puzzled. "Things like her jewelry, watch, money, clothing." Garrett bent to his knees about to pray, I thought, but his arms were shaking.

"Are you okay?" He gagged like he might throw up. "Take deep breaths. Do it slowly," I said and knelt beside him. "Don't worry. This is normal. Happens to me, too." I put an arm over Garrett's shoulder, waited. Finally, his body calmed down.

"Tell me what to do," he said.

"First, before anything else, I want you to try to remember everything you see here. It's a list only for you. Don't think about who she is – only about making a mental record of everything you see. Add one thing at a time to your list. What is she wearing? Focus on specifics. Is there a ring or watch? What are the injuries? Where are they? Take your time. Say each detail in your head. It'll help you get through this. The details you remember will also be useful later when you talk to the family." I lifted Garrett's elbow to help him stand. "When will she be ready to fly?" I asked Benton.

"The Lufthansa flight tomorrow night," he said.

"They'll embalm her and put her in a pressurized casket," I told Garrett. "Always make sure you get a pressurized one, if you can. Altitude decomposition looks worse on a body than the zombies in *Night of the Living Dead.*" Garrett smiled, a sign he was finding balance. I snapped on a pair of latex gloves, lifted Mandy's damaged arm, sliding three silver rings off her middle finger and another from her thumb. They came off easily. Her body was not bloating yet. "Sometimes you have to use cooking oil to get rings off," I told Garrett.

I removed an ebony bangle from Mandy's wrist, two gold-colored elephant earrings. I laid each piece along a side of the steel table. Every item would be listed in a logbook and returned to her next-of-kin. I felt for a necklace under her hair, my fingers moving slowly. No necklace, only a stickiness of drying blood at the back of her head. Neither had I found a wristwatch – which was unusual. I wiped my gloves on a towel. "Did anyone find a necklace or watch?" I called to the attendants. Each looked around, as if the one standing next to him might know better, but no one said a thing.

I unclasped a petite chain encircling her broken ankle. Several of the gold links had been pushed under her skin and smeared with blood. From her feet, I worked my way up her legs, running my fingers under her rolled up skirt, searching the pleats, feeling around her thighs, across her hips. Even through my gloves I noticed her unusually smooth skin – like fine satin.

I searched above her waistline, under the straps of her tank top, feeling across her chest.   Under one breast I touched something rigid – not soft tissue or fluid. With a scissors I cut through her tank top and bra and pulled them away. A money belt was cinched around her ribs, like a tiny saddle. The collision had pushed the belt up from her waist and under her large breasts. I unfastened the clasp and handed the belt to Garrett. "See what's inside," I said. "If there's any cash, count it twice."

From the things in our car, Fred brought in a clean skirt and matching blouse for dressing the body later, before it would go to the airport. I carried the jewelry, as we left the morgue. Outside, the ambulance was gone. Only our vehicles remained in the lot. Garrett had the money belt and $357 in American money, plus some local currency. I showed Garrett the personal items from the highway. We added those items to our inventory, describing each one, and then wrote in the cash, the money belt, and the jewelry. Fred found four empty cardboard boxes to pack her belongings. "Anything broken or bloody we don't send to the family," I told Garrett. "Enter it at the end of your list, as 'damaged property.'"

We transferred the four boxes of Mandy's belongings to the Peace Corps vehicle. Late afternoon shadows blanketed the parking lot in blues and grays. Fred threw the damaged suitcases into a dumpster. "I'll follow you to your office," I said. "We still have to get in touch with her parents." Garrett thanked me for my willingness to help and then drove off. Fred was waiting for me in our vehicle, the engine purring. We pulled out of the parking lot and onto Unity Road, a tree-lined boulevard leading to the Statue Park roundabout. Traffic was heavy – Umbikan rush hour.

A poet once wrote, "Mothers and fathers live until their children die." Driving back to the center of town, I was thinking about Mandy and how we expect children to outlive their parents, not the other way around. I had never raised a child, so I could not know for certain what it was like to lose one. Even so, I knew that getting a call telling me my twenty-something daughter was dead had to be the cruelest news any parent could receive. Mandy Weinberg's passing would leave a hole her family could never fill – I had no doubt.

Chapter 24
Sommerville, Mass

One misconception newcomers to East Africa have involves temperature. Few know how cool the nights can be during the dry season, especially at higher altitudes. The night Fred and I drove to the Peace Corps office was the coldest since I had arrived in Umbika. I rubbed away the evening chill while standing in Garrett's office and waiting for him to speak with his local staff. The Umbikans had remained there after quitting time, waiting for him to return from the hospital. They were desperate to know which of their PCVs had perished.

"They're taking it hard," Garrett said, returning to his office. "Mandy's only the third volunteer they've ever lost."

"It's morning in Boston," I said. "After we call the parents, you should touch base with your desk officer." Garrett settled into his chair. I lifted the phone and dialed Mandy's home number in Somerville. Remarkably, the call connected on my first attempt. I gave Garrett a thumbs-up. "Hello," said a woman on the other end. There was a slight echo, but not enough to redial.

"May I please speak with Mr. or Mrs. Weinberg?"

"This is Nora Weinberg," said the woman.

"Are you Amanda's mother?" I asked.

"Yes, I am. Who is this?"

"Mrs. Weinberg, my name is Joseph Kellerman. I'm the American Consul at the United States Embassy in Umbika – in Africa." I kept my voice steady, trying not to rush or jumble my words. My goal was to speak with authority and control the conversation. At the same time, I wanted to sound respectful and sympathetic. Announcing a loved one's death from ten thousand miles away required complete concentration. "Is Mr. Weinberg home?"

"No, he's at his office."

"That's fine, ma'am," I said. "What I'm going to tell you, I'll repeat a second time to make sure you understand. If you have a paper and pencil handy, I want you to write down what I say. Do you have a paper and pencil?"

"I have them right here – next to the phone." Although Mandy's mother sounded more confused than anything else, I could tell her concern was growing. Everything in her mind was processing quickly. Her brain was sorting out the logical connections as to why I called.

"I will telephone you again in twenty minutes," I said, "once this news has had time to sink in." I did not pause in my delivery. I did not want to give her time to solve the puzzle on her own. If she did, she would not hear anything else I said. "Remember, I'll call again in twenty minutes. Now, I'd like you to sit down, Mrs. Weinberg." I didn't wait for her to tell me she was seated. I only hoped she was. "I'm very sorry," I continued. "I have extremely sad news for you and your husband. Your daughter, Mandy, died here in Africa this afternoon, in a traffic accident."

"Oh, no," the woman said. "No. No." The mystery was revealed – then came seconds of silence that seemed to go on for minutes. Countless dreams and plans were collapsing around the woman sitting alone on the other end of the line.

"I'm very sorry for your loss, Mrs. Weinberg. Again, my name is Joseph Kellerman. I'm calling from the American Embassy in Umbika, Africa. With me here is the Peace Corps director, Garrett Livingston. Write his name on your paper, please. Garrett Livingston. He was Mandy's supervisor. As I said, Garrett and I will call back in twenty minutes and answer any questions you have. But first, I want to make sure you've written down our names and phone numbers. When I hang up, you should call your husband or another relative or a friend. Tell them to come over to your house right now. I'd like you to have at least one other person with you when we call back. Is twenty minutes enough time to get someone to your house?"

Mrs. Weinberg's voice was shaky. She said again that her husband was at his office, but he could be home in twenty minutes. I repeated our names and phone numbers and then said goodbye. The call to Somerville had lasted three minutes.

Garrett was staring at me, still in shock, I think. "Always contact the next-of-kin twice the first day," I said. "The surprise from the first call is so great they don't remember what you tell them." I closed Mandy's personnel file on Garrett's desk and leaned back in my chair. "Now, we wait."

Twenty minutes after the first call, I dialed the Massachusetts number again, connecting on my third attempt. "This is Saul Weinberg," answered a man. For a second time, we were lucky. There was little echo, but other voices were in the background and the sound of a woman crying. I identified myself and repeated the news of Mandy's death. Mr. Weinberg asked about the accident. I told him what I knew, without being too specific about his daughter's injuries. He asked if I saw the body. I told him I had.

"Garrett Livingston, our Peace Corps director, is sitting next to me here in Umbika. He'd like to speak with you, sir. I'm going to pass the phone to Garrett now." Garrett took the phone. He spoke eloquently about Mandy and his sorrow over her death. He talked for fifteen minutes, until I gave him a sign it was time to hang up.

"You get to a point on the first day," I said, after the call ended, "where no one's listening to you anymore. Their questions go in circles. They're only talking because of desperation. They want to keep connected with you, because you're nearest to the deceased." I got up to leave. "What you say the first day is more important than anything else. It's about them. It's never about you."

I was tired, hungry. I still needed to stop in my office before heading home. Garrett was weaving together his fingers and staring at the floor. The whole ordeal was haunting him – the news, the hospital visit, seeing the damage to the young woman's body, the call home.

"It gets easier each time," I said in my most sincere voice, even though I knew what I was telling Garrett was a lie. By that point in my career, I had handled more death cases than I cared to remember. Mandy Weinberg's had been as tough on my nerves as the first.

Fred dropped me outside the Chancery. The offices were all dark, but the exterior security lights around the building reflected off the white stucco walls as brightly as sunlight. I punched my access code on the heavy back door and went inside. A handwritten message was lying on my desk.

> *Sir:*
>
> *Mr. Maurice Hightower, AMCIT, has telephoned this afternoon. There was rioting in Katembeyna, some people killed he wants you to know. Have a good evening, Sir.*
> *Violet, Grace*

I immediately telephoned the three best hotels in Katembeyna, but Hightower was not registered at any of them. I dialed the first hotel again, the Koo-Kat Hotel, where Embassy personnel stayed when in town. The desk manager rang Blake's room, but Blake was out. "Would you leave a message, sir?" the manager asked, cheerfully.

"Not now, but I have a question."

"You are most welcome, sir," said the manager.

"Were there problems in Katembeyna today? I heard about a riot." I waited a long moment for the manager to respond.

"I would not know that, sir," he finally said, his voice serious and guarded now.

"I'm calling from the American Embassy," I persisted. "Do you know if anyone was hurt today?" Again, the manager went silent. "Was anyone hurt?"

"I am sorry," he said. "I know nothing about the shooting, sir."

"There was shooting?"

The manager hung up. I dialed Lew Trestle, an American, my principal warden for the Northern Province. Lew lived east of Katembeyna three miles. He would have heard if something happened in town. My call to his house phone failed to go through on five attempts. I tried his school number. The one time the call connected, no one picked up. I tried Lew's deputy warden, Jerry Adams, and three other Americans in Kat, but none of these calls would go through. I finally reached a retired schoolteacher from Ohio. There had been trouble near the High Court that afternoon, the woman said. She did not know how bad. Her husband was in the yard, checking fences. She said they were afraid to stay at their property tonight, but more afraid to leave.

I drove to the Happy Lion and found Connie leaning against the bar, talking with men from the French Embassy. "The country's falling apart," she said when I reached her through the thick crowd. Voices in the packed room were pitched, unusually high for a Wednesday night. I leaned in close, between Connie and two Frenchmen.

"CPU was closed," I said. "What do you know about gunfire in Kat?"

"Blake called it in, and I wrote the cable," she said. "Two dead, both locals. The Foreign Ministry claims it was all a misunderstanding, a zealous policeman reacting to agitators."

"What did Blake say?"

"Bullshit," she said. "Blake says it was a warning for people to stay away from the Chitsaya trial." The tart smell of Umbikan banana beer blew heavy on Connie's breath. She picked up a glass boot from the bar and drank. She set down the boot and held my elbow. "You want something to drink? I'm buying."

"You hear anything about our VIP?"

"I heard what happened in Ndala," she said. "I warned you about him."

"Did Blake find him?"

Connie shook her head. "You should know what women are saying about the Ambassador's reception. What he did to the German ambassador's wife."

"He didn't do anything to her. I was there."

"I wasn't," she said, proudly. "Why are you protecting him?"

"I'm not protecting him. He's our responsibility."

"I saw police beating a woman on the side of the road today."

"I know, things are falling apart here."

"Men are pigs," Connie said and let go of my arm.

"Connie, we need to talk."

"*Les hommes sont des salauds,*" said one of the Frenchmen, parroting Connie.

Connie lifted the glass boot with both hands and started swallowing beer. She raised her arms high enough for beer to overflow the edges of the boot and the corners of her mouth. Beer ran down her neck and across her chest. She swallowed until her body shook. The Frenchmen were staring at her soaked blouse, the thin white fabric taut against her pointed breasts, and I felt disgusted with myself – because at that moment, my thoughts were the same as theirs.

Chapter 25
Free Fall

Thursday morning, the Ambassador called a crisis-response meeting of the Country Team. Hightower had been on his own for more than a day and unaccounted for. We were receiving reports of additional gunfire at the courthouse in Katembeyna. Army Colonel Red Cadburn, Dave Hardy, Garrett Livingston, and representatives from Admin, Refugee Affairs, and USAID were already in their seats when I got to the conference room. Connie was there too, not in her usual place along the side of the large oval table but seated at the far end. Her eyes carried the glaze of a serious hangover. By the comb of her hair and the careless way her make-up had been applied, I wondered if she had slept the night before, or where. I sat next to her, but she said nothing to me. Alice Jones came into the room and then Ambassador Durhlmann entered and closed the thick soundproof door. He took his seat at the head of the table and set a page of notes in front of him. "I'm very sorry about your volunteer, Garrett," the Ambassador said. "Let me know when a good time is to call the family." Garrett nodded.

"I believe everyone has an idea why we're here. There's been more trouble in Katembeyna. I just spoke with Blake. He estimates ninety people killed and one hundred and seventy wounded this morning at the courthouse."

Everyone around the table, but Connie, exchanged glances. The magnitude of the event had stunned us. Nothing like this had ever happened before in Umbika. "He said Explorers opened fire on demonstrators, after stones were thrown. It all happened while Chitsaya was leaving the court. This is terrible, I know, but we don't want anyone panicking. If we keep our heads on straight, we'll get through this. It doesn't look like any Americans were hurt, but Blake is checking."

"Where were the police?" Colonel Cadburn asked – a question we were all wondering.

"Don't know," said Durhlmann. "Before today, Explorers had never handled security at the court."

"What about Mr. Hightower?" I asked.

"I told Blake to find him and bring him back. They can drive together." The Ambassador then assigned duties. I would write a new travel advisory and contact my warden tree. Connie needed to prepare a press release. The Colonel would touch base with his military sources. Peace Corps was told to recall more volunteers. Alice Jones would review our Emergency Action Plan.

"Listen people," the Ambassador continued. "The Embassy is closed tomorrow for Constitution Day. I've decided we're having a volleyball match and picnic at the Residence. I don't want our families listening to rumors and worrying about what might happen. I want them thinking about something else – like hot dogs, fried chicken, and cake and ice cream. I expect everyone to attend."

Later, the Ambassador stopped by my office. His tie was askew, one sleeve rolled up, he was biting his lip. "Blake just called," he said. "It sounds crazy up there, police and soldiers everywhere. But he found where Maurice was staying."

"Great."

"Unfortunately, Blake missed him. Maurice had already checked out. If he's on the road now, he should be back here by seven, maybe earlier. On your way home, I want you to stop at the Intercontinental. Wait for Maurice. See what he knows about what happened at the court. If you can, find out if he's writing an article about it. Maybe he'll quote us, give us a chance to look like we know what we're doing."

After work, I drove to the Intercontinental Hotel, not far from the Embassy. I parked in a lot surrounded by towering palm trees. Gold carpet directed me into the hotel lobby, where bamboo fans above the reception desk hung motionless. The concierge, a short camel colored Umbik man with a shaved head, said he remembered Hightower, but he had not seen him since Tuesday, the morning we drove to Ndala. I said Hightower was expected any minute. I would wait for him in the whisky bar adjacent to the lobby. The concierge nodded politely, and I walked away.

The bar was sparsely populated during the dinner hour. I ordered a beer and chose a stool with an unobstructed view to the lobby. Two white businessmen, sitting on stools not far from mine, were conversing discreetly. Each seemed an opposite of the other. One was older and more trim – thin shoulders, bony pink face, short white hair. His companion was a handsome bull – thick biceps, smooth facial features, glossy black hair. They were too different in appearance to be related by blood. They could be co-workers or neighbors. They spoke English with South African accents and were talking about airline fares.

I gazed deeper into the bar. A small Oriental woman in pressed bush pants and matching shirt was sitting in a leather armchair large enough to swallow her whole. She had black hair and a pretty face, but I realized grave worry or severe unhappiness was obvious within her from her relentless biting of fingernails. Two older male companions, Orientals as well, sat at opposite ends of a coffee table in front of her. The men puffed unfiltered cigarettes, the smoke hovering over the coffee table like a spell. Shoulder patches on their shirts confirmed they were Koreans, working for a wildlife NGO. Their voices were clear but hyper-tense. Even though I did not understand the language they spoke, I picked out words like "Katembeyna" and "Explorers." They were talking about the massacre at the High Court. The hands of the man who wore thick glasses moved in exaggerated arcs, which was not common to Koreans I had met before. His companions watched him intently. He then stood up and continued his pantomime. I realized, finally, he was explaining how Umbika was free falling towards hell.

The two white men sitting at the bar were whispering now, though I was near enough to hear every word. "I shipped off the little ones and Frannie this afternoon," the younger man said. "They're on their way to Granny's."

"That's a smart move, Jacko."

"Won't be back, 'til these buggers sort this crazy business."

The older man nodded. He understood. "Val's booked on the SA flight to Jo-burg in the morning. I insisted she go on without me. If we all left now, there'd be nothing in the stores when we got back."

"That's how it is, Hennie."

"Val knows the score."

'Yeah, she's a smart one," said the younger man.

I waited in the whisky bar until nine, but Hightower never arrived. It was illogical that he would go to another hotel. He still had a room at the Intercontinental. In case he had decided to move, I drove to five lesser hotels around the city to see if he had checked in. He hadn't. I then drove out to the Bolo Wayside Inn, a one-star hotel, on the far northern edge of the city, past the granary spur and across from the cut-off leading into the airport. The Bolo Wayside was a guesthouse frequented by prostitutes and long-haul truck drivers, the first lodging Hightower would have come to upon arriving from Katembeyna. It seemed a long shot, but if he wanted to be on his own, he might have chosen to stay there.

Five flatbed trucks and six cars were parked in the lot. To the south, the glow of the city radiated into the dark sky like a foggy orange dome. I went inside and checked at the front desk. The night manager had not seen Hightower. Outside again, I walked to the north end of the gravel lot, past where the big rigs were parked. The air was quiet and crystal clear. Not one headlight or cooking fire shone in the vast darkness to the north. Above me, however, stars glittered through the infinite reaches of space. The vast Milky Way galaxy occupied the entire middle of the sky. I wondered if Hightower, wherever he was now, could be watching the sky at that same moment. I was certain now that Hightower had not returned to the capital city. So, where was he? I went back inside the guesthouse to use their phone. I called the Residence. The Ambassador did not sound overly concerned about

Hightower's safety, nor was he ready to concede our visitor was missing. He wanted to wait for Blake to get back from Kat the next day and hear more about what had happened at the court. I left and drove home, still wondering where our visitor could be.

Chapter 26
Picnic

With the Embassy closed on Friday, I stayed in bed until nine, reading a year-old bestseller about the cosmos. Normally on Constitution Day, one of Umbika's most important holidays, the American Ambassador went to State House with other senior diplomats for eight hours of traditional dances, patriotic songs, and laudatory speeches spotlighting the Life President. Ambassador Durhlmann decided it was more important he remain with American families at the Residence this year. He sent our country director for USAID in his place.

Embassy children, off from school, arrived early for a day of splashing in the Ambassador's heated pool. Miriam Durhlmann handed out chocolate chip cookies to them and reminded the children about the Embassy's Halloween party in the coming week. Adults commandeered the volleyball court. Connie was a no-show, despite the Ambassador's announcement that attendance was mandatory. Alice Jones remarked candidly that someone better talk with her soon because her corridor reputation was in a nosedive. On the court, I played through one match, but mostly I called ins and outs. I was never good at standing around and making small talk. I needed to be doing something, even if it was just keeping score. All in all, the picnic was working as planned. For several hours we forgot about Umbika's troubles, and our own.

Blake arrived from Katembeyna early afternoon, but before lunch. I saw him slip around the back of the house and walk directly to the Ambassador, who was at the barbecue grill, chatting with a cook. Blake and Durhlmann found a spot on the lawn, away from everyone else, and talked for several minutes. Then, Durhlmann waved me over.

"Benny called," the Ambassador said. "Washington is having a shit-fit, wondering what the hell is going on here. Maurice's sister saw a report on the news about the shootings in Katembeyna. She telephoned her brother's editor, who contacted the White House. I couldn't sidestep the question anymore. I had to tell Benny we don't know where Maurice is."

I looked at Blake. "I couldn't find him, Joe," he said. "I talked to traffic police at the south checkpoint. No one remembers seeing Hightower leave Kat. I rechecked the hotels and guesthouses. I even stopped at the car rentals. No one's seen Hightower since yesterday. It's like he disappeared."

I didn't know what to make of Blake's news. A man of Hightower's presence and stature does not disappear, yet no one had any information on where he might be. The Ambassador's contemplative pose next to his lush flower garden, looking deeply concerned I assumed about our VIP and probably Washington's next move, reminded me of Pietr Ritt-Boorman's posture only days earlier, standing before his vast acreage of tea, calculating the future of his country.

"I've been resisting this," the Ambassador said, "but now I think it's safe to say, Maurice Hightower is officially a missing person." A cheer rose from the volleyball court. Blake and I instinctively turned towards the distraction. "First thing in the morning," Durhlmann commanded, "I want both of you on your way to Katembeyna and looking for him. Check restaurants, the hospital. Check with the police. I want the whole nine yards. When you get near a phone, update me. There's probably a logical explanation for where he is, but I want him found and brought back here." Across the lawn, Miriam called to everyone that it was time to eat. The Ambassador waved to her. "If there's more trouble in Katembeyna, like yesterday," he said, "I want to know immediately. We'll draw down if we have to."

Cooks carried platters of food to tables already set up on the patio near the pool – heaps of chicken breasts, wings, and hot dogs – piles of sweet corn – bowls of potato salad and cole slaw – a tower of buttered rolls. Off to the side were trays of pies and cupcakes, containers of ice cream. We were looking at an all-American picnic. The Ambassador's cooks must have been working all through the night. Embassy families gathered at one end of the buffet and formed into a long neat line. Children – bundled in Disney towels – laughed and sang songs as they moved along the food tables. Volleyballers argued lost points. When it was my turn, I filled my plate as those before me had, agreeing with everyone around me how delicious it all looked.

Chapter 27
Perseverance

Even on a full stomach, I didn't sleep well that night. My mind was spinning a web of worry about Hightower and whatever trouble he might have gotten into. His visit had grown more complicated by the day, and I was at a loss about what could be done to solve the problem. At one point I turned on the lamp on the nightstand next to my bed. I sat up and drafted a new to-do list, key places to search in Katembeyna, people to contact. Perseverance, it has been said, is not one long race, but several short ones strung together. That, I decided, was how I would approach my search for Maurice Hightower, a series of trials and errors. After arranging by order of importance the places in Katembeyna to visit and the people to see, I numbered them. I had a list of eleven. Only then was I able to fall back asleep.

Early the next morning, I parked in my normal spot behind the Chancery. A row of trees to the east gripped the Embassy grounds in cool blue daybreak light. Even more telling, a winter-like chill hung in the air. It was the dry season at its peak, cool and crisp. Blake was waiting for me at the motor pool with Fred and Maxwell, Blake's regular driver. They stood between two white Embassy Land Rovers, engines running.

"You remember it this cold last October?" Blake asked, rubbing his hands together.

"I got here after the rainy season started. I've never seen it like this," I said.

Blake and I rode together so we could discuss our search plan. We went with Fred. Maxwell followed. Our search party started off at 7 a.m., and within minutes we passed the site of Mandy Weinberg's accident, skid marks still evident on the gray pavement. I didn't know if Blake had heard of her death, but I didn't bring it up. I let my thoughts of Mandy recede behind us. Her body was in an airplane somewhere, on its way home. At the airport turnoff, we passed the Bolo Wayside Inn, its parking lot full of trucks and trailers. A little farther north, we came to the first of several security checkpoints between the capital city and Katembeyna. Three sleepy policemen and six army soldiers stood with hands warming in their jacket pockets, automatic weapons slung over their shoulders. The men scarcely glanced at our CD plates before motioning us around the barrier. The inconsistency of security procedures in Africa could be unnerving one day and welcomed the next. This early in the morning traffic didn't slow us down either. The highway was nearly deserted.

Katembeyna and the capital city connected through one of the smoothest highways in Africa, the M-2, yet an hour into our five-hour journey I began to feel car sick. I sipped water and cracked open my window. Minutes later, I was feeling better. Off to our west, five large rock columns jutted out of the earth, like the fingers of a giant hand. The low angle of the morning light cast long purple shadows behind the columns. One rock in particular stood out from the others because of its strange mushroom-shaped top. It reminded me of a similar rock I had seen almost fifteen years earlier, in Nigeria, not long after that country's civil war ended. A high school science teacher from Idaho had disappeared in the bush. The man was an amateur photographer, traveling alone and visiting a remote area known for its abundant wildlife. The manager at the hotel where the teacher was staying had notified Nigerian police when the man did not return after three nights away. The police then notified the U.S. Embassy, and I was dispatched with a Jeepload of Nigerian police recruits to search for the missing American. Over two days we covered 150 square miles without a single lead. Our luck changed on the third day.

The proprietor at a roadside station where we had stopped for petrol asked us why we were in such a remote area. He then took us to see a village headman nearby, who showed us a rental car abandoned in the village and said a *mzungu* with a fancy camera had walked into the bush two days earlier. We followed the photographer's trail, and four hours later located our missing man – forty miles from his hotel and ten miles from his car. He was sitting on a mushroom-shaped boulder the size of a small garage, delirious from dehydration and buck-naked. He also had a broken leg, just above the ankle.

The police recruits jerry-rigged a rope and pulley to lower the man to the ground. We splinted his leg and gave him water and a candy bar. The man's skin was blistered and covered with insect bites. It took an hour in the shade and two more bottles of water to get his brain working again. He remembered his name and date of birth, but nothing about what had happened.

Another hour later, he finally could tell us that he had gotten lost while following a herd of zebras. He said he had walked in circles, completely disoriented, when a pack of hyenas picked up his scent. The hyenas stalked him until sunset. He kept them away by throwing rocks, but hurt his leg when he tried to climb a tree. The hyenas finally cornered him against a massive mushroom-shaped boulder and began nipping at him from three sides. Out of anything left to throw, he said he had prepared himself to die.

A family of elephants must have heard him shouting. They came and chased away the hyenas. The biggest elephant in the herd used its trunk to lift the man to safety, placing him atop the mushroom-shaped rock.

The police recruits and I shook our heads, a miracle in the bush. I had kept Claire up half that night, retelling the teacher's story. My first missing person case.

As we continued north now towards Katembeyna, I imagined Maurice Hightower in the bush somewhere, lost and disoriented, nursing a bad ankle, sitting on top some funny rock, waiting for us to rescue him. Suddenly, Fred braked hard. My body lunged forward, slamming my shoulder into the back of the front seat.

"Damn it, Fred!" Blake shouted. Blake had been napping. He too was thrown into the seat in front of him. Fred swerved right, just missing a group of ladies walking with woven baskets on their heads, having drifted into our lane on the asphalt, their backs to us.

"I am sorry, sir," Fred said.

"Don't they know enough to walk facing the traffic?" Blake said.

One of the ladies turned and acknowledged us with an embarrassed smile as we passed. "Umbik women are cheeky ones," Fred added, with emphasis.

Eventually, our first hour to Katembeyna slipped into a second and then a third.

Chapter 28
Guts

Blake had fallen asleep again, his head propped at an odd angle between his headrest and side window. I was drifting in a road trip daze, staring beyond the windshield at the centerline, licks of white paint on gray pavement, a series of dots and dashes rushing towards me like an endless transmission of some secret code.

Having a driver was the only time on a road trip when I could sit back and let my mind wander. Sometimes, I just slept or stared at the centerline, but oftentimes I made up mental games, like visualizing the front door of every post I had been to, the face of every ambassador's secretary I had worked with, the living room furniture of every house and apartment I had lived in. These peculiar memories came back to me in a series of phantom images, just like the broken centerline I was watching on the road to Katembeyna, one odd ghost after another. At one point on the M-2, I tried estimating our speed by timing the white dashes, but I soon lost focus and the tally went nowhere. Then, like Blake, I gave in to sleep.

"How long have I been out?" Blake's words woke me. I opened my eyes. His hands bumped the roof and the side window, as he stretched wrinkles out of his body.

"You've been out at least an hour," I said, checking my watch. Blake leaned forward and let his arms drape over the front seat. He squeezed blood back into his fingers.

"How long 'til we get there?" he asked Fred. Fred pointed towards a narrow cord of asphalt we were passing on the right. The old tar surface disappeared into red earth to the east.

"Here is the cutoff from Losei," Fred said. "It is one hour to Katembeyna."

A mile later, traffic police waved us through another security stop. Blake spotted a pencil-thin radio mast sticking out of a field tent pitched beside the checkpoint. "That's odd," he said, writing in his notebook. "Traffic police didn't have radios here yesterday." I stretched my neck and shoulders.

"I'm worried about Connie," I said. "She's falling apart."

"Once he's gone, she'll be okay. She told me she dated a couple of guys like him in college, younger, of course. Sounded like it didn't turn out well."

"Umbika should not have been her first posting overseas."

"You're probably right." Blake said and leaned in closer to me. "Our visitor got into some trouble at the court on Thursday."

"What kind of trouble?"

"A stupid move, but I give the guy credit," Blake whispered. "He's got balls." I waited for details, but Blake said nothing more. He turned and looked out his window. After a minute, he leaned in again. "Nearly got himself killed." Blake had my full attention now and could see I was waiting. "Tell Fred to turn on the radio," he said and motioned towards the front seat. "Some African music."

Fred found a station – tribal drums. The beat pulsated through the vehicle.

"I was going to write up a cable about this, but the Ambassador isn't sure how much he wants Washington to know."

"What happened with Hightower?" I asked. Blake stretched more soreness out of his fingers and wrists. He cracked his neck.

"I got to the courthouse around quarter-past-seven," he said. "Usually, for a big trial, police are in place by seven. They line up around the steps and out to the road. But this time there were no cops anywhere. Do you know the park next to the courthouse?" I shook my head. He used his hands and the space between us on the back seat to lay out where the Chitsaya trial was taking place. "There's a park here with grass and trees. An access road comes in from the main road and circles the park, then runs in front of the steps here. The steps go up to a plateau and the courthouse overlooking the park. I was with other diplomats at the top of the stairs when troop trucks arrived. They parked on the far side of the park. A hundred NEGs jumped out, each with a shiny A-K. We had no idea they were coming."

"I cabled Washington about those guys," I said. "A Norwegian aid worker spotted them outside of Kat, at the teachers college. He said they had new guns."

"New uniforms too," Blake said. "Black and gray camouflage now, with gray berets and black storm trooper boots. We knew they were NEGs, of course, by the A-Ks and sunglasses." After independence, President Mulenga had issued the first of many weird declarations that would trademark his presidency. He decreed only he, his Explorers, and foreigners could wear sunglasses in public. He said people should be able to look in their neighbor's eyes and know what he is thinking. Dark glasses became a symbol of Mulenga's repressive regime.

Blake continued. "Below the courthouse, the NEGs formed a line facing the main road, across from where Wisdom Chitsaya's supporters had gathered – a thousand protesters eye to eye with a hundred NEGs. The two sides were only fifty yards apart. At quarter-to-nine, the prison convoy brought Chitsaya to court, sirens and flashing lights. A big black van circled the park and stopped at the bottom of the steps. Chitsaya was led out in handcuffs. When the crowd saw him, a cheer exploded from the road. People started singing and dancing. Chitsaya paused halfway up the stairs. But before he could wave, the guards hustled him up and into the courthouse."

"Hightower was there?" I asked.

"He was standing against a railing, not far from me – all decked out in this spectacular yellow suit, stunning threads, impossible to miss. The courthouse looks big from the outside – like a Greek temple – but inside it's small, gives you a tight feeling. When I went in, Hightower was behind me. He sat with the press, next to the guy who's always touching that band-aid on his nose."

"Roland Verre, BBC," I said.

"That's a guy who needs to get out of Africa."

"Was Chitsaya's family there?"

"Yeah, six or seven of them. They sat in the balcony. He looked up at them from time to time. Chitsaya stood in the dock, alone, of course. Never sat, never was asked a question, never said a word. The prosecution called police officials to lay out what Chitsaya had done and a law professor to explain the laws – pretty boring. Then, at eleven, the judge adjourned."

"That's it?"

"That was it for the morning. When I got outside, I was surprised. The number of demonstrators had grown to thousands. Some were singing and dancing, but mostly they were just watching, waiting for Chitsaya. I found my spot along the railing, at the top of the steps. Chitsaya came out in handcuffs, one guard on each side. Halfway down the stairs, he stopped and looked to the road. In a second, the crowd quieted. His guards were caught unaware and kept walking. Chitsaya raised his arms and shook his handcuffs at the sky. The crowd roared. The sound was like cannon fire rolling across a battlefield, loud enough to frighten the NEGs, who shouldered their weapons.

"The guards hurried back up the steps and pulled down Chitsaya's arms. He resisted or his feet got tangled, either way, he tumbled down the steps." The thought of a handcuffed man falling down a flight of cement steps made me wince. "He wasn't seriously injured, but his nose was bleeding. The crowd saw the blood and the guards pushing Chitsaya into the van. They screamed at the NEGs as his motorcade pulled onto the road. Some fool in the first jeep started firing his weapon into the air, in front of Chitsaya's supporters – taunting them. The crowd went nuts and started throwing rocks at the motorcade. Guards were hit. A couple car windows were smashed. You could hear the breaking glass all the way where I was. The motorcade sped off, but the crowd was pissed. They started throwing stones at the NEGs in the park. Guys were getting hit left and right. An officer just below where I was standing took twenty men and ran to the front. They formed a new picket line closer to the crowd."

"Where was Hightower?" I asked.

"At the railing, about thirty feet from me," Blake said. "He was watching like the rest of us. Demonstrators had formed a forward line of their own, across from the NEGs. Young men took off their shirts and started dancing like warriors, with imaginary spears and shields, acting aggressively – as if they were about to attack. Some made monkey gestures at the soldiers. Stones kept coming from the back of the crowd. Most missed, but in every ten, one would hit someone. When a NEG up front got hit in the forehead, an officer raised his Uzi and fired over the crowd. Full automatic. The sound was loud. Everyone froze. The officer fired a long burst again. Hundreds of people dove to the ground. Many others retreated in a panic to a high-density neighborhood behind them. That's when I realized Hightower had gone down to the park. I saw him gesturing wildly and going from one officer to another, talking to them, right up to the front."

"What was he saying?"

"Who knows?"

"Was he okay?"

"Ha. It was a stupid-ass thing to do. Hightower was halfway across the park when the crowd surged ahead. The officer with the Uzi got hit in the face with a rock. It knocked him down. He got right up, but there was a lot of blood on his face. He was enraged and fired right into the crowd, not over anyone's head this time, but chest high. Full automatic, until his clip ran out. His men started firing too. In a couple of seconds, it was total chaos. Bullets were flying everywhere. Some ricocheted around us. People ran into the courthouse. I got behind a cement flowerpot."

"What about Hightower?"

"He kept moving to the front. I could see his yellow suit in the smoke. When he was close, he must have shouted something at the officer with the Uzi, because the guy spun around – the gun still smoking on his hip. Hightower raised his arms in surrender. I was sure he was a dead man."

"Jesus, Blake."

"Get this – Hightower was arms up, but his chin was out, still jabbering at the little shit with the Uzi. He wouldn't stop – this black giant in a yellow suit – calling out the little murderer. I don't know what he said, but all of a sudden, the NEG lowers his weapon – just like that. The others did the same. Most of the crowd had retreated, those who weren't lying on the ground. I went down to the park. NEGs were scurrying away like bugs in a spotlight, and regular police were arriving. I saw one NEG go from body to body, kicking to see who was still alive. When he found one, he shot him in the head. He would have shot more, but a policeman ran over and punched him in the face. It broke the guy's sunglasses. The coward ran off."

"Where was Hightower?"

"I looked for him," said Blake, "but he was gone."

"Was he shot?"

"I don't think so. I had seen him after the gunfire stopped, standing on the road. If he had gone down, I would've seen his yellow suit among the bodies. It was a mess, but I would've seen his suit. Police were on their knees in the blood, vomiting and crying – ." Blake stopped talking, though his lips kept shaking. He rubbed his eyes. He had remembered all he could for now. I shook my head.

"What?" he asked.

"What made Hightower do something crazy like that?"

Blake thought for a moment. Finally, he said, "It's no secret – I don't like Hightower. I don't like his politics, or his my-way-or-the-highway arrogance. Hell, I don't even like the way he dances. In fact, I think Hightower's a royal prick. But the truth is – a lot more people would've died if he hadn't gotten that asshole with the Uzi to stop shooting. That took more than guts."

Chapter 29
So-Pretty-Pretty

After the turnoff to Losei, the highway rose in elevation. Soon, we had reached the Northern Province and then, as bicyclists and people walking on the road increased, we were at the outskirts of Katembeyna. Katembeyna was a gem of the North, a city of wide avenues, green spaces, and lush gardens, as well as the center for provincial government and trade. Early in the colonial period, the town had served as the capital of the entire territory, because at 3,200 feet above sea level Katembeyna had a low risk for malaria. Today, it was most known for the richness of its soil, growing a healthy variety of cash crops, including tomatoes, maize, and cassava with the average farmer selling more than enough to make ends meet. The area was also homeland to the Tolog people. Tolog prosperity was evident along the road leading into town. Not only were properties neater and more organized than in the South, but tin sheets replaced thatch on roofs, and clear glass replaced cardboard on windows.

Our car crested a hill, another wrinkle in the increasingly textured landscape, and a security checkpoint came into view at the bottom of a gradual decline. We moved towards it. A line of cars and trucks in front of us was waiting to enter Katembeyna. On the other side of the road, the row of vehicles waiting to exit the city was even longer. We rolled to a stop at the back of our queue. Explorers were running this checkpoint, twelve to fifteen of them, more than I had ever seen at a traffic stop before. Under a baobab tree across the road, two NEGs were searching a green pickup, its cargo bed filled with household items secured by a web of white rope. The truck's driver, a dark Tolog man, stood expressionless as an officer scrutinized his papers. One of the NEGs searching the green pickup held above his head an old hunting rifle he had found hidden in the back of the truck, a bolt-action relic wrapped in oil cloth. I watched the discovery from the backseat of our vehicle, content to wait our turn in line. At that moment Fred decided otherwise and steered us onto the shoulder, bypassing the vehicles in front of us. Maxwell followed a car length behind. Sensing the trouble he was in, I assume, the driver of the green pickup took off running south, up the highway.

Bang! The sound shook the air around us. A NEG standing under the baobab tree had shot the running man in the back. The body tumbled down a gravel shoulder – arms swimming in air – and landed face first in a ditch, a faint halo of dust rising above him. Fred kept driving to the front of our queue.

Three NEGs standing behind the barricade stepped forward. They quickly brought their AKs shoulder high and aimed them at our windshield. Blake yelled, "Jesus Christ! Stop already!" Fred slammed on the brakes. We lurched forward. Our tires carved a rut in the earth, stopping us just before a pair of oil drums – and swirling more dust into the air. Maxwell skidded behind us, nudging our bumper before he came to a halt. "What's with these morons?" Blake shouted. "Can't they read a fucking license plate?"

When the air settled, the NEGs were still holding their deadly aim on us. I was about to tell Fred to get out and talk to the men, but from across the highway – where a camouflaged tent was pitched – a NEG officer sauntered towards us, moving as if all the time in the world belonged to him. The officer was a young man, in his mid-twenties. He wore fancy aviator sunglasses with gold designer frames. As he got closer, I could see his creamy brown skin – the color of milk chocolate, skin free of blemishes and discolorations. A man with skin this perfect had the purest Umbik blood in all of Africa and came from the same district in the South as President Mulenga. It was skin that Umbiks referred to as "Royale" and Tologs as "so-pretty-pretty." The officer stopped at Fred's side of the car and adjusted his dark glasses. Fred rolled down his window.

"Ask him if he's seen Maurice Hightower," I said to Fred, but before he could say a word, the officer leaned into the open window.

"Who do you think you are!" he demanded.

"Sir?" Fred replied.

"You are a reckless driver!" the officer shouted. "What do you care to be doing here!"

Fred stammered something in the local language, in a tone of voice that only surfaced when an Umbikan feared for his life. Despite Fred's apologies, the officer refused to soften. He stood upright, like a steel post, waiting beside the window for god-knows-what. His black lenses were meant to intimidate, and they had that effect on Fred. Without being asked, Fred handed the officer his nationality card and Embassy ID, as if they might make a difference. The officer glanced at the documents and then tossed them back at Fred through the open window. Fred caught one card in midair, but the other tumbled to the floor. The officer bent over again and peered deeper into our vehicle, his gaze settling on Blake and me in the back seat. "Paper!" he demanded.

"This is a diplomatic vehicle," Blake said, unmoved by the man's self-importance, and not a bit intimidated. "You have no right to stop us or interfere in our travel. Take a good look at our license plates."

The officer's head cocked, and then his voice exploded. "Show me paper!"

The shout got the attention of the NEGs manning the barricade. They jumped forward and refocused their aim on Blake and me in the back seat. The NEG who was dragging the pickup driver's body along the road dropped what he was doing and ran over and took a defensive position directly behind the officer with Royale skin. Blake sat back in his seat and folded his arms over his chest, acting as if we had reached a stalemate. "What an asshole," he said, under his breath. "Looks like the bad guys are running the show up here now." I slipped my hand into my coat pocket.

"Let's give him what he wants and get out of here," I said and handed my blue diplomat book to Fred. Blake seemed reluctant, but he did the same. "Tell the officer the car behind is with us," I said to Fred.

Blake leaned over the back seat and called to the pretty NEG officer. "Hey man, who are you looking for?" The officer pushed his sunglasses down his nose and looked eye to eye at Blake, his tiny dark pupils surrounded by a circle of yellow haze that I took for one form of jaundice or another.

"I am looking for confusionists," the officer said, snidely. "I am looking for enemies of my country. They are everywhere, you can be sure." The officer slid his sunglasses back up his nose and walked across the highway, disappearing into his tent with our official diplomat books. We waited for the officer to return, but he didn't. His men refused to let any vehicles pass through the barricade, so the back-up continued to grow. More minutes passed. I could see other motorists behind us, animated in their vehicles, growing disgusted, but no one ventured a formal complaint. Then, an Explorer we had not seen before, a very young guy, only a teenager, exited the tent and jogged across the highway. He handed the blue diplomat books to Fred and motioned to his comrades to let us pass. Fred put the Rover in gear and pulled forward.

"Wait!" I said. Fred stopped. "Ask this kid if he's seen a black American come through here." Fred called to the young Explorer, who came back to our car. Fred asked my question, but the kid shook his head. He had not seen anyone like that. He called to some of his buddies who were pushing the green pickup off the road. They considered the question, but then shook their heads. No one had seen anyone matching Maurice Hightower's description.

Chapter 30
B.O.M.A.

The Koo-Kat Hotel was situated in the center of Katembeyna, on a corner where the M-2 crossed the Jito River. The intersection of the highway and river cut the commercial district into quarters. Ex-pats considered the Koo-Kat the best hotel in the North, a three-lion rating with reliable service and the only above-average restaurant for hundreds of miles. Blake and I were given rooms on the second floor in the east wing. After hanging up my shirts and extra suit, I washed my hands and went downstairs to meet Blake for lunch. He was already in the restaurant, waiting at a table on the patio overlooking a flower garden and kidney-shaped swimming pool. Several species of exotic African flowers were in bloom. But it being late October and too cold to swim, the pool had been drained for the season. Two other tables on the patio were occupied, each by a middle-aged black couple, both of whom appeared to be Kenyan. Several empty tables separated us from them.

"Could be we're the only Westerners left," Blake said. "The front desk told me a lot of ex-pats checked out this morning." He carefully opened a package of saltine crackers wrapped in cellophane, his fingernail proceeding like a dissection.

"You've seen more countries come apart than I have. What's your gut telling you?" I said.

"Exactly what yours is, Joe. This place is ready to blow."

"I was hoping you'd say something like, 'J.J. won't lead his people over a cliff.'"

"Ha. J.J.'s not that smart, or that good." The waiter approached with our lunch plates, set them on the table, and left. One of the black couples had finished eating and was getting up from their table. We watched them walk past us and exit the restaurant.

"I have some business outside of town to take care of," Blake said. "But afterwards, I'll poke around the hotels and guesthouses, see if I can scare up something about our missing man."

"My first stop after lunch is police headquarters."

Blake paused the work of his knife and fork on a medallion of beef. "You know, it's funny and sad," he said. "Hightower preaches his America-is-racist crap. How the system is rigged against him because he's black. But look who's sent to save his ass when he gets in a jam – two white guys."

"I tried not to talk with Hightower about race," I said. "But he turns every conversation into a lesson on black history."

"You mean, the world according to Maurice Hightower."

A short while later, the waiter cleared our plates and brushed breadcrumbs off the tablecloth and into his hand. He then brought us coffee and set our bill on the table.

"We got into an argument after leaving Pietr Boorman's estate. He wanted to know what it was like for a white person, like me, to live in a country of black people."

"Hightower is just another guy who hates the life he's been dealt," said Blake. "Black or white, that unhappiness defines a lot of people." A breeze blew across the patio, so Blake put his hand over the bill to keep it from flying away. "But then, there's that crazy business at the court."

"I've been thinking about that," I said and handed Blake money for my part of the bill.

"Even if I don't like the guy, it's..." Blake paused, searching for the precise word.

"Is 'complicated' the word you're looking for?" Blake arranged our money into a neat pile on the table and put the bill on top.

"Close enough," he said. We left the restaurant, agreeing to meet for dinner at eight.

Fred and I drove across town to the BOMA, a colonial-era military fort converted after independence to the headquarters for the National Police Force, Northern Province. I was becoming increasingly worried that Hightower had been arrested. His actions outside the court must have upset a lot of important people. Questioning the authority of the President's Explorers was only a shade less severe than questioning the authority of the Life President himself. The police may have had no choice but to lock him up – which meant I would have to get him released. At the BOMA gate, a guard lifted the red and white striped pole blocking our path and then saluted as we passed his station.

Fred parked in front of the administration building, a long one-story structure whose forest green color had faded so much since independence that splinters of bare wood showed through on most of the old planks. The building was topped in a hip roof, finished with orange half-round clay tiles – a typical government structure from the Colonial Era. Like the building's neglected walls, its roof had also lost its luster over the years. The clay tiles were chipped and cracked, and fragments had slid off the roof and were lying on the ground, creating a faint outline of orange crumbs around the perimeter of the building.

Fred waited in the car. Where I stood in the damp entryway, a circular fluorescent tube hung on a black cord from the high ceiling. The cool blue light helped my eyes adjust quickly from the brightness outside. I started down a long somber hallway, towards a police sergeant sitting behind a wooden desk at the end of the corridor. Both the desk and the sergeant had long ago seen their best years. An empty cigarette pack had been folded and placed under one leg of the desk to keep it level. The sergeant's hair was spotted gray and thinning on top, his stern cheeks drawn to the bone.

Kneeling on the floor next to the desk was a man about my age, in gray shorts and a white tee-shirt. He was cleanly shaven. His face shined a glossy richness, like polished obsidian. He was not barefooted, as I would have expected, but wearing a pair of woven leather sandals – expensive footwear in Umbika. Normally, a man kneeling in a police station was under arrest, but this man's hands were not bound by restraints. He was not a criminal, it turned out, but the victim of a crime. I listened to the man's precise English as he pleaded with the police sergeant to help him. Five of his relatives were missing, including his two teenage nieces. It was a sad story, for sure, but the sergeant did not seem to care what the man was relating. He scolded the man for wasting his time. He said the complaint was a local matter, best taken up with the police in JiJi, three hours north of Katembeyna, the town where the kneeling man lived. "Go home and wait," the sergeant ordered. He closed his logbook and put down his pen. "There is nothing I can do."

The sergeant turned his attention to me, as if the man on his knees was no longer there. I took out one of my business cards, an official one from the Embassy, its bald eagle embossed in gold and perched in the upper left corner. The eagle's talons clutched a bundle of arrows on one side and an olive branch on the other. Handing out a card from the U.S. Embassy was an impressive conversation starter, so that is how I began. "I'm Kellerman from the American Embassy. I'm here to see the officer-in-charge." The sergeant stared for a moment at the white card, running his thumb over the gold eagle.

"American," he said, unimpressed.

My official title was printed under my name. Every policeman in Umbika above the rank of private knew the American Consul was one of the highest-ranking diplomats at the U.S. Embassy. I am certain the sergeant had noticed my title on the card, but for whatever reason he decided to show me less respect than the title deserved. He paged through his logbook, but it was a false show. He already knew what he was going to say. "You have no appointment."

"I know. I came without notice," I said. "I apologize for that, but my business is urgent." The man flicked the edge of my white card with his thumb, producing a stiff, unwelcome sound. I sensed he was not sure what to do about a diplomat arriving without an appointment, on a Saturday afternoon no less. Making things worse was the superstition among Umbikans that foreigners showing up unexpectedly brought bad luck.

"What is your business here?"

"I'm trying to find an American who is missing." The sergeant considered my answer. Then, he got up from his chair.

"Wait." He walked away, down a hallway to my left. I watched him turn a corner at the end of the hall. I went over and sat on a worn wooden bench, facing the sergeant's old desk. A few minutes later the sergeant returned. "Mr. Mwenda, the police commissioner, will see you," he said.

"The commissioner is here on Saturday?"

The sergeant didn't reply. I followed him through a succession of halls to a door with a frosted window. Traces of adhesive tape – probably decades old – stuck to the glass in an array of mysterious symbols, like remnants of an ancient and forgotten language. The sergeant knocked once on the glass. "Enter, please," said an officious voice from within.

The sergeant held the door open for me and then closed it as he left. A paunchy Umbik man, mid-fifties, was seated behind a battered gray metal desk. He wore a khaki shirt with two gold stars on each shoulder and four navy blue chevrons on the sleeves. The man's gold cap rested atop a jumble of file folders on the desk, beside an old black telephone. His fat fingers held my business card. "Joseph Kellerman," he said, flicking the edge of the card with his thumb, much as the sergeant had. "American Consul." He rose and extended his small hand. "I am Peterson Mwenda, Commissioner, National Police Force, Northern Province. You are most welcome."

"It's an honor to meet you, sir," I said, shaking his hand. "I've heard your name, but this is our first face-to-face. Thank you for seeing me on a Saturday. I didn't expect the commissioner himself to be in the office on weekend."

"These are busy days, Mr. Joseph. Please sit."

I sat on the only guest chair in the room, a straight-back steel remnant without armrests. The commissioner's office had the same lofty Colonial ceiling as the hallway. In the past, there might have been a fan suspended there, but not now. Against one wall stood a plywood armoire, its two doors padlocked. No curtains or blinds dressed the only window in the room. The view looked out onto a plot of dry grass and a barracks with a tin roof. The window was half open, letting in the faint scent of diesel fuel. A cork bulletin board was mounted on one wall. A clipboard hung from it by a piece of thick packaging string tied to the head of a nail. The other walls were naked, except for blisters of gray paint. Next to the commissioner's desk was a stenographer's table, and on it rested additional file folders. The office seemed undersized and shabby for a senior police officer, but with Mulenga's funding priorities as they were, this was probably the best someone could expect in the Northern Province.

"How may my office be brought to your assistance?" Mwenda asked. Peeking from around the corner of the armoire was the banana clip and wood butt of an automatic rifle. The shiny butt rested on the floor, the barrel hidden by the corner. Although I didn't need prodding, the gun reminded me why I was at the BOMA.

"I'm looking for an American journalist," I said. "He's missing."

"We seem to have many people missing these days," the commissioner replied. "Why is your journalist?"

"That's the mystery, sir. He never returned to the capital city. We don't know what happened to him. He was here in Kat on Thursday. No one has seen him since."

"Is he a confusionist?"

The police commissioner's question took me by surprise. "No, he's definitely not a confusionist."

"Then what is he?"

"He's a writer," I said, emphasizing the last word.

"Is he a missionary writer, writing church business?"

"No, he writes for the *New York Times* and the *Washington Post*. He's a professional writer." I was tired from the long road trip, and the tone in my voice was revealing my frustrations with the odd questions the police commissioner was asking. I watched his eyes drift away from mine, disinterested it seemed in my visit, gazing somewhere behind me, though nowhere in particular that I could tell. Maybe his thoughts were roaming the cracks in the wall at my back, wondering if it was time to repaint the room. Maybe he was just bored on a Saturday, hoping I would walk out and leave him to his business. The buzz of the fluorescent light overhead was all that filled a very long pause.

"Is he here to write about the drought?"

"No. My missing man is sixty-six years old. He has black skin," I said. "He's tall, much taller than me – gray hair and a beard. He might be wearing a yellow suit. He's an important person in my country." Then, I added something that stretched the truth a little. "He came to Umbika on the wishes of the President of the United States." The police commissioner was staring at me again.

"I think I know this man," he said with renewed interest. The tone of his voice sounded optimistic, almost like he had experienced a revelation. I was greatly encouraged, and my heart began to fly.

"That's terrific! Do you know where I can find him?"

"Mr. Joseph. I did not say I know where this man is. I only said I think I know who he is." My rising optimism was short-lived, brought quickly back to earth. The commissioner adjusted his posture, sitting straighter in his chair. "On Thursday morning, inside the High Court, there was a dark-skin foreigner in a yellow suit. Later, he was outside on the commons."

"That definitely sounds like the man I'm looking for," I said. "He was at the court on Thursday. His Excellency, the Life President, invited him to observe the Chitsaya trial." My mention of Hightower's connection to Mulenga was the first time the police commissioner seemed surprised at something I had said, but it lasted only a moment.

"These are difficult days," the commissioner said. "Many people want to harm my country. First, there was the Chitsaya fellow. Now, our Speaker has been murdered."

"My missing man doesn't want to harm your country."

"Are you certain?'

"Of course, I am. He's just a reporter."

"But reporters write about mistakes, do they not? They identify failure. When they do not have all the facts, they confuse people. And their stories encourage criminals to challenge our weaknesses and kill our leaders." I finally realized that a chill had been descending on the room since I'd sat down.

"This man is not here for any of that. In fact, it's just the opposite." I tried to breathe some warmth into the conversation. I smiled. "He knows your president. He's met him. He likes him." The police commissioner smiled.

"You Americans, you expect everyone to stop what they are doing when misfortune comes your way." He picked up my business card from his desk. "What makes your people more important than my people?"

"Nothing, my job is to help Americans," I said. He flicked the edge of the white card.

"What does it require to be the American Consul? Is that a university degree?"

"It's not a degree, but I went to law school."

"You are a solicitor."

"I didn't finish."

"You gave up?"

"My father died, but that's not important now. The man I'm looking for is missing. He could be in danger. That's why I'm here. That's my job. Wouldn't you do everything you could to help someone from Umbika, if he needed you?"

"We have a proverb, Mr. Joseph. It says, 'A person who has not travelled thinks his mother is the only cook.'" I did not recognize the African saying and had no time to figure out how it related to why I was in Mwenda's office.

"Would it help if you knew the missing man's name? You could check your records," I said.

"I know his name." The police commissioner's statement surprised me as much as a slap to the face. "Your American is Mr. Maurice. Is that not correct?"

I had been played for a fool since entering the police commissioner's office, maybe since entering the BOMA. I wanted to know why that was, but asking that question would lead nowhere useful. I needed information about Hightower. "Yes, Maurice Hightower. That's who I'm looking for," I said. The man leaned back in his chair and put his black knee-high leather boots up on the desk. He crossed his small feet only inches in front of me, a gesture so disrespectful in Umbikan culture that I had never heard of anyone doing it to a foreigner, let alone to a diplomat.

"Your journalist interfered with our national security."

"That's not possible."

"Is it? On Thursday morning, he obstructed justice. He prevented the Life President's National Exploring Group from carrying out their official security function at the trial of the confusionist, Chitsaya."

Now, everything was clear. The authorities already knew it was Hightower who had confronted the officer with the Uzi, when hundreds of demonstrators were shot at the court. "Did you arrest Mr. Hightower?" I said.

"No," replied the commissioner, "but I spoke with him at the court. I saw what he did. I told him he was fortunate not to be shot with the others. I reminded him that few are so lucky a second time."

"Mr. Hightower had no intention of interfering with your national security. He was covering a news story. After you spoke with him, where did he go?"

"I wish I knew. I have more questions to ask. He left with a driver."

Sarcasm had finally gotten the best of me. "Mr. Hightower isn't locked up in a jail here somewhere, is he?" My undiplomatic attitude was noted by sudden eye contact from the Commissioner.

"If he was locked here, you would have a right to see him. You are the American Consul, yes?" The man's animosity was unmistakable now. I would get nothing from him.

"Let me ask you this, sir," I said, already planning where to take my search next. "Where do you think he went?"

"I don't know. But when you find him, tell him to go back to America."

"Mr. Hightower is a guest of the Life President," I reminded him. The police commissioner grinned. He seemed immensely satisfied. Was this the moment he had been waiting for since I first entered his office?

"I believe your information concerning the Life President is in error," he said with confidence. "Mr. Maurice is welcome in my country no more."

Chapter 31
Seeds

Fred and I left the BOMA and drove to the west side of town. Fred pointed at the dozens of young men we passed along the edge of the road, thin dark bodies standing in long lines, like starlings perched on telephone wires, nervous birds waiting for the onset of winter. The young men craned their necks at each passing vehicle, eyeing who was inside the car, wondering if they were friend or foe. Fred said he had never seen behavior like this before. I told him I had seen it a couple of times, when a powerless community was afraid and no longer knew who it could trust.

The next name on my search list after the police commissioner's was Winfrey Locke. Locke was an Englishman in his seventies. I had mentioned Locke's name to Hightower in Ndala and thought it possible he might contact him when he was in Kat. Locke had lived his entire adult life in Umbika and built a successful business selling supplies to farmers in the Northern Province. He sold everything from shovels and rakes to fertilizer and irrigation tubing. Most of his sales came from seeds. Half of the seed stock sold in the North was purchased at his stores. Because Locke charged fair prices and stood behind his products, the average guy on the street trusted him. He was also a patient listener to people's problems and an elder in the church, so Tologs in the North saw Locke more as a lay clergyman than a businessman. That trust helped his business thrive all the more. At the Embassy, we knew Locke had regular contact with Umbikans in all walks of life, so whenever one of us was in Katembeyna, we made a point of visiting him as a potential source of information and political insight.

At the closed gate to Locke's property, two barefooted guards armed with shovel handles peered nervously into our car, then motioned us ahead. Normally, Locke's home was an island of tranquility, but not this afternoon. The jumpy guards quickly shut and barred the gate behind us. A garden boy sprinted ahead, as we drove to the main house. Locke came to the front door before we were out of the car. "Mr. Kellerman," he said, as we shook hands. "I apologize for the dramatic arts at the gate. Everyone is on edge after what happened at the court."

I too apologized, for dropping by without calling first, and explained my search for Hightower. "We haven't seen him since Thursday," I said.

"He was here for dinner Wednesday evening," Locke said.

"You saw him?"

"Yes, he was in fine form."

For a moment, I felt relieved.

"I'm sure you know he's rich with humor," said Locke. "I enjoy that in a journo." That Hightower had a sense of humor was news to me. "We talked until ten. He held a determined point of view on the Colonial Period." Only an ex-colonialist who had earned two fortunes in Umbika – one before independence and one after – could cast Hightower's deep bitterness towards white rule as a "determined point of view."

"I'm concerned for his safety," I said.

"You spoke with the police?" he asked.

"I did, but Mr. Hightower has some problems with the police now because of what happened at the court." Locke walked with me through his garden, just the two of us. Tree orchids were his specialty. He pointed out several varieties.

"Mr. Hightower knew I was active in the diocese."

"I'm afraid I told him," I said.

"That's fine, Joseph. He said he was writing an article, UFreeMo and its role in the Church."

"I didn't know UFreeMo had a role."

"He was looking for a connection, but I told him I stay out of politics. He asked if I could arrange an audience with the Bishop. I said I could, but not until next week. Bishop Gregory returns from the UK on Monday. Mr. Hightower said he'd ring me, but he never did."

That was the extent of what I learned from Winfrey Locke, the smallest of leads. It was late afternoon when we left the seed dealer's home. My first two stops in the search had turned up some intriguing information about Umbika, but nothing about where Hightower was now.

"Let's drive out to the Nazarene School," I said to Fred.

Lew Trestle, director of the Katembeyna Trade School of the Church of the Nazarene, was an American from Wheeling, West Virginia, and he served as my warden for the northern part of the country. Lew had lived in Umbika since the year after independence. His church's Board of Superintendents had sent him to Africa for a one-year sabbatical, with the charge of opening a small trade school to train carpenters and seamstresses. Lew soon fell in love with the African people and their pace of life. He never left. Lew's first wife came with him from West Virginia. Jenny died of lung cancer seven years after they arrived in Umbika and was buried now in the cemetery next to the trade school. Lew met his second wife, Lisa, a few years later, when they sang together in a church choir. Lisa joked that it was not Lew's baritone voice that first attracted her – but his distinctive black hair. Lew kept it greased and combed front to back with a pompadour loft, like Elvis's. Lisa, the child of a Presbyterian missionary couple, was called *Binti* – or daughter – by students at the trade school, because she was twenty years younger than her husband. Such a difference in ages would have aroused scandal in Wheeling, but in Katembeyna no one cared the least.

Lew was coming out of a work shed with a sewing machine across his arms, when Fred and I drove onto the school's property. He saw us and broke into a wide grin. "God bless!" he called. "I didn't know you gentlemen were headed this way."

Lew was as organized and as resourceful as anyone I'd met in Umbika, which was why I had tapped him as my warden. He set down the sewing machine and came over to our car. "The trip was a last-minute decision," I said, as we shook hands. He greeted Fred and asked about his family.

"Can you stay a while, Joe? You owe us a visit, you know."

"Thanks, but I came with Blake. We're already checked in at the Koo-Kat." Lew started to say something, but he caught himself. He motioned for me to follow him inside. When we came in, his wife was sitting at the dining room table with a yellow pencil held crossways between her lips. Spread on the table were a pile of receipts, a ledger book, and a hand-cranked adding machine. Lisa looked up from her work and took the pencil out of her mouth.

"My, my," she said cheerfully. "How nice is this!" We hugged. Lew pulled out a chair for me at the table.

"I suspect you're here because of the trouble at the court," he said.

"It's connected."

"That was so awful," Lisa said. "So many people killed."

"Our staff lost family. The pain they're carrying is unbearable."

"We remind them, Joe, that Jesus didn't come to free us from pain," Lisa said. "He came to give us the strength to bear it." I nodded respectfully. Lew and I had spoken on the phone on Thursday, when I called each of my wardens with the new travel advisory. Now, I gave him more details about Maurice Hightower at the court and the gist of what the police commissioner had said. Lew's body seemed to absorb the news of Hightower's predicament, not just hear it. His shoulders caved. He stared at the ground for a moment, and then he stood.

"We need to talk, my friend," he said. "I'll get us something to drink."

I sat at the table across from Lisa. She continued to write in her ledger and punch keys on the adding machine. Directly behind her, on an antique wooden sideboard, rested an enormous aquarium – fifty gallons or more. At the bottom of the crystal-clear water, cichlids hovered around tiny air bubbles escaping a treasure chest half buried in pink gravel. The beautiful fish were a rare variety found only in Lake Ziwa – their super thin bodies like oversized coins, adorned with vertical striping in red, white, and yellow. Long graceful streamers – both blue and silver – trailed their bottom fins. No other fish in the world looked like these. Collectors in Europe paid outrageous sums to get even a few.

I watched the pattern of Lisa's bookkeeping process, every motion of her fingers and arms, all in perfect harmony with the keys and hand crank of the adding machine. Lisa had the appearance similar to other expat wives I had met over the years, hardened women who had lived on the Continent longer than they had lived anywhere else – ladies with remarkable faces, heroic faces – drawn and tired, yet beautiful and resilient – appearing as if they had made it through a dreadful war but still found the capacity to dream. Lisa glanced up at me watching her. Her machine fell silent.

"I know that look, Joe," she said. "Are you thinking he's been in an accident?"

"We don't know," I said.

Lew returned with three bottles of Orange Fanta and a bowl of salted groundnuts. He pulled up a chair, close to the table. "I didn't want to say anything outside, you know. Never sure what the locals tell one another, who talks to the police and all that. I phoned the Embassy around noon today, hoping to talk to you. But it's Saturday, so I got your duty officer. He wouldn't tell me where you were."

"Sorry about that," I said. "It's policy."

"Lisa and I were at the market this morning. We bumped into Dr. Martin Polk."

"Do you know Martin?" Lisa asked.

"The name sounds familiar, but I can't place it."

"You must have met him," Lew insisted. "He's the new American doctor at the hospital up here. Comes off a little like a know-it-all."

Yes, now I did recall Dr. Polk, a physician from Yale, spending a year in Africa on a teaching fellowship. A few months earlier, just after Polk arrived in country, I had met him at a reception the Ambassador was hosting for visitors from the Centers for Disease Control. I remembered Polk less for his name or his pedigree and more for his pursuit of Connie Saunders. He was a ladies' man of the first order. Connie had just arrived in country herself and was feeling her way around the community. Polk zeroed in on her early in the evening. "Looks like the bulldog's got a scent," Blake had remarked. The nickname stuck as the reception wore on. Polk's moniker soon morphed into "hound dog," because every time Blake saw him talking to Connie, he seemed to be salivating and either touching her arm or slowly brushing invisible particles off her bare shoulder. By the end of the evening, Blake had shortened the handle to "dog" when we learned the lucky Yale doctor would be driving Connie home that night.

"I remember Dr. Polk. A good-looking guy with a ponytail," I said. "And a little full of himself."

"That's Martin," said Lew.

"Once you get to know him, he's really sweet," Lisa added.

"Martin told us he'd been with Mr. Hightower for a couple of days."

The news was invigorating. This was the first solid lead we had had since arriving in Katembeyna. "I need to see Dr. Polk, right away. Can you tell me how to get to his place?"

"Take it easy, Joe," Lew said. "He's not here now. When we saw Martin this morning, he was on his way to the capital. Mr. Hightower wasn't with him."

"God damn it!" I blurted. No sooner had the words left my mouth, than I regretted saying them. The Trestles forgave my anger and my language. But they could sense my frustration. I asked if Polk had mentioned where Hightower was, if he too was headed for the capital. A hesitant tone seemed to clutch at Lew's voice.

"Mr. Hightower wasn't headed south," he said. Then, he began his story.

Hightower and Polk had met on Thursday at St. Michael's Hospital in Kat. Polk was in a classroom, lecturing nursing students, when someone rushed in to say there had been a massacre at the High Court, only a mile away. Wounded were already arriving in the Emergency Room. Polk attended to a queue of the injured bodies that already stretched from the ER, down a hallway, and out into the parking lot. Some were expiring on the floor. Others before they even got inside the hospital. Victims arrived on the back seats of cars, stretched over the handlebars of bicycles, dragged in on planks of cardboard. Family wailed over the lifeless. Then, Hightower appeared out of nowhere, this tall black American in a beautiful yellow suit. He approached Dr. Polk and asked how many people had been killed.

"Martin told your friend there wasn't time to count the dead," Lisa interjected. "He called the Emergency Room a 'war zone.'"

"Your guy found rubber gloves and insisted on helping," said Lew. "He wouldn't take no for an answer. So, Martin put him to work."

"Tell Joe about the little boy."

Lew described the final victim Polk and Hightower treated that night. He was about ten years old. A bullet had shattered his femur, and a lot of blood had been lost. Polk was not sure the boy would survive. He decided the leg had to be removed.

"Mr. Hightower worked the saw," said Lew. "Must have been tough." He added more details about the operation, which caused Lisa to leave the room. My thoughts drifted for a moment to the winter night years earlier when I injured my own leg, my back to the pavement, my eyes gazing up at a streetlight, cool snowflakes falling on my face, warm blood soaking my pants leg.

"Martin called your friend a hero, Joe," said Lisa. She had returned to the dining room with a cup of tea, her hands hugging the vessel for warmth. "A real hero."

Lew said that Dr. Polk had asked Hightower why he had insisted on helping with the injured, seeing that he had already witnessed so much bloodshed at the courthouse. "That's when your guy made a strange comment," said Lew. "Only in old age do people finally realize you can never make up for all the mistakes you've made in life. Even so, you should try."

"What?"

"No, you must try," Lisa corrected her husband.

"You're right, honey. Not 'you should try,' but 'you must try.' Sounds strange, Joe, don't you think?"

I nodded and asked, "Did police come to the hospital?" A surge of desperation coursed through my chest. I was so close to finding Hightower, but Umbika was spiraling out of control, and Jimmy Mulenga seemed as volatile as ever. I had to get to him while it was still possible to move about the country, before the police or the NEGs found him. But my most promising lead, the bulldog from Yale, had already left for the capital city.

"Martin never mentioned any police," said Lisa.

My conversation with the Police Commissioner had told me President Mulenga already knew about Hightower's interference at the court. J.J. would not tolerate a foreigner's meddling in Umbika's internal affairs – no matter whose guest he was. The best scenario for ending this was Mulenga giving Hightower the cold shoulder – maybe ordering him to leave the country. But things could get far worse. If it looked like Hightower was taking sides in Umbika's politics, such as caring for wounded confusionists or writing an article that put Mulenga's regime in a bad light, Hightower could be thrown in jail. Or he might even disappear. I was confident Mulenga had not made the leap from courthouse to emergency room yet, but it was only a matter of time.

"Where did Hightower go after the hospital?"

"Martin figured it was safer if they slept at his house Thursday night," said Lew. "On Friday, they drove to the Seven Hills. Martin needed to check on a baby he delivered last week. They stayed overnight in the mountains and drove back this morning."

My mind and my body were exhausted. I wanted to call it quits for the day. Major pieces of the puzzle were still missing, and my best lead so far, Dr. Martin Polk, was probably five hours away by now, somewhere in the capital city, perhaps even visiting Connie Saunders. I reached for my orange soda, but the bottle was empty.

"You want another Fanta?" Lisa asked.

"No, I'm good, thanks. Where do you think Hightower is now?"

"That's why I tried to get in touch with you today, Joe. Martin thinks he's headed up to the Highlands, to find UFreeMo."

My head started to throb, a deep pain digging in behind one eye. The pain grew so intense in a couple of seconds that my teeth hurt too. I opened and closed my mouth, relaxing my jaw as much as I could. "Do you have a couple of aspirin, Lisa?" I asked.

Riding back to the hotel, I tried to imagine Hightower's line of reasoning for going to the Highlands. What was he thinking? What clues had he noticed? Where were those clues pointing? Did he believe UFreeMo rebels had infiltrated Chitsaya's supporters at the court and plotted to provoke the government into using lethal force? In that case, an overreaction by a few arrogant NEGs might be enough to enrage thousands of Tologs in the high-density neighborhoods around Katembeyna. The massacre at the court could have been anticipated by rebel plotters and intended to tip the North towards civil war – in other words, a UFreeMo setup.

There was another possibility, just as plausible. What if Hightower had begun to suspect Mulenga's regime was not the victim of the chaos at the High Court – but its choreographer? Hightower knew the Life President had sworn to oppose multiparty at any cost. What if that cost would be far greater than anyone imagined? What if the NEGs had deliberately provoked Chitsaya's supporters to riot, giving Mulenga the justification he needed to show the world how far he would go to stop dissent and preserve his regime? The only way for a fair reporter to sort out the truth was to travel north and meet with the rebels. JiJi, a truck stop and logging mill town on the M-2, three hours north of Katembeyna, was the gateway town to the Highlands and epicenter of rebel support. JiJi was where Hightower would begin trying to find his answers. I needed to get to JiJi as soon as I could.

Chapter 32
The Zazzy Lounge

Fred dropped me at my hotel at quarter-past-six. Daylight was spent. The evening sky was already dark and filling with a glitter of stars. In the room next to mine on the second floor or maybe across the hall, I was not sure how close, a baby was crying. The sound surprised me because I had not seen any children in the hotel, or anyone other than Blake on our floor, since we had arrived. In my room, I phoned the Embassy. Ambassador Durhlmann was still in his office and more agitated than usual.

"I just got off the horn with the Secretary. The Secretary," he emphasized. "That's not a happy camper, Joe. Neither is his boss. The disappearance is causing big waves in Washington. Have you found anything to help us out of this mess?"

I considered how I should respond. What was clear was the police were already looking for Hightower, and he was on his way North to find the rebels. The police were not following me yet, as far as I could tell, but it was only a matter of time. Triple S was certainly eavesdropping on our phone calls. I was not about to reveal over an open phone line Hightower's likely new direction, but I had to give the Ambassador something.

"I have a lead I want to follow, sir."

"I hope it's a good one."

"I think it is. Try to follow me on this, sir," I said. "It'll sound a little silly, like a puzzle. But there's good reason for it."

"Go ahead, Joe. Lay it out."

"When I got up here, let's say the cupboard was bare. No breadcrumbs, nothing. But I found one clue. It's distance specific and means I need to go from Raleigh to Richmond. Everything points to the South's old capital as the next stop on the train." I figured it would take the plodders at Triple S a day to decipher what I was talking about – if they bothered trying at all. It took the Ambassador only seconds to catch on. The idea seemed to give him hope and excite him.

"Well, if that's the way out of this mess, then go for it, man!" he said. "Just keep me in the loop. Time is running out, Joe. Security in your neck of the woods is sliding downhill fast. I assured the Secretary we had our best officer on the case."

"Will do, sir," I said and hung up.

It was six-thirty. Blake and I were to have dinner at eight. I phoned an Umbikan lawyer I knew and arranged to have a drink with him in the hotel's bar at seven. For a few minutes, I lay on my side on one of the twin beds to rest. I gazed up at the ceiling, sorting out in my mind what I wanted to take away from my meeting with this lawyer. In a high corner of the room, my attention was drawn to an intricate cobweb. The web was almost as large as my hand and dense like a silky nest. It was not the discovery a guest expects to find at the best hotel in town, but there it was. I figured from its dark edges that the web had been there for some time.

I was curious to see what was inside. I lifted my head and blew a lung of air towards the muddle of filaments six feet away. If a spider were hiding there, or a gecko, I was hoping to arouse it a little, make it curious enough to poke its head out. Yet even the thinnest strands remained still against my breath, I got not as much as a flutter. I formed my lips into a perfect circle and exhaled again, as hard as I could, but the web refused to budge. No movement, nothing coming out to see what was going on. I raised myself off the bed and tried a third blow, a long hard effort, but only got the return of my headache.

Lying flat again, I shifted my gaze from the web to the ceiling directly above me. I let my eyes lose focus, so my mind could drift beyond any thoughts of the web or Hightower or my meeting with the lawyer. Instead, I imagined my body passing through the hotel roof and rising up into the starry night sky. I imagined floating high above the city, only the pinpoint lights of Katembeyna below me and the endless array of stars above. As a Foreign Service Officer, I had travelled a lot. I had overnighted in many hotels across Africa and lain on many rented beds. I had stared at more blank ceilings than I cared to remember, and plenty of times, before falling asleep, I had wondered how, among all the possibilities in the universe, I had ended up on that particular bed, in that particular hotel room, on that particular night, at that particular moment in my life. The only explanation I ever came up with in all of my travels, the only explanation that made any sense, was that everyone had to be somewhere.

Just before seven, I got up from my bed, slipped on shoes, and walked two flights down to the lobby. No one was in the lobby when I got there, no guests, no porters, not even the concierge. I crossed in front of the reception desk and turned down a long hallway, past floor-to-ceiling windows of the hotel's gift shop and travel agency. Both businesses were dark, closed for the night. The hallway then curved left, ending on one side at double doors going into the restaurant, where I would meet Blake at eight. Across from the restaurant was a single door to the hotel's bar. Over the door hung a sign made of wood. Carved in cursive letters and outlined in yellow paint was *Lake Ziwa's Zazzy Lounge*. Rifts of African electro-jazz pulsated behind the door. I went inside.

The room was in the shape of a triangle, each wall about the same length. Behind the bar, against the wall to my left, were shelves of liquor bottles and empty glasses. Straight ahead, a series of wide curtained windows was the second wall. The windows looked out onto the hotel parking lot, though their burgundy curtains had been drawn over the glass, except for a narrow slit at the middle. To my right, the third wall was blue felt, floor to ceiling, decorated with several black and white photos of famous jazz icons, such as Louis Armstrong, John Coltrane, and Dizzy Gillespie. Music was coming from a boom box on the bar, near the bartender, a honey-skinned Asian man in a pink shirt and black bow tie. Three white men sat on stools at the far end of the bar, their suit coats and ties piled neatly on an empty chair. At the center of the room, four Asian men in suits drank cocktails and beers around two square tables pushed together. Empty bottles and glasses crowded the limited table space. The whites at the bar spoke quietly, individual words impossible to hear. The banter among the Asians, however, was loud and animated. They seemed to be arguing sports. I was glad to hear it. The noise suited my purposes fine. I did not want anyone to overhear my conversation with the lawyer.

"You are most welcome," said the bartender when I came in. He had an Indian or Pakistani accent. "What is it tonight?"

I ordered a whiskey and carried the glass to a chrome table near the blue wall. Except for the bartender and me, everyone held a cigarette or had one burning in an ashtray. Silver smoke hovered in the room like a gathering storm cloud, chest-high. At seven-fifteen, Tommy Nguru walked in. I waved him over and asked, "What can I get you?"

"I prefer a light," Tommy said, "something imported."

Tommy Nguru practiced law in the capital city, but he also had an office in Katembeyna, his hometown. I was introduced to him at the Embassy's Fourth of July picnic earlier in the year, after reading several classified reports laying out important political and legal perspectives he had provided the Embassy over the years. Tommy had attended a small college in Texas on a church scholarship, and that U.S. connection had led him to a series of friendships with officers at the Embassy.

I returned to our table with a green bottle of beer and an empty glass. "Asante sana," Tommy said and poured the amber liquid into his glass, carefully angling the glass and the bottle neck to create as little foam as possible. A trick, he said, he had learned as a student in the U.S.

Two men entered the lounge, dressed in matching brown suits. They were short and heavy-set, and remained standing at the end of the bar, even though empty stools and tables were available. The bartender glanced at the two when they came in, but he made no move to serve them.

"Don't turn around," I said to Tommy. "Looks like Triple S followed you here."

Tommy nodded. "They've been on me for days," he said. "When I pass my door, they follow."

"Is the League a target now?" I asked, referring to a small group of activist lawyers who only months earlier had founded Umbika's first human rights organization. Tommy was secretary of the group.

"They are on us all – the general secretary and the electeds. They wait outside our homes and offices."

"Has anyone been threatened?"

"We feel no more danger than others," he said. He turned his chair enough to look directly at the two agents standing at the bar. "The Life President is waiting for the League to buckle. He thinks harassment will fill us with panic and end us. He believes he can stop fish eagles with brown hippos, like those two old men at the bar. But hippos are fat and lazy. And there are more eagles than J.J. knows, many more." Tommy's voice sounded strong and confident, without any loose threads, no trace of indecision or fear. "When you rang me, Joe, you said nothing of what concerns you. I am assuming it is important."

I nodded and deliberately looked towards the men in brown at the bar, but when I did, they looked away. "Did an American journalist come to see you," I asked.

"The one who is Maurice."

"Yes," I said, my interest aroused by Tommy Nguru's sighting of our missing man. "He was coming to Kat, so I gave him your name."

"Maurice stopped in my office on Wednesday – the day before the 'hiccup' at the court. That's what the government is calling the murder of a hundred Tologs – a hiccup." Tommy shook his head, as a long-time cynic might. He took a swallow from his glass and looked to the bar. "Maurice was a bit rude at first. He asked me, 'Was I proud to live where the color of my skin was not an issue?'" Tommy shook his head again. "That one knows nothing about us. I told him this is a fine place to live – if you are brown and Umbik. He told me he was a guest of the Life President, so I tended my words." Tommy took out a pack of Marlboros, lit one, and blew a perfect ring of smoke. I assumed another trick picked up in the U.S. "I said to Maurice, 'Come live in the North with us, where hippos follow you night and day. Come if you want to be hanged as a confusionist, like Wisdom Chitsaya will be.'"

"What did he say?"

"He became angry."

I nodded. "He doesn't like it when someone disagrees with him."

Tommy laughed. But what escaped from within his chest was not the sound of someone having fun. More the murmur of someone being consumed by despair. The confidence Tommy had shown minutes earlier had deserted him. "Maurice said, I should see how bad living is in the U.S., for someone with dark skin like mine. But I told him, even the darkest African would sacrifice anything to be in America."

"What did he answer?"

"He said I've seen too many Hollywood movies. Ha."

"Did you tell him you met your wife in the States?"

Tommy shook his head. When I asked him why not, he shrugged. "Your blacks do not understand their good fortune," he said. I checked my watch; it was eight o'clock. Blake would be waiting in the restaurant.

"Mr. Hightower is missing," I said. Tommy looked surprised.

"Missing, how?"

"He checked out of his hotel, but never returned to the capital." Tommy's dark eyes stared into the distance, not at the Triple S hippos at the bar, but beyond the burgundy curtains far across the room, as if he could see suspicious movement in the parking lot.

"I saw Maurice a second time – at my office," he said, "Thursday past. But only a minute. Maurice was shaky-shaky. Like malaria, but no fever. I thought he was ill, but he said he had only now come from the High Court. Then, I understood. I had heard the guns from my window."

"Why did he see you again?" Tommy cocked his head to one side. It was an Umbikan reflex I had seen before. He knew something important, but he was not sure if he should share it.

I persisted. "Why did he see you a second time?"

Tommy leaned in closer. "He asked me to fix a meeting with the other side – with the ones who went to the village of the Speaker."

"You can arrange a meeting like that?"

"Of course not – I want no part in violence. The gun and machete is not our answer. I only offer advice." Tommy's voice again turned to whisper. I could barely hear him, even though our heads were nearly touching. "I told him, 'A journalist could drive to JiJi. If UFreeMo wants to meet, they will find you, if it is safe.'"

"Do you think he went north?"

Tommy Nguru finished the last of his beer and got up from the table. "I do not know," he said. "I must leave now. My wife is one to worry."

We shook hands. I watched Tommy cross back to the other side of the room, through layers of cigarette smoke. Shortly after he was out the door, the two men in brown suits followed in his wake. I pushed back my chair, drew a bill from my wallet, and placed it on the table. The meeting had been good. It confirmed my suspicion about Hightower's next move.

Chapter 33
Rome

Blake never showed for dinner. I waited until eight-thirty before ordering food, and by then, I was the only customer left in the dining room. When I finished, it was after nine. On the way to my room, I stopped at the front desk to check for messages, but there was nothing. That night, I had trouble falling asleep again. I was concerned about the mess I had put the Ambassador in, but more so, it was the whereabouts of Blake and Hightower I worried about. The last thing I remember before drifting off was thinking about the day Claire and I flew into Washington after two years in Nigeria.

Lagos was my first tour abroad as a junior officer. It was also the first time either Claire or I had been out of the U.S. We had left for Africa less than a year after we were married and returned two years later on a gray Sunday morning, a couple of weeks before Christmas. When we got off the plane, our clothing smelled stale. Our eyes were red and swollen from too little sleep. Our bodies ached. But we were excited to be home again. The Immigration Officer at Dulles stamped our black passports and handed them to us. "Welcome back," he said with a smile. I felt on top of the world. Claire said she felt the same. We were only twenty-six years old, but we had accomplished something important to the both of us. We had honorably represented our country abroad, in a strange and mysterious part of the world we had known little about. Most of all, we had done it together.

Outside the arrivals terminal, we took a Red Top Cab to a Howard Johnson a block off DuPont Circle. Our plan was to stay there until we found a furnished apartment we could lease through March. Travel orders had us leaving the U.S. on the first of April. My onward assignment was the American Embassy in Rome, a reward post for a job well done in Lagos. On our drive into Washington, Claire pointed out the bleakness of the Virginia landscape. How difficult it was to distinguish the grays along the road from the browns and blacks. Nothing was like the scene we had left in Africa. No brightness here in DC – not even primary or secondary colors. Claire said, if despair were a color it would be the color of the lifeless shrubs we saw on our way to the hotel. Making matters worse, ominous clouds swirled overhead, some dropping low enough to touch the barren tree branches. December in Washington was not supposed to be this depressing, but our transatlantic pilot had warned us that winter had arrived early in the U.S. An arctic front had slipped down from Canada earlier in the month, pushing hard on the eastern seaboard. The first big snowstorm of the season was expected to hit the region in less than a week.

"I'd forgotten what it was like in the District between fall and winter," Claire said. "Maybe a fresh blanket of white will help."

"Not to worry," I promised her. "Rome will be great."

But we never made it to Rome that spring. There was the accident. And the next few months of winter were the most difficult months of my life.

The first morning in Katembeyna I was up at five. By seven, I had finished breakfast and gone outside. Fred was standing in the parking lot next to our Land Rover, the rear door already open for me. "I'm sorry you're missing church," I said to him.

"It is not a problem, sir," Fred replied and slid in behind the steering wheel. "My wife will go for both." I got in back and set my briefcase, two water bottles, and a plastic sack of snacks on the backseat. I asked if we had a full tank of gas.

"I topped off last night, sir."

"Blake never returned to the hotel overnight. Did you see Maxwell at the hostel?"

"He was there last night," Fred said, "and this morning. But Mr. Blake took his vehicle."

"Did Maxwell say where Blake was going?"

"No, sir."

I then explained to Fred that the best lead we had for finding Hightower was the rebel town of JiJi. His eyes immediately revealed uneasiness. We talked about Fred's reluctance to travel there and the danger Hightower was in. "I could really use your help when we get up there, Fred. I have no good idea where he might be."

Something sparked in Fred, because he shifted into gear and started us off. "We are there in three hours, sir."

We drove for two blocks, under a canopy of purple jacaranda blossoms. The petals revealed only a blush of color, but were ready to explode into a deeper hue once the spring rains arrived. Fred eased us onto Loyalty Way, the town's main thoroughfare. North of town, Loyalty Way ran parallel to the river and became the M-2 highway. I leaned back in my seat and let my eyes rest. Soon, my mind followed. Fred's promise of three hours to JiJi made me optimistic again. It was still possible to salvage at least some of the Hightower visit. We could be in JiJi by ten o'clock, find our missing man, get him to a phone to call anxious family back home, and then return to Katembeyna before nightfall. Once Hightower's family knew he was safe, the worst of it would be over.

At the northern edge of town, Fred steered through a succession of six roundabouts, and by the last sweeping turn, my stomach had gone sour again. I took large swallows of bottled water and set my gaze on the horizon for balance. I had never before travelled north beyond Katembeyna. The scenery was pleasant. Hundreds of small holder farms spread out on both sides of the highway, as far as the eye could see. The individual farming plots were outlined with white strings in a grid pattern, the shifting contours of land looking like enormous pieces of graph paper. Each tract had been seeded and was waiting for rain. Fred claimed the coffee-brown soil in this region was so rich and fertile you could cut off a tree branch, stick it in the ground, and watch it grow.

The Jito River was always within sight from the highway. The river was the country's main waterway, its headwaters far to the north, in the Highlands. The Jito meandered south from the Highlands for five hundred miles through the heartland of Umbika, much like the M-2 itself. From Katembeyna south to the capital, the river and the highway were only a mile apart, but north of Kat where we were, and all the way to the Highlands, no more than a hundred yards separated the highway from the river.

One hour north of Katembeyna we entered the Lower Jito Valley. Its straw-colored hills rose gradually on either side of the highway. To our left, egrets stood along the muddy shoreline. Black and white fish eagles perched on a dead branch high above them. The water level in the river was low, on account of the dry season, but a steady current still pushed southward at midstream. Beyond the river, turkey vultures circled on warm updrafts rising off the sunlit hills, as our wide tires caressed the even pavement of the M-2. The soothing sound of the rubber tread carried me near to sleep again.

Then, thwack! My briefcase slid off the backseat. I snapped awake. Fred had braked heavily, coming out of a curve. Up ahead, a large tree branch lay in the middle of the road, blocking our way. The limb had been hacked violently from its trunk, the cut end facing us like a fist of white splinters, the sharp spikes daring us to pass.

Chapter 34
Substation

"I am sorry, sir," Fred's voice strained to reach the back seat. "Explorers ahead!"

Four menacing NEG thugs were standing beside the branch that blocked our way. Each was pointing his AK-47 at our approach in a ready position, posing frozen like four deadly marionettes. "Explorers should not be so far north," Fred added, his voice unsteady "Traffic police run the stops here."

"Just pull up to the tree in the road," I said, trying to remain calm. "We haven't done anything wrong. I'll sort this out."

A big rig pulling an empty trailer was in the process of turning around ahead of us, apparently having been ordered to return south. We rolled past the truck and stopped in front of the sharp end of the felled branch. Off to our left, between the highway and the river, were six more NEGs, seated in chairs around a folding table. They were playing cards and listening to music from a portable radio. None paid any attention to us. A piece of fabric, possibly a large blanket, had been tied as an awning between two trees on either side of the card table, offering the soldiers an island of shade. Behind them was parked a military truck, hand painted in camouflage, greens and tans and browns. One of the NEGs on the road approached us.

"Good morning," Fred said in the local language. The young Explorer, in his late teens, did not answer. He peered into our vehicle, first at Fred, then at me. He raised two fingers towards his comrades. Then, he walked full circle around our car. A second NEG, slightly older, looked at our license plate and wrote something in a small notepad he had taken from his chest pocket.

"What is your business?" the second NEG demanded, at Fred's side of the car.

"We are finding an American, who is missing," Fred replied politely. "I am taking my boss in the direction of JiJi." The man considered Fred's response. Then, he straightened.

"You cannot go to JiJi today," he said, dismissively. "Come back tomorrow."

I did not wait for Fred to reply. I slid over and leaned my head and forearm out the window. I handed the young man my business card, the gold American eagle glinting sunlight. "You can keep that," I said, pointing at the card. "I'm from the American Embassy, in the capital. Yesterday, I met with Peterson Mwenda, Commissioner of the National Police."

"I know Mwenda," the man said, rubbing his fat brown thumb over the embossed gold eagle on my card.

"You are most welcome," I said. "My business is official and extremely urgent. The Commissioner was very helpful. He advised me to look for our missing American near the lake. He assured me there were no problems on the road." Although I could not see the man's eyes through his sunglasses, he seemed to be studying my card closely. "We don't have to go to JiJi, if the road is closed," I continued. "We only need to get to Lake Ziwa. I know there's a cut-off to the shore road, before we reach the High Bridge." It was stretching the truth again, but I plowed forward. "Our travel is authorized by the Police Commissioner himself."

The man left without saying another word. He walked to the card table and gave my business card to an older man who was holding a full hand of playing cards. The two NEGs talked for a minute. Then, the younger one returned to our car.

"Confusionists are creating problems at JiJi," he said. "It is dangerous to be travelling now."

"Is it?" Fred replied, exaggerating his concern. I could see Fred's reflection in the man's inky lenses.

"You met with the Police Commissioner?" the man said.

"I did, yesterday."

"You will go only to the lake?"

"Yes, only the lake."

"Not to JiJi."

"No, sir. Not to JiJi."

"You know the cut-off to the lake?"

"I know it. I've driven it before," I said – another lie. I had only seen it on my map. "It's not far up the road from here, maybe an hour."

The officer nodded. "If you go beyond our position, we cannot be responsible for your safety. There are confusionists in JiJi District. The road is not safe."

"I understand," I said with a smile. "Thank you for your assistance." The man gestured to the other NEGs standing on the road, and they pulled back the ugly branch. Fred did not wait for instructions. He let out the clutch and drove around the barrier. A minute later, we were back to cruising speed. I patted Fred on the shoulder. "Good work back there," I said.

We drove another hour before coming to a small bridge, a solid concrete structure from the colonial era. Fifty feet long, but barely wide enough for two cars to pass at once – a spot where head-on collisions seemed inevitable at night. Under the bridge, a stream flowed right to left, crystal clear water from Lake Ziwa sixty miles away. The stream fed the much wider Jito River, no more than a stone's throw to our left.

"Why haven't we seen any road traffic?" I asked Fred.

"I cannot say with assurance, sir. It is Sunday."

"Even so, we should have passed someone."

"It could be Explorers have blocked the north road as well, sir."

We rolled across the small bridge. Fred pointed to graffiti on the concrete siding. A painted black fish eagle was outlined in white, its wings spread. Beneath the bird was the word "UFreeMo" in bright red. Here was the first evidence we had entered rebel territory. Just past the bridge we came to a telephone substation, on the right side of the road. It had the size and look of a small shed – block walls, no windows, a steel door and tin roof. Beside the substation was one lone telephone pole. Thick black telephone wires came off the tin roof and connected to the top of the pole. The wires continued north and south, linking other poles along the M-2. There was also a second wire coming off the roof. Thinner than the first and gray, it disappeared to the east, carried on poles standing parallel to an old tarmac road. Most travelers would pass the substation and never notice the side road, or next to it the small signpost in the shape of an arrow with the words "TO LAKE ZIWA" painted on it. This was the route I had assured the NEG at the checkpoint we would be taking to find our missing American. But Fred did not slow for a turn off. He made no move to exit the M-2. He continued straight ahead, towards JiJi, the direction he knew all along we would keep to. I loosened my tie, took off my jacket. I had no alternate plan if JiJi was another dead end. But I told myself we would never return to the capital city defeated. We were close to finding our missing man, and we would not give up until we did.

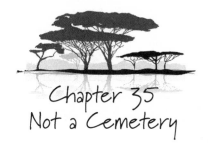

Chapter 35
Not a Cemetery

Though nearly blinding us in the empty sky, the mid-morning sun also warmed our fine leather seats, so I lowered my window to let in a cooling breeze. The incoming air carried a definite fragrance of pine needles. We were getting closer to the Highlands and its dense primordial forests. I was daydreaming now and staring blankly at the shift knob, thinking about the next steps in our search, when Fred grabbed the shifter, giving me just the extra second of warning I needed to brace myself and reach for the safety strap over my head. Fred quickly downshifted, rapidly slowing our speed. I looked ahead, expecting to see another tree branch blocking the road, or a disabled car or truck in our path, perhaps a pedestrian skittering across our blacktop, all common risks when driving on the Continent. There was nothing up ahead, no people at all, only the long dark strip of asphalt pointed north. Fred yanked hard on the steering wheel, angling us onto the gravel shoulder. Soon, all four tires were off the road, bouncing us roughly over untilled field.

"What are you doing?" I shouted, my hand clinging to the safety strap.

"There!" Fred said, raising his hand off the shifter to point towards the river. I saw nothing unusual there, only scrub trees and a dense tangle of bushes at the water's edge. The Jito appeared as nothing more than reflected light, a shimmering thread glimpsed through narrow openings in the brush. It was towards one of these openings to the river Fred was aiming us. "See!" Fred cried. "There!"

I finally spotted what Fred was frantic over – colorful objects bobbing near the riverbank. How he had noticed them from the highway, seventy yards away, was anyone's guess. We stopped atop a knoll of dry wheat-colored grass, just short of where the plateau dropped off precipitously to the muddy shoreline below. The intricate weave of the river's many gray currents was easy to appreciate now so close to the water.

"Oh, Lord!" Fred gasped.

For a moment he sat stunned behind the wheel. Then, he shut down the engine and sprang from the vehicle. He jumped to the shoreline. Before I was out of the car myself, Fred was moving waist deep in the shimmering water. He waded towards an enormous fallen tree, downed by lightning years earlier, its bare branches and wide trunk half submerged in the shifting water. Fred reached out and unhooked a piece of blue fabric snagged on the tip of a limb. With the fabric came the body of a small Ebony-skinned boy, a Tolog. Fred carried the body to shore and handed it up to me. I laid the dead child on the dry bed of grass. Fred headed back into the water, towards another swatch of color entangled on the tree. "Keep steady, sir," Fred directed from the river. "There are more to pick. But creatures could be approaching me – in the water or grass. You must stay alert."

Waiting on the knoll above the river, I watched the river intently, its deepest shadows alternating gray and blue. Was I seeing real movement below the surface, a threat to Fred, or only random reflections in an ever-changing current? I wasn't sure. Crocodiles and hippos were common along Umbika's riverbanks – as common as cobras and pythons. Any of them could be hidden, out of sight, lurking in the thicket of grass around me, or submerged in the dark shadows at the tree trunk. During my years in Africa, I had been taught to let the ears hear what the eyes can't see. So, I listened. I listened to the wind, to the water, to the blades of grass. I listened to my own breathing. But no sound was out of place. Danger, I also reminded myself, might be nowhere near us at all. Uncertainty – that was one of the great mysteries of Africa.

More so than anywhere else on the planet, in Africa you never knew what might happen next.

Fred waded towards a shirt caught on a branch. He tore the white sleeve and freed a second boy, though a corner of the fabric stuck to a twig like a tiny flag of surrender. Fred carried the boy back to shore and lifted him into my arms. I laid the second body next to the first. Two tiny orphans, resting side by side on a mattress of dry grass, as if napping in the warm sun. But there was evidence of nightmares in their sleep. Powerful bullets had entered the boys' ribcages and burst out through their spines. The damage was vicious. I tried to understand how something so horrible could happen to children.

"Look!" I called to Fred and pointed upstream. More colors were approaching in the current, a bob of purple, another pink, something green. Fred waded towards them, moving deeper into the river. When the muddy bottom fell away, darker water rose past his waist. The currents were strong mid-channel, even for the dry season. Fred's frame was much thinner than mine and too buoyant to keep his legs planted for long. His feet began to bounce off the bottom. Water reached Fred's ribcage. Despite his best effort to fight it, the river was forcing him downstream. "Come back!" I yelled.

"Thank you, sir!" He waved.

"I mean it! The water's too dangerous!"

"I am there!" He was five feet from a body in a purple shirt, but the river was deepening even faster than Fred's advance. The water approached his chest.

"Can you swim?" I shouted.

Fred's balance was struggling against the undercurrent. It seemed like the force of the entire Jito was pulling him downriver. He reached for the purple shirt, but the water's force spun him half circle, pushing at his knees and waist. In seconds, Fred was fifteen feet farther downstream. The river was too deep where he was, the current too strong. The look of failure on Fred's face was heartbreaking. He knew he would never reach the three bodies before they floated past. He spit out a mouthful of water. "I am returning, sir!" he called.

Maybe it was Fred's brave effort or the boys' broken bodies. Maybe it was my having been a lifeguard for two summers in college. An impulse took hold of me. I quickly pulled off my shoes and socks, removed my shirt and pants. Fred stumbled out of the water, two hundred feet downstream, and he collapsed on the riverbank. I put my shoes back on, and wearing only white underpants and black wingtips, I limped out into the current. Remembering what Fred had said about creatures hiding in the shadows, I scanned the water's surface, looking for anything unusual. By the time the river reached halfway up my thighs, I realized I was far enough away from shore that I could never get out of the water fast enough if a crocodile or hippo came for me. The hopelessness of that possibility provided its own odd relief, and I began to move with less caution and more urgency.

The water was colder than I expected, especially deep below the shiny surface. A chill pressed against my testicles, as if the river had turned to ice. As the water rose above my waist, I found it harder and harder to breathe. When I got to the middle of the river, water covered my chest.   Purple and pink fabrics had already floated by. I was able to reach for the last one, an old man in a green jacket. I grabbed him at the ankle and pulled him back to shallower water. I left him floating at the riverbank and waded over to the tree. A striped piece of clothing, a woman's blouse, was hooked on a branch. I unhooked it, but the blouse was empty. I maneuvered around the tree, over to the far side. Two bodies lay trapped in a tangle of branches. They were larger than the boys or the old man. Heads were submerged, but the wide hips floating at the surface said they were female. One was naked from the waist down.

I broke a branch to free the lady dressed in a yellow skirt. I did the same for the other, who was wearing only a red top. Interlocking my arms with an arm from each, I towed yellow and red to shore and used a sidestroke kick when the river's bottom fell away. Their dark skin had begun to decompose, swelling the arms and legs like balloons, but it also added buoyancy and made it easier for me to move them, which meant I could devote more energy to fighting an undercurrent that seemed determined to carry us all downstream.

Fred and I worked together to lift the women and the old man up the embankment. We lined them beside the boys, making an uneven row of five. They had been in the water at most a day, but the smell of death was already in the air, as was the faint smell of sulfur. Four had been shot in the chest. The woman in the yellow skirt had also lost part of her forehead. Fred brought his jacket from the car and covered the woman-in-red's private parts. Then, he knelt on the grass and prayed. I laid my shoes on the warm hood of the Land Rover, hoping to dry them before I needed to wear them again. I rung out my underwear and laid it beside my shoes. I stood naked for a few minutes, drying in the warm air. Then, I put on my pants, socks, and shirt and asked Fred what he thought had happened.

"It is part and parcel of the trouble at the court," Fred said, sadly.

"But the bodies came from upstream," I said. "You think UFreeMo did this?"

"Those four are Tolog," he said, pointing at the dead. "But this one, she wears an Umbik dress, but an Umbik from the North." The subtleties Fred described were details I simply could not recognize.

I asked him again if the rebels had done this.

"UFreeMo does not shoot women and children. UFreeMo is not the guilty party. I cannot say who is." I wanted to remind Fred that UFreeMo had already killed six villagers at the Speaker of Parliament's home, but now was not the time. Fred knelt beside one little boy and folded his arms over his chest.

"We better get on the road," I said. "It's quarter past twelve."

"You are most welcome, sir," Fred said, but didn't move.

"I'll report this to the police in JiJi."

"We must bury them," Fred said matter-of-factly.

I shook my head. The day was slipping away, and we still had much to do. We did not have time to bury anyone. "We have to get to JiJi and find Mr. Hightower," I said. "I'll tell the police where the bodies are. They can investigate."

"Police will not investigate," Fred said.

"Of course, they will. These people were murdered."

"The government will not come."

"Look, our mission is to find Mr. Hightower. I don't want to miss him in JiJi. And I don't want to be driving on the road after dark." Fred smoothed wrinkles on the lady's yellow skirt. He fiddled with the collar on the old man's green jacket. He was wasting time and not listening to me anymore. "This is not a cemetery," I reminded Fred. "How are we supposed to bury them?"

Fred got up and bowed, like he was trying to please me. He scurried over to the Land Rover and reached under the back seat, where he pulled out a green shovel, an army tool that folded on itself, a soldier's implement designed to be tucked inside a backpack, used for digging a foxhole or field latrine. Every U.S. Embassy vehicle in Umbika carried a shovel like this in case of a breakdown. Never knowing what might happen next, we also carried a hand ax, three road flares, a couple of blankets, and a trauma kit. Fred unfolded the shovel's steel blade and screwed it tightly into the short, wooden handle. When he was done, he proudly held it out in front of himself, like an Eagle Scout showing someone a special knot completed for a merit badge.

"Okay, okay," I relented. "We'll bury them. But we have to work fast."

Fred was immensely satisfied. He began digging with the shovel at the head of the first boy. A few shovels full became a mound. I joined him on my knees, pulling soil out of the expanding trench with my bare hands. It took two hours to dig five graves. I lifted the first boy into a hole his size and pushed dirt over him. I followed with the others, one by one. Fred fashioned crosses out of driftwood and braids of dry grass. When all five were secure in the ground, we pressed a cross into each mound of soft earth above them and laid out a rectangle of river rocks around the entire plot, like an elegant necklace of gray pearls. Then, Fred got on his knees and prayed again.

After our makeshift funeral, we drove across the same uneven ground we had taken to get to the river. Bouncing out of the last ditch, our tires reached for the smooth blacktop of the M-2, the thick rubber treads catching hold and not letting go, as if they knew how desperate we were to escape the horrors we had witnessed. "You were right," I said, when we were riding steady on the highway again. "We couldn't have left without burying them."

I put my hand on Fred's shoulder, but he didn't say anything. He was crying.

Chapter 36
The High Bridge

I put the burial behind us and returned to my worries about Maurice Hightower. It was half-past-two. The air was the most comfortable it had been all day, but the sun was no longer directly above us. It had slid to the west, into its declining arc towards evening. I lamented the fact we should have been in JiJi hours earlier, found our missing man, and already been on our way south to Katembeyna. But our direction was still pointed north, and we were empty-handed. There was time enough to find Hightower and be back in the city before dark, but it would be cutting things close.

We still had not seen another vehicle since the trailer truck turned back at the checkpoint in the morning. I suspected Fred was right, the NEGs had shut down traffic both ways because of the trouble at the court, but there was no way of knowing for certain. Commercial radio reception was spotty this far north, and what little radio we heard was recorded music, not news. Until we got to JiJi, there was no way to contact anyone at the Embassy and find out what was happening. All we had in our 4x4 was the factory-installed AM radio and the Embassy's emergency FM transceiver, top range 60 miles.

To our left, an organized line of pines blocked a clear view to the river. Early in the 20th Century, lumber was Umbika's most profitable commodity.

British logging companies planted millions of saplings, pine and ash, throughout the Northern Province, a region already thickly forested. Over the years, volunteer seedlings had sprung up along the M-2 and grown to fifty and sixty feet tall now. Through a few breaks in these trees, I could see the river had widened. I checked my map for our location. I found where the Jito came in from the west, turned 90-degrees, and widened like a small lake within itself, maybe a quarter mile across, a noticeable bulge, similar to what an animal caught in the belly of a python looks like.

Flakes of golden sunlight reflected off the lake's surface through the trees to our left, nearly blinding us. I had never seen the Jito as stunning or peaceful as it appeared now. Ahead of us, the highway inclined gradually. According to my map, a mile in the distance the road would curve left, right, and then left again, matching the turns in the river. As we drove over a rise in the road, the four steel towers of the High Bridge came into view in the distance. The bridge was the official gateway to the Highlands. Behind the four towers, ancient green mountains stretched up into a deep blue sky. Bursts of light and shade danced across the emerald slopes. Before now, I had never seen the High Bridge or these mountains. As we approached, the sight filled me with awe. Yet, even more so, I had my first feeling of accomplishment in a long time. Reaching the Highlands was a milestone for us, a sign of progress, the encouragement we desperately needed. For the first time in days, I felt like I could relax a little. We were closer than ever to reclaiming our guest and setting things right. The town of JiJi was only thirty miles up the highway. I breathed in the cool mountain air, the rich smell of pine.

The Land Rover moved into a sweeping turn. Beside us, the trees quickly thinned out, and a steep embankment sloping down thirty feet to the water's edge came into view. The angle of sunlight hitting the river changed too. Dancing reflections that had captivated me minutes earlier were gone. The water was gray and dull again. The small lake within the river now spread out to the side of us. What I saw, then, made me gasp. I struggled to breathe. Bobbing in the middle of the lake were scores of dark-skinned bodies, like the five we had just buried, a new and much larger caravan of death held together by the pull of the Jito's current. There were too many bodies to count now, maybe a hundred, maybe two. Most were caught in the middle of the wide sweep of water, where the current was strongest. Some had been flung beyond the channel and were floating along the lakeshore, in shallow pools below us. A sudden sickness rose from my stomach to my throat, the acid burning my mouth.

Fred had been alerted by my gasp. His foot eased from the accelerator, and the Land Rover coasted into the next curve. "This is more than we can bury," I said to him, not realizing the absurdity of my statement. "Keep driving!" I commanded, "Just keep driving. We'll tell the police in JiJi." Fred pushed on the accelerator. No protest this time. The car lunged forward. We had already witnessed so much since leaving the hotel, enough for me to draft a couple of "Immediate" cables to Washington, when I got back to the Embassy. I grabbed my notebook and pen. I had to record the details now of what we had seen or they would become a jumble in my head. I put my pen to a fresh page, but my hand seemed frozen. I could not decide where to begin taking notes.

I squeezed out a few sentences, as the M-2 straightened again. Now, we were entering a long downward slope to the High Bridge, a straight shot through rows of dark pines bordering the highway. The steel superstructure lay just in front of us, a few hundred yards away, but something on the road ahead seemed out of place. A blue and white police jeep was parked in the middle of the highway, blocking our path over the bridge. Uniforms scurried around the jeep. One figure stepped forward, a man with gold epaulets. He waved for us to stop. These were not Explorers on the road, as at the first checkpoint. These were common policemen in blue uniforms with white cuffs.

Fred stopped before the officer and rolled down his window. The officer kept his distance. "You cannot go through! The bridge is closed!" he shouted at us. "Go back!" He moved his hands in circles above his head, motioning us to turn around. Fred tried to explain our business in JiJi, but the officer wanted none of it. "Go, now!" he shouted.

I had stopped paying attention to the officer. Instead, I was focused on the bridge itself, less than half a football field away. It was an impressive piece of engineering, enormous steel pillars, massive cement footings, and hundreds of feet of braided cable as thick as my leg. At the center of the bridge was parked a flatbed trailer. Beside the trailer, two policemen were lifting a body. Two other policemen, standing on the flat bed, took the body by the legs and arms and laid it on the trailer, at the end of a row of bodies already there. More police were along the riverbank, but it was difficult to see what they were doing. I stepped out of our vehicle and moved forward.

"We need to get to JiJi," I called to the officer, though I was looking at the bridge, not at him. The officer grabbed a carbine from one of his men, and before I could say anything else, he fired. Crack! Crack! Crack! Three shots. The bullets sliced through the air just above my head, close enough for me to hear one round snap the air as it passed my ears. I raised my hands in surrender, my arms shaking without control. Smoke and the smell of gunpowder spread across the highway.

"Go out!" the officer shouted. "Bridge is closed!"

I was shaking with fear, but I will never forget the even deeper fear in the man's eyes. He was not looking at me as much as around me. He did not appear afraid of Fred and me, but of who could be coming behind us or who might emerge from the surrounding forest. I glimpsed the river for only a few seconds, but it was time enough to see a dozen policemen with white handkerchiefs tied over their nose and mouth, like bandits. They were harvesting a tangle of bodies wedged between the far riverbank and one of the supporting piers. A sort of bucket brigade had formed along the bank, the dead being handed from one officer to the next, all the way to the men standing up on the flatbed trailer. Before I could ask another question, two policemen beside the jeep raised their rifles. I jumped back into the Land Rover. "Let's get out of here," I said to Fred. "There's no way we're getting through to JiJi today. I think we've already seen more than we should have."

Fred turned the car around, and we fled south, back towards Katembeyna. I hunted for my notebook and pen and found them in the crease of the back seat. I tried to write notes, but my hand was shaking too much. For several miles, Fred and I said nothing, because nothing we could say would make any sense. We eventually passed the spot where earlier we had left the highway to bury five souls rescued from the river. I looked towards the gray water in the distance, expecting more swatches of color floating downstream, but there was nothing. I took a bottle of water and drank eagerly, my hand still quivering. I passed a second bottle up to Fred. We shared a bunch of bananas I had pilfered at breakfast and a tin of groundnuts. It was not much of a meal, but what we ate calmed us and filled our stomachs.

By half-past-four o'clock, the sun had moved far beyond its crest. Violet shadows covered the empty road in front of us. I had been writing notes for half an hour, but I set my pen aside and took out my map of Umbika. I studied an area northeast of Katembeyna. It took me a while, but I eventually found the connection I was hoping for. "Take a look at this," I said to Fred. He stopped in the middle of the deserted highway and studied the thin black line I was pointing to on the map. "It's out of the way, and hardly more than a trail," I said, "but I think it might be what we need."

"I know that one," Fred said of the tertiary road printed on my map. "There are plantations where they trade cashews."

"Is this where Wisdom Chitsaya had his farm?"

"No, sir. Chitsaya is from the other side of the river."

"Can this road get us back to Katembeyna, without the NEGs and their checkpoints bothering us?"

"That one is old, sir, but we can find tarmac, here and there. That one cannot bring us back in the rainy season, but it can now."

"Then, let's go for it," I said, and on we drove.

Soon, we turned onto the hard-pack side road from my map. The sun having slipped behind the hills to the west, a chill now descended upon the Jito Valley, as evening settled in. We rolled up our windows. It would be dark soon, and though this thin road was almost certain to be free of NEGs or police, we were still many miles from Katembeyna.

In my long history of days, the drive to the High Bridge was one of the worst days I could remember. On top of everything else that had happened since leaving the hotel this morning, I had again failed to find Maurice Hightower. I hoped Ambassador Durhlmann would see our inability to reach JiJi as nothing more than bad luck, or perhaps as another consequence of a country falling apart. Either way, he was the one who would have to answer to Washington for my failure, and I regretted that. Yet Durhlmann's being reprimanded or his disappointment in me was not what upset me most. What bothered me was the great disappointment I felt about myself. My father's strong work ethic never let me accept my own shortcomings. Riding in the back seat now, I knew I could have done things better.

I closed my eyes and realized the dangerous rhythm my heart was pounding out. I tried counting the beats, but it was a pointless game. They were coming too fast. I searched for a cadence in my heartbeat to focus on, something that was constant and regular. Something I could hold on to, like the rhythm of a familiar song – anything to help me relax.

But the horrifying images we had seen in the river kept infiltrating my thoughts – the wounds of the two little boys lying on the grassy knoll – the lady without a skirt – the one without a forehead – the mosaic of many more colors, of countless shirts and skirts, death floating in the current of the Jito River, like a shattered rainbow. The more I tried to forget the dead, the more I thought about them. My heart ached. My head ached. The beating in my chest carried up my neck and into my skull. My body refused to relax, so I sought a different strategy. Instead of thinking about my heart, I worked to slow my breathing. I closed my mouth and inhaled deeply, through my nose, slowly filling my lungs to capacity, holding the air in, then letting it seep out. Think of nothing but the flow of air in and out. I tried this pattern several times. It did not work. The smell of gunpowder still lingered over my breath.

Chapter 37
Blake

That night, we slipped into Katembeyna under cover of darkness. Fred had fussed about driving dark, but when he spotted the lights of Katembeyna, he was fine. We avoided all NEG checkpoints outside of town, but we did run into a police stop near the center of the city. The sleepy officers passed us through without a second look.

No message from Blake was waiting for me when I returned to the hotel. The concierge said I was the only "European" he had seen all day. I went to Blake's room and knocked on his door. No one answered, but a housekeeper working down the hall opened the room when I explained my concern. Blake was not there. The housekeeper said that when she cleaned the room that morning Blake's bed had not been opened from the night before. I returned to my room and telephoned Ambassador Durhlmann.

"You know, Joe, I like an officer who can think on his feet, always have," the Ambassador said immediately. "What I don't like is when he puts my ass in a sling." I had no idea what my boss was talking about, but it was clear he was upset. "You remember Lovemore Andelebe," Durhlmann said, "head of the National Police. William's father?" Only when the Ambassador was extremely perturbed did he revert to sarcasm.

"Of course, I know him."

"Lovemore came to my office today. He said you gave some Explorers a line about having special permission to go through their roadblock this morning." That Durhlmann had already heard about my encounter at the NEG checkpoint, north of Katembeyna, surprised me.

"I exaggerated the permission part. I told them what I had to, in order to find our missing man."

"Did you find him?"

"Not yet." I waited through a long pause.

"Did the Police Commissioner for the Northern Province give you permission to use his name?"

"Not in so many words," I said.

"Then, first thing tomorrow, I want you to visit the Commissioner and apologize for misrepresenting him. Lovemore advised me the M-2, north of Katembeyna, is closed to all traffic until further notice. It's a safety issue, he said."

"What did he mean, sir, a safety issue?"

"Lovemore said they're having problems with the road."

"I was all over that road today, Mr. Ambassador. Other than its centerline needing paint, it's in perfect shape. It's one of the best roads in Africa. Lovemore Andelebe's problem is with dead people in the Jito River."

"What are you talking about, Joe?"

"We saw at least a hundred bodies floating down the river, mostly women and children."

"They had drowned?"

"The river didn't kill them. They were shot and dumped in the water."

The Ambassador and I shared an awkward silence while the full effect of my news was felt on his end of the line. "My god," he said and then told me other embassies had reported hundreds of people arrested in Katembeyna during a Chitsaya rally this morning. And eight Chitsaya supporters were killed trying to rob a bank. "Has Blake filled you in on anything?" he asked.

"I haven't seen Blake since yesterday at lunch," I said. "And he hasn't been back to the hotel."

"Have you tried him on the radio?"

"We did, but his unit must be turned off."

"He hasn't contacted us, either," said Durhlmann.

"Do you want me to look for him?"

"No," the Ambassador shot back, his voice blustery cold. "I want you to stay put. I have enough to worry about."

"I think I came close to finding our man."

"Things are changing, Joe," Durhlmann said. I wasn't sure if he was talking about Hightower or something happening that I wasn't part of. "Tomorrow, after you apologize to the Police Commissioner, I want you to camp out at the hotel, sit next to your phone. I'll call at noon. I'm hoping we'll have heard from Blake by then."

Time was running out for finding Hightower, and now Blake might be in trouble too. I was not happy being stuck at the hotel. It was not the time to move cautiously, but Durhlmann's order did not surprise me. From what I knew of our ambassador, he was not a cowboy. Durhlmann was a true believer in diplomacy, always looking for what he called "the win-win," where no one loses everything. The Foreign Service was not a constant test of Durhlmann's manhood, as it was for some officers, especially political appointees. The day they tapped Durhlmann on the shoulder to be an ambassador was probably the happiest day of his life – just as he had planned it. For thirty years, he had worked his way up the promotion ladder, one rung at a time. Reading Durhlmann's résumé, you could see he had left nothing to chance. He had punched all the right boxes on his dance card – staff assistant, desk officer, hardship tour in Haiti, sabbatical year at the War College, a stretch assignment in Southeast Asia, and a few deputy assistant positions in the Department. But there is a well-known saying in the Foreign Service, about officers like Durhlmann – There are bold officers and there are old officers, but there are no bold, old officers. Over thirty years in government service, Durhlmann had never dropped America's diplomacy banner, but what real difference he had made – in even one individual's life – was open to debate. We had a good chance now to find Hightower and bring him home. Not wanting to step on any toes, however, the Ambassador had taken us out of the game.

After the phone call, I took off my clothes and lay on my bed to rest. When I awoke again, it was morning. The first pink rays of dawn glazed my windowsill. I was lying face down on the bed, naked. I remembered nothing from my sleep, no images, no dreams, not even an urge to pee. I showered, put on clean clothes, and went down to the front desk. Again, there was nothing from Blake. The hotel restaurant was open, so I got in line for the breakfast buffet, filling my plate with ham, eggs, fried potatoes, and wedges of freshly cut mangoes.

At seven o'clock, I was returning to my room, when Lew Trestle ran in through the front entrance. His long black hair was pasted against his forehead. Lines of perspiration trickled down his dust-covered face. We met on the bright red carpet at the foot of the staircase. "What's going on?" I asked. Lew rested his hands on the rail to keep his balance. He wiped his eyes with his shirtsleeve. An African couple that I had noticed our first day in Kat, when Blake and I were eating lunch, rushed in from outside and passed us without a glance, as they hurried up the staircase.

"The NEGs have roadblocks everywhere," Lew said. "They wouldn't let me bring my car in town, so I jogged the last two miles."

"Come on, Lew," I motioned. "Let's talk out back."

I led us past the gift shop and travel agency, which were just opening. We went across the restaurant patio and down a flight of steps. I stopped beside a retaining wall above the deep end of the empty swimming pool. Over us, on the veranda, a few Africans were having breakfast, but none within earshot.

"Your guy's dead," said Lew.

His unexpected words paralyzed my thoughts, made me dizzy. I needed something to grab onto, something solid, but there was only the brick wall. I leaned against it. Then, I realized I did not know if Lew meant Hightower or Blake. "Which guy are you taking about?" I asked.

"The one you're looking for – the journalist. They shot him and dumped his body in the river." I went and sat on a chair beside the pool's bar. Lew sat next to me. He was still out of breath.

"Who told you Hightower is dead?"

"A kid who carves wood for me," Lew said. "He went home to visit his family in JiJi and phoned me last night. He was really shook up. He said a lot of people had been killed in the Highlands and one was an American – a tall American with black skin. I figured it had to be your guy." My thoughts crashed into one another. Adrenaline reached every corner of my body. I could feel the wild power in my fingers and toes.

"How'd the boy know the tall black man was American?" I said, trying to appear calm.

"He heard the police in JiJi talking. They were upset that an American had been killed."

"Does the boy know who killed him?"

"No one said."

"Did he see Hightower's body?"

"No. The police only talked about an American. One who wasn't *mzungu.*"

"So, it's possible Hightower is still alive."

"I guess, it's possible, Joe. The boy saw a lot of bodies – but no American. He only heard them talking."

"Who did the shooting?" I asked again.

"Like I said, no one is saying. But if the police have your guy's body, or the NEGs have him, they'll keep that a secret as long as they can. Once word gets out someone killed an American – the Life President won't stand for it. Not the negative publicity. There'll be hell to pay for whoever did it." Lew waited for me to ask another question, but I was already planning my exit from the city. He saw the faraway look in my eyes. "If you're thinking about heading up to JiJi, you better leave soon," he said. "Something's going on in town here. I don't know what, but the NEGs are pretty worked up. Things are gonna get worse." I quickly told Lew about our visit to the High Bridge and then hurried to my room to get my map, so he could point out the villages where the boy thought the dead were from.

Fred was waiting beside the Land Rover when I came out of the hotel. It was half-past seven. I handed him a bag of things I had just purchased – a bunch of bananas, a six-pack of Coca-Cola, four bottles of water, a couple candy bars, a box of vanilla wafers. "It's not much of a picnic," I said as I got in the car, "but there's no time to stop at the market. There's trouble in town."

Fred set everything on the front seat beside him. "Yes, sir. Barriers are forming at every chokepoint," he said.

"Then, let's get on the road before they completely shut down the city. We're going back to the Highlands." Fred started the engine without protest. I pushed my briefcase across the back seat and was about to close my door when I heard someone calling my name. Across the parking lot, approaching in a gallop, was Blake. He had removed his jacket and carried it like a saddle roll under his arm. His dress shirt was ripped and dirt-stained at the sleeves, as were the knees of his pants.

"It's all falling apart," Blake said, catching his breath beside the Land Rover. "Chitsaya hanged in his cell last night. The news is spreading like a brush fire. NEGs are everywhere and more are on the way."

"Chitsaya hanged himself. Why would he do that?"

"He wouldn't," Blake said. "Whoever did, really screwed the pooch, man. There's a shit storm coming back at those bastards this time." Blake noticed the Coke and other gear on the front seat. "If you're going somewhere, the roads are a mess. Those pricks wouldn't let me through the stops, even with CD plates."

"Maurice Hightower is dead," I blurted out.

"No way," said Blake.

"I'm going up to JiJi to get the body and his personal effects."

"Man, that's a tough one," Blake said. He seemed stunned, even sad. So did Fred. "Are you sure he's dead? I didn't see that coming." I filled Blake in on what Lew Trestle had told me. I then briefed him on our drive to the High Bridge and the bodies in the river.

"The Ambassador told me to stick around the hotel today, but I have to go to JiJi – while I still can."

"He'll be pissed, Joe."

"He'll be pissed if I go or don't go. But he doesn't know yet about Hightower. Will you tell him for me?"

"I'll call him now."

"And make sure Dave Hardy activates the warden system and lets our people know what's going on." Blake had his breath back and motioned for me to follow him to the rear of the 4x4.

"I don't want Fred hearing this," Blake whispered. "The less Fred knows, the safer he'll be. But since you're going up there, I think you better hear it." He paused for a moment, deciding, I guess, if he had second thoughts about telling me. He noticed a cut on his forearm and sucked on the wound to cleanse it. "The NEGs have a couple of special units working in the Highlands," he said, finally. "They've been up there a few days." If he thought the news was going to surprise me, it did not.

"What's a special unit?" I asked.

"Death squads, Joe – probably the guys who killed the people you saw in the river. I have sources inside the Explorers. One told me J.J. sent the special units up here after the Speaker was killed. Their orders are to eliminate anyone providing assistance to UFreeMo."

"Eliminate?" I said. Blake nodded. "Jesus."

"To top it off, these guys are posing as rebels," he said. "You know, dressing like them."

"Why pretend to be rebels? That doesn't make sense. UFreeMo wouldn't kill northerners."

"Jimmy Mulenga's not a rocket scientist, but he's not stupid either. He knows the average villager will get confused by the news. They'll hear UFreeMo was seen killing people in the North. If Mulenga can discredit UFreeMo even a little, some of its supporters might turn against the rebels. But even if most people see this as another government plot, the bottom line is they will know not to cross the Life President."

My job as American Consul was limited to issuing visas and tending to Americans who needed help, nothing more dramatic than that. I had paid attention to local politics in every country I was posted to, but I never got deeper than that. Even knowing about death squads made me uncomfortable. I think Blake could see the anxiety on my face.

"You sure you have to go back up there?" he asked. "Special unit guys are cold blooded. You don't want to mess with them." Not far away, the popping sound of gunfire broke the morning stillness. "I know you like to finish things you start, Joe, but you and I can stay here and wait for the locals to hand over Hightower's body. What's the difference – you going up there or them bringing his body here? With everything that's going on, Durhlmann might want us to pull pitch and get the hell out of Dodge."

"I'm not sure Hightower's dead," I said. "If he is, I have to get his body before it's too late. Once those 'special units' figure out who they've murdered, they'll come back for the evidence. His body will disappear forever. I need to get him before they do." More gunfire sounded in the neighborhood, and it was moving closer to the hotel. "And if he's not dead, he'll need my help to get back to the Embassy."

Seconds later, a hundred terrified people were running along the narrow street adjacent to the hotel, what I imagined a cattle stampede might sound like. The chain-link fence on the edge of the property was the only thing preventing the mob from streaming across the hotel parking lot.

"You better take off," Blake said and extended his hand. "Let's plan on a nice, quiet dinner tonight."

"That's funny," I said as we shook.

Blake hurried away. I then remembered I wanted to ask him where he had been for more than a day, but he was already entering the hotel. "Get us out of here," I said to Fred. He took us to the far end of the parking lot and around a corner of the hotel. He made the turn as if he had travelled the route before, and maybe he had. At the back of the building, we slipped through a gap in a fence, the narrow opening hidden behind a maintenance garage. The back road we took was gravel and empty, except for a frightened dog running aimlessly down the middle of the lane. She was a nursing mother, her teats red and swollen, and she paused in the white dust to watch, as we flew around her.

Chapter 38
Multiparty!

From the center of the city, Fred took us northeast, circling a sizeable hill and the high-density neighborhood of neat huts covering it like a quilt. Within minutes, we had avoided two NEG checkpoints because of Fred's great anticipation and cunning use of empty lots and back passageways. The commercial center of Katembeyna receded behind us. Even at the outskirts of town, people we passed knew something was happening in the city, though the news of Chitsaya's death could not have been more than an hour or two old. Parents clutching small children darted between shops and houses. Young men gathered in open spaces at crossroads and on patches of yellow grass, their wild conversations punctuated by gestures directed towards town.

We came upon a drainage canal that forced us to stop, one of several like it laced throughout the city to control flooding. The canal was dry, but its cement containment wall was deeper and wider than the undercarriage of our vehicle would allow. We could not reach the other side from where we were. I looked up and down the canal a hundred yards in each direction, but there was nowhere for us to cross. Fred looked behind us towards the city, in the direction we had come. Plumes of black smoke were rising in the distance. "We're not going back to town," I said to him.

"No, sir." Fred shook his head. "I know where we can find our way."

We retreated around some same row houses and open fields. We grew closer to the city again, the smoke darker now and billowing overhead. We cut across a new plot of dirt, crisscrossed with footpaths. The back and forth movement of our escape was churning my stomach acid, so I followed my normal remedy – bottled water and an open window. Finally, we arrived at an old railroad bridge. Fred said it spanned the same dry drainage canal as before, now twenty feet below us. Fred eased the Land Rover over the worn ties to where we straddled the iron rails. Bouncing on more wooden ties for fifty yards, we finally reached the far side of the canal. Fred turned down a narrow road lined with mud huts, and then down an even narrower lane. He braked abruptly.

"What is it?" I asked.

Fred sat motionless, ear to the wind. In the distance, I soon heard it too, what sounded like thunder, the call of an approaching storm, though the sky was pure blue, clear and bright. This thunder increased rapidly and then turned into the roar of a lion. The fury was right behind us. In an instant, hundreds of Africans swarmed our vehicle, an angry tempest wedged between us and the nearby huts. Men, women, and children rocked our car. Moving past us, they pounded on our windows and doors. They carried machetes and hammers, waved sharp sticks and heavy clubs. Blake was right when he said a storm would descend upon Katembeyna because of Wisdom Chitsaya's death. We were in the eye of it. "They go to City Center," Fred shouted above the din. "It is for Chitsaya."

Fred rolled down his window. He shouted at the people to stop hitting our car. They ignored him. Their expressions turned from anger to bewilderment, though, when they looked inside our car and saw a *mzungu* in a suit and tie sitting in the back seat. A few stopped running and stared, making sure what they thought they were seeing was real. Even so, our vehicle was still being pounded. Fred extended his arm out his window, roof high. "We must show them we are with them!" he said and formed his fingers into the "Victory" sign. "Multiparty!" Fred shouted out his window. "Chitsaya! Chitsaya!"

I called the same refrain out my window. "Chitsaya! Multiparty!"

When the mob heard our yells, their rage turned to joy. The pounding ceased. They smiled. We were part of them. Someone started singing, and others took up the song. The mob became a war choir, a river of revolution with its own melody, flowing deep and dark and in perfect harmony through the long and narrow street. An old man with poor teeth stopped in front of our car. In his hand was a rock the size of a grapefruit, large enough to open a sizeable hole in our windshield, even with the weakest toss. He raised his arm and looked directly at me, grinning. It took a second to realize he was not intending to smash our window. He was showing off his prize and letting us know he had plans for it elsewhere.

The crowd seemed like it might keep passing around us forever, but as quickly as it had come, it was gone. Fred and I sat for a while, without moving or speaking, only watching the dust settle on our windows and hood. Then, Fred started the engine and drove until any trace of Katembeyna was behind us. Outside the city, I recognized a Catholic church and adjacent school block of red bricks. I had glimpsed them in shadows the night before. We were on the cashew road again, moving away from the city now, headed north. Our search for Maurice Hightower back on.

Chapter 39
Déjà Vu

Umbika gained independence from Britain when Africa was an important playing field for Cold War rivalries. The East and West courted dozens of newly-independent African nations, spending large sums on everything from private armies and airports to luxury sedans and hospital beds – whatever a country's leader wanted. One foray in the battle for Sub-Saharan Africa was West Germany's offer to build a suspension bridge over the Jito River, in the Northern Province. For many years, missionaries in the North had been recording rainfall amounts, river levels, and flood damage in the Jito Valley. The missionaries knew exactly how many weeks each year the roads were impassible. They knew how many villagers were prevented from accessing medical care and food distributions during the rainy season, and how many had died because of that. The Germans were aware of the Danish Parliament's commitment to building new highways in Africa, including one in Umbika's Northern Province – if the Jito's flooding problems could be resolved. A new suspension bridge could solve those problems.

When plans for the modern bridge reached Umbika's new president, he vetoed the project on two counts. First, Jimmy Mulenga reminded the Germans he had never asked for a bridge to be built in his country. Second, he told the Germans he had plenty of projects that needed funding, but none were in the North. The Germans responded with a revised offer to Mulenga – it's the bridge or nothing.

Umbika's economy was fragile, and Mulenga did not want to lose German money. He also did not want to appear to other donors as being ungrateful. He tried bargaining with the Germans behind the scenes – offering kickbacks and special favors to delegates – but when the Germans refused to budge, Mulenga's arrogance got the best of him. He went on radio and railed that "confusionists" from abroad were offering false hope to the Tologs in the North. An expensive new bridge in the Highlands was a waste of resources and would do nothing to improve Tolog lives. He compared the German Chancellor to a witless undertaker, who allows a bereaved family to place a priceless bracelet on the wrist of a corpse before burial.

The German government was not amused by the analogy. The German and Danish alliance gave Mulenga an ultimatum. He would lose funding for the bridge and the highway unless he relented. The High Bridge was completed a year after the M-2 and stood as the most magnificent suspension bridge in East Africa. The project surpassed in grandeur even the Soviet-funded hydroelectric plant recently completed in Tanzania.

The first thing anyone sees when approaching the High Bridge from the south is its four tall towers, charcoal gray in color and standing like sentinels before the Highland's lush green mountains. On a clear day, the tops of the four spires are visible from two miles away. Each tower was forged of Krupp steel and set on massive concrete piers that were sunk deep into the riverbanks. Two lanes of steel decking connect one side of the channel to the other, a span of 220 feet. For pedestrian traffic, a cement balustrade runs along each edge of the deck, the long wrought-iron handrail held up by dozens of waist-high pillars, fitted with Ionic capitals. When the Germans built the High Bridge, classical architecture was unknown in East Africa. In the minds of local villagers, the elaborate Greek flourishes on the structure make it appear otherworldly.

Even stranger is the sound the bridge makes to this day. During the rainy season, when afternoon winds pick up in the valley, vibrations along the cables create an eerie noise – a high-pitched whine – like the cry of a child. On a very windy day, the sound can carry for miles, downstream through the valley. Uneducated villagers, not understanding the physics of the phenomenon, believe the bridge is possessed by spirits. They refuse to walk across the bridge whenever it is crying. This superstition led to a start-up ferry business under the bridge. From sunrise to sunset during the rainy season, shirtless men with dug-out canoes and long poles transfer wary villagers from one shore to the other.

At 11 o'clock, Fred and I passed the small lake at the bend in the Jito River, where only a day before the dead bodies floating downstream were too numerous to count. Now, the water was as calm and clear as a mirror, its surface reflecting only blue sky. All evidence of a killing field had vanished. In this our second attempt to get to JiJi, we had encountered no checkpoints or other vehicles on our backcountry route through the cashew farms. The AM radio carried no news about what was happening in Katembeyna, only canned music. I had rehearsed a speech to give the traffic policemen once we got to the High Bridge, explaining my orders. I needed to convince them of my duty and my desperation to reach JiJi and collect the body of a dead American.

Now, on our approach, the towers of the High Bridge were in view again, the four spires rising dramatically over the pines, four knights guarding entry to some royal kingdom. Fred downshifted twice. We slowed to a crawl. Unlike the day before, no one stood on the road ahead of us now, no one waving us to halt. There was not a policeman or Explorer to be seen.

Fred slowed until our front wheels touched the concrete lip of the bridge. "Stop here," I said to him. There were no tents or tables off to the side of the highway, no trailers or trucks parked on the decking, no sign of life or death anywhere around the bridge. It was like arriving at a familiar house, finding the front door wide open, but after going inside, discovering no one there, not even furniture. The fear of an ambush crossed my mind, but the thought seemed absurd, so I let it slip away.

"We must not stay, sir," said Fred, his voice stressed and dry.

"Just for a minute," I said and got out of the vehicle.

Fred rolled down his window. "Sir, this is not good. Traffic police are always here, guarding the bridge."

Fred was right, of course. On normal days, policemen or soldiers would be posted at both approaches to the High Bridge. That was standard procedure throughout Africa; bridges had strategic importance and had to be protected at all cost. Now, in a country sliding towards civil war, when everything had to be protected, no one was here protecting anything. The bridge had been abandoned. I walked out onto the deck and stopped a quarter of the way across. I was high above the channel, a drop of thirty feet to the water below. I leaned over the balustrade, on the side facing upriver. Three dugout canoes rested below me on the near bank – part of the local ferry service. They were positioned keel up, parallel to each other, on a patch of brown mud. Their bows pointed downstream. I spotted two more vessels hidden in the reeds. On the far bank, the spot where a day earlier I had witnessed policemen passing bodies like a fire brigade, only clumps of trampled grass remained and footprints locked in the mud.

"Everyone from yesterday is gone," I called to Fred, who had remained in the car. "They're all gone."

"We must return to Katembeyna." The apprehension in Fred's voice was unmistakable.

"No need to worry," I assured him. "Just follow me to the other side."

Fred released the handbrake and drove onto the deck, keeping an even distance between us. I recalled my rainy night on the highway from Molo, when my tire went flat. I wondered if someone was watching us now from the trees, like then. Could UFreeMo rebels or one of Blake's "special units" be out there, measuring our interest in the deserted bridge, deciding if we posed a threat?

The steel platform supporting my feet was in excellent shape, but the cement columns holding up the balustrade could have used paint. Up close, their grey undercoat showed through in several weak spots. The iron railing itself had started to rust, bleeding orange stain down the white flutes. At the middle of the bridge, I leaned over the railing again. The water level was low, but the current still carried power. I estimated the midstream depth at twelve to fifteen feet, shallow enough to see the bottom, but only in shadows. Upriver, I spotted a thick stick floating my way. It rocked from side to side like a vessel having lost rudder and sail. I watched it pass below me and become trapped in a swirling eddy around one of the piers. For a time, the driftwood ship circled and circled, unable to escape the water's spin. Then, a second stick arrived from upstream and bumped the first stick out of the vortex. Both floated under the bridge and out of sight.

A hundred yards upriver, I saw the place where two smaller tributaries from the mountains joined to form the wide single stream that passed under me, the Jito River. Two herons circling overhead suddenly dove towards the spot where the tributaries merged, but before the birds touched water, they leveled out and then glided side by side to my left, disappearing behind a fence of trees abutting the shoreline. As I stood there gazing upriver, I felt something oddly familiar about my vantage point. I was certain I had stood at this same place before, had seen the same blue-gray shadows on the water, and had known what those herons would do before they did it. I had been here before, I was sure, but that was impossible. During my time in Umbika, I had never been this far north.

It was then I realized it was not a previous morning in Africa I was seeing again, but a day much earlier in my life. I was seeing something from twenty years before, a vision from the end of my high school years, a moment I had never wanted to remember.

Chapter 40
Prom

It was the weekend of senior prom, just before my high school graduation. I was eighteen, but taking a fifteen-year-old freshman to the dance. Samantha Anne Spencer was her name. Sam was unlike any other girl I had met. She spoke her mind, took initiative, and got things done. Although her given name was Samantha, she believed the name sounded old fashioned. She wanted everyone to call her Sam or Sammy. Her rebellious side intrigued me, as did her incredible cuteness – full lips, turquoise eyes, hair the color of the sun, and a figure that had developed earlier than other girls' her age. Sam came from a respected family in town, a fact my father pointed out to me more than once. Yet despite my clear attraction to her, it was Sam who had asked me to the prom. Somehow, she had heard I was the smartest boy in the school, and she was fascinated with smart people. A month before the big dance, she started passing me private notes in the halls and leaving small gifts at my locker. A couple of weeks later, she asked me to be her date.

Mary was Sam's best friend. Mary's boyfriend was Ed. For prom weekend, Sam organized a Saturday afternoon picnic for the four of us at Long Lake State Park. Afterwards, the plan was to dance until dawn at the Armory in town. Because the others were not old enough to drive, I ferried us in my father's Impala. At one end of the lake was a picnic area, with a sandy beach and public boat ramp. At the opposite end was Fisherman's Point, a hard-to-get-to but beautiful peninsula. Dense forest separated one end of the lakeshore from the other. Wanting to avoid the crowds that were headed to the beach, the four of us decided to hike to the peninsula and have our picnic at Fisherman's Point. From the nearest parking lot, that meant a half-mile trek on a narrow path through thick forest.

Ed was a big guy for a freshman, so he lugged our grill and cooler. Mary carried a bag of charcoal. I was in charge of the folding table and blankets. Leading us through the woods was Sam. She carried two grocery bags of food. We followed our guide along the seldom-used footpath, and for the first quarter of a mile everyone kept up with Sam's determined pace. Then, Ed and Mary began to lag behind. When Sam and I came to a small wooden bridge over a sizeable stream, the others were trailing us by fifty yards. My forearms ached against the weight of the table, but I was so happy to be with Sam, and so intent on pleasing her, that I ignored my own discomfort. In fact, I was so lost in thought about her that I had not noticed the trouble she was having with the things she carried. "I need to stop, Joe," she said at the center of the wood bridge. Just then, the bottom of one bag gave way. "Oh, no!" she cried.

Mustard and ketchup bottles fell on the bridge, along with some napkins, a jar of pickles, and two bags of chips. Sam reached for the pickle jar before it rolled off the bridge and into the stream, but she wasn't fast enough. The jar plopped into the murky water and sank. "I'm so sorry, Joe. I know how much you like pickles," she said, clearly upset, and knelt to gather the other items.

"Not to worry," I told her. "I can live without pickles." Sam looked up at me with the sweetest smile I had ever seen. She put her hand on my leg, behind my knee, and kissed me lightly on the thigh, on the stiff fabric of my new jeans. At that moment, my life could not have been better.

"You're a doll," she said and squeezed my thigh. She then gathered the napkins and the ketchup and mustard bottles. Mary and Ed had caught up to us by then. "Do me a favor, will ya?" Sam cooed to me. "Reach me those chips." My head felt as light as a leaf, my brain still dizzy with the touch of her hand on my leg. I gazed at her perfect face, her innocent eyes, her full lips. My next words escaped my mouth effortlessly, without any forethought or higher purpose. At that moment, all I wanted was to sound clever, so she would like me even more.

Returning her smile, I asked, "Who was your nigger last year?"

Sam's moist lips parted, but no sound escaped them. Her turquoise eyes widened and turned a steely gray. The silence that continued I quickly recognized as the sound of ruin. At the same time, Sam's creamy face flushed hot pink, and she turned away from me. In the one good sack left, she rearranged her picnic items and then got up and hurriedly continued across the narrow bridge. Mary and Ed followed a step behind.

I remained in place for some time, trying to make sense out of what had happened. I wasn't sure but figured the words I had said had offended the others, though I didn't see what the big deal was. The expression I had used was not alien to any of us. The phrase was a joke, something I had heard a hundred times. It meant nothing to me. Even my father said it now and then.

Standing alone on the footbridge to Fisherman's Point and gazing upstream, I saw high in the distance an owl circling. I watched it turn on its wing and dive towards earth. I could not tell what it was after – a chipmunk along the bank, a garter snake in the weeds – but before the owl hit the water, it repurposed its flight. It leveled off, glided a ways, and then disappeared behind a dark green windbreak to my left. When the owl did not return, I picked up my table and blanket and continued to Fisherman's Point.

The others were standing around Ed's grill, watching wieners sizzle over bright red coals. I apologized to Sam and the others, hoping that would help. They nodded and talked about the classes they would have the following year. I wanted to believe everything was as it had been earlier, but I soon realized that my senior year had ended back on the bridge. Sam and I would never get together. My life was no longer anchored to high school, not even to my hometown. Three weeks later, I received my diploma. The time had come for me to cast off, to move on. Five years from there and in my first year of law school, I met and then married Claire.

It has been said that shame is the worst curse put on an honorable person. The more he struggles to do what is right, the more disgrace he feels when he makes a mistake. That weekend of senior prom, I had not fully understood the extent of the mistake I had made on the footbridge – how easy it is for a few words to destroy all that is good between one person and another. But over the course of my life, such an understanding would eventually become clearer to me.

Chapter 41
The Meadow

From afar, Umbika's High Bridge looked amazing. Up close, it was even more impressive. To walk onto the bridge was to walk inside a piece of abstract art. I marveled at the web of braided cables crisscrossing the air around me – creating hundreds of unique shapes and patterns. I wondered if the bridge's strange geometry was another reason why villagers were afraid to cross it. I had lost track of time while gazing up stream and thinking about my journey from high school. I looked to the Land Rover again. Fred was still with me, hands wedded to the wheel, shoulders hunched forward. I waved him on, to follow me to the far side of the bridge, where I searched the gravel farther along the highway for any sign of why the bridge had been abandoned. But after another fifty yards of walking, I had found nothing. I got back in the car. Fred was silent and made no move to shift into gear.

"Yesterday was a bad day," I said, sensing Fred was feeling uneasy. "We saw some terrible things. But now, we have to stay focused on our goal, which is to find Mr. Hightower. I can't do this without you, Fred. I need your help. Mr. Hightower's family is counting on us." Fred removed his hands from the steering wheel and let them slump in his lap.

"Old people here say the devil lives at the High Bridge," he began. "I never believe their stories. They are hill people. They are not educated. But yes, there is evil here. I feel it." I let Fred's comments settle. Then, I asked how much farther it was to JiJi. He studied his wristwatch. "We are there, half-eleven, sir."

Only twenty minutes to our destination, but there was little commitment in Fred's voice to get us there. His mind was set on returning to Katembeyna and then heading south to the capital. I opened my briefcase and removed my map.

"Lew Trestle said there's a side road up ahead that leads to a footbridge. The footbridge is where the villagers were killed. It's where Mr. Hightower died."

"We need to go back," Fred said. "The police are gone."

"Before we go to JiJi, I'd like to see the place where they died."

"No, sir. The forest is not safe."

Fred knew the land as well as anyone, but I could not force him to help me. "Your country is falling apart," I said, trying a different approach. "You see it as well as I do. The trouble in Kat is more than a hiccup, Fred. Nowhere is safe now – not JiJi, not Katembeyna. For all we know, the capital is shut down." Mention of the capital city aroused Fred. His shoulders twitched. He seemed to be reassessing our situation. Maybe he was thinking of his family.

"We have our jobs to do," I continued. "My job is to locate Mr. Hightower's body. Your job is to get me where I need to go. We're the only ones who can make sure he is returned to his family. I promise you, we'll drive to JiJi and then to Katembeyna, after I see the footbridge." I checked my watch. "We've still got time. It's not even noon." I watched Fred do the math in his head, calculating if we could be back in Kat before dark.

"I am transporting us for the family of the American who has passed," he said and put one hand on the steering wheel. He then shifted into gear, resigned or resolved to continue as my driver and guide. Half a mile up the M-2, Fred pointed to a clearing on our right. At the back of the clearing was a narrow opening. I would have missed it without Fred. "This isn't on the map," I said. "But it looks like the place Lew was describing. Have you been this way before?"

"No."

"Let's give it a try."

We turned off the highway and drove a while, along something not much more than a trail, passing through groves of old trees. Off to the side, a fat baboon balanced on a branch, eating a yellow fruit. He watched us pass. At bunch points on the trail, the tips of branches scraped the sides of the Land Rover. I kept on the edge of my seat to help navigate our way through. We rounded a sharp bend.

"Watch out!" I shouted. Fred hit the brakes before we fell into a pothole the size of a bathtub. He steered around the hole and then around another. For ten minutes, we dodged one depression after the next. "Stop, I'm going to throw up," I told Fred. He stopped the car. I got out and tried to vomit. One mouthful came up. I stretched my leg.

"Look, sir," Fred said, pointing to a worn opening in the undergrowth. I checked my map again. It could be a thin line on the map that in half a mile intersected the western headwaters of the Jito River.

"Let's go for it," I said and got back in the car. Fred steered onto the new trail, but the going was slow. Thorny bushes scratched at us both left and right. Finally, the path opened, and we drove into a grassy meadow, half the size of a soccer pitch. "There!" I pointed.

A wooden bridge lay ahead of us, on the far side of the field. Fred stopped at the old structure. We got out to examine the wooden construction. It was basic bush work, a simple platform over the water, function over frills. The stream from the mountains flowed with force under the bridge, gurgling around thick sunken posts. The posts supported wood joists linking both shores. Floorboards were bolted perpendicular to the crossing beams. No handrail for pedestrians, no Greek columns. Just a simple deck made of planks. I bounced on the bridge. It seemed sturdy.

"Let me know if anything moves out there," I said to Fred, pointing upstream at the dense reeds growing along both shorelines. I walked across the meadow to our left, taking an angle parallel to the stream. The dry grass reached to my knees. "If this is the place," I called, "there should be evidence."

A third of the way across the meadow, I spotted a shoe, a petite pink little girl's dress shoe with a silver strap. It was lying on its side. I reached for it and noticed a woman's *chitenji*, yellow and blue in the grass, an arm's length from the tiny shoe. A large corner of the woman's wrap was stained dark red. "This is the place!" I called.

Continuing forward, I found deep impressions in the grass, tire tracks made by a heavy truck. I followed them upstream, until they curved back towards the center of the meadow. Then, without warning, there came a fierce noise in the grass in front of me. My body froze. My senses, on alert, quickly concluded the sound was not moving towards me, but away, heading towards the water.

"Crocodile!" Fred shouted from the bridge. He pointed upstream, where the reptile had just splashed into the river.

"You'll tell me if you see any more?" I called.

"You are most welcome, sir, but that one is large."

I backtracked along the path. Snakes, I knew, often travelled in pairs, and I wondered if the same held true about crocodiles. Midway back to the bridge, I noticed sunlight reflecting off something in front of me. A small brass object was suspended knee-high on a blade of grass – a rifle cartridge. I picked up the empty cylinder and held it high for Fred to see. Then, I spread blades of grass at my knees and discovered dozens of the spent cartridges, some caught in the grass, others pressed into tire tracks. Not all were the same size, not all from the same caliber of weapon. I stuffed a selection of them into my pants pocket – someone at the Embassy would know the kinds of guns they came from.

I studied the opposite bank. Something looked out of place, so I crossed the bridge and walked along the topside, avoiding the shoreline, where reeds were thick and shadows uncertain. I came to the spot I had noticed from the other side, a thick burgundy blotch of color lay curdled in footprints locked in mud. A rancid smell invaded my nose. Black flies swarmed above the blood pools, preventing me from going any farther up shore. I rejoined Fred on the bridge.

"The shooters were over there," I told him, pointing to our left. "Most of the villagers were on the other side of the water, but not all of them. Later, a truck arrived – regular police from JiJi, I think. That's what Lew said. Someone must have sent the police to collect the dead. They parked in the field, where the gunmen had stood. Before the police got here, some of the bodies either fell into the water or were dumped in and then floated downstream. Those are what we saw yesterday at the High Bridge. But this can't be the only killing field. There must be others. There were too many bodies in the river yesterday. Not all of them came from here."

I unfolded my map and laid it on the hood of the Range Rover. Fred came in closer for a look. "The village of Suleko is a mile north of here," I said, pointing at a mark on the map. "Do you know it?"

"They are hill people, sir."

"Do they support UFreeMo?"

"I cannot say. Perhaps they are." Fred was fidgeting with his car keys.

"What's the matter?" I asked.

"We are far from the highway, sir. I want to go."

"You're right, Fred," I said and closed the map. I had pushed my driver too much for one day. "We've seen enough here. Let's get back on the road. We'll get Mr. Hightower's body in JiJi and then head home."

Chapter 42
Matthew

Back in the car, I handed Fred a bottle of water and kept one for myself. Fred backed up onto the grassy meadow to turn around. "Jesus Christ!" I shouted. The sound was so frightful Fred's foot slipped from the clutch, stalling the engine.

What had frightened me was pressed against my side window – the face of a zombie, or so it appeared, its one eye staring directly at me, the other eye only a gory empty socket. Fred saw this phantom too and hurried out of the car. He went to the thing and put his arm around its shoulder. I then realized my mistake. This was not some terrible Highland spirit, but the face of a child, a boy no more than thirteen years old. He was grossly injured, the black hole where his one eye should have been a crater outlined in clots of blood. The boy was wearing gray pants, cut off at the knees, and a baby blue tee-shirt, stained red. Hundreds of insect bites covered his bare legs and feet. Above his shoulders were more bites, as well as scratches running across his cheeks and weeping yellow fluid down his neck.

Fred and the boy spoke in a dialect I did not recognize. I got out and examined the boy's eye wound. The flesh around the socket had melted like plastic in a fire, the intense heat from a powerful bullet. The eye itself had been vaporized, but the bullet had not breached the boy's skull. Blood vessels behind the eye had been cauterized by the heat, keeping the boy from bleeding out. He was lucky to be alive. "This one is Matthew," said Fred. The boy was trembling as he stood in front of me. "He was here with the others."

Although schooled in basic English, Matthew spoke to Fred in the local language and told us about the killers. He said he did not know who they were. They were dressed like rebel soldiers – except they weren't UFreeMo, he said. The boy's village knew UFreeMo. Men from his village had joined UFreeMo. I was certain the killers were from one of the special units Blake had described.

Matthew said the men arrived in the morning and collected everyone from two villages, Suleko and Bildi. They marched everyone to the meadow here, next to the river. The soldiers started shooting people. The next morning, police came to get the bodies that the river had not already carried downstream. Crocodiles and hyenas took some too.

"This one, they thought was dead," Fred said, pointing to the hole in Matthew's face. "He failed to show for the police and hid in the bushes over there." Fred gestured to a dark clump of vegetation on the other side of the footbridge.

"He should've run the hell away," I said.

"Some did as you say, sir, but Matthew stranded himself. His mother and sisters were killed beside the water. He showed himself to us because he is hungry and you are *mzungu*."

"Did he see Mr. Hightower?" I asked. Fred questioned Matthew again, and their dialogue went on for some time.

"Matthew says he saw the black giant in a yellow suit. He came like a god to save them. The soldiers shot him too." It was what I had feared. This was where Maurice Hightower had died.

"What happened to Mr. Hightower's body?" Fred asked my question. The boy watched me carefully, while he explained something to Fred. Fred became alarmed and asked the boy another question. The boy nodded.

After the killers had disappeared into the forest, Fred said, five ladies were passing by. They checked the bodies along the shore. The women discovered three survivors in the reeds, two small children and Hightower.

"Hightower was still alive?"

Fred nodded. The women then made a stretcher out of tree branches and the skirts from dead women, he said. They strapped Hightower and the children to the stretcher and carried them away, east, in the direction where the women had come. Matthew thought about going with them, but he was afraid. He thought the ladies were too slow and would be caught and killed by the soldiers. So, he remained hidden.

"Where did they take Mr. Hightower?"

"This one cannot say," Fred said. "They are from a village the boy does not know." I retrieved my map from the car and located the tiny dots that were the villages of Suleko and Bildi, a mile upriver. Following a broken line on the map, I traced the footpath the women would have taken east from the bridge. It meandered through forest, and then split in two directions, a couple miles east from where we were. One branch veered north and one south. On my map, the village nearest to the split was unnamed, but it was on the route going north. It was only five miles from our current spot and the closest village where they could have gone.

"If we can get to this village," I said, pointing at the map, "we can pick up Mr. Hightower and avoid JiJi altogether. We can drive down the escarpment at New Castlebay, take the lakeshore road, and still be back in Kat before dark." Fred thought over my proposal, which was a better idea than returning to the High Bridge. He nodded his approval.

"What about this one?" he asked.

"We'll take Matthew with us. Someone in this village will know what to do with him. But first, I want to clean that wound. You can give him something to eat."

I opened the Land Rover's rear hatch and handed Fred a bottle of water and the package of cookies I had bought. I slid out from under the back seat a large first aid kit, what all U.S. Embassy vehicles carried with them – bandages, tape, antibiotic cream, scissors, and because of Africa's dangerous roads and wildlife, exotic ointments, prescription medications, needles and syringes, two glass bottles of intravenous solution, and a snakebite kit.

I broke open the security seal and unfolded two large pouches. A magnifying glass helped me see into Matthew's wound. His eyeball was completely gone, and only a thin crescent of white cheekbone remained between the socket and Matthew's ear. The trauma had been so shocking, the boy probably never felt any pain from the bullet's impact. With a piece of gauze, I dabbed rubbing alcohol around the wound. Matthew flinched, a good sign the tissue was still alive. A bright red drop of blood trickled down his cheek.

As far as I could tell, infection had not set in. I squeezed a third of the tube of antibiotic cream onto another gauze pad and plugged it over the empty socket. To secure the plug, I looped a long ribbon of rolled gauze several times around Matthew's head, like a white crown. Strips of adhesive tape finished the job. "He can ride with me in back," I said.

To limit weight on the old timbers, Matthew and I followed on foot as Fred drove up onto the bridge. The platform was not built for cars, so a careless driver could easily slip a wheel over the edge. Fred was as skilled a driver as anyone. He got the vehicle to the other side without any problem. The trail through the woods was flat, though we came upon an occasional depression filled with water. The hit and miss showers known to precede the rainy season must have already begun in the Highlands. There were no scuff marks on the trail. The ladies were carrying the stretcher, not dragging it. Where I could see sky, wisps of yellow clouds had moved in, a reminder it was afternoon at the end of the dry season. I checked my watch, 1:35.

Minutes later, Fred stopped. "Here is the three-way," he announced.

The trails to our left and right were wider than what we had traveled since the footbridge. I looked at my map again. "The trail to the south makes a big loop before turning towards the escarpment," I said. "The nearest village, that way, is ten miles. I don't think they could've dragged the stretcher that far. The village to the north is only two miles from here."

Fred did not wait for an order from me; he turned north. Soon, the cover of branches above us grew denser. Deep purple shadows covered our path. Only an occasional breach of sunlight flashed across our hood. Ahead of us was a blind hill, and when we came down on the other side, four men were walking towards us on the trail. The lane was too narrow to turn around, but it was not an option anyway. The men had heard our engine. Each one pointed an automatic rifle at us.

Chapter 43
Ziwande

"Slow down," I said to Fred, as we neared the soldiers on the trail. "But don't stop, unless you have to. We'll try to pass by."

Earlier, I had noticed on my map a tarmac road coming up the escarpment from the lake. It ended at the town of New Castlebay, atop the high plateau. I knew from my warden list that a family from Nebraska, named Cooper, oversaw a Presbyterian mission near there. I told Fred, "If these guys ask where we're going, tell them New Castlebay. American missionaries there have a new baby. And tell Matthew to get on the floor and keep quiet."

Matthew slid onto the floor next to me, and I pulled a dark blanket over him. Fred attempted to steer around the four gunmen on the trail, but they refused to give way. He stopped only inches in front of them. Other gunmen slipped out from their shadowy cover in the forest on either side of us, and we were now fully surrounded. All of the men carried automatic weapons of various types, but they did not look like soldiers. Some wore camouflage, others blue jeans and shirts, exactly the way witnesses described the UFreeMo band that had raided the village of Enro Muswaya and killed him and his people. I had no way of telling if these men were rebel fighters or NEGs play-acting the part. "Don't turn off the engine," I said to Fred. "We might have to leave quickly."

The men in front held their blocking position, but they did not move towards us. A new man slipped out from the trees and tapped a chrome revolver against Fred's window. He wore a green beret and aviator sunglasses with yellow lenses, which seemed comical, given the lack of sunlight on the trail. Fred rolled down his window. "Turn down the motor," the man commanded. Fred did as instructed, no hesitation. The man peered into our vehicle. If he was surprised to see a white man wearing a suit and tie, he did not show it. "Are you lost?" he asked Fred. The man's command of English was good enough to get an Umbikan student high marks in language class. Fred told our story, exactly as instructed. This man, the leader of the group, leaned in through Fred's open window and spoke directly to me. "You are American," he said.

"Yes, I'm from the American Embassy. We're on our way to the Christian mission at New Castlebay. There are missionaries waiting..."

"Yes, yes," he interrupted me. I wondered if he knew the Coopers and that we were lying about the new baby. Instead he asked, "What do you know about *ziwande*?"

I was familiar with the African word, a folklore term meaning demon or devil. Two centuries earlier, Arab slave traders had raided this part of East Africa. *Ziwande* was what the native people called the traders. Lake Ziwa, or Devils Lake, was named for the Arabs who ferried kidnapped Tologs and Umbiks across the lake on their way to merchant ships waiting on the coast of the Indian Ocean. Many Umbikans believed the spirits of the *ziwande* still lived in the forests of the Highlands and were looking to abduct the careless or lost.

"*Ziwande* are demons," I said.

"Very good, my friend." The leader smiled. "You know, then, *ziwande* may be around us in the forest."

"You've seen them?" I asked. The man ignored my question.

"Your driver says you came from Katembeyna this morning."

"We did, but we missed the cut-off to the lake. We're trying to get to the Mission this way."

"Did you pass the Jito River today?"

"Of course, we did. We passed it for hours. It's right next to the highway."

"What did you see in the river?" The question was unexpected, and I hesitated. It is a mystery how fast the brain can process one's options sometimes. In two seconds, I read the man's body language, made sure he could not read mine, and tried to decide three things – Was he testing me? Was he being sincere? Was he setting a trap?

"What did we see in the river?" I said. The soldier's face was pointed directly at me, but because of his yellow lenses, his eyes appeared distorted, and I could not tell if he was looking at me or past me, into our car.

"*Ziwande* are killing villagers – and floating their bodies in the river," the leader said.

"What are you talking about?"

"Did you see bodies in the river?"

"*Ziwande* don't exist," I said. "They're a myth."

"Did traffic police stop you at the High Bridge?"

"There were no police at the bridge," I told him. "The bridge was empty."

"That's because *ziwande* have frightened the police away," the man said with confidence, as if he had finally proven his point. I reached behind me into the cargo bay and grabbed the six-pack of Coca-Cola. I rolled down my window and handed him the drinks.

"This is from the people of the United States of America," I said. "With your permission, we'd like to continue to New Castlebay. The missionaries are expecting us." The man accepted the sudden gift and handed it to a lieutenant behind him. He then reached into the chest pocket of his OD jacket and extracted a long narrow ribbon of yellow cloth. He knotted one end to the top of our antenna, the free end trailing across the hood.

"There are others like us in the forest," he said. "If they see this, you can pass."

"I'm grateful for your help," I said, relieved. The man rested his chrome handgun, a large and powerful weapon, on the ledge of my open window. The silver barrel pointed at my chest like a shiny cannon.

"Not long ago, I met an American," the leader said with the indifference of a conductor on a commuter train. His glasses faintly reflected a silhouette of my head. "He was not from your Embassy. He was a journalist, a tall man with dark skin. Do you know him?" The leader of this band of forest soldiers, that may have been a death squad cut from the President's private army, was smarter than I had estimated. It took all of my willpower not to grab the bait.

"You met an American negro, here, in the Highlands?" I said. It was the best surprised voice I could produce. "There aren't any Americans like that in Umbika, at least no one I know about."

"Were you sent to find this man?" I held the direction of the leader's gaze, or where I imagined it to be.

"There's no one I know like that, but I'll ask about such a man, when I return to the Embassy. I'd like to meet him."

The leader held his pose, and I held mine. Then he straightened and waved his pistol in the air, signaling the men blocking our path. "Go," the leader said with a smile. "But do not forget this lesson, my friend. Devils live in these woods."

Fred pulled forward. The man's wicked grin and the wide barrel of his chrome-plated handgun were images I would not forget for a long time. I did not turn to look back at the soldiers. Once we passed a second rise in the trail, I lifted the blanket and motioned Matthew to get up off the floor. "Were those men UFreeMo?" I asked Fred. Fred tilted his head in thought.

"Some are Tologs, for sure. They can be UFreeMo, sir. But I do not say for certain." Fred asked Matthew if he had recognized the leader's voice, but under the blanket, he had heard nothing but muffled sound.

The trail alternated between forest and grassland as we traveled through the mountains of the Highlands. I noticed a family of antelope and three zebras grazing on a hill, a pair of turkey vultures sitting in a dead tree, plenty of baboons. If we had been tourists, I would have snapped a few photos. We arrived at a sign fixed to a post. The sign's metal edges were serrated, due to rust and weathering, and the name printed on it had grown faint with time. Enough paint remained to show that we were entering the village of WiJJ. It was the unnamed dot on my map we had been traveling to. Fred stopped at the center of what was left of twenty structures. All were in some stage of ruin, having been abandoned years earlier. No window glass or wood trim remained on any structure. Some walls had crumbled into piles of useless bricks, sprouting tufts of grass. It was impossible to tell which structures had been houses and which were shops. "Wait here," I said to Fred and got out of the car.

In the calm air, I listened for sounds of life, but heard nothing. I walked to one building that had its roof intact, but found no clues that people were still living there. No, WiJJ was a ghost town. I had convinced myself we would find an injured Hightower at this dot on my map, but there was no evidence his rescuers had come this way. I got back into the Land Rover and told Fred to crisscross the village, circle every building and every pile of rubble. Fred was as frustrated as I. He went around some plots three or four times, until I told him to stop. The ladies had taken Hightower somewhere else, but where?

It was mid-afternoon, and failure and fatigue had taken hold of me. Fred was feeling the same. I took out the bag of groundnuts, scooped a handful, and passed the bag to Fred and Matthew. For a few minutes in the center of WiJJ, we ate the peanuts and drank water. I studied my map again. I considered every line on the paper, every grade of elevation, every symbol. Had the ladies continued to a village beyond WiJJ? Three more villages were north of our spot, five or six miles away, all with actual names on my map. But they were deep in the Highlands and uphill, too difficult to get to for someone carrying a wounded six-and-a-half-foot man.

The more I studied the map, the less convinced I was the ladies had turned left at the three-way. I was not convinced they had turned right either. The trail to the right was too long, ten miles at least. The nearest village on that circuitous route was the village of Yulemo, sitting on the edge of the escarpment overlooking Lake Ziwa. Maybe there were other villages, not on the map, but that was impossible to know. Then, I realized another possibility. The women might have continued straight ahead at the three-way, going overland through the forest, an unmarked shortcut to Yulemo. My map showed a ribbon of consistent elevation through the mountains between the three-way and the escarpment. A shortcut through the forest there would reduce the distance to Yulemo by eighty-percent. The ladies could manage that, even with a stretcher.

"We have to go to Yulemo," I said to Fred and pointed out the elevations on the map.

"The soldiers are behind us. It is too dangerous."

"You're right. We can't trust going back. But if we go first to New Castlebay, I can phone the Embassy. From the Cooper's mission, we can take the road along the escarpment to Yulemo."

"Will we drive dark, sir?" Fred asked – the dread of violating official procedures was obvious in his voice.

"We'll be fine, as long as we get off the plateau before nightfall. There's a way down the escarpment at Yulemo. At the bottom, the road is flat along the lake. We'll be in great shape after that."

Chapter 44
New Castlebay

The drive from WiJJ to the mission at New Castlebay took twice as long as estimated, as the trail was more uneven than I had expected. I asked Fred several times to stop, only for a minute or two, so I could rest my stomach and put my legs on solid ground. Near the end, we crested a succession of hills before Fred spotted the mission, a cluster of red and white buildings a mile ahead, squatting on a grassy plain. Just after the buildings, the plateau dropped 2,000 feet to the lakeshore below. With the late afternoon sun to our backs, the view to the mission was a palette of pastels, soft browns, greens, and yellows. Beyond the mission lay the rich aqua-blue water of the lake. Everything appeared in perfect harmony. "This is gorgeous," I said to Fred. He agreed. A glimpse of paradise, it would seem.

I didn't remember much about these American missionaries, only that their surname was Cooper and they were from Nebraska. I had never met them. They were another name on my warden list. As we got closer to the property, fruit orchards, vegetable gardens, then a large house, a church, and various outbuildings came into focus. A tall red brick carillon with a cross on the roof loomed over an open gate guarded by a pair of smaller brick towers. Past the gate, white-washed mud huts lined the road leading up to the church. The mission property appeared to be the essence of order in what was becoming a chaotic country. Stones painted white, and arranged like runway lights, marked the edges of the driveway and the footpaths that connected the numerous outbuildings. The grassy areas were uniformly cut and neatly raked. Not a leaf or twig or blade of grass out of place. As we drove through the property, I expected to see parishioners working in the gardens, children playing beside the huts, a dog or two sleeping in the warm sun. But there was no sign of life anywhere, only some sheets hanging on a clothesline.

"Drive over to the main house," I told Fred.

It was an East African two-story, covered in white stucco, plantation-style, its large roof a thick bed of faux thatch. Fred parked on crushed rock in front of the house. Only after he had turned off the engine did I notice the Coopers' front door was wide open.

"Tell Matthew to stay in the car," I said. "Let's you and me find out what's going on."

Instead of heading straight inside, I decided to circle around to the back of the house. Along the way, I noticed no signs of struggle in the yard, nothing tipped over or scattered about. The windows were not broken. Flowers were picture-perfect in hanging baskets. I checked one pot and found its soil moist. Towards the rear of the house, a black garden hose lay perfectly coiled under its faucet. Caged tomatoes and green pole beans were growing in a private garden, ready for picking. Everything I saw told me people had been living here recently.

Then, as we came around from the backside of the house, I discovered the cut wire. A telephone cable had been severed on the first floor where it entered the house. Deep cut marks scarred the white stucco where the black cord slipped inside the wall. The wire had been hacked to pieces, probably with a machete. Only a stubby sheath poked out from the wall. Above us, the service end of the phone line dangled from the roof, its other end connecting to a nearby telephone pole. Someone had disabled the cable, as high as he could reach.

Fred and I returned to the front of the house and then walked up on the porch. The frame for the front door had been smashed with the same violence as the phone line. Splinters of mahogany lay scattered across the threshold, along with a broken lock. I paused before going inside. With everything we had seen in the past two days, I prepared myself for the worst. I called ahead of us, "Is anyone home?" There was no reply. Fred followed me in. We crossed the wide foyer and the spacious living and dining rooms. I paused at a staircase. Its white railing and ebony spindles led to the second floor. "See what's up there," I said to Fred. "Check every room, look in every closet, but be careful. If we're not alone, I don't want to spook anyone. Call me if you find anything."

I watched Fred climb the stairs. He moved with an abundance of caution. I continued on to the back of the house – first, an office, then three small storage rooms, then a closet for the water heater, and beyond it a laundry room. Finally, I came to the kitchen at the end of the long hall. Cupboards had been ransacked and drawers left open. A potato peeler and a rolling pin lay dead on the floor. Two kitchen chairs were overturned and lying next to an oak table. In the refrigerator were warm bottles of water and a single Orange Fanta. The rest of the refrigerator had been cleaned out and its electrical cord pulled.

Thieves in Africa did not steal things that needed constant cooling, so the unplugged refrigerator suggested the Coopers had gotten out alive. Even so, the thieves had pillaged the family's pots and pans and most of the staples from the pantry. Only a few odds and ends remained – canned peaches on a top shelf, three chocolate cake mixes, a pack of cookies. In the washroom, I opened the door to a linen closet. The space was empty, except for one blue pillowcase and a stack of washcloths. Completely overlooked by the thieves, however, was a supply of medicine, hidden behind the mirrored door of a vanity cabinet above the bathroom sink.

I could tell that the thieves had extremely practical and transportable needs. In the dining room, china and silverware were left untouched. A television and video player sat in place on a table in the living room. Videotapes, some still wrapped in cellophane, were neatly arranged on a shelf beside the TV. A brass trumpet lay atop an upright piano.

While assessing the damage, it struck me as odd that only the front door and phone line had been destroyed. If anti-American or anti-white hate was on the intruders' minds, the destruction would have been much worse. The thieves seemed focused only on getting things they could use, not on revenge.

Fred found me standing in the living room. "There is no one up there," he reported.

"What about anything unusual?" I asked. My question appeared to confuse Fred. "Is anything disturbed up there," I said. "You know, are the rooms a mess?"

"Nothing is disturbed, sir."

I noticed a black phone was lying in pieces on a rug under a window in the office. I examined the fragments, giving special attention to the handset and the rotary dial. Both had been hacked violently, damaged beyond repair. I looked behind an armchair, where the outside phone line entered. The plastic junction box was hanging in splinters. Machete cuts scarred the inside wall. "I'm not sure why they wanted to keep the Coopers from making phone calls," I said.

I then spotted a wire coming down through a hole in the ceiling. It was painted the same beige color as the office wall, its own sort of camouflage. A casual glance would likely overlook it. I ran up to the second floor. In the bedroom above the office, a pink telephone – what was called a Princess phone – sat on a nightstand beside a twin bed. It was untouched, just as the Coopers had left it, and exactly what I was hoping to find. Fred and I went outside with the small device. Matthew stood next to our car, his bandage still snug around his head.

"Before I call the Embassy," I said, "we should see if anyone is on the property, someone who might know what happened."

We left the house and walked to the church and from the church to a tool shed. About to go inside, I noticed Matthew was several feet behind us. He had not remained with the car, but had been trailing us.

"This one is afraid to stay alone," Fred explained.

"We're all afraid," I said and motioned for Matthew to join us.

Every outbuilding we looked in was deserted, including the church. Fred noted hand tools missing from the woodworking shop, and not one egg or hen in the chicken coop. We came to a garden shed, one of the buildings farthest from the house. Matthew pointed to a cluster of fire ants swarming over a white marker stone. Ahead on the path, he pointed to more fire ants on white stones. We followed the ant trail to a borehole at the back of the property, where the shirtless body of a long black man was lying face down in the dirt beside the well. I felt my insides collapse again.

To travel so far, was this how our search would end? It was the worst of my fears.

Chapter 45
Rescue Plan

A dark spot of blood, the size of a playing card, was high center on the man's back. A bullet had entered between his shoulder blades, just below his neck. We got closer. The long figure wore blue shorts and green sandals – not a fine yellow suit. My body started to relax. While very tall, the man had the darkest black skin I had ever seen, darker than Hightower's. My guess was he lived at the mission, remaining behind when the Coopers left. He had been shot nearer to the house, and then stumbled to the well, before he collapsed and died. Why someone shot him in the back was a mystery I did not expect to solve.

Beside the borehole was a cement platform for washing clothes. I climbed onto the wall around the platform to gain a better view of the Coopers' property. Nothing appeared out of place. I looked across Lake Ziwa, the water's surface as smooth as glass. Beyond the lake was a ridge of mountains, Umbika's neighbor to the east. The late afternoon sun colored the peaks in multiple shades of purple, yellow, and orange. This view to the east was peaceful, nothing in the least bit threatening. Yet below me lay a dead body, where fire ants feasted on open flesh and black flies circled like a gathering storm. T-I-A, I thought.

It was five o'clock now, and we still had more than an hour's drive to Yulemo. Part of me felt like giving up, but I fought the urge. We could stay at the mission overnight and set out for Yulemo in the morning. I considered that option, but concluded it was not safe at the mission, and I would not be able to sleep anyway until we found out if Hightower had been taken to Yulemo. "It is night soon," Fred said. We both understood what that meant. We would not get back to Katembeyna before tomorrow. Regardless of what we found in Yulemo, we would have to stay there tonight and then descend the escarpment in the morning.

"We better get going," I said.

Fred was numb to death by now. He made no plea to bury another casualty of Umbika's decline. I was of the same mind. In the past two days, we had encountered too many of the dead to feel a responsibility for burying one more. Maybe our hearts were too small to carry all of the sadness we felt and we needed to break away. Maybe it was easier to move on because we knew none of the dead by name. Unlike the anonymous victims in the Jito River and the one lying here beside the well, Hightower was someone we knew. He had a name. That name made a difference. It made him real to us and helped us to keep our search alive.

"Take Matthew and get whatever you can from the kitchen," I said.

Fred gathered bottled water and the Fanta from the refrigerator and cans of peaches from the pantry. In the dining room, I found a steak knife and Phillips screwdriver. Outside, I hauled an extension ladder from a shed over to the side of the house. I mounted the ladder and grabbed the cut telephone cable dangling near the roof. I shaved away plastic insulation and separated the four thin strands of copper wire inside. Then, I connected each colored wire to its mate in the Princess handset. A dial tone purred through the phone's earpiece. I smiled at my handiwork and spun the dial six times. Instantly, the familiar voice of the Embassy's switchboard operator greeted me. "American Embassy, how may I direct your call?" he said, his Umbikan accent as clear as if he were standing on the ladder with me.

"This is Mr. Kellerman," I said. "Please pass me through to the Ambassador's office." Durhlmann was on the line within seconds.

"For chrissakes, Joe! Where the hell are you?" I brought the Ambassador up to speed on our convoluted road trip, the narrow escape from Katembeyna, and the deserted High Bridge. I mentioned nothing about the meadow or Matthew or where we were, however. I planned to reveal my news about Hightower when I was about to hang up. Because Triple S eavesdropped on all calls into and out of the Embassy, their agents had probably already started to trace my call. Fortunately for me, a phone trace in Umbika could take an hour or more, and we would be long gone by the time they figured out where I was calling from. Even so, someone would be sent to look for us, so Hightower's safety, as well as ours, depended on staying one step ahead of a search party. "Katembeyna is a mess," Durhlmann said. "A lot of property burned today. Dozens of people were killed. The country is under martial law tonight, Joe. Police have orders to shoot on sight."

"Did you talk to Blake?"

"He's holed up at the hotel, says he's going stir crazy. He explained why you had to leave, so I understand. By the way, the Foreign Minister confirmed the bodies in the Jito River, near the High Bridge, just like you described. He claims UFreeMo murdered them."

"We might want a second opinion, sir."

Durhlmann's voice turned solemn. "The Foreign Minister knows that Maurice went to JiJi, to interview the opposition. He believes UFreeMo killed him. He said the last time anyone saw Maurice was Saturday morning."

"Why would UFreeMo kill him, sir?"

"I don't know. It looks like Maurice just ended up in the wrong place at the wrong time. I'm really sorry about that." The Ambassador's voice carried a melancholic tone that signaled closure, the sound of something familiar ending unexpectedly and our knowing, sadly, it would never come again. I was tempted right then to break my news to the Ambassador and lift his spirits, but the time wasn't right. "Have you located the body?" he asked me.

"The answer to your question is, no, sir. I don't have a body yet. But it's more complicated than that."

"We need the body, Joe. This whole thing's becoming a Chinese fire drill. The White House called us twice this afternoon. They're organizing

Maurice's funeral, not the family. It sounds like it's going to be a big deal. Getting that body stateside is your top priority. Tomorrow night, there's a British flight leaving here and going through Heathrow. The Foreign Minister will help us get Maurice's body on the plane." I could not be sure if what the Ambassador was saying was for me to know or something to satisfy Triple S agents listening in, but the time had come to break my news.

"There's one more thing."

"What's that, Joe?"

Before another word left my mouth, I was blind-sided by doubt. In an instant, my confidence had deserted me. I weighed the consequences of what my next move could mean. Maybe, telling the Ambassador that Hightower had survived was not smart to say over an open phone line. The news would only confirm what Mulenga and his death squads already suspected, that a credible witness to state-ordered murder was hiding in the Highlands. Mulenga's special units would have even more urgency in finding and eliminating the witness. On the other hand, saying nothing about Hightower carried its own risks. Without Durhlmann knowing that he might be alive, Fred and I were on our own. There would be no need for help from the Embassy. We were witnesses to terrible things too, but Durhlmann didn't know most of it yet. If we were never heard from again, no one would know who was responsible for the massacre in the meadow.

"Are you still there, Joe?"

I decided to explain everything we knew, everything Matthew had told us, but then stopped. If the NEGs heard how much Fred and I knew and then caught us on the plateau or at one of their checkpoints, we would be eliminated for sure. We knew too much. I could not reveal it all now.

"Mr. Ambassador," I said, "our missing man was wounded, but did not die with the others. Someone found him and carried him away. I'm trying to find out where he is now." A prolonged silence followed my news. Finally, the Ambassador spoke.

"You're telling me Maurice Hightower is still alive?"

"There's a good chance he is, but it's also possible he died after being rescued. I don't know how bad he was hurt. I'm on my way to find out. I think

I know where they took him."

Durhlmann knew what was at stake if we could bring Hightower back alive. He sprang into action. "What can I do on this end, Joe?"

"It's dangerous up here, sir, and it'll be dark soon. We need to spend the night. Can you send some Marines from the Embassy to Katembeyna and have them wait with Blake at the hotel? Tomorrow, I'll need them to escort us home."

"They'll be in Kat by dawn," Durhlmann said.

"I think tomorrow morning, they should buddy up with the traffic police in Kat, a lot of traffic police, regular guys, if you know what I mean."

"I got it, Joe."

"When I'm in range in the morning, I'll radio from our car. We can decide where to meet."

"Consider it done," Durhlmann said. "And I'm coming too, god damn it. We'll have the flags flying, all the bells and whistles. The Foreign Minister said he'd help, if he knew where you were. But I'm coming myself. This will be a miracle, Joe. The best ending anyone could hope for." I had never heard a Senior Foreign Officer so excited. Then, Durhlmann's voice trailed off. He had realized the other possibility. "If you get to him and he's gone, Joe, make sure you take charge of the body. We'll need it just as much. Remember, the White House has been planning his funeral, and this is an election year."

I was about to hang up when I remembered something else. "Mr. Ambassador," I said, "has a family from Nebraska, by the name of Cooper, checked in at the Embassy?"

"Hold on, I've got a list right here. Dave Hardy put it together," Durhlmann said. The sound of shuffling papers filled the pause. "Yes, their name's here on the list. They came to town yesterday and are staying out at the Bible College. Do you need us to get in touch with them?"

"No, that can wait," I said. "I'll see you tomorrow." I disconnected the handset from the black cable and got down off the ladder. I hid the pink phone in a rose bush next to the house and returned the ladder to the shed. I was surprised how good it felt to hear the Ambassador's voice.

When I got to the car, I told Fred and Matthew to eat whatever they wanted. I went back inside the Coopers' house and filled a paper bag with first aid supplies from the medicine cabinet. I found a vial of motion sickness pills, so I swallowed two of the bitter tablets, even though I usually stayed away from them because they made me sleepy. By the time we left the mission, it was half-past-five. The village of Yulemo was an hour away, which would put us there after dark.

Chapter 46
Ngumbi

Just outside the mission and at the edge of the plateau, where the escarpment dropped 2,000 feet to the lakeshore below, we stopped at a crossroad. To the right was the trail we had taken from the Highlands meadow. It had gotten us this far, but we would not be backtracking. To the left was the town of New Castlebay half a mile distant, where a series of precarious switchbacks descended to the lakeshore road. I wondered if anyone in New Castlebay knew what had happened at the mission. I considered driving into town for an answer, but I chose not to. I was not sure who we could trust there. Ahead was our only good option, the old colonial road running along a cliff, thirty miles to Yulemo. We set off ahead in late afternoon amber light. To our left the view of the lake was breathtaking, a vibrating sweep of blue color turning darker the farther east I looked, all the way to a deep purple swatch at the far side of the lake. Ziwa was part of the Great Rift Valley, though not as large as the lakes Victoria, Tanganyika, or Malawi. It was ten miles across and fifty miles long, but deeper than the others, and home to more species of birds than any other lakeshore in Africa.

When we came to a rise in the road, the sun had declined enough that the lake was hiding now in shadows. The mountains of the Highlands were to our right. We watched the last remains of the day slipping away, one final brushstroke of blood-orange sunlight fading behind a magnificent charcoal ridge. Between us and the mountains the plain was dotted with acacia trees in silhouette against the failing light. And there were termite mounds as big as garden sheds, crouching on the plain like so many resting warriors. Two or three miles away, a wisp of gray smoke rose into the twilight. Whether it was from the cooking pot of some innocent villagers or an encampment of UFreeMo rebels keeping warm in the cooling air or an assembly of "special unit" soldiers planning their next deadly move, I couldn't tell. But a fire was burning out there. We were not alone.

My map showed we had left the escarpment now and veered inland. Night had arrived in full. Fred turned on our headlights because without them we could no longer see the crumbs of asphalt that were the old colonial road. Ahead, a curve disappeared into a clump of black trees. Fred stopped the car. "We are driving dark," he said. "We must stop."

"We can't stop in the middle of nowhere," I countered.

"I can drive no more."

"Look, this is not the time to follow every rule in the book," I said. "I won't tell anyone if you drive dark. We need to keep going."

"I will lose employment, sir."

"You won't lose anything," I assured him. "We have to get to Yulemo."

"I cannot, sir." He shut down the engine.

"Come on, no one will know," I pleaded.

"You will know, sir."

"It doesn't matter."

"Matthew will know."

"Matthew doesn't know anything, and I don't care."

"I will know."

"Just turn on your brights and let's get going."

Fred's resolve didn't waiver. He just sat there.

"We have to find Mr. Hightower in Yulemo."

"We do not know he is there, sir."

Fred was not going to drive another mile.

"Okay," I said and got out of the car. "I'll drive."

I opened Fred's door. The idea of my driving us to Yulemo seemed to catch him by surprise. He wanted to say something, but he had no words ready. He climbed over the console, and I slid in behind the wheel. "You can sit in my place in back, if you want," I said, "with Matthew. You don't have to sit up front."

His reply was firm and left no wiggle room. "Front is good," he said. I started the engine, switched to high beams, and let out the clutch. We were moving again.

The first white flare streaked across the outer reach of our headlamps not long after I had taken over the wheel. Like a tiny shooting star, the white light was there one moment and gone the next. Soon, the streaks were coming in twos and threes. Then, it was a full blizzard. We barely had time to roll up our windows before the road looked as if we were passing through a downpour of white rain.

"Ngumbi," Fred said.

En-GOOM-bee. I repeated the word to myself. Flying termites.

"Have you ever seen them so thick?"

"Isn't it," Fred said. "It means the new rain will come tomorrow or the next. It is a good sign for maize and cassava."

The life cycle of the ngumbi, precisely the African white ant, includes one spectacular night a year when these otherwise grounded insects take flight on enormous translucent wings. The timing of the spectacle varies across the Continent, influenced by anything from latitude and altitude to regional weather patterns. Yet whenever it happens, two things remain constant – the flight of the ngumbi happens at nightfall, and it coincides with the start of the rainy season. A few days before the first heavy rain, a brief morning shower signals these termite colonies to ready themselves. Each colony has already determined who among the new offspring will become flyers. When the right night arrives, the flyers begin their difficult climb out of the nest, up the long cone-shaped mound of mud. Their wings are so large that the weight prevents the flyers from making the climb by themselves. They need hundreds of worker ants to push them to the top of the long neck of the mound. At the opening, the flyers emerge into the night air and begin flapping their giant wings. Once a flyer is airborne, it begins searching for a mate.

Ngumbi couples are monogamous and remain together until they die, sometimes many years later. Flyers travel fifty or a hundred yards to find a partner, though some have been known to go over a mile. The distance a flyer travels is not important. What matters is that the flyer gets off the ground. Unless both partners have flown some distance, a couple will never be able to reproduce.

The flurry of white ants flying across the beam of our headlights now reminded me of snow – of childhood winters in the Midwest, sleds and ice angels, snowball fights. My memories continued to drift. There was that Washington in December, the year Claire and I returned from Lagos. The coldest holiday season on record.

Chapter 47
Yulemo

Despite blustery Canadian winds swirling through the streets of Northern Virginia, we were immensely happy, Claire and I. Christmas was only a few days away, and the thought of spring not far behind – the time we would leave for Rome, our next adventure together. I was enrolled in a series of short courses at the Foreign Service Institute in Rosslyn, things I needed to know for Rome, like Innovative Assessment Management of Visa Compliance Regulations; American Citizen Services: The Benefit Accountability Formula; and Tracking Dependent Status for Permanent Resident Adjustment Claims. To stay busy herself, Claire was substitute teaching in Arlington.

Snow started falling at noon that Friday. Streets were already slick with slush by two in the afternoon. By half-past-three, snow was heavy across the entire region, from North Carolina to New York. Normally, a December snowfall in the Washington area meant little or no accumulation. Most would melt as soon as it hit the ground. But that year, an unusual jet stream was producing frigid temperatures as far south as the Florida panhandle. From my classroom window on the fifth floor of FSI, I watched the big flakes settle on the cars parked along Key Boulevard. The white blanket spread over the George Washington Memorial Parkway and the hardwoods along the

Potomac. Across the river, snow covered every rooftop in Georgetown.

At five o'clock my class let out, and I went outside to wait for Claire. We had arranged to meet under the pedestrian bridge on North Nash. Claire had spent her day at Washington-Lee High School, and was driving into Rosslyn on Route 66. As always, she was on time. I saw her turn the corner at Key Boulevard and head towards me up the long hill. Claire navigated our small rental car through the slipperiest spots on North Nash and stopped at the curb where I was waiting. I opened the passenger door.

"You want me to drive?" I asked.

"I want you to sit and relax," Claire said. "You look tired."

I tossed my briefcase in back and got in. We kissed. "We need to stop at Woodies," she said, pulling away from the curb. "I still need a couple of gifts for Julie's kids. I want to mail them in the morning."

At Wilson Boulevard, we turned right. Claire could have gone back to Fort Meyer Drive and cut over to Highway 50 to get out to Seven Corners and the shopping center there, but she said it was safer staying on Wilson, even if it took longer. We continued past Veitch and the Courthouse, heading towards Clarendon and the busy intersection with Washington Boulevard. The snow was falling as hard as it had been all afternoon. Five inches, thick and wet, already stuck to the pavement.

"The principal wants me to come back after the first of the year," Claire said, proudly.

"That's because the kids love you. All kids love you. You're a great teacher."

Claire said a ninth-grade student had approached her that morning at the end of General Chemistry. The girl said she had wanted to be a chemistry teacher too, but thought it impossible, until seeing Claire in class. The regular science teachers at the school were all men. Now with Claire standing at the front of the science room, the girl believed her dream was actually possible. "She gave me the biggest hug," Claire said. "I didn't have the heart to tell her I'd been an English major." We laughed.

Traffic leaving Washington was light that evening, probably because of the deteriorating road conditions. After North Fillmore, traction got worse, and Claire had to brake for two cars that were slowly turning left onto North

Garfield. We were waiting in the intersection for the second car to complete its turn, so I leaned over the console and inserted my hand through the opening in Claire's half-zipped parka.

"Nice," I said and held my hand around one of her large firm breasts. "I thought of you all day." Then, I kissed her on the cheek.

"You thought of me all day," she said with a smile, "or just part of me?"

Screaming down North Garfield from the south came a gypsy cab, a bullet neither Claire nor I had noticed when we entered the intersection. In a flash, the old Sedan de Ville hit us squarely at the center of Claire's door while we waited in the intersection. The force of the collision was extreme. My passenger door was literally blown off its hinges. I was ejected from the car and flew thirty feet in the air before hitting the pavement. I tumbled another ten, only stopping because my left leg had hooked around a steel utility pole at the curb. My head never touched the ground, which was the miracle that saved my life. The utility pole, however, had shattered my femur and knee.

Later, the State of Virginia's accident reconstruction team determined the Cadillac had been travelling no less than forty-seven miles per hour at the moment of impact. In court, the cab driver's public defender argued that her client, an undocumented immigrant from Haiti, was "going forty, tops," as if that would have made any difference in the outcome. When the cab driver took the stand, he recounted in broken English how he had seen the red stoplight and applied his brakes. But the weather was so bad, he said, his taxi skidded on the slippery road, before colliding with us. The reconstruction team, however, reported finding no evidence of braking anywhere on the road.

The noise of the collision was like an explosion. People living near the intersection said they thought a plane had dropped out of the sky. They ran to where we were. Some came to me, some to the cab driver, and some towards our crumpled car. The first police cruiser arrived in only a few minutes. The officer checked the cab driver first, probably because he was lying in the middle of North Garfield. Witnesses later claimed the driver had attempted to flee on foot, but he had collapsed in the street.

All I remember was a cluster of people leaning over me as I lay along the curb. Because snow continued to fall, an old lady held a red umbrella above me to keep wet flakes from landing on my face.

I read court documents that detailed how our sedan was kicked back onto Wilson Boulevard, how rescue workers had drawn a blue tarp over the wreck while they tried to cut Claire's body from inside. The Cadillac's grill had sliced her nearly in half, but it was a blunt force trauma to the top of her head that killed her instantly when the roof support collapsed.

Shame, it is said, cuts a person from the outside inward. Guilt, on the other hand, eats at him from the inside out. My hand, selfishly slipped inside Claire's coat, had distracted both of us at the worst possible moment. It had kept each of us from watching out for the other. For a long time after the accident the guilt I felt made it impossible for me to talk about what had happened. The Department gave me medical leave and said that, once I got back on my feet, I could go anywhere in the world I wanted for my second tour, anywhere.

While recovering, I sat in a wheelchair at FSI and paged through post reports, looking for a destination that would make me whole again. I found no such place anywhere on the planet. I was sinking in grief. I wanted to give up. I had lost more than a loving wife and companion. The very compass I needed to chart a meaningful course in my life was gone.

One afternoon, I noticed the FSI librarian flip over a page on his wall calendar. The new glossy photo that appeared was for the month of April. It pictured Japanese cherry trees encircling the Tidal Basin in DC, their branches in full bloom. The sky in the photo was royal blue, the grass bright green. The big pink blossoms blushed in the sunlight. But the photo was far from representing the truth of the day. That spring was the coldest Washington had been for a hundred years. There wasn't a blossom on any tree within two hundred miles of the capitol. People had begun to wonder if spring had been lost for good. The FSI librarian, however, refused to give up. He took out a black marker from his drawer and defiantly wrote in tall letters across the cherry trees on his calendar, "Even in the grave, all is not lost. – Poe "

The librarian's cynical quotation was meant as a joke, perhaps, but I saw what Poe was getting at. I wheeled myself back to the shelves of post reports and started paging through them again. I stopped after only a handful. I had my answer. It did not matter which post they gave me, as long as they sent me to Africa. Africa was where Claire and I had spent the best two years of our lives. Africa was where I had to be. I was not ready to surrender yet. That afternoon, I committed myself to my work. Single again, work became my sole purpose and companion.

Memory of the snowstorm in Washington, spurred by the flying ngumbi, was the first time in years that I had recalled the moments leading up to the loss of my wife. Thinking about that terrible day, however, no longer made me feel lonely or sad, which surprised me. Though I continued to sense a deep loss, a feeling of what might have been, too much time had elapsed, I guess, to still feel those other emotions. Now, my memories about the accident were simply distant facts, like something I might read in an old newspaper article. The only truth that mattered was that Claire was gone, and I was still here.

Fred was first to spot the yellow glow in the distance. We saw, as we got nearer, that what had looked like a large cooking fire was a bonfire. Figures jumped around the towering flames in a crazy native dance. The air above the fire pit was thick with ngumbi, thousands of white wings darting this way and that, attracted to the bright light.

We pulled in next to the pit. People, who had been jumping during our approach, froze in place like statues. I parked and turned off the engine. Fred got out and went over to talk to an old man, who was sitting on the only chair around the pit.

Soon, Fred returned to the Land Rover. "This is Yulemo," he said. "They thought we were Explorers, come to punish them."

No longer sensing a threat, the villagers started jumping again, swiping at the air with sheets and blankets. It was a harvesting ritual we were witnessing. A tradition dating back to the beginning of time. While adults flapped the air, children scooped the falling insects off the ground and plucked away their wings. Then, they put the wiggling bodies into wooden bowls, saving them for later. A mother, cradling a baby near the fire, broke a termite in half, feeding one part to her infant and swallowing the rest herself.

"They thought we were Explorers here to punish them? Why would NEGs punish these people?" I asked.

"The one we search for is resting here."

Chapter 48
Survivor

"Hightower, he's here in the village?" I said, excitedly.

Fred nodded.

"He's alive!"

Fred could not hold back a prideful smile. "That one is the village headman," he said and pointed across the fire pit. The old man sitting there, Yulemo's traditional chief, was gazing at us through the dancing flames. Fred said he had explained to him our connection to Hightower and my responsibility to help the American get to safety. "He is ready to bring us," Fred added.

Even across the pit, I could see in the headman's eyes his wish that none of us had ever come to his village. He knew there would be dire consequences laid on his people if the government found out they were sheltering a witness to government murder, and our presence only made matters worse.

Matthew stayed at the fire, and we followed the headman in his slow walk through the village. The glow of the fire receded, and we proceeded in increasing darkness. President Mulenga's electrical grid did not reach Yulemo. Only light from the stars above us illuminated our way. We passed several huts and the village church, which was nothing more than three tall brick walls supporting panels of corrugated fiberglass and a cross. Votive candles in vases of red glass were alight on a table in one corner of the church. Yulemo was a Catholic village, Fred said. Once a month, a priest from the lakeshore came up to say Mass.

We approached a row of mud huts on the far edge of the village, beyond which all shadows ended and absolute darkness began. My anticipation for seeing Hightower again was stirring inside me. At the last hut, tawny light escaped from the open door and spilled onto the ground in front. The headman entered first. On my turn, I froze before the threshold. A row of white onions, cut in half, had been laid along the doorway. The sign was familiar to me, so I scanned the ground around my feet, looking for movement. Fred noticed my hesitation. "It is safe," he said. "They have not seen any since breakfast."

I stepped over the onions and into the hut. An old woman was standing at the center of the small room, the headman's wife, Fred said. She backed out of our way. Several candles burned atop a wood crate on the dirt floor, next to a thin mattress on which lay Maurice Hightower. He was flat on his back, his torso and legs covered by a sheet. Hightower turned his head at the sound of our voices. His movements were sluggish. His eyes had been drained of their normal edginess. Yet he was alive, that much I was certain.

"The cavalry has arrived," he murmured. I knelt beside him.

"I wasn't sure we'd ever find you," I said. "We've been looking a while."

The small size of the hut and narrow mattress made Hightower appear even more like a giant than usual. His feet and ankles stuck out beyond the mattress and the sheet covering his legs. "I knew you'd come," Hightower whispered, "just didn't expect it now, not while I was still kicking." One hand was wrapped in a bloodstained cloth. The other squeezed my arm, a show of emotion that took me by surprise. I held his good hand. The grip was weak, affirming what I already suspected – it would be difficult transporting him.

"First thing in the morning," I said, "we're taking you to Katembeyna. They've got doctors there." Hightower closed his eyes. "Are you hurt anywhere, other than your hand?" He lifted a corner of the sheet and grimaced. I was surprised by how much pain it caused him to perform such a simple motion. Hightower was naked under the sheet. A towel had been folded and placed on his abdomen. A stain looking like spilled coffee had soaked through the towel – he had been shot in the stomach too. "Go to the car and get the first aid kit," I told Fred.

Hightower tried to lift the rest of the sheet from his legs, but the reach was too painful. I lifted it myself. A bloody piece of yellow fabric was wrapped around his knee. "You have three wounds," I said. "Are you cold?"

Hightower shook his head. "Hot."

I gathered the sheet in a bundle, using it to cover Hightower's private parts, but leaving the rest of him naked to the air. "You're going to be okay," I assured him.

"I keep telling myself, this ain't happening," he said, his body shaking. "I'm not ready to go – not now." Hightower readjusted his position on the mattress, but it hurt to do so.

"Conserve your energy," I said. "We'll get you to a doctor." He stared up at a corner of the hut, as if he had spotted something there in the dark. His lips moved, but his mouth made no sound. He reached for my hand again.

"I have something to tell you."

"What's that?"

He whispered, "Can't feel my legs no more." He turned his head away. I heard soft crying.

"Don't worry," I said. "The doctors will know what to do."

Fred returned from the Land Rover and set the first aid kit on the dirt floor, next to the mattress. "I'm going to take this towel off your abdomen and see what the wound looks like," I said and then lifted it away. Fred, the village headman, and his wife stood behind me as I worked. Soon, the putrid odor of decaying flesh filled the small room, the smell so harsh that Fred and the others stepped back. It took all my willpower to keep working. The stomach wound was grossly infected, some of the surrounding tissue already dead.

Chapter 49
First Aid

Hightower's stomach wound lay just below his ribcage. Though only the diameter of a pencil, the ugly hole was outlined in bright pink and puffed up like a swollen knot. Burnt red syrup oozed from the hole and pooled in a glaze on the mattress. Fortunately, the bullet had missed arteries and vital organs, or else Hightower would have already bled out. What worried me now was infection inside him.

"Did the bullet go out your back?" I asked. Hightower shook his head. "Maybe I should turn you over and check."

"It's still in me," he said.

"Have you eaten anything?"

"Corn meal porridge," he whispered. "But I couldn't keep it down." His eyes were dry, his lips cracked. It took all his strength to speak even a few words. "My stomach's on fire. It burns real bad."

"We need to get some fluid in you."

"They tried already. I choked."

"Let me see what I've got in this bag." I took out everything I needed from the first aid kit and placed it in a neat row beside the mattress – tubing, needle, a bottle of glucose solution, scissors and tape, a blue tourniquet.

"You can smell it, can't you?" Hightower said.

"That's the infection inside. I'll put some antibiotic cream on the wound."

"No cream's going to do anything, Joe." He reached out and took my hand again. "I know the truth. I can see it coming. I'm not making it back." His forehead was warm and dry.

"You aren't a doctor and neither am I. We don't know who's making it anywhere. All I can tell right now is you need liquids in you."

"You got something to stop the pain?"

"I saw some pills in the bag."

"Give me some."

I opened a zippered pocket of the kit and took out an amber vial. DEMEROL 100 MG – TAKE ONE TAB ORALLY EVERY SIX TO EIGHT HOURS AS NEEDED FOR PAIN. Along the cap, a paper seal, like a postage stamp, had been affixed to the bottle. I cut through the paper band with my thumbnail. At the bottom of the vial were four white tablets. I showed Hightower the vial. "You're supposed to swallow them with water."

"I can't drink."

"I know."

I picked up the glass IV bottle and looked at the metal cap. It was factory-sealed, no way to pry it off and put something inside. "Let me suck on one," Hightower said. I disinfected my fingers with an alcohol wipe and shook out a pill from the vial. I placed it on his tongue.

"Let it dissolve in saliva. Don't try to swallow it."

Hightower closed his mouth around the pill. He worked his tongue back and forth, coaxing the pain pill to dissolve. Once the protective coating was gone, however, Hightower started gagging. The bitter taste of the medicine was so intolerable he spit it out. The pill landed on the dirt floor. The gag reflex sent painful spasms across his abdomen. I lifted a capful of water and a gauze pad to Hightower's lips. "Rinse your mouth," I said. "Then, spit it out." It took half a dozen rinses for the gagging to stop. I sat back on my haunches. Hightower let his head fall back on the mattress.

"I'm sorry," I said. "Let me first get the IV in for some fluids. Then, we'll figure out the pain."

I opened a paper envelope containing a pair of sterile examination gloves, and put them on. Putting the IV pieces together was intuitive. I mated one end of clear plastic tubing with the end of the IV bottle. Opening and closing the flow wheel, I forced air out of the line. I gave Fred the bottle of fluid to hold. "Keep it high," I said and drew an imaginary horizontal line in the air, four feet above the mattress.

I had never put a needle into anyone, but I had seen it done. I wrapped the tourniquet around Hightower's arm, above the elbow, and wiped his skin with an alcohol pad. The vein should have popped up with the tourniquet in place, but it didn't. "I can't find a vein," I said.

Hightower exhaled deeply. "Use the back of my hand."

The back of Hightower's hand, at his age, was a web of thick dark veins. I cleansed a spot with another wipe and laid the short needle against his skin. A plastic catheter was wrapped around the needle, and a bridging tube extended out the back of the needle like a tail. I unscrewed a tiny cap at the end of the tail and lined up the needle with a blood vessel. The headman, his wife, and Fred were intrigued with my work, watching intently. They only moved when termites, attracted by candlelight, flew into the hut. Then, they snatched them out of the air and plucked off the wings.

"You and me, never started on a good foot, Joe," Hightower said. His voice was shaky. I made no reply. The needle was extremely sharp and required all my attention. "I believe what I said." I pushed the tip through his skin and into the vein. The angle proved correct on my second attempt, a triumph. "But I've been told I sometimes sound full of myself." Blood flowed backwards into the clear tail and dripped from the end where I had removed the cap. I slid the needle out from Hightower's hand, leaving the catheter in place. "You might say things too, if you knew Jim Crow like I did." I connected the tubing between the IV bottle and the catheter's tail. I opened the finger wheel, and fluid started dripping through the tube. "You've got to go there, to know there," he said, his speech sounding sleepy, almost confused.

With a strip of adhesive tape, I secured the tubing to his hand. I had Fred find some twine and a short stick, and when he returned, I hung the glass bottle from a roof beam and taped the stick to Hightower's forearm as a splint. "I'm not an easy person to live with," Hightower said and closed his eyes again. "Divorced three times, imagine that..." The bullet that had cut through Hightower's other hand had exited on the palm side, leaving a large wound. "Beautiful ladies, all three..." I cleansed the front and back with alcohol and used a tweezers to pull away dead skin. I re-bandaged the hand with a clean dressing, and did the same to his knee, where another bullet had clipped the end of his thighbone. "Black women... expect too much of their men," he continued. "They got tired of me." Unable to get used to the smell of infection, I breathed through my mouth. Perspiration ran down the sides of my face. "My last wife was white."

"White?" I said.

He smiled. The wound on Hightower's abdomen was the most serious. I disinfected around the opening, wiping away blood and green pus draining from inside. When I finished cleaning it, I was not sure what to do next. A first-aid kit, even a large one, is not an operating room, and I was no surgeon. Somewhere lodged inside Hightower's gut was an infected bullet, and there was no way for me to find it or remove it. I squeezed antibiotic cream around the swollen wound and worked the cream into the skin. I pushed the last of it into the hole.

After half the glucose IV water was in him, Hightower's face showed the first true signs of life. The sallow tint invading his cheeks receded, and a normal shape returned to his lips and chin. His eyes glistened again. Still, these improvements did not tell the full story. Hightower's strength was fading. His pulse was weak. Pain urged him to give up. Along with its benefits, re-hydration had unintended consequences as well. Nerves throughout Hightower's body, refreshed now by the sugar solution, were transmitting stronger pain signals to his brain. The agony he felt was getting worse.

"I'd give you another pill to suck on, but I'm afraid you'd just spit it out again," I said and laid five gauze pads soaked with water across his warm forehead and temples. When I was done, they looked like playing cards in a game of solitaire. Hightower opened his eyes.

"Give 'em to me behind," he said.

I stared at the journalist, not sure if I had understood what he said.

"You heard me, Joe," he said, turning to look at me. "The backside. Years ago, they did that to a friend of mine. In his mouth was a tumor, so they gave him medicine from behind."

"In his. . ." I couldn't get myself to finish the thought.

"Yeah, like a . . . suppository."

I was feeling panicked now, not sure how to respond. "Why didn't they give him a shot?" I asked.

"I don't remember."

"They could have injected the medicine in him."

"They didn't." Hightower was getting annoyed at me.

"They could have put it in an IV."

"I don't know, but that's what they did!"

Finally, I said, "I can't do that."

"Hell-yes, you can!" Hightower bellowed. The outburst started a coughing fit, which made his abdomen spasm again. When his body calmed down, he said softly, "I'd do it myself, if I could reach there. I'd do it for you." My face flushed. No one had ever suggested something so outrageous to me. My imagination was spinning with foreign images. I leaned back and glanced up at Fred and the others, but as soon as they met my gaze, they looked away. They had been following our conversation about the pain pill, with great interest, and seemed as embarrassed as I was about Hightower's unusual idea.

I shook my head. "I don't think it'll work."

"It works. I know it. You're not afraid to put your finger up an old black man's ass, if it'll save him, are you?" The village headman's wife hurried out of the hut. I wanted to flee with her, but Fred and the headman were watching me intently, waiting to hear my answer. Hightower spoke before I could, though his breathing was labored. His pain appeared intolerable.

"Wasn't right to say that, not with a lady in the room," he said. The lines of age around Hightower's eyes winced on every breath he took. "I need your help, Joe."

Hightower let his head fall back on the mattress. His shoulders trembled. I told Fred and the headman to wait outside. When they were gone, the room became powerfully quiet, as quiet as a frozen river. The silence ended with the buzzing of a ngumbi, flying lost in the thatch above us. Hightower's eyes opened, perhaps to locate the flying insect, or maybe just searching for any distraction to help him forget his pain. He breathed with his mouth open, as if the air he struggled to swallow might ultimately save him. At that moment, I believe, Hightower was ready to die, maybe even wanting to die.

It was also when the inevitable became clear to me, as difficult as that was to admit. I now knew that this larger than life character, who had millions of people reading his words every week, words that had immeasurable influence over how they thought about their own lives, was not going to make it to Katembeyna in time for doctors there to save him. This giant man was going to die right here in Yulemo. I reached into the first aid kit and took out the last envelope of sterile gloves. The amber vial of Demerol was also easily reached.

Chapter 50
The Meadow Revisited

"If you could turn on your side, this would work best," I said. "But I know you can't twist like that. So, I'll try to fit my hand in from the front, between your legs."

I snapped the latex gloves, and a dusting of powder drifted for a moment in the air between us, a sudden white aura. Under different circumstances, I might have taken it as a sign of hope, but not now. The dust settled after a second or two. I held up the small vial for him to see. "I'm ready when you are." Hightower nodded, then covered his eyes with his big black forearm. "The directions say one tablet, but I'm going to give you two, unless you think you need three."

"They're powerful?"

"I think so."

"Just give me two. This is our first date," he said and laughed. His joke was unexpected and coarse, but I laughed with him. I shook two tablets from the vial and poured water over them. It took a minute to rub away the protective shells. I lifted the sheet covering Hightower's privates. The journalist's long body was naked, except for three white bandages on the wounds I had dressed. I had never seen a black man without clothes before now.

"Tell me if you get cold," I said.

I spread his legs and bent his uninjured knee, the one nearest to me, at a forty-five-degree angle. "Can you feel me moving your legs?"

"No," he said.

With one hand I cupped his private parts and delicately lifted them on top of his pubic bone, holding them out of the way. The candlelight offered only enough illumination to see the general area of insertion. I would have to feel my way to the target. I tried not to think too deeply about what was happening, what I was doing, just about the process. With my thumb and index finger, I took one tablet and reached into the shadows between mattress and flesh, feeling with my middle finger until I hit the mark. Hightower flinched at my touch, and I quickly withdrew my hand without having inserted the pill.

"Go on," Hightower said.

"But you felt something."

He assured me it was nothing, but I wanted to rejoice. He still had feelings that far down. Was there a chance he could make it to Katembeyna? I lingered on the hope I had created, even though the violation I was committing with my hand bothered me greatly. I considered telling Hightower the awkward thoughts that were going through my mind – the renewed hope, my embarrassment. Instead, I continued my work in silence. I found the soft spot again and inserted the first pain pill into his body. I recalled the night in the rain with Mr. Mkandawire, and how his blind fingers at the back of my Land Cruiser had freed my spare tire. How he had saved me that night. I pushed the pill with my middle finger, up into the warm, tight space as deeply as I could, knowing that the muscles of Hightower's rectum were beyond his control and would try to expel the medicine if the tablet did not go in far enough. I inserted the second pill the same way.

"That went well," I told him. "I'm going to add four aspirins for fever and two penicillin pills I found in the bag."

"I'm allergic to penicillin," he said.

"Okay."

When I finished the treatment, I lowered Hightower's bended leg and let gravity return his privates to a more natural resting place. I rearranged the sheet to cover his feet, hips, and abdomen, and then removed my examination gloves and tossed them on top of the pile of garbage collecting at the foot of the bed.

The first bottle of glucose finished. I swapped it for the second and readjusted the drip to once every five seconds. Hightower's forehead was on fire again. I wet more gauze pads.

Hightower then asked me something so softly I could barely hear him. I asked him to repeat it.

"At the door, you saw the onions?" he said.

"Yeah, I saw them when we came in."

"I don't smell them anymore."

"I don't either," I said. "But the onions are still at the door. I can see them from here."

Hightower craned his head, trying to see the entrance to the hut. "Snakes hate onions," he said. I was busy repacking the first-aid kit and did not answer, but I did know about snakes and onions. "This morning, the old woman found a cobra by my feet."

"You had a cobra in here?" I said.

"Sleeping down there, by my feet. Scared me, scared her too." My back was to Hightower, as I closed the last side pockets of the first aid kit. He started laughing. "Imagine that, a cobra, in my bed!"

"Where did it go?"

"Men killed it in the yard," he said. Hightower's speech was improving. The IV fluid was working. "They cut onions to protect me."

"I know," I said, and went outside.

It took a moment for my eyes to adjust to the darkness. Fred and the others were all together, crouched on their haunches, in front of the hut. They stood. I thanked the village man and his wife for their help in caring for Hightower and placing the onions in the doorway. I asked Fred to go to the car to get me one of the cans of fruit from New Castlebay. "Make sure you and Matthew eat something too," I said.

When I returned to the inside of the hut, Hightower was talking to himself. "Cobras in my bed," he said when he saw me. "This is Africa. Isn't that what they say?"

"Yeah, it's what they say," I replied. I had been mulling over a question since Fred and I were at the meadow. Now was the time to ask it. "Do you know who shot you?" I said.

Hightower answered immediately and with conviction. "Rebels," he said.

Some of his strength had returned. For several minutes he talked about the day he was shot. Much of what he said came in fragments, so I had to fill in the gaps, but he seemed determined to tell me everything he could remember.

According to Hightower, once Dr. Martin Polk left for the capital city, Hightower had found a minibus driver in Katembeyna who was willing to take him north for a hundred U.S. dollars. Hightower was his only passenger. They arrived in JiJi at noon. For another hundred dollars, Hightower coaxed the driver to find someone who could arrange an interview with UFreeMo. The go-between turned out to be JiJi's baker, who demanded another hundred dollars. An hour later, the baker had set up an apparent rendezvous with UFreeMo in a forest not far outside JiJi.

"Looking back, it seems too easy now," Hightower said. "But I told myself, the rebels were desperate for publicity."

He and his driver left JiJi and followed the directions given them by the baker. They headed south and turned onto a dirt road just before reaching the High Bridge. They then travelled up into the hills. After a while, they were all turned around and not sure if they were still on the right trail or had gotten lost. They were about to go back, when they came upon a man urinating in the middle of the path, a rifle slung over his shoulder. The minibus driver stopped immediately.

The man on the path did not look up until he finished relieving himself. In the meantime, more men with guns had slipped out of the trees on either side of the minibus. They pointed their weapons at Hightower and the driver and ordered them to step out of the vehicle. Another soldier, I imagined, wearing half-frame reading glasses hanging from a strap around his neck, scrutinized the driver's identity card and Hightower's passport. He waved towards the surrounding trees, and more men with rifles emerged, about fifteen in all. A tall man, with a handgun strapped to his waist, was the last to emerge from the trees. A soft soldier's cap was planted on his head. Pinned on the front of the cap was a gold five-pointed star.

Hightower explained who he was, but the man acted confused. He did not know the baker in JiJi. Even so, he agreed to an interview on the spot. The conversation lasted five minutes, and throughout it, the soldiers behaved oddly. They constantly looked up and down the trail, acting as if remaining out in the open too long posed a serious threat. The man with the star said he was UFreeMo, but he permitted no photographs when the interview was over. Hightower and his driver got back in the minibus and turned around. They headed south through the forest, back towards the M-2. They had travelled a ways, when they heard gunshots.

The double dose of Demerol was slurring Hightower's speech now. "We should've kept going," he said. "But my driver noticed a path towards the shots, so we took it."

They drove into a meadow, the spot where Fred and I later met Matthew. Across the stream, dozens of villagers were huddled in terror. Children clung to their mothers. Teenage girls crouched together along the muddy bank. Boys and old men stood in clusters at the top of the bank. On Hightower's side, twenty soldiers stood in the meadow. They wore no special uniforms, only blue jeans and shirts. They looked similar to the rebels Hightower had talked with only minutes earlier, on the trail. What was odd, though, was that the soldiers barely glanced towards the sound of the minibus engine when the vehicle entered the meadow. None of the men pointed a weapon at them. No one appeared surprised or interested in the intruders; it was as if they were expecting them. I told Hightower what Blake had revealed about special units of Explorers posing as UFreeMo rebels, and the possibility seemed to intrigue Hightower. His thoughts drifted, and I had to ask him to continue with his story.

The minibus parked next to the footbridge, Hightower said, and he got out. The first thing he noticed was five or six bodies on the meadow grass in front of a man with a pistol in his hand. An elderly villager stood in front of the man with the pistol, his thin old arms raised high above his head. While Hightower walked through the grass towards the man with the pistol, he subtly clicked photos, holding his camera at his waist, almost out of sight.

"I called to them, that I worked for the *New York Times*," Hightower said, "but no one cared. I don't think they had ever heard of the *Times*."

Without a word, the commander raised his pistol and shot into the chest of the elderly man, who fell where the other bodies had fallen before him. The gunshot startled Hightower. He took out his passport and waved it over his head, calling out that he was an American journalist.

"'What have these people done to deserve this?' I shouted. 'Let me talk with you.' No one paid me any attention. It was like I wasn't there."

The man with the pistol gave a command, and his men took aim across the stream. Children were crying. A few women made the sign of the cross. A tragedy was unfolding quickly, Hightower said, so he hurried through the grass, towards the man with the pistol. A teenage girl, huddling in the muddy grass across the way with her friends, scurried up the riverbank on all fours. Drawn by the sudden movement, the armed men turned to watch her. The girl hiked up her long dress, as high as her thighs, and at the top of the bank she made a dash upstream.

"Very black skin, beautiful long legs," Hightower said, reflecting on the memory.

The girl was halfway to a stand of trees when a terrifying roar paralyzed the air over the meadow. Children screamed. Five or six rifles were shooting, all on full automatic.

"Sounded like chainsaws cutting wood," Hightower said.

In an instant, the girl's body was beaten to death by a hail of bullets. I could see the pink mist trailing in the air where she had been sprinting, hanging there for a while, even after her body tumbled like a rag doll down the riverbank and into the water.

"I didn't want the other kids running away like the girl, so I hurried across the bridge and told everyone to stay down, stay where you are." Hightower looked at me with what I believe was the vast depth of regret in his eyes. "I was wrong," he said, softly. "If they had run, if they hadn't stayed in place, some would've made it."

"Some did make it," I assured him. "We brought one of them with us here. A boy. His name is Matthew." News about survivors seemed to give Hightower comfort, but his face was sweating again. I wiped away the perspiration.

Hightower said he positioned himself between the shooters and the villagers, and had shouted at the gunmen to go away, to leave the field, but they continued to ignore him. Soldiers took turns picking off villagers at the edge of the crowd, knocking them over as easy as cardboard targets – one shot here, another there. Bodies tumbled into the water, some stuck in the mud. The shooting went on for a while. The crack of each round rolled over the meadow and up into the surrounding hills, its echo returning as a reminder that another innocent had died. Yet, despite the bodies falling around them, the villagers never moved. Whether their paralysis was a result of fear or obedience to his instructions, Hightower could not be sure, but he carried within him the guilt of the latter.

The shooters, Hightower thought, took special care to direct their aim away from him, however. He had just put away his camera and passport, when a sharp pain shook his body. It took a moment for him to realize a bullet had grazed his knee. He pivoted on his good leg and saw, through a veil of blue smoke, the soldier across the stream who had shot him. The commander with the pistol went over and slapped the shooter in the face. The man dropped to his knees and put his forehead to the ground in front of his boss, the most extreme Umbikan plea for mercy. The commander brutally kicked the man in the side of the head with the heel of his boot.

Hightower heard crying behind him and turned to see a little girl and little boy sitting amidst mangled bodies. He gathered up the girl in one arm – she weighed almost nothing – and picked up the boy in his other arm. Balancing on his good leg, Hightower turned to face the soldiers across the stream. He stood there, defiantly.

The commander put away his pistol and took a rifle from one of his men. He methodically brought the rifle butt to his shoulder, aiming it like a skilled marksman towards Hightower. All shooting stopped for the longest moment.

Then, the commander's first shot blew off the crown of the little boy's head, and the tiny body jumped out of Hightower's arm and landed in the river. Hightower clutched the little girl even tighter against his chest and shielded her with his arm. That was the last thing Hightower remembered, until he woke up in Yulemo.

"I think the next bullet went through my hand, through the girl, and into my stomach," Hightower said. He lifted his bandaged hand and put it over the wound on his stomach. The puzzle pieces fit together perfectly.

The irony, though, was more difficult to accept. The girl he had tried to save was probably Hightower's own undoing. Had his hand and her body not slowed the bullet, the slug may have passed clean through Hightower's body and out his back. Instead, the bullet had caught inside him, trapped where its poison was festering still.

Chapter 51
A Request

While Hightower was recalling what had happened at the meadow, the ngumbi harvest in the village came to an end. Mothers put children to bed, their little stomachs filled. Men sat around the fire pit until the bonfire was reduced to embers, and then they followed their families to bed.

"I think they wanted you to be an eyewitness," I said to Hightower. "But something went wrong."

"Be a witness to what?" he asked.

"To what you thought was UFreeMo at their most cruel. They knew you would write about it. The government wanted you to think UFreeMo was murdering innocent people."

"You really believe people were killed just to fool me?" Hightower whispered. Telling his story had taken most of his energy.

"You don't think that's possible?"

"The Life President isn't so foolish."

"I'm not saying it's the only reason. It's not even the main reason. Those people would have been killed even if you never went to JiJi. But having an American journalist poking around up here, that was a lucky break, an opportunity the government couldn't pass up."

Hightower shook his head, slowly. I could imagine the dilemma he was facing. How could Jim Jimmy Mulenga, one of the patriarchs of the African independence movement and one of the Continent's only living lions, permit evil like that in his country? "The president would never kill his own people, or me," Hightower said.

"This killing is bigger than you and your visit," I said. "Mulenga needs to disrupt the opposition in the North, or it'll keep growing. It'll spread elsewhere. He can create panic, if people think UFreeMo is on a killing spree. Fred and I saw a couple hundred bodies in the Jito River yesterday, more than what died at your field."

"Why kill me?" he asked.

"President Mulenga never knew you'd show up at the field when you did. He didn't want you killed. This is on the guys who were there. They made a mistake. They're probably only realizing right now how bad this is for them. Whoever pulled the trigger on you might not even be alive anymore."

I could have added what the Police Commissioner had said to me, how Hightower's standing with the Umbikan government had reversed itself because of what had happened at the court, but I saw no purpose in troubling him more.

Fred returned with a spoon and an open can of peaches for my dinner. I ate with great determination. Halfway through the can, I realized Hightower's eyes had shut again, and I could not see his chest rising or falling. "Are you okay?" I said. Hightower's eyes did not open, but he spoke.

"I want to be buried in Africa," he said. The words came out of his mouth clearly and matter-of-factly, albeit in a whisper. He gave added emphasis to the word buried, as if he had been thinking about that word for a while. "Bury me in this village, or somewhere else around here. You choose, Joe. Just don't send me back to New York. I want to stay in Africa." Fred was crouched on the dirt floor, not far from the mattress, listening intently. He stood up and addressed Hightower.

"Sir, you are most welcome in my country. Resting here forever is not proper."

"Let's not worry about that now," I said to Fred.

"We must worry," Fred insisted. "A foreigner cannot have his grave in Umbika."

Hightower propped himself up on an elbow. "Who's to know who's buried around here?" he said.

"I'm sure there's a ton of red tape," I said, though I knew nothing about the requirements for burying a foreign national in Umbika. The idea had never been suggested to me before. Even so, I was certain that getting permission was complicated. Given Hightower's part in recent events, I could not imagine President Mulenga going along with the idea.

"You seen any cemeteries around here?" Hightower asked, looking first at me and then at Fred. "We're in the wilderness. There's nothing here. Just dig a hole and drop me in. That's all I ask."

The angle of the IV catheter and the pressure on Hightower's elbow to support his weight, made him wince in pain. He fell back on the mattress and stared up at the thatched roof. "I know you have to bring me back," he said, every word uttered a strain on his lungs. "That's what you do."

"It's done for your family."

"Ha. You won't see my wives fighting over where I'm buried."

"There could be others who have a stake in it."

"Maybe, but I have a right to be buried where I want," he insisted. "Give me a piece of paper to sign. You'll have proof this was my choice, not yours." It made no sense to argue with Hightower.

We got him a pen and a page from my notebook. When he finished, he pushed his final wishes across the dirt floor. The handwriting was scratchy, but anyone could read what he had written. "I'm trusting you to do right by me, Joe," he said. I said nothing. "Help out an old man, will you?"

"In the morning, Fred and I are taking you down the escarpment and to the doctors in Katembeyna."

Hightower stared at me and then looked away. "You know better than that," he said. There was sadness in Hightower's reply, a reflection of the disappointment he suddenly felt for me, for feigning hope. Quite unexpectedly, I felt embarrassed for losing his trust.

Finally, I said, "You're right. I do know better." I folded the piece of notebook paper and tucked it into my pocket. "I'll do whatever you want," I promised him.

After a while, Hightower said, "Can you carry my bed outside? I want to see the stars."

Chapter 52
Stars

Fred and I could not carry Hightower's mattress to the fire pit by ourselves, so we went to find a few men from the village to help. We had not walked far, when Fred took hold of my arm, something he had never done before. "Sir," he said, "we cannot bury this man in Umbika. It is not our way. He must return to the U.S."

"Don't worry, Fred. We can let him believe what he wants. He's dying. It won't hurt anyone if he thinks he'll be buried in Africa. I'm okay with it, if it gives him peace. We'll do what we have to, later." Fred seemed relieved by my answer. He let go of my arm. Above us was the night sky that Hightower wanted to see. Stars covered the middle of the heavens like a wide sequined belt. Some travelers claimed the night sky of southern Africa was the most beautiful of any on earth. The sweet scent of burning cedar grew heavy in the air as we got closer to the fire pit. Termite wings crackled under our shoes. "What worries me most is NEGs finding us," I said. "They know Mr. Hightower is a witness to murder. Soon enough, they'll figure out that we know what he knows. They'll come for all of us. We have to leave here at first light."

"I will be ready," Fred said.

It took Fred, me, and four drowsy men to carry Hightower from the far end of the village to the fire pit. The hardest part was not Hightower's weight, but keeping his long body balanced atop the mattress and not rolling to the ground. At the fire pit, we set the mattress beside the Land Rover. The other men returned to their beds, but Fred and I remained with Hightower, who lay with his head cocked towards the last red embers still glowing in the pit. There was no foul odor of gangrene about Hightower now; in the cool air, only a scent of old age lingered, oddly, the same staleness I remembered from childhood visits to my grandparents' house. I secured Hightower's IV bottle to our car's radio antenna, using the yellow streamer still hanging there. I slowed the drip interval to ten-seconds. The second bottle was already half empty. Hightower shifted onto his back, his eyes gazing skyward. Fred left to find more firewood.

"The sky is moving," Hightower said. "Or is that the pain medicine?"

"It does look like it's moving. You ever see a sky like this in New York?"

"Ha, not in Harlem. But as a boy I did, in Mississippi."

Fred dragged a dead branch into the fire pit. The dry needles ignited in a burst of bright yellow light. He set a second branch off to the side. Leaning against the Land Rover, I felt hungry, so I opened another can of peaches and bent back the jagged lid. I could see Hightower's eyes scanning the stars, his curiosity very much alive, even though his body was failing. I asked if there was anything I could do for him. He said, no. I regret not saying more. I wanted to know what he was feeling, what he was thinking – what he would miss, what he thought came next. But I said nothing.

I ate until the peaches in my can were gone. Then, I dipped my spoon into the sugary juice at the bottom of the can and lifted the spoon to Hightower's lips. "Try this," I said. "Just a taste," I said. "I don't want you choking." Hightower parted his lips for the sweet syrup.

"That's good," he said.

I fed him two more spoons. Fred returned with a wicker chair. He set it next to the mattress. "I am off now, for sleeping, sir," he said. "I am at the one with the green door, if you call for me." He pointed to a hut beyond the fire pit.

I motioned for Fred to walk with me in the direction of the hut with the green door. When we were away from the fire, I stopped. "If Mr. Hightower makes it through the night, or not, we have to leave here at dawn," I said. "When you wake up, find a clean sheet and some rope. If he passes, we'll wrap his body and take it with us. If he's alive in the morning, he'll ride in the backseat."

Fred went to bed, and I returned to the fire. The branch was still aflame. As the dry wood popped, tiny flecks of fire arced out over the pit, like shooting stars. I let my mind get lost in their flight. It was a convenient distraction, and for a while I thought only about these streaks of light. But the distraction could not last forever. I had to face the truth. Lying next to me was a famous person, who I had so famously lost. Here was a man I had not met until a week ago, but someone who would be linked to me forever. The firelight added a warm, golden radiance to Hightower's face. He appeared at peace, gazing up at the sky.

Never, before now, had I waited with someone who was about to die. Never had I witnessed the transition from being to nothing. As a U.S. Consul, I had handled death cases several times, but only after a life had ended. It was the same in my family. My grandparents had died in towns many miles from mine. My father had died of a heart attack while I was away at school. I was only five, waiting at home with my aunt, when my mother died at a hospital, in childbirth along with my sister. And with the accident with Claire, I had been a patient for five days in an ICU before they told me she had died at the scene.

Sitting in the wicker chair, I fought sleep. I did not want to miss what happened next. I craned my neck and shoulders, stretched my legs. Yet no exercise made me feel more comfortable or less tired. I was also worried. We were caught in a maelstrom. A nation was collapsing around us. Innocent people were dying. Killers were searching for us. It was only a matter of time before they traced us to Yulemo. We had to keep moving. We had to keep evading. But I was so tired.

And my head swirled in contradictions and irony. There was Hightower's family back in the U.S., already in mourning and awaiting his body. What if they knew that he was still alive but unable to be saved? How much worse would that be for them, or for us? There was the man himself, only an arm's length away, a man sliding towards death, yet content in knowing he would be buried in Africa. What if he knew what Fred and I were really going to do after he was gone? And there was the White House, planning a national funeral just before Election Day – a day to celebrate a man they despised. Would voters care if they knew the truth about the journalist's trip to Umbika and the President's intentions?

Hightower was still looking up towards the stars.

"What kind of funeral do you want?" I asked.

"I don't want to talk about it," he said. "I know you'll do right by me, Joe."

"What about a will? What should I tell your family? Is there anything you want them to know?"

"Do you know which ones are planets and which are stars?" he asked.

He had effectively cut off my line of questions. I pulled my chair closer to his mattress. During fifteen years in Africa, I had learned to recognize the more well-known constellations, but on this night the sky was so vivid – the stars so bright and the rest so black – I could barely separate one bright cluster from another. It took a while, but together we found Leo, Orion, and the Southern Cross.

"They look close enough to touch," I said.

"Some aren't real, you know," Hightower said. "They burned out millions of years ago. The light just gets here now."

"That's how big it is out there, the universe," I said. Then I asked, "Are you in any pain?"

"No pain," he said. "My family will ask about pain. Tell them about the pills you gave me."

Our conversation jumped around from there. He wanted to know why I was not married. I explained about being married to Claire for a couple of years and the accident. He asked about children.

"I guess you didn't have any either," I said.

"I do," Hightower replied, "Boy and girl. They call that a 'million-dollar family.'" He told me about his children, what they were doing, and then he turned so he could look at me. "You know what hurts most?" I shook my head. "Knowing your kids will die someday." Unexpectedly, I suddenly felt homesick, but for a home I did not have. I had pretended Africa was my home for so long that I had started to believe it. Yet the only things anchoring me to Africa were my job and the fact I had nowhere else to go. I had no roots anywhere. Africa was no more my home than the U.S. Hightower had claimed I had remained in Africa because I was hiding from something here. Maybe he was right. Hiding in plain sight.

Hightower turned his vision skyward again, away from me. I was glad he looked away when he did. There was a barrenness on my face that I didn't want him to see. Physical and mental fatigue had also overtaken me. The night was consuming me, as well as him.

Hightower's breathing became more and more shallow, and his throat wheezed. I fought to remember every detail I could about what was happening. I would want to tell his children someday. I pulled the second dry branch into the fire pit.

"I know what you did outside the courthouse in Katembeyna," I said. Hightower's strength was nearly gone. The last bag of IV fluid was empty.

"You weren't there," he mumbled.

"No, I wasn't. But I heard you were a hero."

"I was just showing off."

"You saved a lot of people."

Hightower looked at me. "What do you remember most about your wife?" It was a totally unexpected question. I had to think for a while before answering.

"Claire's skin was so soft," I said, finally. "It was like touching powder. And sometimes when I dream, I hear her voice, exactly like it was. But when I'm awake, no matter how hard I try, I never imagine it like it really was."

In the firelight, I watched Hightower's body closely. When he did not move for the longest time, I became worried and touched his hand. It had taken on the chill of the night air, but he still had a pulse. The sheet covering him was not long enough to reach over both his feet and his shoulders. I got up and took a blanket out of the Land Rover and put it on him from the waist down.

"I've been thinking about your wife," Hightower said, his voice only a background whisper to the crackling fire. "What happened to the cab driver?"

For years, I had carried the memory of this evil person with me, a man who had changed the course of my life in a few awful seconds. "He got three months in jail," I said. "But only because he was drunk. He had a good lawyer who made him the victim, as much as Claire and me." Hightower could hear the sarcasm and hatred in my voice. I did not try to cover it up.

"The guy's a nobody," Hightower said. "I spent most of my life carrying around nobodies in my head, Joe. Don't make the same mistake." The light from the embering branch illuminated Hightower's face. His eyes stared at the starry night above him. I ran my hand over his forehead and felt it cool and dry. I remembered his comment, to the Yale doctor in Katembeyna, Martin Polk. People do things later in life to make up for what they failed to do when they were young. I was about to ask Hightower what he had meant, but a sound from another world rose from deep within his chest, not like a cough or a whistle, but the sound of something letting go for good, the release of a lifetime of tension. The opportunity to get an answer to my question had passed.

In the failing light of the fire, I saw Hightower's deep brown iris flicker. A tiny electrical impulse was surging from one side of the eye to the other. I wondered if he could see it too, a final moment from the inside looking out. I took his hand, but there was only weight to it, nothing more. Hightower's eye flickered again, and the pupil tightened, frozen in place. The blanket covering his chest was frozen too. I pulled back the blanket and stared at the sheet beneath it. Red-gold reflections from the fire pit danced across the thin fabric. I urged the sheet to rise again, to dance with the remaining flames of the fire pit, to return Hightower to where I was waiting. But the material remained still. His long body was already cooling in the cedar-scented air. It was then that a profound and frightening sensation of loss came over me, an overwhelming realization of how great the distance is between what is and what was. I let go of Hightower's hand and sank back into my chair.

Chapter 53
Lessons

The next morning, I awoke to wood doves cooing in a nearby tree, their sunrise call soft and reassuring. I had fallen asleep the night before watching the second branch burn to ash. It was only when the fire was out did I accept as fact that Maurice Hightower was gone. Alone in the darkness, I had felt vulnerable, even afraid for a while, but I had been too tired to drag another branch into the pit for company.

I got up from the wicker chair and watched the pink light of dawn wash over the village. Two skinny mongrel dogs arrived at the fire pit, circled it, paused to look at me, and then picked up a new scent and followed it past a row of huts. I watched until the dogs had disappeared around a distant corner. I removed adhesive tape from the back of Hightower's hand. His eyes were still open. His skin was cold and stiff. I pulled out the IV catheter. The puncture released a drop of dark blood. I set the splint to the side, untied the IV bottle from our antenna, and added to the pile of refuse gathering on the ground. I then pulled the blanket over Hightower's face.

Yulemo sat atop the Highlands escarpment, on a bluff overlooking Lake Ziwa, but I could not see even a hint of blue water from where I stood. A grove of cedar trees blocked my view to the lake. A well-worn footpath entered the trees, and I decided to follow it. I walked in eerie quiet alone, through damp air and morning shadows. I emerged from the trees and found myself on the perimeter of a field of tilled garden plots, five or six acres in all. Each plot was separated by neat ditches lined with dry grass. The gardens were all that lay between me and the drop off to the lakeshore below. In the distance Lake Ziwa sparkled, a morning palette of pink and gray color spreading out for miles. A lake breeze gusted up the cliffside of the plateau and against my face. A trio of fish eagles glided on the updrafts.

I wove around the garden plots and came to the edge of the escarpment. Standing on a rocky promontory, I now had a clear idea of what lay ahead of us going down to the lake road. Several switchbacks had been etched into the steep rocky face. I estimated it was over two thousand feet from top to the bottom, a precarious drive, the lane only wide enough for one vehicle. But we had no other option. This was the first step on our way home. At the bottom of the escarpment was a tarmac road, the single gray thread skirting the lake's shoreline. Up and down the lakeshore, blue smoke from breakfast fires started to rise over villages no bigger than dots. Frothy waves, like thousands of white scars, crashed against the beach. That was when I noticed a storm building to the east. I had expected to see the sun as a big, bright ball, rising in the morning sky, but instead, a jam of dark red thunderheads was gathering across the lake. A fierce storm was coming, and I needed to return to the fire pit, find Fred, and pack up everything before it reached us.

I crossed back around the gardens. Before I reached the grove of cedars again, I noticed a mother with her young son, tending to a small corner of one of the dirt plots. She was in the middle of a lesson, instructing her boy how to work the soil. She showed him how to place his feet astride the row they were tilling, how to grip his hoe, how high to raise it before striking. She chopped the earth, and the boy copied her move for move. I watched every turn of her blade, matched by a turn of his. The mother constantly spoke to her son. She re-directed his actions, repositioned his hands and arms, until she was satisfied with his progress. When she shook dirt from a root, he did the same. When she threw the weed onto a pile, he added to it.

The distance between us was too great for me to hear her words, or even the tone of her voice. It was her mannerisms that held my attention. Finally, I figured out why they seemed so familiar. It was my father's movements that I recognized in hers. My father's attention to detail, the repetition he practiced until he got something right, the code he had lived by, day in and day out – the desire for perfection. The mother was exhorting her son with the same refrain I had heard a thousand times as a boy, my father's question that became the mantra guiding my life – How could you have done this better?

The storm clouds continued to build over Lake Ziwa. I listened to the wind, wishing to hear my father's voice again, the sound of a time when days seemed longer and simpler than now. At the corner of my eye, Fred was moving quickly, approaching in a jog from the village. He came to where I stood. "I am sorry, sir," he said, his lungs out of breath. He held his head down, clasped his hands. "I am sorry Mr. Hightower is gone."

"I am too, Fred. He passed in the night."

"The car is ready for us, sir. Men are wrapping him now and laying him in the boot. You can see, a storm is coming." I looked at the heavy clouds already leaning over the lake, sure to be a severe start to the rainy season. I nodded. Fred and I started to walk.

"I want to ask the village headman if we can bury Mr. Hightower here in Yulemo," I said. My news caught Fred unprepared.

"Sir, you said we will take him with us."

"I've been rethinking that. If he is buried here, that would be according to his last request."

"We cannot leave him here," Fred protested. "He must go home. This is not his village."

"I know, I know," I said and continued on a line towards the cedar grove. "It's not his village, sure, but he asked to stay here. It's Africa."

Fred was beside me in the trees now. The cool smell of cedar was refreshing. "The Ambassador is coming for us in Katembeyna," Fred said, a reminder of another reason for taking Hightower with us. Many careers were on the line.

"They're coming for us one way or another," I answered.

"Failure will bring more trouble."

"Look, Fred, if we had gone back earlier, without finding him, the people of Yulemo would've been responsible for Mr. Hightower. They would have buried him here anyway."

"We did not give up, sir. We found him. He belongs to you now."

"You heard him, Fred. He wanted to be buried in Africa."

"He does not know where he is buried, sir. He is gone."

Fred was right, of course. Hightower would never know where on the planet his body had been put in the ground. At this time, the location mattered to no one but me. Yet in a few hours, after what I had done became known, the whereabouts of Hightower's body would matter to many people. Leaving Hightower in Africa would cause a lot of trouble for me in Washington. The White House was planning a big funeral show with national media coverage, only days before a close Presidential election. To say Washington would have a fit wouldn't cover half of it. As is the case everywhere, there are rules and regulations in place, orders that must be followed. Corridor reputations. The purple star on my personnel file would certainly be replaced.

For Ambassador Durhlmann and others at the Embassy, their careers could suffer almost as much as mine. I wondered how bad it would get for them. I would have to make the Department understand that this choice had been all mine. As for punishment of me? If Hightower's claim that Africa was where they sent diplomats who had fallen out of favor, where could they send me? I had already spent my entire career here.

"There is a reason you want this for him," Fred said, waiting for more explanation.

"There is," I said.

Chapter 54
Rituals

When we emerged from the grove of cedar trees, the women of Yulemo were lighting breakfast fires. The wood kindling burned brightly, and the blue smoke rose above the huts. Wood smoke in Africa had always carried a mysterious fragrance for me, fresh not stale, light not weighty, and so sweet, like a second chance.

Word about the passing of the black American man had spread across the village. The women stopped working to watch us walk by. They clasped their hands towards us and curtsied. Three men were lifting Hightower's body into the back of the Land Rover. They had wrapped a sheet around the body and bound it with yellow twine. Fred said something and the men laid the body back on the dirt. Fred turned to me. "If you do this, sir," he said, "you will need a coin, and a gift." He had stopped trying to change my mind. I think he knew there was no sense in arguing anymore.

"I know about the coin," I said, "but why a gift?"

"It is Tolog custom. The family offers a gift when someone dies, asking the village headman to let God know one more soul is coming to him."

"Can I give paper money?"

"No, the gift is small, but it must not to be a common gift like money."

Fred led us through the village to the headman's house, a whitewashed structure that was twice as large as any hut we had passed on our way there. Its roof was shiny tin, where others' had thatch or scraps of fiberglass like at the village church. Trim around the windows and front door was painted bright turquoise, similar to the color of Lake Ziwa in sunlight. At the front of the house was a porch, a space large enough to hold meetings. I stood with Fred in front of the porch and tossed my coin through the open front door. Within seconds, the village headman came outside. Fred knelt in front of him. "You are most welcome," the headman said. "How is it?"

"The American has passed," Fred replied.

"So, it will be."

"Good morning, sir," I said and stepped forward. I shook the old man's hand in the traditional African manner. "As Fred said, the American you assisted, he died during the night. I am responsible for him now." The headman listened attentively, as I explained that Hightower had been an important person in our country. I described Hightower's bravery at the meadow and at the court. "Late last night, he knew he was dying and asked if he could be buried in your village. I know this is unusual, but it's what he wanted. Is it possible for him to be buried here in Yulemo?"

"Do you speak for his family?" the headman asked.

"His family is in America. I speak for him now, sir." I handed the old man two cans of peaches, the last of our stash from the pantry at New Castlebay. "This is our gift for you."

He took the cans and said, "The man's family must arrange burial."

"We have the same tradition in America, but Mr. Hightower did not want to return there."

"But he has no family here. He must rest with his family."

"That is true, sir, he has no immediate family in Umbika, but he believed Africa was his true home. Africa is the continent of his ancestors." The headman was thinking, weighing the arguments for and against. I did not feel I had made my case strongly enough, so I plowed on. "He saw himself as an African, sir, so he won't be resting here alone. He'll be with other Africans. It was his final wish."

The headman and Fred talked back and forth in the local language. Then, the old man asked me a question. "There is a problem with your government?" I glanced over at Fred, who averted my gaze. Obviously, he had told the old man that official protocol decreed that an American's body be sent back to the U.S.

"It's not my government's business to decide where one should be buried," I said. "A man should be free to decide that for himself. Mr. Hightower wanted to rest here, for eternity, but only if you agree, of course. I saw a piece of land, overlooking the lake. It's a beautiful spot, and I'd like to show it to you, sir."

I had made the best arguments I could. To say anything more would be counterproductive. I folded my arms over my chest. The headman stood stiffly on the porch, looking down at the two big cans of peaches in his hands, whose weight was pulling on his thin arms and shoulders. Finally, he looked up at me.

"It is my honor to assist your friend. We will bury him in Yulemo, according to his wishes. The body must be prepared this morning. That is our tradition."

I reached out to shake the man's hand, but he was holding the peaches. "On behalf of the United States of America," I said, "thank you very much." They were the only words that came to mind at the time. Fred and I returned to the fire pit.

"We're doing the right thing," I assured Fred along the way.

"Yes, sir," he replied, but I could tell he did not believe me.

Men from the village came and dug a shallow basin in the ground next to the fire pit, long and wide enough to surround Hightower's body. Slats of fresh wood from a banana tree were placed over the top of the basin. Four men unwrapped Hightower's body and laid him naked on the wood slats. An old man washed him from head to toe, while younger men formed a human screen around the area so children and women could not see what was happening. I was standing at the back of the Land Rover, when the headman's wife approached me.

"Your friend," she said, "carried these." She handed me Hightower's camera, passport, gold watch, wallet, and notebook. She explained that

Hightower's yellow suit had been stained with blood, so it was burned when he arrived in the village. I thanked her for the belongings and laid them on the hood of the car. Fred arrived moments later.

"They are waiting for us, sir," he said.

At the edge of the escarpment, the headman and a few men were standing with shovels when we arrived. I showed them the burial site, a wedge of land on a promontory overlooking the lake. I arranged four rocks on the ground to mark the corners of the grave, as I imagined it. Then, I lay on the ground myself, inside the four markers, using my height as a guide. I readjusted the rocks for the dimensions of the hole to be dug.

The headman then walked around me, like a surveyor. He eyed the site from several angles. He moved the rocks outward, tugged at a tuft of dry grass, and scooped up a handful of soil, fingering its consistency. He looked across the garden plots behind us. Finally, he nodded, and the village men started digging. I asked to join them, but the headman would not allow it, because I was "family," he said.

When a shovel hit a rock too large to pry out with the blade, the men cleared dirt with their fingers, before lifting the rock out with their hands. Children came and sat on the grass around the hole, though they appeared more interested in me, the *mzungu*, than in the digging. The sky turned overcast, and a soft yellow light filled the air around us.

I anticipated the first words Ambassador Durhlmann would say when I told him Hightower's final request and what I had done to honor it. He would say, "For chrissake, Joe, what in the hell were you thinking!" I had no idea what I would answer. In my pocket was the note Hightower had written, but I knew one piece of paper would never justify to the White House my ignoring their direct orders. I recalled the mother in the field, who had shown her son how to work in a garden. Not even my closest friends would understand how she might be the reason for my disobedience. Fred and I had agreed that neither of us could ever reveal where Hightower was buried. If we did, someone was certain to come one day from the U.S. and retrieve the body. Even worse, the Life President would know the people of Yulemo had assisted, and they would suffer terrible consequences.

Chapter 55
Lookout

Hightower's body was washed according to Tolog custom and then wrapped in a white sheet, with only his head exposed. The body was placed on a wooden litter. Villagers processed in front of him, at least 300 in all, marching from the fire pit, through the cedars, and across the garden plots to the grave site overlooking the lake, where Fred and I were waiting. Women were at the front of the line. Their mournful chorus drew my attention as the procession emerged from the trees. I watched the mourners snake around the gardens. At the back of the line, Hightower was held up high by six men. Behind them walked the village carpenter and three assistants, carrying on their shoulders a long empty coffin and its lid, which they had just built.

At the gravesite, Hightower was transferred from the litter to the coffin. The carpenter put a first nail into the lid, but I stopped him. I withdrew Hightower's notebook from my coat pocket, its pages stained and warped by blood. Into the notebook, I slipped the letter explaining his desire to be buried in Africa, and I slid the notebook into the coffin. Fred was watching me, and he looked confused over what I had just done. I nodded to him across the gravesite that everything would be okay. I stepped back, and the carpenter finished nailing the box shut.

Men with ropes lowered the coffin into the grave, and the same gravediggers who had dug the deep hole now filled it with dirt. It took some minutes to cover the coffin completely. A young girl came forward and handed one of the diggers a cross made of pine. The man planted the cross at the head of the grave, tapping the shaft into the soft earth with the back of his shovel. I did not know what religion Hightower followed, if he even had one, but the simple cross made the burial look complete. From the lakeshore, the first clap of thunder from the approaching storm rolled up the escarpment's rocky face, all the way to the plateau where we stood, the sound so sudden the women stopped singing. A thin and very dark man stepped forward. He carried a bible. A crucifix with red and black beads hung around his neck. The man stood at the head of the grave. In the local language, he read a passage from his bible, and at the end of the reading, everyone said, "Amen."

"It is the family speaking now," Fred said to me in a whisper.

"What do you mean, the family?" I asked.

"That is you, sir."

It would be safe to say I had not anticipated being called on to speak at the service. I had prepared nothing. Fred would later tell me Umbikans believed God listens most carefully to the last person who speaks at a funeral. Normally, this is a parent or child or another member of the departed's family. Today, it was me.

Another clap of thunder mounted the bluff and rolled back at us, echoing off the rocky hills to the west. The storm was close now. A towering thunderhead stretched over Lake Ziwa. Children looked to their parents for direction and reassurance, but the parents were looking at me, waiting for me to say something. I stepped forward, my mind a blank slate. A sudden cloud of dust, whipped by a breeze rising off the lake, battered us at the gravesite. Villagers covered their faces with hands and arms. Hightower's U.S. passport was in my shirt pocket. I took it out.

"This man's name was Maurice Hightower," I said and opened the passport to a familiar page. "His middle name is Jeremiah, and he was born in the state of. . . Georgia." I paused. I had thought he was from Mississippi. "He was a citizen of the United States of America." I returned the passport to my shirt pocket. "I am also a citizen of the United States. This man and I shared the same country, but we did not know each other well. He came to Umbika not even two weeks ago. That was the first time I met him. One of the first things I noticed was how tall he was." Villagers nodded in agreement. "He was a tall, tall man," I said.

A human cry sounded to the west. It was a child's voice, and it was calling from the grove of trees between us and the village. Everyone turned towards the noise. A boy then emerged from the grove and sprinted towards us. He was shirtless, only a teenager, no more than fifteen. We all watched him run. When he reached the gravesite, he collapsed on the ground in front of the village headman. He was a messenger and had run a long distance. The boy was breathing heavily. His eyes had rolled back in their sockets. His body shook, as if convulsing, but this was not a seizure. He babbled African words. I was unable to tell where one report of his ended and the next began. The headman knelt beside the boy and took his head firmly in his hands. He forced the boy to look at him. I finally recognized one of the words the boy kept repeating – *Ziwande*.

Chapter 56
Looking Ahead

Seeing the familiar face of the village chief, the boy calmed down. The old man let go his firm grip on him and coaxed the boy to sit upright. Villagers standing closest to the grave listened intently to the old man's questions and even more so to the boy's replies. After a minute of this dialogue, villagers quickly gathered children and hurried away. Gravediggers took their shovels, carpenters their tools, all following the rest. The headman asked the boy one final question. After answering, the boy jumped up and ran off with the others. Only three of us were left at the gravesite.

"*Ziwande*," the headman said to Fred.

Fred nodded. He turned and looked at me and said, "Demons."

"I know what *ziwande* are, Fred."

"It is Explorers, sir," he added, giving clarification. "The boy has seen them. They are coming to Yulemo." Fred pointed to a green hill in the distance, perhaps a mile away. "They are wearing the clothes of UFreeMo, but they are not UFreeMo. They can be the ones we saw in the forest. Twenty-three, the boy counted."

"They're coming for us," I said. Fred nodded. "Where did everyone go?"

"My people will find white missionaries at the lake," said the headman.

"They will keep them."

"We have to leave too, Fred," I said. "Was the boy certain he saw NEGs?" My level of worry was rising rapidly, but I tried to remain calm.

"This village gives men to UFreeMo," Fred said. "These soldiers are not UFreeMo." I had little doubt now that these men were one of the death squads sent to find us.

"The boy was sure they're coming this way?"

"Yes," Fred said. I could tell he was growing impatient with my questions. "Because Mr. Hightower came here and then us, and what happened at the river, boys were sent to watch for intruders. This one was watching."

"How much time do we have?"

Fred didn't know.

"They are here soon," said the village headman. I expected him to start off for the village, with us to follow, but he stood in place, looking at me.

"What are we waiting for?" I said.

"He is waiting for you to go," said Fred.

"Why me?"

"He is the chief. He must be the last to leave the gravesite."

I took Hightower's camera from my pocket, framed a quick shot of the grave, its fresh dirt surrounded by dry grass, the cross. I made sure nothing in the background could give away the location. I clicked the shutter and took a second shot from a different angle. Then, I pulled the wooden cross out of the ground and flung it over the edge of the promontory.

"Forgive me, sir," I said to the headman. "I don't want them finding this place."

The headman nodded, and we started for the village.

When we reached the fire pit, the village headman hurried off in the direction of his home, nothing more said. Red coals from breakfast fires were still glowing beside their abandoned cooking pots. Two men, kneeling on the ground beside our Land Rover, pushed dirt with their hands into the shallow bath where Hightower's body had been washed. All around us entire families were streaming southward, some with suitcases, some with plastic bags or tubs of clothing, everyone headed towards the switchback road that would take them to the lakeshore below, where British and French missionaries could shelter them.

I gathered tubing and IV bottles, the tin cans and other used items, and stowed them on the back seat of the Land Rover, leaving no obvious trace of our visit. Fred got in the car and started the engine. Instead of sitting in the back, as was protocol, I got in front next to Fred. He looked at me for a second and then released the clutch, and we churned ahead, steering around the fire pit and picking up speed as we headed out of Yulemo. In my side mirror, I saw no sign of the death squad's having entered the village yet, but I glimpsed a young man with stalks of straw or brush in his hands. He was jogging behind us, smoothing over our tire tracks in the dirt, erasing all evidence of our having been there.

Fred had to brake often to avoid hitting villagers fleeing on the road. We passed Matthew, who was running with the others, his head still wrapped in the white bandage. By the time we arrived at a fork in the road, half a mile south of Yulemo, we had gained a hundred yards on the speediest villagers. Without my having to say anything or look at the map, Fred took a left turn, and moments later, we were descending the escarpment.

Before we had gone very far, I told Fred to stop. I got out and bundled the evidence of Hightower's wounds, the empty bottles, the bandages and tubing, the whole nine yards as Ambassador Durhlmann would say, and threw it over the rocky cliff beside the road. If we were stopped on the road by soldiers or police, there would be nothing directly implicating us with Hightower or the meadow.

As we continued down the escarpment, the switchbacks were steeper and our descent became more treacherous than I had expected. We could slip over the edge at any time. Fred kept a foot on the brake and let gravity do its work. He held us to the center of the narrow lane, as best he could. Halfway down the mountain, I lost sight of Lake Ziwa. Storm clouds had reached the escarpment, and within seconds the rain was upon us. It started as small pellets, whipped against our windshield by a wind of gale force. Then, the sky turned so dark we could not see the lightning flashes any longer, only hear their thunderous explosions.

When the full force of the storm hit, rain came in waves and beat against the Land Rover's metal skin. Jabs of charged air, swirling left and right, rattled our windows and side panels like a series of targeted punches. Streams of water surged down ruts in the road, faster than we could descend. I hung my head out the window, identifying the gullies ahead of us, so Fred could slow in time. At one point, we could not see where we were going, not at all, and I thought we would roll over a cliff any second, but soon the road leveled out. We had reached the bottom.

Fred pulled to a stop. The asphalt road I had seen from above as nothing more than a gray thread far in the distance was now directly in front of us, its surface surprisingly smooth. Just beyond the asphalt road was Lake Ziwa. Jagged whitecaps covered the navy-blue surface, as far out into the agitated lake as I could see. Fred turned southward, gently easing our wheels up onto the surfaced road. The thick rubber tires welcomed the familiar flat surface, and the Land Rover accelerated smoothly. Minutes later, with rain falling heavily around us, our car's wipers were still doing all they could to help us see where we were going, but the sound of thunder had become more elusive, more distant.

Since turning onto the lake road, I had been having second thoughts about my decision to bury Hightower in Yulemo. Maybe second-guessing was to be expected. After all, Fred had looked at me like I was crazy when I first told him my plan. At the gravesite, I had convinced myself that I was acting rationally, acting on behalf of Hightower's final wishes. Now, I wondered if that were true.

Maybe I had done it for something altogether different. Maybe it was to soothe my guilt – or the shame I felt. Maybe I was just being sentimental, or arrogant. I wondered if my only reason now, for questioning my decision, was the fear I had about what would happen once everyone knew I had disobeyed orders. As we continued along the lakeshore, looking for the turnoff that would lead us back to Katembeyna, my mind spun these threads of doubt into a tapestry of second guesses.

I soon realized it was foolish of me to question my decision at all, because only one thing was completely clear. The choice could not be undone now. There was no turning around and going back up the escarpment. Our only direction was south, towards Katembeyna, where Ambassador Durhlmann and U.S. Marines would be waiting for our radio call. Maurice Hightower's final wish was to be buried in Africa, and I had honored that wish. Why I did it mattered nothing at all.

We travelled another mile along the lakeshore. A thick mist had started to rise from the earth, frontal fog it was called, a weather condition created by warm rainfall meeting cooler land.

"A sign!" Fred called out. "There!"

He slowed the 4x4 to a crawl and pointed ahead. Somewhere out in the mire, he had spotted something important.

"Do you see it, sir?" he asked. Fred's words sounded surprisingly joyful, his voice resonating with more delight than I had heard from him in days. Whatever dangers were still awaiting us were anyone's guess, but I could tell Fred was not worried in the least. He was happy to be on his way home.

I peered beyond the wiper blades that were drumming a dutiful rhythm. My eyes probed the gray soup, scanning both sides of the road, searching for whatever marker Fred had seen, while the din of heavy rain continued to pound our roof and hood.

Up ahead, through a narrow crease in the fog, I spotted a square plate of wood, nailed to a guidepost driven into the ground. As we drew alongside the board, I saw the hand-painted arrow and the rest of the message: M2 - 49 MILES.

"I see it, Fred," I said. "Yes, I see it now."

Fred took the turn gracefully. With Lake Ziwa pressed against our back, her deep blue water churning and spitting, the edge of the shoreline began to recede. We leveled out on the new road. It was worn to dirt in many places, but the mist rising off the ground no longer seemed as impenetrable as before.

"It was a tough decision I had to make with Mr. Hightower," I said, as the air continued to clear. "Just remember, none of this will be on you, Fred. Whatever happens is my problem. It's all on me."

We continued along the new road, without either of us saying anything for minutes. The rain subsided for brief periods but then returned in drenching gusts. At one point, as a new wind was pounding our car, Fred glanced over at me, and our eyes met for only an instant, but it was long enough for me to know that something was on his mind. I waited several moments, and then he spoke.

"Do not look where you fell, sir, but where you slipped." Fred was staring not at me now but straight ahead, both hands on the wheel. He kept to that pose for some time.

Outside, lightning flashes seemed as powerful as when we had descended the escarpment, though now they were a few miles distant, off to our right and up on the plateau, the dark gray front moving deeper into the higher land.

Acknowledgements

As it has been for many other writers, my journey to see this story published was long and circuitous. I will always be grateful to the many people who assisted me along the way and kept me moving forward.

To Karl Elder, a friend of four decades.

To the many readers over the years who offered their opinions, suggestions, and encouragement: Nancy Devaney, Brenda Elder, Jodie Mortag, Janet Rosen, Lisa Vihos, Diane Krause-Stetson, Elizabeth Trupin-Pulli, and Greg Scholtz. It all helped. And a special thank you to Wendy Varish, who long ago read the first completed draft of the book and made me feel I had created characters and a plot which were believable and worth talking about.

I am especially grateful to Dawn Hogue at Water's Edge Press for all she did to get this story in print and in the hands of readers. Thank you to Meg Albrinck for her very careful final look at the novel. Also, to ever-so-talented Monique Brickham for designing the book's cover and map.

I want to thank the writing teachers who inspired, guided, and prodded me much earlier in my life; though all gone now, I think of them often: Grace Paley, George Garrett, and Hannah Green.

And finally to fellow writing students who befriended me when I was young and living out of my element in New York City and having this wild thought that I might become a writer: Randy Sullivan, Jane Bernstein, and Mary Wallach. And Mike Graves, who walked with me often from one end of the island to the other during those same years, talking about the poets and storytellers we admired and wanted to be like.

About the Author

Jeff Elzinga graduated from St. Olaf College and Columbia University. He has lived two rewarding careers. As a foreign service officer of the U.S. State Department, he served in Tunisia and Malawi. Then, for more than 20 years he was a college instructor, retiring in 2018 as Emeritus Professor of Writing at Lakeland University in Wisconsin. He is married and has three children. This is his first published novel.

Learn more at jeffelzinga.com

12271933R00207